Ania K Pasek has been writing and blogging for several years. Passionate about English, she studied English philology with a particular interest in English as a foreign language (EFL) and in particular how first language acquisition techniques can be mimicked in learning a second language. Since graduating, she has been teaching EFL to both adult and young learners.

Ania has long been fascinated by psychology and the powerful interplay in personal relationships and often uses her writing to explore ideas on these themes.

She lives in Warsaw, Poland, and loves listening to music and reading.

A K Pasek

THE CONFESSION

AUSTIN MACAULEY PUBLISHERS™

Copyright © A K Pasek 2022

The right of A K Pasek to be identified as author of this work has been asserted by the author in accordance with sections 77 and 78 of the Copyright, Designs and Patents Act 1988.

All rights reserved. No part of this publication may be reproduced, stored in a retrieval system, or transmitted in any form or by any means, electronic, mechanical, photocopying, recording, or otherwise, without the prior permission of the publishers.

Any person who commits any unauthorised act in relation to this publication may be liable to criminal prosecution and civil claims for damages.

This is a work of fiction. Names, characters, businesses, places, events, locales, and incidents are either the products of the author's imagination or used in a fictitious manner. Any resemblance to actual persons, living or dead, or actual events is purely coincidental.

A CIP catalogue record for this title is available from the British Library.

ISBN 9781398448377 (Paperback)
ISBN 9781398448384 (ePub e-book)

www.austinmacauley.com

First Published 2022
Austin Macauley Publishers Ltd®
1 Canada Square
Canary Wharf
London
E14 5AA

Table of Contents

Prologue   7

Part 1: Ania Is Impulsive   13

Thursday 2 May 2019   *20*

Friday 3 May 2019   *41*

Saturday 4 May 2019   *46*

Sunday 5 May 2019   *69*

Tuesday 7 May 2019   *94*

Wednesday 8 May 2019   *101*

Part 2: Ania Is Lost   125

Saturday 11 May 2019   *125*

Sunday 12 May 2019   *129*

Monday 13 May 2019   *145*

Part 3: Ania Is Alone   153

Saturday 18 May 2019   *153*

Part 4: Ania Is Impetuous   172

Friday 21 June 2019   *172*

Part 5: Ania Is Broken   186

Part 6: Ania Is Rescued   215

Part 7: Ania Is Restored   **228**

    Saturday 22 June 2019   *228*

    Sunday 23 June 2019   *242*

Epilogue   **245**

Afterword – Dominika   **247**

Prologue

This is very hard to put into words. It is shameful and a disgrace, but I'll do my best to explain what happened during May and June 2019…

During those two months, I went to the brink of the abyss and knew despair and anguish almost beyond all endurance. It was one of the most traumatic experiences of my life and what makes it even worse was that it was absolutely all my own fault. I'd put selfish desire above everything that really mattered.

The price I paid was high, too high, and I lost almost everything that is dear to me.

But before I get into all that, let me start by telling you a bit about myself, starting with why I write.

I have always been better able to say how I feel through my passion for writing. For me personally, it's always been my best form of self-expression as I am naturally quite shy, and despite what you are going to read, quite introverted. I'm that person in the room who says little but listens a lot.

It was only natural for me to write as only I know how to. The words flowed, but so did the emotions, which cast me into a paradoxical maelstrom as I've found reliving the whole experience to be both painful and therapeutic.

My words have been a lamp that has shone a light on everything that happened, but where there is illumination there is also shadow. The darkness at times was relentless and all-consuming, but writing it all down has helped me to put everything into perspective. What helped was that despite everything I kept writing my diary even as some of the events were still unfolding. It proved to be invaluable in my recollections and subsequent reflections on what happened.

The additional reasons for why I have put things down in writing will become clearer as you read on.

Everything that happened goes way beyond the realms of normal experience, even for somebody as broadminded and adventurous as me. While I can't wholeheartedly vouch that it is a totally accurate portrayal, it's my best and sincerest attempt to describe everything that happened.

Such tumultuous events and strong feelings, that pushed the limits of my sanity, can often lead to confusion. Writing has helped to order my thoughts and I've done my best to lift the fog. Time has clarified some memories, but others have blurred as events collide, merge and move around each other. It's only natural that some aspects are still clouded, despite my best intentions.

Similarly, conversations have not always been reproduced verbatim; this would of course be impossible. I have a good memory, but there is no way that I can recall with the accuracy of a live recording everything that was said and especially in the situations that were particularly emotionally charged. Rather, when I can't recall specifically what was said, conversations have been paraphrased or stylised to fit with the events as they happened.

The content of such dialogues still reflects the intent and meaning of the conversations as I recall them. Dominika has also read them and didn't raise any questions or have any problems either. So on that basis, the accuracy of our exchanges can be assumed. It has constantly been my aim to be as true as possible and in this regard, it's totally honest, even if allowing for some inevitable mistakes as the result of an occasional memory lapse.

I'm sure you can forgive me.

Central to my confession is the trouble that my lies and deceit got me into. So this was an additional motivation to do the best I could. It was a chance to set the record straight and finally be totally honest with myself. Obviously, I've done my best to be as open and accurate as possible.

So now my reasons are clear, I should make a start...

I'm originally from Sosnowiec in the south of Poland, and contrary to mum's wishes, I had successfully applied to study in Warsaw. Mum had wanted me to study closer to home, but I was determined to become more independent and break away from her stifling love. Moving to Warsaw also meant that I needed to find a place to live, and this was how I met Dominika.

Dominika is about two years older than me, but only one academic year higher because she took a year out in England. She was already established in Warsaw and we met after I saw her advertisement for flatmates in the university atrium. Her previous flatmates had graduated and moved out and now she was looking, on behalf of her landlord, to find some new students to share with.

I moved in September 2015 and at the same time two other new girls, Emilia and Kasia, joined us. The flat only has three rooms so I ended up sharing with Dominika in the biggest room. She had a bed and I slept on a sofa-bed. The other two girls had a room each.

I found out later that Dominika had fancied me from the first moment she'd seen me and had deliberately contrived things so we ended up room sharing. I'd known for some time that I am bisexual and so with time, I had no problem with accepting my growing feelings for her. My inclinations definitely lean more towards girls even though I'd only ever been with one girl for what, in the end, turned out to be a one night stand. I'd also been with a couple of guys before moving to Warsaw, but it didn't even come close to what it felt like to be with a girl.

Dominika is slight, almost tiny, with wispy blonde hair and much smaller than me. She came across as so together and clear-headed with a towering confidence that just gave her an incredibly powerful presence that appealed to my submissive nature. It was therefore only natural that I became more drawn to her in a very short space of time. Within weeks we were dating and it took maybe another six months for Emilia and Kasia to get together.

All four of us are fairly liberal-minded and play together from time to time, although this is almost entirely just between us with no one else invited. The first time it happened was after we all got a bit drunk just before Christmas 2015 and it was really just—shall we say—youthful exuberance. It happened just a couple of months after Dominika and I had got together, but a few months before Emilia and Kasia were an item. As I look back now though it might have been part of what drew them together.

Back to Dominika and me; we'd been going solid for about three and a half years. She was my love, my life and my everything. But we were rapidly approaching rocky territory. To begin with it was only distance, but it was becoming an ever-widening chasm that led to a stupid moment of madness that almost destroyed me and everything we had.

To an external observer, our relationship must appear to be quite unconventional. She is the Domme (or Dominatrix) and I am the Sub (or Submissive) in what is often described as a D/s relationship, otherwise known simply as a BDSM lifestyle. These are roles that suit both of us, for differing reasons. The bonds of trust and complexity and the levels of intimacy we have are far stronger than I have experienced or observed in, for want of a better term, normal relationships, which I will henceforth refer to as *vanilla*.

Probably to apply the simplest of definitions, for the unacquainted, it is fair to say that Dominika serves my masochistic tendencies that are deep-rooted and born out of my personality and upbringing. My predispositions and mentality will become ever more apparent as you read on. Conversely, while Dominika is not a true sadist, our lifestyle also serves her need to be in control and conforms to her strictly black and white worldview, where everything fits together in neat little boxes. This may seem inflexible, but it provides clear boundaries, understanding and security—in truth for both of us.

One further element of our BDSM lifestyle is that, to give me what I need, Dominika never defined our relationship as exclusive. Sometimes Emilia and Kasia join us, it adds to the intensity of our sexual experience and, frankly, it's more adventurous and more fun. Dominika has to rein in some of Kasia's more sadistic impulses and Emilia joins in because she's just as free-spirited and open-minded as the rest of us.

As I have already made plain, I am bisexual and from time to time Dominika allows me to indulge with a man or even on one occasion two men at the same time. Since getting together I've had a few adventures, but always with her full knowledge and consent. She's always been present on such occasions to protect me and keep me safe, while allowing me to embrace my deviancy and make no mistake that was exactly what I was doing.

The way Dominika sees things is that if she knows about and has agreed to something, however sordid it may seem to be, it's fine. Simply she just has to know. Her only demand is absolute honesty and openness and she despises secrecy and deceit.

However, I'm not writing about BDSM here. So if anybody is interested, please research it thoroughly, stay within safe boundaries, with limits and safe words and make sure that everything is *consensual*. Where there is no consent, there is abuse. Always remember that as trust is important in all relationships, it is especially true within a BDSM lifestyle.

I'm responsible for myself and I'll repeatedly remind you that I'm not blaming Dominika at all, even though it might seem like it at times. My constant reminders are deliberate because my guilt is central to what happened, and that can never be forgotten. Dominika told me to write down as much as I could remember to deepen my understanding of what I did and the catastrophic consequences that followed. Of course, there is the possibility that Dominika will also have a greater understanding of why I did what I did—not that I am trying to justify myself.

This account that I present to you now is an attempt to lay everything bare and be as open as possible about what really happened in those two months and it is why I have called it *The Confession*.

Writing everything down has given me the chance to analyse and reframe my thoughts as part of my healing process. Healing is something that I have come to understand more and more as an absolute necessity. Each word is tearfully considered, and each memory evoked both excites and condemns me.

Above all, Dominika is fair, even if she comes across as harsh at times. There's one incident in particular when you might even consider her actions to be cruel, but in the end, I have to be honest about how she reacted. To me, under the circumstances, her actions were fully justified. Dominika making me admit to my sins here will not bring absolution, but it will bring me into the full light of the consequences of my actions.

My guilt is complete.

This memoir is made up almost entirely of my thoughts and memories, but I have left the last word to Dominika, as her opinion is important too. Here too, she'll explore her foundational views on the interplay between domination and submission. Even though she is a Domme and I am a sub, she needs others to know that I'm an independent free-thinking person who willingly submits to her and that there is never any coercion on her part. My writing gives me a voice that'll always be independent of hers and in that her wishes are fulfilled. With that in mind, it's still important that she has a chance to present her point of view. Additionally, she has taken the opportunity to explain both Emilia and Kasia's attitudes and actions, especially towards me. Understanding Kasia in particular needs a little more effort.

After reading what she had to say, it only reaffirmed my guilt. It also showed how decent and fair she is. Most importantly though, and maybe surprisingly to the reader, it puts beyond any shadow of a doubt her love for me. It's plain for all to see, even to those who don't know us, let alone understand the nature of BDSM relationships and our relationship in particular. I too have come to a greater understanding of how immense her love is for me.

As always, my writing will feature a lot of erotica, but if you are looking for BDSM then you will probably be disappointed. There are still some small elements of domination involved, but nothing that compares to the real BDSM experience that forms the central core of our relationship.

The truth is what it is, and this is what Dominika has demanded.

Finally, I must make it absolutely clear that everything that happened, while possibly shocking and extreme, was done between *consenting adults*. There was never a moment when anybody was taken beyond anything they'd freely agreed to. Borders were respected and limits were tested, even if that meant skirting right on the edge of them at times. This is most apparent when I describe what I endured in the hotel room towards the end of my confession.

So I give you my confession, my dark secret and confirm my guilt before all.

Ania P.
September 2019 (revised April 2020)

Part 1: Ania Is Impulsive

The mild winter had turned into glorious spring, but everything was changing.

It's hard to pinpoint when but while I can't put a specific date on it, everything started to change when Dominika reached a crucial point in her studies. She was in the last few months of her MA in English philology and was working hard on both her exam revision and her final thesis which is about the Psychology of Classroom Management, a fitting subject match to her personality. Dominika is a perfectionist and any thought of slacking off or doing something that's *just good enough* is totally incomprehensible to her…

She researched, checked her findings, researched again and confirmed her data before she finally wrote, revised, re-revised and redrafted again in an endless process as she looked for that perfect synergy of flawless prose underpinned by exhaustive research.

I'm sure you can see where this is going already, and if you've read my introduction it's already patently obvious. So I won't beat about the bush and get straight to the point…

Poor, neglected little Ania was feeling so sorry for herself and missing the attention that she was so used to getting, that she did something really stupid…

…and I mean really stupid!

But getting back to the beginning…

I was really interested in Dominika's thesis, as I'm studying for the same degree, only I'm an academic year behind her. Next year it'll be my turn. Getting some insight into her perspectives on control also reflects on the nature of our BDSM relationship, in which I have relinquished all control to her.

It was immediately apparent that my interest was an unwanted distraction. She was very nice about it, in that she asked me to be quiet so she could concentrate or she moved away.

At first this distance manifested itself physically, but it also become increasingly emotional. The end result was always the same. Maybe I was being a bit paranoid, but it seemed that she retreated into her own space almost every time I went anywhere near her.

Even taking a coffee to her while she was working became difficult, because she often said she was in the middle of writing a sentence that became lost forever because I was distracting her. I still made her drinks and brought her sandwiches. Usually, I ended up just placing them wordlessly in front of her.

Dominika's evening study sessions turned into long nights and her side of the bed was cold and unused. Night after night, light filtered in from the kitchen, where she was studying, seemingly selflessly, so I could sleep. The reality couldn't have been more the opposite. Her absence was keeping me awake and I found myself staring at the chink of light creeping under the door until finally in a zombie-like state I would fall into a lonely sleep.

Generally, I had no idea what time she came to me, but from time to time I was vaguely aware of her climbing into bed next to me. At first, she would lay a gentle affirming arm around me, but with my responses dulled, I might sometimes mutter something barely audible. To begin with, we still made love but it was sporadic and felt rushed and after some time even this, the slightest of physical contact stopped. Her life became an endless cycle of study and sleep.

I longed for her touch, but she wished only not to disturb my sleep.

Tired in the mornings, conversation was minimal and desire was unfulfilled.

Even on her birthday, which fell on a Saturday and gave hope for something more, Dominika took just a few hours off. We went to a restaurant and had a really lovely time, even if the damp cold weather wasn't the greatest. For just a while it felt like I got my Dominika back, but as soon as we got home she went back to her books.

Easter was probably the hardest because I'd been waiting for the long weekend. Even if we visited our parents and didn't get a chance to play, at least we would have some time away from her accursed studies. I thought we were going to my parents' first and then to see her mum and sister. So I was devastated when just a couple of days before we were due to go, Dominika announced that she'd stay at home and keep working. She more than strongly suggested that I should go and spend time with my family. Mum and dad are very religious so Easter is an important event for them. I buried my disappointment because I knew how crucial her work was to her, but it almost felt like she was pushing me out of the door. I know it wasn't her intention, but you feel how you feel and that's just the way it is.

All too often the truth is brutal, and my feelings were more than a little bruised.

So after finishing university on what is known in Polish as 'Great Thursday' I went alone to Sosnowiec and spent the entire weekend with mum and dad. The weather was gloriously hot and sunny, but the sun was the only thing that shone. I smiled and played at being the dutiful daughter, and even went to church with them. I carried the Easter basket to be blessed on Saturday morning like I used to when I was a child, and I even went through the ritual of meditating on the Way of the Cross, especially to keep mum happy. Externally I was the perfect, obedient Catholic daughter, but there was a deep hole deep inside me, a frustrated anguish that cried out to my soul. When the priest reminded us of Christ's words on the Cross, 'My God, my God, why have you forsaken me?' it echoed hollowly in my heart.

My Dominika, my Dominika, why have you forsaken me?

It was the longest weekend of my life and the longest time I'd spent apart from Dominika since we'd started dating. We chatted online or by phone every evening, but it just wasn't the same. I missed her so much and I needed her more than ever.

When I got back to Warsaw in the late afternoon on Easter Monday, she did put her books down for me. She even came to meet me at the train station. I was so happy when my eyes met hers on the platform. We took time for us, nothing was rushed, and I hoped it would lead somewhere. My expectations were high, but after we got home and I moved towards her, once more a restraining hand found its way onto my wrist and stopped me.

'I can't—not this week—as much as I'd love to.'

Her woman's *curse* had got in the way and now even nature was against us. She must've seen something in my eyes because she didn't go back to work again until after I'd gone to bed and for eternal moments we just held each other close. I know she loves me, but to have something—but not everything—wasn't enough and left me more frustrated than ever. I have needs, and the longer I waited the less likely it seemed that anything would ever happen again.

Periodically throughout this time, in despair and loneliness, I reached out to Emilia, who was very supportive and sympathetic. She was clear that she couldn't get directly involved and insisted that I tell Dominika how I was feeling. Of course, Emilia was right.

If only I had listened to her, everything that followed might have been avoided.

In many ways, Dominika is very straightforward and simple. I mean that in a positive way, in that she prefers direct communication without silly games. In her mind it's better to say something straight up and get it out there and over and done with. I knew her studies were such an important part of her life and weighing heavily on her mind so I felt that I couldn't distract her from her work simply because I wanted some attention.

She hates it when I behave like a brat.

If I had a *grosz* (Polish penny) for each time Emilia told me just to talk to Dominika, I'd be so rich; eventually, even she lost patience with me.

'Look Ania, I have told you what you have to do, so just get on with it.'

I know Emilia is all sweetness and light, but do not confuse this with softness. In her own way she can be as hard as Dominika and even Dominika has never told her what to do. If Dominika wants something from Emilia, she only asks or suggests.

This is Emilia.

With Easter being so late, *Majówka*, the long Polish Bank Holiday which included Labour Day on 1st May and Constitution Day on 3rd May, was rapidly approaching.

Finally, I thought to myself, *Dominika will take some time out for me.*

This year's Majówka would be perfect as the Bank Holidays fell on a Wednesday and Friday respectively and thus it was quite normal to take the Thursday off too. This made for a very long weekend; Wednesday to Sunday. It'd be great.

After the disappointments of her birthday and Easter I more than hinted to Dominika that we should maybe do something together; it didn't need to be a session or something so emotionally or physically demanding, but just take some time out for each other, to linger in bed and enjoy each other, to rediscover our intimacy. She was non-committal and was worried that she was still behind on her thesis. Of course the truth is that we'd stopped communicating long ago.

Even Kasia had noticed, although I didn't realise this until later.

Finally, Dominika did something she never does. We were sitting in the kitchen early on the Friday morning before Majówka and she uttered a word that I didn't even know existed in her lexicon.

'I'm sorry, Ania. I know it's hard for you too, but I have to get this done. Just a few more weeks and then things can go back to normal.'

Dominika sorry! Wow!

And the truth is that her unreserved apology makes the confession that follows even harder. My loving Dominika had reached out and I went on to do the worst thing I possibly could to her.

She kissed me passionately, and a flicker of life returned. I pulled her to me and wanted more. I wanted her to rip my dressing gown off and take me, on the table or on the floor or simply anywhere and anyhow. But, yet again, she placed restraining hands on my shoulders.

'Soon Ania, soon.'

I pouted and played coy in the most seductive way possible.

Take me, Dominika, use me like you used to, my unspoken voice cried out, but she just returned to her coffee. There was an awkward pause which was broken by a fatal suggestion.

'Just because I have to be boring and stay at home and study it doesn't mean you have to. I know you were looking forward to Majówka. Go out and enjoy yourself.'

I even understood it how she meant it and didn't feel like she was pushing me out again.

So this is what I did and it was fun, while it was happening. One of the many lessons I've learnt through this experience is that this is the nature of sin. It's great in the moment, but catastrophic in the consequences that follow.

With Dominika having a home study day, I went to university on my own on that fateful Friday morning. In class I asked around to find out what people were up to over the long weekend. Most were going home to their parents.

Then I asked Elwira.

Now, Elwira and I have a bit of a strange history. A couple of years ago, she and I had had a very strange conversation which is still as clear as day to me. For some unknown reason she asked me if I shave down below. Such an intimate question, out of nowhere, had taken me by surprise and puzzled me. I still don't know if it was because of the shock or just the way I am, but I told her openly and without embarrassment that I do. She responded by saying that she did too. Then she went on and even asked me if there were any good creams for shaving rash and how itchy it can get when the hair starts to grow back.

It was all very strange to me.

At the time, I told Dominika about our weird conversation. We decided that it was probably a clumsy attempt, on Elwira's part, to check out my sexuality. Maybe she was fishing to see if I was interested in her in more than a platonic way. Dominika even considered seeing where this could go. If she really was into me maybe, with Dominika's permission, of course, she and I could play together and maybe even she could join our little family as a fifth member.

I remember now, chatting on social media with an early mentor about it. He advised caution because he felt that while two couples (Emilia and Kasia, and Dominika and me) or four of us is balanced, five most certainly is not and it could cause a lot of problems. It turns out his words were prophetic, although not quite in the way he'd foreseen, but he never even realised.

I can't remember if we discussed it with Emilia and Kasia, but we probably did. In the end it all became irrelevant anyway because nothing ever happened. Elwira and I grew as friends and would catch occasional coffees together between lessons or meet up as part of a group for a night out, but that strange obscure conversation never came back up or was even mentioned again. Dominika would often tease me by saying that it was like I was keeping Elwira dangling on a fishing line—just in case.

Just like that early mentor's prophecy, Dominika's playful joke also became a terrible reality.

I must also admit to fantasising about Elwira. I found myself dwelling on her shaven treasure. *What does it look like? How does it taste?* As my lust grew, my vision widened and I imagined her in her naked glory and the things we could do together.

Why had she put that image into my mind?

Later I dreamt of her making love to me or even her joining us in a fivesome. Nothing ever happened, and with time these waking dreams were slowly replaced with other fantasies and realities as life moves on and things change.

I hadn't even thought about Elwira sexually for months.

As it happened, Elwira wasn't going away so she and I discussed hanging out on the Thursday because everything would be closed for the public holidays on the Wednesday and Friday. We decided to meet in Promenada, a shopping centre quite close to where I live and go on from there. It was also convenient for her, as there is a direct bus from where she lives in Stary Mókotów.

When I got home, I told Dominika that I'd taken her up on her suggestion and made plans. I stopped short of telling her who with. Dominika didn't probe and I didn't volunteer the information, she simply trusts and accepts me. She wasn't in the slightest bit suspicious and that only makes my betrayal all the more cutting.

My dormant fantasy had reignited. Somebody was interested in spending time with me. It might have been wishful thinking, but in my mind there was good reason to think she might want more than just to hang out. Old desires reappeared and I was enticed by the sweet imagination of her touching me and in turn, me enjoying her. Thoughts of vibrant pleasure and intimacy filled that gaping void in my mind. It was an irresistible and exciting temptation that, if circumstances played out, would more than meet my needs and satisfy my greed.

Mum always says God tests us to build character and strengthen us and never beyond what we can handle, but my resistance and self-control were already teetering. Possibilities overwhelmed me, but I kept telling myself we were only going to hang out—an attempted reality check to keep things under control.

The truth is that it was all a self-deception. I was in denial, but a little part of me knew I was lying to myself. I wanted something to happen and I knew it would so long as Elwira was up for it.

I kept all this to myself and I didn't even tell Emilia what I was up to. After not telling Dominika, I was already feeling a bit guilty about my inner lust, so to tell another would've been even more wrong. It was almost as though I'd already sinned and done the deed and slept with Elwira.

This kind of thinking was what led me into the mess that followed. Sin is incremental and creeps up like a dark spectre and it may not even cross the line in the beginning.

I recently heard on television that a person is dark as their secrets.

But back to the present…

Emilia's birthday fell on the Monday before Majówka, so she and Kasia went out on the Saturday night before. I was disappointed that we didn't all do something together for the occasion or even on Emilia's actual birthday on 29th April, but Kasia and Emilia clearly wanted to enjoy their time as a couple—*and why shouldn't they?*

So that self-same evening, when I'd expected and hoped to go out I ended up on my own again. My mind was filled with a sense of abandonment that left me feeling more alone than ever, I remembered bitterly how we'd all played together over the last couple of years whenever one of us had a birthday. We hadn't for Dominika's birthday and now we didn't for Emilia's and I was convinced that Kasia's birthday—in about three weeks—wouldn't be any different. Emilia and Kasia were fine as a couple and totally entitled to do things that couples do, but I felt so left behind.

It was almost as if Dominika and I were no longer a couple. At that moment I wasn't even sure we could be described as best friends. We were drifting so far apart and consequently, the four of us seemed less secure than we'd ever been. A foundation was crumbling and I was powerless to do anything about it.

I think this was how Kasia noticed that not everything was right between us.

Emilia and Kasia were getting on with their lives, Dominika had deserted me for her studies and I was an irrelevance stuck in a corner. I was sad and alone and living in a virtual fantasy with my online friends, without substance or satisfaction. I came through the point of denial and fully accepted the truth that Elwira was looking a more attractive proposition every minute and even if nothing happened, regardless of my wishes, at least I'd be spending time with somebody who wanted me around.

I couldn't wait until Thursday… it couldn't come soon enough.

Thursday 2 May 2019

The flat was quiet with Emilia and Kasia gone. They'd decided to go away for the weekend and had left on Tuesday for Sopot on the Polish coast to make the most of their time. They were also taking the opportunity to stay overnight with Emilia's family in Bydgoszcz because although not exactly on their way it was roughly in the same direction.

I was awake before Dominika and lay in bed thinking about what the day might bring. Although my stomach was tight with anxiety and more than a hint of guilt, I refused to let it get in the way of my hopes for the day. I was just a couple of hours away from some of the attention I was craving. I was as excited as a child before Christmas and more nervous than a virgin in her last moments of purity.

My mind was made up. I cast my eyes around, fully aware that my heightened senses had already made me fully conscious. I didn't want to disturb Dominika, but I really didn't want to drag the early morning out either. For the first time since meeting Dominika, I was keener on leaving than staying by her side. I wanted to be on my way, and the sooner the better. I only had a mind for

Elwira. My thoughts were scary, deliciously naughty and irresistible at the same time.

I'd arranged to meet Elwira at 10.00 and couldn't really hang about. I slipped out of bed as quietly as possible and made breakfast. This has always been our routine. Whichever one of us got up first usually did this and it would look strange if I didn't. Despite my best attempts to be as quiet as possible she soon joined me with sandy eyes and a white towelling dressing gown tied loosely around her waist. Her first glimpse of me was when I thrust a more than welcome steaming coffee in her direction.

She looked absolutely adorable, and if she'd asked me to stay and taken me back to bed, I would have been so happy. I'd have changed my plans, in the blink of an eye and given the whole day over for her. That small thing would've pulled me back from the brink, but I had no expectations and of her doing so and they weren't disappointed even if I was—at a deeper more needy and emotional level—when she didn't.

As soon as breakfast was done, Dominika was straight back into her work. I cleared everything away and finished getting myself ready. Finally, I kissed her and told her I was going out as I'd arranged. She simply, with as few words as possible, wished me a good day and so I left without mentioning exactly who I was meeting.

She never asked and I never told.

The glorious spring weather had become much cooler in the last week or so. Since Easter, it could best be described as unpredictable. It could change from hot to humid to cold, in a matter of hours and today was no exception. It'd taken me a good while to figure out what to wear and I'd eventually settled on the safe option of jeans, top and jacket. The only easy choice was my trainers. Boots would've been too warm and sweaty and something more elegant ran the risk of getting ruined if it rained or at the very least my feet would get cold. When I stepped outside into the weather I realised immediately that I'd made the right decision. It was definitely much cooler than it'd appeared to be from the kitchen window.

I was so excited about meeting Elwira and now it was going to happen. As I put one foot in front of the other I was leaving Dominika behind and moving closer to my desires. The thought tickled my stomach in eager anticipation.

Public transport isn't that helpful for getting to Promenada. So I decided to walk. I quickly left our little street and went by Auchan, between the buildings before using the footbridge to cross Ostrobramska Street to get there.

It took about 20 minutes and as I was walking my imagination began to run wild. I felt like I was going on a first date and my greed and libido spurred me on as lust and desire flooded my consciousness. My thoughts were racing, as numerous scenarios that would lead to us being intimate ran through my mind. I could almost feel her warm body in my hands as I ambled along lost in my fantasy. As I walked, with my mind filled with a flow of erotic images, I could feel the yearning damp between my legs grow with every passing moment.

I knew exactly what I wanted, but whether I would get it was as yet to be seen.

When I arrived in Promenada, Elwira was already waiting. I saw her first, sitting in front of Costa, by H&M. She was looking around with searching eyes and when they met mine I resisted the urge to run to her and close the gap between us as quickly as possible. I didn't want to seem desperate. She smiled upon recognising me and got up and started towards me. As she came nearer, I took the whole of her in. She was carrying a light jacket across her arm and wearing skinny black jeans and a light top, with puckered sleeves that came just over her shoulders. She was carrying a small black handbag and in many ways, she is so typically Polish, just like me.

She's slim and blonde and stunningly beautiful with perfect pale skin. Her dark top dipped at the front just enough to give me a delicious glimpse of her cleavage which I saw it as a sign of hope as yet unfulfilled. Even though she's really slender she has surprisingly large breasts, which almost gives her a corseted, but not quite waspish, appearance from a bygone age. Her figure is incredible, most skinny girls like me, are quite small in that department, but she almost looked like a Barbie doll, but she's definitely far more intelligent!

Her physical perfection had an immediate effect on me. My inner longing, barely contained anyway, was immediately attuned to her and my desire to have her became almost overpowering. Despite this, I embraced her with an affectionate hug and small cheek to cheek kiss that was no different to our usual greeting and an effective mask that concealed the greed and lust that was I feeling for her.

I want you…

I was almost drooling over her.

Patience, Ania! A bit of self-control. Let's just order coffee!

We went into Costa and ordered. We chatted casually while waiting for the barista to prepare our coffees before finding a quiet corner where we could sit and talk. Unusually for a coffee shop, there was a certain intimacy to the seats we found, as there was a discrete seating area around the back. As we sat down, we naturally fell into easy conversation, picking up where we'd left off just a moment earlier. I'm not much of a talker but she is, so it made everything very natural and comfortable. We chatted about classes and gossiped about everything and anything that came to mind.

As we talked I kept glancing at her neck and the tantalising sliver of a shadow that disappeared down her top. I wondered what it would be like to feel her, nibble on her breasts and tease her nipples until they became hard and sensitive. I wanted to know the feel of her hands on my body and as fantasy ruled my mind, I had a strong desire to touch myself, but daren't. I couldn't ruin it all with one stupid move when we were getting on so well.

The first hour flew by and we were well into the second hour when I decided to call Dominika. I just wanted to let her know that I was fine and what I was up to (or what I *wanted* her to think I was up to). It was a deliberate and conscious act and all the more devious for it. I left Elwira for a moment, feigning that I wanted to go to the toilet, which was nearby, but outside Costa. Elwira wanted to come with me, but I persuaded her that it'd be easier if I went alone, so she could keep an eye on my coat.

In that moment, with my wish to play at normality with Dominika, I deceived Elwira too for the first time.

Dominika was fine, but still studying hard. I told her we were—without telling her exactly who *we* were—thinking of going to the city centre maybe for some shopping or at the very least to browse around some shops.

'Go and enjoy yourself, Ania. I'll break this thesis this weekend or next and then we'll have more time for each other. I love you.'

I whispered back, 'I love you.' Our last words before temptation became sin.

When I'd finished, I came out of the toilets and re-joined Elwira before leaving Promenada, We used the same footbridge I'd used earlier to get to the bus stop on the other side of Ostrobramska Street. From here there were at least two different bus services that would've been perfect for getting to the city centre, but then another bus, the 168 service, came first.

I was facing Elwira and had my back to the bus when she suddenly noticed it and interrupted our chit-chat. 'Hey Ania, this is my bus. It goes right by my flat. Do you want to come to mine for dinner instead of spending more money in the city centre?'

This is music to a student's ears. Not only would it save money but it'd satisfy my curiosity about her flat. The thought that it might give me an opportunity to be alone with her in private wasn't lost on me either.

I dared to hope and let my mind delve further into the fantasies that were only just being kept off the boil, and simmering under the surface anyway. I hungered to know her body and for her to know mine. I wanted to feel her lips on mine and to climb up the mountaintop with her. I wanted her so badly and just hoped that she felt the same way. The warmth in my loins was growing again and I was just so happy that my dark jeans wouldn't let any dampness show.

Let's see what happens. Stop running before you are walking. I thought to myself. *If it leads to something it will be...*

I don't want to say amazing again, but I couldn't think of any other way to describe it. The chase has always been a part of the game and the mixture of fear and adrenaline, that often goes with it, makes it at least as sweet as securing the victory.

I somehow reined in my excitement and tried to play it down and simply said understatedly, 'Great.' Then I added, while deliberately not inflecting a question, 'Maybe we can browse in the shops later.'

I said it, but shopping was the last thing on my mind!

So with that, we were on the bus and on our way to Stary Mókotów. It passed through a new district that seemed quite nice with well-spaced modern apartment blocks on both sides of the main road. Soon we were in Mókotów, that unlike our area, is an older part of Warsaw (*Stary* actually means old in Polish) and feels like a proper city, rather than just row upon row of anonymous blocks. Even new districts, like the one we'd just passed through, tend to feel like this.

A few minutes later, we were off the bus and then we just had to walk a couple more minutes to hers. When we got there, I saw that it was a tenement building on a main road.

'Is anybody else going to be in?' I asked as we got to the door to her stairwell.

It was something I'd been longing to know since we'd set off, but was struggling to find a natural moment to ask. I already knew that like us, she too was sharing a flat with other students.

With delicate fingers, she entered the code and pulled the door open. I was so consumed with her that I couldn't help but think of those same fingers touching me, caressing and stroking my most delicate parts and probing the centre of my existence.

She held the door open for me and said simply, 'No, my flatmates are all away. Come in.'

My heart skipped a beat as I concealed my joy at this news. In my mind the possibility was turning into more of a certainty with every passing moment.

As I followed her up the stairs, I couldn't keep my eyes off her curvaceous ass which I had a much better view of from below. Her skinny black jeans perfectly accentuated her perfect shape and to me there is nothing better than a pair of good jeans to show off a good ass. I couldn't quite get a glimpse of her most secret place through her jeans, but I could only imagine…

We went up some stairs and reached her flat door which she unlocked and we entered. I slipped my shoes off and handed her my jacket as I looked around. She quickly hung my jacket up in a built-in wardrobe to the left of the door while I gazed around. I was curious, but not intrusive and into everything. Mum and dad always stressed the importance of being a good guest, even though mum can be quite pushy.

As with many older buildings, the rooms were bigger than those in our flat and the ceilings were much higher. It was painted a simple white and had an old polished parquet floor that probably dated back to when the flat was built. Knowing Warsaw's tragic history this probably meant immediately post-war, although it could've been a pre-war building that'd been repaired after the Nazis had destroyed it. The kitchen, where we were heading, was a narrow space with units on one side and a table on the other.

'Do you like pasta?'

'Yes,' I replied as I sat at the table. I had eating in mind, but food wasn't what I was thinking about!

Elwira then made some tea and started preparing the food. As we had all morning, we continued chatting comfortably, as she cooked. She again carried most of the conversation, but it never became awkward because she had plenty to say for the both of us. I felt a bit bad because I wasn't helping her, but reasoned that I couldn't really do anything because I didn't know where anything was. Besides she seemed to have everything under control.

As part of my confession I must tell you I was mesmerised by her figure and particularly her ass. I kept being drawn to it. I had no idea whether she even noticed, but it was pulling me over the line of temptation, not that I was fighting it. My self-control was almost completely gone as all semblance of decency fell into pure unadulterated lust.

I must have you.

The fantasy that I'd just about been keeping under control since the early morning was now fully unleashed. I was consumed and I couldn't think about anything else. I visualised what it'd be like to feel her, to touch her, to be touched and to have the companionship and fulfilment that I'd been starved of for far too long.

The intensity of my feelings was working on my body too and when she wasn't looking, I touched myself briefly between the legs. A wet, clammy warmth through my jeans confirmed that the fire indeed was being stoked. My fantasy was in danger of taking over. I stroked myself gently, in anticipation of what I ~~wanted~~ needed (deletion deliberate). As much as I love touching myself, I couldn't keep my hand there, for the risk of being discovered, while unlikely because Elwira had her back to me, could ruin everything.

As she carried on, I occasionally touched myself, but daren't leave my hand there. Even so, the risk I was taking was a massive turn on and my heart was pounding in my chest with hollow dread. There was no way I could let her catch me, but pushing the boundaries was stimulating me way beyond anything my gentle stroking was doing. I soon realised that the more I carried on, the greater the chance of discovery.

I had to stop.

It was difficult, but being forced to physically restrain myself dragged my mind back to reality.

Soon the pasta was ready and she dished it up before joining me at the kitchen table. As in the coffee shop, I was sitting opposite her and took in once again her face and shoulders and amazing chest. In stark contrast to my greedy mind, the conversation, nice as it was, was just so mundane and ordinary. Between mouthfuls of delicious pasta delicately seasoned and complemented with a cheesy sauce, she told me more about her flatmates, and I told her about Dominika, Emilia and Kasia without explaining the exact nature of our relationships. There was no need to freak her out. When I told her that we go to England and work for two or three months every summer she told me that she'd never been to England. She more than hinted that she'd like to come with us this year if possible.

It'd be nice—but no chance; especially if I get what I want today…

When we finished eating I helped her clean up. At least I could do that. She washed up while I wiped down the sides and as we finished she suggested moving elsewhere, as it would be more comfortable. Leaving the kitchen spotless, I followed her through the hallway and as I stepped over the doorway, that marked the threshold of her bedroom, I willingly, with careless abandon entered the blissful abyss and destruction awaited me.

Her room wasn't as expansive as the rooms I'd already seen, but looked larger than it actually was because of its white walls and high ceiling. It was sparsely furnished in that way that marks out student rooms throughout the world. There was a desk, which was clearly her working space and home to her laptop which was open, but turned off. Next to it notes and textbooks were sorted into tidy piles, with colourful pieces of paper sticking out. I'm sure that each highlighted information that was important to her. Her chair was unadorned and pushed under the desk. Most noticeably, there was a distinct lack of clutter. It seemed that Elwira is a very studious, neat and organised person.

Or maybe she's tidied up, just to make a good impression on me?

On a cork noticeboard, mounted on the wall above her desk, there were a lot of photos and her timetable among other little personal touches such as wristbands from concerts and a rainbow array of even more little post-it notes. The narrow single bed, pushed into a corner, was big enough for one but tight for two.

Even skinny girls like us.

At the end of the bed was a small television on a chest of drawers that I hadn't originally noticed and that was about it.

Other than the chair there was nowhere else to sit so fairly predictably she invited me to sit on the bed. I leant with my back against the headboard and my feet up and she kind of reclined on her side, slightly curled up nearer my feet with her head resting on a hand somewhere near my waist.

It was probably just my imagination, but for there was a palpable tension in the air, a feeling that something was about to happen. There was a hiatus, the hopeful anticipation of an unexpected adventure. I had no idea what she was thinking, or if my feelings were being driven entirely by my lust. Her thoughts and feelings didn't really matter to me though because with the sexual undercurrent I was feeling I decided to take a risk and try to move things along. At worst it might be a bit embarrassing and look like I was simply satisfying an old curiosity, and at best it would be the catalyst to start moving things in the direction that I was lusting for.

The reward definitely made it worth the risk.

'Do you mind if I ask you a weird question?' I asked suddenly as I politely, almost over-delicately, cut across the forgettable thing we were talking about. 'Will you promise not to be offended?'

Caught by surprise, she sat bolt upright and looked deeply into my eyes. She hesitated for a few seconds, with flickering trapped eyes as she grappled with my intentions and her own thoughts, before gesturing in agreement. For just a second my courage and my voice deserted me as insecurity rose from within. I'd created an opening and this was my moment. I just had to push through if I really wanted something to happen. I had nothing to lose and everything to gain.

A girl can always hope.

'Can you remember asking me a strange question a couple of years ago?' I paused as though waiting for approval. She didn't say anything but rolled her wrist as if to say *get on with it*. 'You randomly told me that you shave down below and then asked me if I do.'

She nodded, as though remembering.

'It came from nowhere,' I continued, 'and I really didn't know what to say. It was kind of surreal and I think I just told you that I do without even thinking. I was so surprised that I just blurted it out, but ever since then I've always wondered why you asked me.'

Her cheeks pinched a delicate, delightful, pink and her porcelain neck mottled red as she blushed. It was obvious that she remembered the conversation like it was yesterday. She smiled demurely. It was a slight toothy cheeky grin that could've been embarrassment, but to look in her eyes, she seemed almost relieved that I'd brought the subject up, almost as if she'd been waiting for it.

She was so adorable. I wanted to kiss her there and then, but that still rational part of my mind urged restraint. She might have been ready, but I was still unsure as my nerves rose. So I just smiled back at her.

She took a breath before haltingly answering, 'Yes, I remember… Sorry if I shouldn't have… I was just curious because I'd just started shaving and…'

She stopped dead.

Now I beckoned her to carry on. In an almost ironic reversal of roles, I now imitated her rotating hand that she'd urged me on with just a moment ago. I really wasn't sure what she'd say, even though I hoped it'd open the door.

'You've got to promise you won't laugh or hate me.'

I don't know if it was clever manipulation on her part, but with that she somehow flipped everything around and suddenly the pressure was on me.

'I promise,' I said earnestly.

What else could I have said?

'I like you. I mean I really like you, but more than a friend I think,' she said quickly before pausing. 'I felt—and to be honest I still feel—attracted to you. You're in my mind and I find myself thinking about you even at totally stupid times, like in the middle of a class. I can't explain it. I was so confused and I really didn't know if I should tell you or hide my feelings.'

I sat and smiled at her. She may have started hesitantly, but now it all came out in a continuous stream of words.

'I felt a bit guilty about my feelings for you, like they were unnatural and wrong, and that just made it even harder. I thought I was going crazy, but I couldn't get you out of my mind. Just everything about you, your smile, your energy, just you as you are. I was caught between two worlds and I was torn about what to do. So I thought sharing something so personal with you could show me if there was a chance, but then I got scared and backed off and have hidden my feelings ever since. I knew I'd die of embarrassment if I told you and you didn't feel the same way.'

Can you imagine how her words hit home? She was into everything about me. She was so straightforward and was making everything about me. I just carried on listening to her, smiling all the time. After so much neglect, her words trickled like honey into my ears.

Most importantly, I felt wanted.

Suddenly, fear flashed across her face and she lowered her eyes. 'You're laughing at me—*awkward!*'

And with her comment, she created a tension that hadn't been there. I was happily enjoying her little monologue and now she'd gone and pressed the self-destruct button. There was a real danger of everything being lost. The silence between us was growing and becoming more uncomfortable with every passing second.

I had to do something.

No words would prove that I wasn't mocking her and more often than not actions speak louder than words. So I leant forward and kissed her. It started with just a peck on the lips. I kept my lips pressed to hers and reached out and took her cheeks in my hands and presented my tongue between my lips. As they touched her lips they parted and her tongue shot out and found mine. I turned my head a little to my left and she mirrored what I did while at the same time putting her hands on my ribs just below my upper arms. I held her face almost protectively as we kissed deeply and passionately and our tongues became mingled, our saliva mixed and, in that instant, we became one.

This was it. This was my betrayal. This was the instant when I gave myself to Elwira. This was the moment of my sin and the moment I became an offence to Dominika and everything we stood for.

But I wasn't thinking about Dominika.

I don't know how long we kissed for, but it was even better than my waking fantasies and how I'd seen today playing out. From the moment we'd agreed to meet and especially since I'd met her this morning, she'd awoken the dormant fire inside me and now it was a raging inferno, a simmering volcano just waiting to erupt. Fire unquenchable was consuming me and I fought off an urge to take her there and then—too much, too fast could ruin everything.

We are moving along nicely, so why risk it?

Finally, inevitably, we broke off the kiss and I moved my hands to her shoulders and as I lay back against the headboard, insistent fingers pulled her forwards onto me. She slid her hands down my sides to my hips and I pushed my knees apart so she could get closer and more into my intimate space.

The moment was electric and I hungered for more. I tried to ignore the cautionary voice in my head that whispered repeatedly that I should take my time. I fought every inclination and compulsion that was racing through my brain. I wrestled inwardly as my lust and inner voice contended with each other until I reached down to the hem of her top and took a firm hold of it. In that moment with her top in my hands, my inner voice finally won out and I put the brakes on.

'May I?'

I wanted to tear her clothes off and fuck her there and then, but I knew that I couldn't go any further unless she agreed. The inner voice, my conscience if you like, wouldn't let me go any further. Not just because of my past, but because it is right. Consent has always been essential and this situation was no different.

She started shaking. She was obviously unsure of where we were going, but brave enough to put her nerves aside. Through quivering lips, she uttered a barely audible 'yes'.

I lifted her top over her head and cast it aside before removing my own. With her top off, I got a much better view of her breasts. They were sitting neatly in the two cups of her white bra. As I lusted internally to touch them, I somewhat awkwardly reached behind my back and unclipped my own bra and slid it off in front of me, revealing my pert little breasts. They are not as perfect as hers, but they were firm and ready.

Better I give her something first if she's so anxious.

'Am I going too fast?' I asked cautiously.

Like I'd done just a few minutes earlier, Elwira responded physically. She reached out and stroked one of my breasts, tentatively as though she didn't know how to touch me. I took hold of her hand and pressed it more firmly against my flesh and she groped more enthusiastically and now she knew what I wanted I let go. I paused to let her play and then after a few minutes I eased her bra straps off her shoulders. It was obvious what I wanted, so she moved her hand from my breast and unclipped and removed her own bra.

Her nipples were larger and flatter than mine and her breasts were perfect globes, much bigger than mine. I moved forward again and took them in my hands and moved my mouth to kiss and lick one of them until her nipple hardened in my mouth. She reached under my arms and played again with my more modest mounds while I moved on to her other nipple which I also roused with my tongue and the suction of my lips.

Then I pushed her back as I pulled my legs under me. At the same time her legs bent uncomfortably under her and she had to straighten them quickly as I went. I continued pushing until she was on her back with her feet on her pillows.

I was vaguely aware that I was being quite dominant, but what had started as a reassuring kiss had become full on desire and unless she said anything there was no stopping me now. It struck me that while she was totally into what was happening she didn't really know what to do. So naturally I had to take the lead, even though this was contrary to my submissive nature. I wanted her and I wanted her now. I had been denied for far too long…

Once she was fully on her back, with her head almost hanging off the end of the bed, I kissed her again and rubbed her breasts, which were sitting flatter into her chest. I moved from her lips and nibbled her neck and decorated her body with little kisses as I moved down to her navel. My hands followed and drifted further below while I concentrated on tongue fucking her belly button. I tugged ravenously at the button of her jeans and, once it gave way, I slid the zip down. She could have stopped me at any time, but her hand was on the back of my head and pulling me deeper into her belly, which I was now trying to consume with my whole mouth as my tongue continued to thrust into her belly button. Under my passion she was still shaking nervously.

Is she a virgin?

I opened her jeans and saw the smooth front panel of her knickers, plain and white. I was so hungry that all I could think about was how fast I could take her. Before I could do anything else, she let go of the back of my head and I saw one of her hands come down near my head and hook into her jeans by the side of her hips. She lifted her ass and pushed down. She must have done the same with her other hand on the other side because her jeans and knickers were suddenly tangled around her knees. I sat up to give her space and she pulled everything over her heels and before I knew it, she was completely naked before me.

And I was worried about taking her too fast!

I opened her legs and looked at the fullness of her flower—shaven, but a little red. It seemed to me that she had probably shaved last night or even this morning before we met. Maybe she too had expected something from today?

If that was the case, neither of us was going to be disappointed.

'It's beautiful,' I exclaimed. 'It was so nice you told me about it before, but a shame I had to wait so long to see it.'

I bent and kissed it in adoration, but I wanted more. My kiss soon became a probing tongue with which I explored her slit. I expertly parted her labia with my tongue before introducing a finger, which I slowly pushed into her already wet hole, which enclosed itself around me. She parted her legs further to accommodate me and I went to work. Elwira certainly wasn't my first girl and I knew exactly what I was doing. Her groans and tiny squeals of pleasure confirmed her rising heat.

I lapped on her like a starving dog while at the same time finger-fucking her with everything I had. Within minutes she was arching her back as her body was racked with increasing levels of arousal. Her breathing became shallower and she expelled air from her lungs with guttural sighs that almost purred. Her shaking now was more through ecstasy than nerves as she gave herself to the moment. I recognised her womanly rhythms and helped her to ride through the waves that washed over her, and even when she thought she had reached her summit, I carried on determined that she dragged every last pleasurable second out of her climax.

Ideally, I would have taken my time and enjoyed her body more, but as selfish as it sounds I was desperate for my turn.

I reasoned the sooner I get her there, the sooner I can get there! If that makes sense?

She continued to shudder for some minutes, as her orgasm began to subside. Eventually, she became more tranquil and closed her eyes at peace in a dreamlike trance. Slowly, so not to disturb her afterglow, I eased my fingers out of her and got off the bed momentarily.

'Don't go,' she murmured with a satisfied smile as I got up.

'I'm not going anywhere, Elwira.' My mind was made up. I knew what I wanted and we were far from finished.

I'd only got up to strip off. I quickly removed the rest of my clothes. Now I was naked, I took her hands and helped her to sit up. I rotated her around and used persuasive hands until she was on her back again, only now with her head on a pillow. I then slid next to her. With it being a single bed, the space was really tight. Her clammy hot body pressed against my cooler dry body. It might sound gross, but somehow one body sated and the other waiting to be satisfied pressed together as they were, created a vibrant closeness as her heat radiated through her body and into mine. She rested her head on my chest and I rested my chin on the top of her head.

Intimacy and tenderness—everything I have been craving—well almost!

The fire was stoked and the passion had been ignited, but Elwira wasn't offering anything. Again I would need to take her in hand—literally.

'Elwira, do you want to touch me? You know you can.'

'Yes,' she murmured before pausing, 'but I'm not sure how.'

So that was why she was holding back.

'It's simple. I'm a woman too. I'm sure you play with yourself. Just do to me what you would do to yourself. I'll fine tune you if necessary. This is your first time?'

'With a girl—yes. And you?'

For the briefest of moments I thought of Dominika, but to let my emotions get involved now would be to deny myself this moment.

'I've been with girls before,' I answered vaguely.

Enough talk, other relationships past and present, weren't the right thing to be talking about, especially not at this very moment.

I took her hand and pushed it between my legs. I lifted a knee to give her more room and she began to rub my crevasse. She dipped her fingers ever so slightly into my wet—believe me, I was hot and as horny as hell before she even started to touch me—and then she moved her fingers up and began to play with the area around my love button. I felt flames rise and she definitely knew what she was doing—even if she was just transferring what she does to herself to me.

After a few minutes she rolled so she was over me. One hand stayed between my legs and the other propped her up. As she caressed me with sensitive fingers she lowered her face onto my body and sucked on my little red cherries, first one and then the other. They were already firm and sensitised, more out of anticipation than anything else and it felt so good, a sensual tickle that was taking me to greater heights already.

For her first time with a girl, she's doing really well.

Each little kiss, each little sensation, each little bit of attention was a reminder of what I needed and what I'd been missing. It was so different today—new, exciting and fresh. Elwira's touch was delicate, frequently unsure, but always just right. My body began to respond and her fingers entered me. I gasped in pleasure as at long last I was penetrated again. I pulled her hair, forcing her to move her head back and I kissed her passionately, my tongue swirling in perfect harmony with hers. As our mouths danced their little tango, her fingering became more frenzied and forceful.

She caught me with a fingernail, causing a second of sharp pain, and I grunted in surprise. I felt her try to move her hand away, worried she'd hurt me, but I grasped her wrist and wouldn't let her.

'Keep going, Elwira, don't stop,' I almost begged between breaths.

I rose to the mountain and then higher, as I responded to her touch and all sense of personal abandonment fled in the intensity of the fire. Then, maybe because I'd done the same to her, she kept going even when I reached my apogee. My legs quivered and my skin tickled as my inner being buckled under the waves that were now crashing on my shore. My very being screamed in defiance at the months of denied pleasure I'd endured. My body exploded in one continuous undulating orgasm as my loins tightened and spasmed under her control, and still she wasn't stopping.

Masturbation had been all I'd had for so long and now this—it doesn't even come close.

I pulled her nearer and fucked her fingers with gyrating hips and her still persistent thumb flicked at my clit, making it almost painful to touch. I was already coming down and tightening around her fingers and stinging, but I didn't resist or even mind when it came down to it. Pain is my thing and even incidental pain was making me feel alive once more.

Finally, when I was long over the heights she too stopped, exhausted and probably, and not unsurprisingly, with a cramp in her wrist. An entangled mass of limbs, we pulled her bedding over us and rested in the closeness that is only possible after sharing such a moment. We were facing each other and I had a hand on her hip as she stroked my hair.

Elwira is amazing.

I'd craved this for so long and the reality had matched the fantasy. I'd missed the love and attention so much that…

Then a dark thought suddenly entered my head. *Dominika—shit, Dominika! She will fucking kill me!*

But it felt so good being so close to somebody. Elwira had more than surprised me. I'd met her today secretly hoping something would happen, but this had gone way beyond my wildest expectations. I hadn't resisted and, in fact, I'd kissed her first.

I should be loyal to Dominika, but I was conflicted. I'd been feeling so neglected and with this reasoning I once more pressed down the guilt that was threatening to ruin my afternoon.

Closeness and intimacy were all I wanted and now I have it.

Elwira was first to break the golden silence. 'Did I hurt you with my nail? I'm sorry.'

If only she knew!

'Maybe just a bit, but for me pain adds to the pleasure.'

'You sound like you know,' she joked.

'I'm serious,' I didn't joke back.

There was no conversation that could follow from that so, in the silence, our bodily closeness was enough. Intimacy doesn't need a voice. Once more she was stroking my hair and staring tenderly into my eyes. I was lost in her undivided attention. She was sweeter than nectar and she was all mine.

After a few minutes she seemed to be getting a bit restless, but her agitation wasn't from boredom, but quite the opposite. Her hand slowly, but quite deliberately moved from my hair and down my neck until once more she had her hand on one of my now soft little saucers. She playfully pinched it, and the little nip hurt a bit, but I groaned in pleasure. Compared to previous experience it was nothing, but she was still unsure of herself and the more she could give me what I need, the better it will be—being completely selfish of course.

'You want to play some more?' I asked rhetorically.

She groped my flesh in a firm squeeze of affirmation.

'Bite me if you want to,' I said encouragingly.

She moved her face to my other nipple and bit down on it gently, like the tightening of a vice, while continuing to pinch the first one. At the point when it became too hard I pulled her face into me and smothered her, if I can call it that being as small as I am, causing her to ease off slightly. At the same time I reached down to her and found her rosebuds already firm. I rolled them gently between my thumb and forefinger and she groaned into my chest.

I wanted her again, only this time my need wasn't so urgent. Greed had been satisfied and now I was in a different place. I was determined to take my time and enjoy her so she could enjoy me at the same time. Earlier on we'd both been so intent on satisfying each other's lust that it'd become a frenzy. Now we could just take our time and enjoy the ride as much as the destination.

I pressed myself into her, which meant she had to release my breasts. I nibbled and teased her neck and soon found her earlobes. I took them one at a time into my mouth and sucked as I rubbed my hands down her legs. I actually felt her flesh goose pimple under my touch. Encouraged I tongued inside her ears, again first one and then the other.

Her breathing deepened and her body quivered in delight and I had barely touched her. Once more I was on her neck and expertly caressing it with my lips and nuzzling her throat before finally rolling her once more onto her back.

Her nakedness was fully open for me to explore and enjoy. I only had to remember that she is probably quite *vanilla*—so I shouldn't freak her out by doing something she may consider too weird. As for me, I'm up for almost anything and everything, but I just couldn't take her too far too fast.

This train of thought brought me back to Dominika. She was innocently studying at home, but far too busy for me. The last vestiges of my conscience didn't stand a chance against the calling of my inner fire and this freely available beautiful girl who was laid naked and ready in front of me.

I am sorry, Dominika, but you told me explicitly to confess everything and be totally honest with you.

Once more I found myself in the unaccustomed position of taking the lead and being in a more dominant position. I lay beside her and I traced her body with one hand. Meandering fingers stroked her almost to the point of tickling her. She writhed deliciously and let out the occasional squeal as my touch liberated previously undiscovered sensations. Just for a moment, as I toyed with her unselfishly, I had a different perspective on the joy of giving somebody else pleasure and watching her express it.

My thoughts drifted once more to Dominika, as I suddenly realised this is how she looks at me when giving me what I need. But she hadn't done anything for so long and she wasn't here.

I knew what I was doing was wrong, but I just couldn't stop myself. I'd got myself into this and now I was this far in I couldn't get out without hurting Elwira. And I didn't want to hurt her. Once more I cast my sin away and concentrated on the moment, which meant Elwira—who was absolutely irresistible.

It was a foregone conclusion that my attention would eventually find its way between her legs, but I was determined to enjoy it too. Elwira may be a novice, but she's not passive or submissive and I repeat I'm not dominant.

I changed my position so I was lying in the opposite direction to her on the mattress, and with persistent firm hands I pulled her on top of me. There was no way I was going on top. I could at least manage that. Her legs were spread beside my ears and I found myself looking up at her eager little honeypot. I opened my legs and made it pretty obvious what I wanted.

Then I put my hands on top of her luscious ass and pulled her down onto me so her little slit was almost on my face. My initial probing was serpent-like. With a fast darting tongue I tasted her moisture and at almost the same time I felt fingers part my petals. A warm wet tongue began to work on me and I could feel a steady rotating pressing massage on and around my little switch. I didn't know if it was a thumb or a finger, but I didn't care…

It felt sooooo fucking good.

I moved my hands and used my fingers to pry open her little space and ran my tongue up and down. My saliva mixed with her honey—slightly salted—and once she was oiled up enough with our combined slick I pushed a finger inside her. My hand was now blocking my face and I could no longer lick her, but judging by the sounds she was making she wasn't about to complain—even if she was moaning. She was groaning, but it sounded strange because she clearly had her tongue sticking out of her mouth—it was buried inside me!

I pushed a second finger inside her and she responded by bucking backwards. At first, I thought she was trying to push me off, but then I realised she was trying to embed herself deeper by fucking back on me. Down below, I felt her fingers move as she got a better grip of my labia. It felt like she was pulling me apart, just enough for it to feel like a slight bite and her tongue and what was almost certainly a thumb continued to probe. As she started to succumb to my attentions she was getting increasingly less coordinated. Her movements became more erratic as pleasure racked her body with sensations that were beginning to overwhelm her.

Then she gave up on her tongue. She leant forward a bit more and I had more space to see what I was doing. While keeping her thumb on my clit Elwira immediately pushed inside me. It was more than two fingers and she too was now finger-fucking me.

I really wanted to push a finger in her ass, but thought it would be too much for her. I wouldn't have complained if she had done so to me. Of course, it may just have been that if I had done it to her she might have just followed and done the same. I was her first girl and a mirror and a barometer for her.

Do unto others as you would have them do unto you, I thought with amusement.

Maybe next time?

Ania, you stupid bitch what are you thinking? What about Dominika?

Damn my conscience! Why does it keep rearing its head? The truth was, as much as I love Dominika I was really enjoying my afternoon with this angel of lust and I didn't want it to end. Or when it did end I wanted to come back for more.

In the space of one lustful afternoon it seemed that Elwira had completely consumed me. I was hers.

No, I wasn't; but such was the duality of how I was feeling. I belong to Dominika, but somehow I'm now linked inextricably to Elwira, even more so than to Emilia and Kasia. Maybe the responsibility of leading her into her first lesbian experience was also playing on my mind. I'd taken her lesbian virginity and I was determined that she'd feel better than I did after the first time I was used by another girl for sex.

The aftermath of that experience had left me hurt, abandoned and confused, but the sex had been nothing like I'd ever known before and it'd helped to set me on the path that I'm now following—unless with Elwira I have just changed lane.

Am I straying away from Dominika?

I wanted them both. To be owned by my Dominika who knows me better than I know myself. Only she truly understands my desires and deviancy and knows how to give me exactly what I need. But it'd been so long since anything like that had happened and now I had a chance to play with this delightful sprite of a girl who is now pleasuring me I wanted her too.

Thoughts ultimately dissolve into the living moment and pleasure ended all thought.

In our *sześćdziesiąt dziewięć* (69) position we once more climbed our mountains. With one hand I continued to fuck her with the two fingers I had already penetrated her with and with the other hand I reached under and went for her swollen love button. She was more than ready, far closer than I had expected. She shuddered and rolled her hips as her orgasm hit. I actually saw her legs spasm and her skin twitch as her body relented and lost control. So intense were her feelings that she fucked my fingers back to get as much pleasure out of what I was doing to her as she could, as I drove her over the edge.

Meanwhile, I was getting close and I started to fuck her fingers too by rolling my pelvis upwards. I would love her to push more fingers inside me, *but patience Ania!* My crescendo was building and if I were too greedy it'd come too soon and be far shallower for it.

Elwira's orgasm was beginning to lose strength by the time I neared. It was like we passed each other on a mountain pass, only she was on the way down and I was still ascending. Eventually, waves of the most intense pleasure began to wash over me and I too lost bodily control. I couldn't move too much, because while I wasn't pinned I didn't have much wiggle room with her on top of me.

My whole body tingled as my cum took control. My mind found orgasmic oblivion as she kept going, as she had done earlier. My climax was becoming almost too painful as she persisted on my clit that was now more than over-stimulated.

Fuck me—she's good, and this is only her first time!

Once spent, we collapsed onto each other. Her head rested between my legs and her treasure was on my cheek. I had to turn my head aside so I could breathe, but the smell of her fresh sex lingered in the air as a reminder of the magic we'd just conjured up between us.

I closed my eyes as a wave of tiredness suddenly struck me and we remained in the afterglow of that special intimacy, unmoving for perfect eternal minutes.

It was a shame to finally disentangle, but all good things must come to an end. Only this time she propped herself up on her pillow and I laid my head on her chest and once more she stroked my hair, just like Dominika used to.

Dominika, get out of my head!

I forced myself to concentrate on the moment and realised that we couldn't stay like this forever. Almost mournfully, I forced myself to get up and get dressed. Elwira just threw on a long T-shirt.

I didn't want to run out on her so we made our way to the kitchen and got some tea. I didn't want to leave, but knew I had to. It was getting later and evening was on the verge of drawing in. Dominika would be starting to get worried.

Enough—I have to go.

I stood up and pulled Elwira to me one last time. We kissed long, passionately and for the last time today, I groped her naked ass under her T-shirt. I wanted to stay, so we could fuck again, but knew I couldn't. It was a real wrench when I finally tore myself away from her. I told her I'd call her and hopefully we could meet again on Saturday—Friday would be no good because everything would be closed and it'd be harder to make up an excuse for going out. I coldly calculated that this was the best way to justify my deceit and sell my idea convincingly to Dominika.

What a bitch I am!

I left Elwira's and went to the bus stop and waited for a few minutes before my bus came along. As I sat on the bus I all but convinced myself that Dominika would be able to read what I'd done on my face or in the way I acted. She might even on an instinctive level smell the sex I'd enjoyed. She's always cautioned me that pleasure has a price and as I got nearer home this thought, more than any other, continued to nag me and eat away at my guts. I was terrified of her finding out, but knew I had to do my best to conceal the dreadful truth of what I'd done to her.

It probably took about an hour after leaving Elwira to get home and when I entered the flat everything was quiet. So I went directly to our room and saw that Dominika was still in her books and writing on her computer. She barely even noticed me when I came in. I nibbled the back of her neck as I often do, but today in an attempt to normalise the abnormal.

'Oh hi, darling, did you have a nice day?' she asked pleasantly.

If only she knew what I had done!

'Yes, it was pretty nice,' I answered blandly. 'How's it going?'

'I'm good; I just need to finish making my notes on this chapter for tonight. Can you make us some tea?'

'Ok,' I said with a mixture of relief, because I hadn't been found out, and disappointment because even now her studies were still more important than me. In fact she'd hardly even registered that I was there.

'Thank you, darling.'

I headed towards the kitchen and as I opened the room door she called out, 'I love you!'

But my mind was elsewhere. Sin is forbidden fruit and it is delicious and I wanted more, and I wasn't prepared to wait.

Later in bed, while Dominika was still studying, I gently masturbated, not to get off, but just to feel good, to feel touched and to remind myself of the pleasures the day had brought me. I replayed in my mind everything that'd happened from the moment Elwira and I met to the first kiss and everything that followed and I even dared to fantasise about what might happen next. As I stroked myself I knew that I was no longer abandoned and desire had found its way. Or to put it in other words, my mind was following a single track.

Elwira!

Friday 3 May 2019

Eventually I nestled down into the quilt and closed my eyes. Even though I'd stopped playing with myself and was trying to switch off, sleep was eluding me. I tossed and turned while trying to find my space and I just couldn't get comfortable. My mind was still alive with a cacophony of thoughts, which were delicious, sinful, exciting and condemning. Everything centred on Elwira, who now had an inescapable hold on me. The more I tried to will myself to sleep the more my brain kept racing… and all thoughts led back to Elwira.

I must have eventually succumbed though, because at some unknown moment sleep crept up and finally took me into the safe unthinking oblivion within the depths of my mind. The next thing I remembered was waking up looking at Dominika, but thinking about Elwira.

Unless you have ever been there it is the craziest contradiction in your life— a real mind-fuck; to be in bed with somebody who you profess to love and having your mind totally on somebody else.

Dominika was facing me and I wanted to reach out and touch her pale perfection, but knew I couldn't. Her eyes were soft and closed and at peace. I was torn between guilt and lust. If only Dominika would wake up and use me, like she used to. I'd never go back to Elwira again. I didn't want to rouse her. She has been working so hard and needed to sleep as much as she could and it seemed that last night had been especially late for her.

Her study had become her life and I was paying the price.

The rain that had been threatening intermittently all week was now pattering on the windows and I was surprised that it didn't wake Dominika. She must have been absolutely exhausted when she finally came to bed.

My mind was fully alert, even if my eyes were still gritty. I kept replaying yesterday's adventure, that golden moment; that Judas kiss that had crossed the line. It had been a moment of perfection, but at the same time a moment of utter loss. As confused as I was, my betrayal excited me and my body was screaming for her attention.

Her attention! Elwira had invaded my mind and consumed my body.

I carefully turned onto my back and pressed my hand between my legs. A finger quickly found my love button and in small swirls, I began to play with it and in that so sensitive area just around it. As I flicked it with an agitated finger it soon became a hardened knot of swollen flesh. With my right hand I found a nipple and squeezed hard as I remembered how Elwira had bitten down on it causing me delicious, but totally unintended, pain. Fearful of waking Dominika, I suppressed a groan of pleasure and the need to clench my ass as my body began to respond. I cast a quick sideways glance at Dominika. I hadn't been discovered. She was still as unmoving as the dead.

I opened my legs so I could let myself in and found my slot already gooey with my love juice and I pushed a finger inside while moving my thumb so that I could carry on working my hard nub, while all the time I kept the pressure on my nipple that had now become firm and erect under the torment I was giving it.

I remembered how Elwira and I had tasted each other and got off in a perfect naked entanglement of synergetic desire. My memory was so strong I could almost taste her sex again. I resisted another urge to clench and buck my hips and fuck my finger as my excitement rose.

I must not wake Dominika.

I need to cum. I should really go to the bathroom and have a shower to disguise my lust and get myself off discretely. But the very act of moving might disturb Dominika.

Then I began to think that the best thing could be for her to get up and go to the kitchen and then I could do what I wanted to myself. That'd mean waking her, which I really didn't want to do, and besides the one thing I knew for sure was that she wouldn't take advantage of me even if I presented myself on a plate to her.

Added to that, there was something devilishly naughty about masturbating next to her while at the same time doing my best not to wake her. My heart pounded in my chest in a mixture of excitement and the fear of being caught.

I remembered how in the past Dominika had tested my limits and part of that included the fear of discovery—especially the first time she'd left me naked in the midnight forest a few years ago.

I remembered the forest and the intensity of how it made me feel, but then as the memory's power began to fade my mind wandered again.

I imagined Elwira in the room with us. She climbed into bed next to me and pressed her naked form again mine. Her flesh was hot against mine and her heat fired me up. Once again I suckled her perfect breasts and thrust a hand between her legs.

I moved my right hand from my nipple and sucked my fingers as I dreamt of the taste of her sex.

My bodily responses were no longer completely under control and my loins suddenly bucked against my finger causing it to slip deeper inside.

Careful, Ania! Careful! Fear of discovery isn't the same as actually being discovered.

I'd climbed on this rollercoaster and now must ride it to the end. If I moved my arm as I masturbated I would surely wake Dominika, flexing my hand while keeping my wrist as still as possible I used my thumb to flick my clit more furiously. I had a sudden desire to wear my butt plug or to at least have something inside my ass that I could fuck back against. My lust defines me and makes me feel alive and now this is all I am.

Again my hips jumped and my back arched involuntarily as yet another wave of pleasure shook my body. I tensed up, almost to the point of making my muscles hurt, as I tried to remain still. But the fantasy grew more intense.

Dominika had woken up and seen me with Elwira. She jumped up with a wicked smile and grabbed my throat roughly.

'Fuck the dirty little whore—that's all she is good for.'

I smiled gratefully at Dominika, who was now crushing my throat and I was struggling to breathe. Elwira wasn't bothered. Her hands were holding my hips firmly and her tongue was deep inside me, tasting my honey, while Dominika was strangling me.

My death was imminent, but what a delicious death it would be!

Back to reality, Dominika was still sleeping and now I had two fingers inside while my thumb persisted. I pushed my ass down into the mattress as though I was fucking something, but there was nothing there.

Elwira's tongue became more vigorous and her face pressed into me as she ate me out. She let go of my hips and found my outer lips and pulled me apart so she could take more of me into her mouth. My throat was closing and my consciousness was fading as my last orgasm ran through my body. Dominika was still smiling with an evil stare that was superimposed with Kasia's demonic glare.

I continued to manipulate myself carefully—still surprised that Dominika hadn't started moving about. I brought myself to the peak and as pleasure gripped my body I tightened up so not to move. I forced my mouth to stay closed and breathed carefully through my nose and forced myself not to make a sound. My legs straightened and I felt the muscles harden as I silently and (almost) motionlessly stayed on the rollercoaster until it finally coasted to a gradual stop.

My sight dimmed and darkness surrounded me as I took my last breath and the last thing I heard was Dominika.

'Throw her out with the rubbish when you are done.'

I rested with my eyes closed in the clammy sweat of my personal afterglow. My fantasy had been powerful and unusually dark.

Was my subconscious trying to tell me something?

Stop analysing, Ania! It's not your first dark fantasy and not even your first death fantasy!

There was a difference though. This was the first time I'd ever died at Dominika's hand. Dominika is my love and protector; she is my strength and my all. Never before, even in my darkest moments, had she been the one to take my mortality.

I opened my eyes and reality returned. I needed to shower and rinse off my filth. Light was flooding through the curtains and I reasoned that it was a good time to get up.

I pulled the bedding back carefully and eased myself up and rotated onto my feet. The bed squeaked as I pushed down against the mattress as I stood.

'Are you making coffee, darling?'

Dominika was awake.

'I'm just getting a quick shower. I'll make coffee when I am done.'

Making coffee is no big deal, but today it was a gift for Dominika, an offering to appease my guilt.

'Great. I'm just going to close my eyes for a few more minutes. Wake me up when you're done. I can't lose today.'

With that, the conversation was over. I went to the shower and as I washed myself down the guilt also washed away. I was there for her, but still she didn't want me. She wanted a servant to make her coffee. I wanted and needed more.

I touched myself playfully and let my imagination run away with itself. At the same time I was invoking a memory and a desire, I so wished Elwira that was there to touch me, to make me feel alive.

At least *she* wanted me and with that thought the guilt washed away as quickly as the water disappeared down the plughole.

***

The rest of the day was nothing special. Dominika studied again until late and I dutifully looked after her and she gave me absolutely nothing back. I made her drinks and food when she wanted them and did my best for her. Even in the evening when I made us some supper and suggested eating at the table in the kitchen she told me she was in the middle of a very important part and didn't want to lose her flow.

I don't give a shit about you losing your flow, you're losing me.

I couldn't even go online to my social media. I just knew I wouldn't be able to keep secret how Elwira and I had spent yesterday and even more importantly what I'd done to Dominika.

I was with her, but I was so lonely.

I'd had my doubts about meeting Elwira tomorrow. My masturbation fantasy had felt like a warning, but now I longed for her and nothing was going to stop me.

Fuck you, Dominika, I thought in a defiance that even startled me. A rebellion that was totally out of character for me rose in anger. I *am* going to spend the weekend with somebody who cares.

I am sorry, Dominika, but to repeat myself you insisted this confession be honest and that was exactly how I was feeling.

Emotions are brutal.

Saturday 4 May 2019

I woke up angry.

I am aware now in hindsight that I was being completely selfish, but the way I saw things there and then in the moment was very different. Emotions distort reality. I was really hurt by Dominika rejecting me again last night and any guilt had been replaced with resentment and outright scorn, which found its outworking in a selfish determination to serve once again my own needs.

I will get what I want with or without her.

While I wasn't quite prepared to voice my rebellion to Dominika I had absolutely no qualms about meeting Elwira again.

In writing down everything that happened I'm doing my best to recount everything as accurately and thoroughly as possible. However, in truth, my memory of today isn't as good as it was for Thursday. A girl never forgets her first time and with Elwira, it had been something really special and beyond my furthest expectations. Reality is almost certainly doomed to fall short of fantasy, but on Thursday they'd become almost perfect mirrors of each other.

No, that's not true. I don't know about for Elwira, but for me it'd surpassed even my wildest of dreams. Somehow if I could define what had happened in one word that word would be *more*.

It'd been primal and yet gentle, it'd been wild and yet tender and every little detail had burned an impression into my brain. If you were to ask me if I remember all of my adventures then most would be shadows and ghosts of the past with some particularly illuminating moments. Saturday with Elwira was no different. Some moments stand out while others recede into the past. They become faded relics lost in time.

Dominika was still asleep. Despite my anger and my desire for Elwira, my heart was still Dominika's. I didn't think I was confused, but I guess I was. I was really annoyed about yesterday, but it didn't change my love for her. I so desperately wanted to stay with her and hold her and for her to hold me back. She only needed to reach out and I'd reject Elwira without hesitation. I knew my anger had made me blind and it'd be so easy for Dominika to make it dissipate completely. But in my heart of hearts, I knew and already accepted that Dominika wouldn't give me what I needed.

With the sure knowledge that there was no hope of anything from Dominika, compulsion and greed had taken over. Elwira had invaded my mind and reawakened my lust and even though I wrestled with my feelings for Elwira the truth is that the temptation was just too powerful. She was as irresistible as sweet fresh water in the desert.

Or to put it another way it'd be like ignoring that driving instinctive compulsion, which overpowers all rationale and reason, and never masturbating again.

I thought Elwira was mine, but the truth is I was hers.

I knew Dominika would be studying again and I was unsure whether I should disturb her or not. I got up as quietly as I could and went to make breakfast in the kitchen and despite my best efforts, she came and joined me just a few later.

'I wanted to let you sleep, darling,' I said with a smile, in the pretence of normality.

'Too much to do. I think I'll finally be on top of it by tomorrow evening, and then we can do something special—just you and me.'

My mind was already plotting and planning, dreaming up delicious fantasies of how Elwira and I would spend the day. So I didn't really register what she said and grunted the barest of acknowledgments.

'So what are you doing today?'

My mind was made up. Unless Dominika grabbed me right now my course was set. As the Titanic had, on that fateful night, I too would without conscience, steam headlong into disaster. I put on my best mask and said, 'Going out again, I know you are busy so I made plans so I'm out of your way. Fewer distractions mean you'll get more done faster. Emilia and Kasia get back tomorrow afternoon so I'll probably let you take advantage and go out tomorrow too so you can get even more done.'

At least that wasn't a lie.

'That'd great. Thanks,' was her quick reply.

What I said had made it all about Dominika and her needs, but in reality it was completely indulgent and all about mine. The space I'd offered her was definitely not out of any generosity on my part and at that time I didn't regret it. After all, it felt almost like she was pushing me out of the door again.

It is good that I have made other plans.

Dominika hadn't even tried to persuade me to stay and that last flicker of hope was crushed. My thoughts had proven to be correct and my reasoning sound.

Damn you, Dominika, at least Elwira wants me!

That thought got me. A momentary pang of guilt tore across my stomach. I knew I was still in love with Dominika, but she was making me feel so unwanted and unloved. I knew Elwira would be waiting for me with open arms and open legs. When I'd messaged her last night about meeting today she'd been more than excited about the idea.

Can I really be blamed for my lack of resistance?

Dominika went to the bathroom and while she was there I took a couple of things for Elwira and me to enjoy and put them in a plastic bag in a larger handbag to conceal them. I realise now that the toys weren't just for Elwira and me to enjoy, but they were a scream in Dominika's face. Elwira and I would use our toys. Despite this, I still secretly hoped Dominika wouldn't notice that they were missing, but again that was more out of fear of consequence than any sense of morality.

I doubt if she'll even notice.

While annoyed like hell with her and kicking back I still wasn't willing to voice my rebellion and destroy even what we had left. In my mind it was tattered and broken, but still something.

I decided that I should wait long enough for her to come out of the bathroom so I could at least kiss her goodbye and pretend everything was fine. I was putting my shoes on when the door opened and she reappeared. I gave her an intimate, but far from passionate, peck on the lips as I stepped out the door into our stairwell.

'I'll be back later.'

I just hoped she couldn't taste the betrayal on my lips—although this morning I didn't really care if she did anyway. It's not like she wanted me around.

Again I am sorry, Dominika, when you read this, but you wanted me to be absolutely honest and I promised that I won't lie to you ever again.

'See you later, darling, have fun.'

She was so lost in her studies that she seemed barely aware that I even existed anymore. Surely there must have been some unspoken signs of my unhappiness that she should have picked up on? Emilia knew and even Kasia had noticed. It seemed apparently not; as she closed the door on me and shut me out once again.

As I reflect on how I was feeling I wonder if I would have really stayed if she had asked me, and the answer is a definite yes. As much as I was consumed by Elwira, Dominika and I are twin flames, two halves of the same orange, a perfect match.

Conflicted as my thoughts were the feeling of being wanted and needed by Elwira overpowered any sense of guilt or conscience which left me feeling liberated as I began to make my way across the city.

Elwira and I met nearer her home this time and getting there was a disaster.

It'd have been better to go have gone through the city centre and use the Metro. Alas, this wasn't the way I thought would be best. The route I had chosen this time meant that I had to get a tram a few stops and then change to a bus and it was the bus that took forever. At some point I let Elwira know I was on my way and gave her the impression—mistakenly on my part—that I was going to arrive quite soon. However, the bus got snarled up in traffic near the Chelmska TV studios and from there on it slowed to a crawl. I began to despair about ever reaching her.

What was nice though, when finally the bus broke through the tedious rainbow stream of traffic, was that she was waiting at the bus stop for me. Her face made my heart judder. As soon as her eyes met mine, she beamed like the sun and her grin was shining a lot brighter than the overcast weather that was threatening rain once again.

Just a simple smile screamed at me about how much Elwira wanted to spend time with me. Even if there was a single cell in my body that was still holding back, it too succumbed and I was hopelessly lost in her again.

We hugged as I stepped off the bus and exchanged a Polish three cheek kiss. She held on to me a little tighter and a little longer than what is usual in Poland, but I certainly wasn't objecting. As well as igniting desire it made me feel warm and secure.

To be wanted—is it too much to ask?

'What do you want to do today?' she asked.

I didn't want to be forceful, but at the same time I wanted her again so I played it smart—or so I would like to think.

I answered with a cheeky smile, 'Maybe something like we did on Thursday?'

'We can skip the coffee at Costa if you like? I have coffee at home—but only instant. Is that alright? Do you want second breakfast?'

It was like we were playing chess, but working beautifully together to capture each other's queen, me taking hers and her taking mine. Only, unlike chess, neither of us had any problem with surrendering our queens. It was a fun game where the inference was clear, but the words were indirect. Anyone overhearing our conversation wouldn't have given it a second thought.

'Sounds perfect, let's go to yours.'

I hooked my arm comfortably into hers and we set off. It wasn't too far, but it still took a little while to get there. Our conversation was limited—or I can't particularly remember anything about it—maybe we were both just too excited about the day's adventure that was still before us, or too consumed with memories of Thursday. Whichever it was, it didn't really matter because it amounted to the same thing.

All I was thinking about was getting her into bed and my mind was a tapestry of memories and thoughts of what today might bring.

We got to her flat and entered through the stairwell, and just like Thursday I followed her up the stairs taking in the magnificent view of her perfect ass. When we got in I paused briefly to slip my shoes off and hang my jacket up. Elwira's flatmates were still away so again we were alone. She pounced almost immediately. She wrapped her arms around and slid her hands down to my ass, which she grabbed firmly while pulling me closer. Then she kissed me.

She kissed me deep and long and, of course, I responded. I too reached behind her and placed my hands on that special space just above her ass. That space that hints at intimacy and something naughty, but doesn't quite cross the line into lustful abandonment. It screams desire while at the same time showing restraint. We got lost in the moment and all I can remember was the kiss and the closeness. I have absolutely no idea how long we stayed embraced like that, but if you had told me an hour, and I am sure that it wasn't, I'd have believed you. Time became an eternal moment and lost all meaning enfolded in her warmth.

Finally, when the kiss ended she pulled back slightly, but we were still almost nose to nose.

'I've wanted to do that since I saw you get off the bus,' she breathed on me. Her breath was hot and her desire clear. Her passion was obvious and it fed my lust. I'm not sure what I said, but it was something about not being hungry yet—not for food anyway—or even suggesting we could have second breakfast in bed. Whatever it was we skipped coffee and second breakfast and were soon in her bedroom which was all nice and tidy with her bed perfectly made.

Is she still working hard on making an impression or she genuinely is a very tidy person?

We sat on the bed next to each other and held hands on my lap. We smiled for long minutes while staring into each other's eyes not needing to speak or do anything. We were a perfect toothpaste advert. We just soaked in each other's company. Elwira makes intimacy so simple and effortless.

Then without warning, she let go of my hands and pulled my top out of my jeans and was lifting it over my head. It was an exact mirror of last time, only she didn't ask. Although she caught me slightly by surprise I fell willingly into what she wanted. In fact, I raised my arms to make it easier for her. She then cast it aside and reached round and undid my bra, which soon went the same way as the top.

This was not the unsure, tentative Elwira of Thursday, she was more confident, more sure and willing to assert herself. I'd loved Thursday, but this was already promising to be better. She had a plan—she was in charge—and that suited me just fine.

Once the inconvenience of my bra and top had been removed she eased her face into my chest, first kissing one breast and then the other. She ran her mouth up to my neck and in the meantime her hands found my nipples and began to pinch and tease them. She carried on moving up my neck and forced her tongue into my ear and I convulsed involuntarily as a ripple of pleasure electrified my skin and made me knock my knees together.

I lay back on her bed until my head came to a rest on her pillow and she followed me with her tongue not leaving my ear. At the same time her hands stayed on my now hardened nipples as she tormented them with a combination of little pinches and gentle strokes. I lifted my arms above my head to make myself as open as possible and she read the signs.

She covered my naked flesh with little kisses and ran her hands all over me until she reached my waist and my jeans. She made short work of undoing them and sliding them down, with my knickers at the same time. She then pulled them over my ankles and off, complete with my socks too. Not for the first time in my life I was the first one in the room to get naked.

My exposure and vulnerability raised my temperature even higher.

She pushed my knees apart to expose my little damp flower, and for the first time today, she buried her face into my most delicate part. Her tongue was hot and as it made contact with my already swelling button such a sensation ran throughout my body. Elwira is a quick learner. She concentrated her tongue on the most precious space above my love slit, but within seconds she was penetrating me with firm unyielding fingers, I was so ready that she just slid inside me. I opened my legs further as though I wanted her to eat her up completely. At the same time and unseen by her I began to massage my own breasts and toy with my pink nipples. I pinched them hard to make them hurt as she pleasured me. I desired the pain too because the combination of both was the best way for me to reach the mountaintop for which I hungered.

Before Thursday, I'd been denied for too long and now I was too turned on and full of frustration from the last couple of months that I wasn't prepared to be satisfied with the foothills. Orgasmic pleasure needed the summit and anything less would be a denial of deserved pleasure.

I'd dreamt of this moment for the last two nights and dwelt on it in my waking hours—aside from the dark imaginings my mind had conjured yesterday morning. Dreams can come true and while my Elwira fantasies hadn't *quite* crossed the line into obsession it'd been something that had been playing on my mind regularly since Elwira had asked that rather strange question all that time ago. Although those fantasies had faded to be replaced with others over the last couple of years, new ones had been born since she'd agreed to meet up with me this weekend.

My body responded, my mind submitted as I gave myself to the orgasm she was treating me to. As on Thursday she pushed me beyond the orgasm and continued to stimulate me even after the final waves had crashed on my shore. We had both done this to each other before and so she probably understood this was the only way to do it. She understandably still had gaps in her knowledge—not that I was objecting.

Even though she refused to let up with her vigorous fingers, my responses were weakening and I was becoming increasingly limp, even if my breath remained ragged. My levels of arousal were dropping rapidly and she too, after seeing my responses dull, finally eased to a stop, although she kept her fingers inside me. With the cooling of my fire I started closing and with that came a dull pain that was more of a tightening as my sex gripped her fingers and began to push her out.

I'd been conscious of it throughout, but now, even more than before, it pressed on my mind that Elwira had completely given herself to me. She hadn't even undressed yet. She'd made it *all about me* and I can't even begin to describe how special it made me feel. I was her centre and it made me determined to spoil her and I knew just how to.

'I have a surprise for you Elwira, something I brought from home for us to try? You willing to have a go? I just need my handbag.'

Such enthusiasm. She jumped up and ran out of the room and brought it back before I even had a chance to react. I'd intended to go and get it. Her keenness was sweet and endearing, but it almost felt like she was trying too hard to please me—not that I was complaining. If she was seeking my approval she didn't need to. She already had it—not that it matters anyway—because that can be very judgmental. Neediness can be a problem but it is always initially endearing and after months of neglect it was making a refreshing change.

I know I am being a hypocrite and my neediness is part of who I am; only Dominika knows how to handle this.

The sudden impulsive thought of Dominika threatened our space for a moment, but I pushed it out in the same way as she had almost pushed me out of the flat this morning. Focusing on what I planned for Elwira brought me back from my conscience and helped me escape thoughts of Dominika.

Now I will treat Elwira.

Servitude, which often means an element of passivity, is normally my place and once more I found myself almost in a role reversal and it made a refreshing change.

Elwira is so sweet and I wanted to spoil her and to hold her and keep her forever.

I took the plastic bag out of my handbag and with it a 25cm strap-on. Elwira's eyes opened wide, because even if she'd never seen one before, what it was and how to use it were pretty obvious.

'Do you want to play?' I flashed her my cheekiest and most alluring smile, while all the time knowing that she had absolutely no chance of resisting me. In turn, she nodded unreservedly as though I'd offered her the sweetest gift from heaven.

I put the toy aside on the bed so she was my all, my centre and everything—at least for now. Looking at her I suddenly realised again I was naked and she wasn't.

I'd soon bring balance to that.

Elwira was still standing so I got up and stood in front of her. As much as I wanted to just jump on her I knew I needed to take my time so she could enjoy it as much as possible—at least as much as I'd enjoyed her attentions.

It didn't however mean I couldn't tease and have fun with her in the meantime.

One thing I learnt very quickly about Elwira is that she loves kisses. Once more I kissed her with a hunger born of the famine I'd endured over recent months. At the same time, I tugged at her belt and quickly unbuckled it. A few quick finger manipulations later her button and zip were undone and my hand was inside her knickers and pressing on her shaven treasure, not quite as perfectly smooth as it had been on Thursday, with nubs of stubble that felt like kitten's teeth. I found the top of her groove, but couldn't push any further down because her jeans were tight into her crotch. The heart of her forbidden flower was tantalisingly out of reach.

Not for much longer.

Her breathing deepened and her heat rose and under her top, her breasts heaved, I suspected, more out of anticipation than real arousal. Then I pulled my hand out of her knickers and clasped both of my hands around her back just above her ass. I pulled her close and pushed her head aside with a persistent mouth before nibbling her neck. I hadn't really noticed before, but she was almost as tall as me, just a tiny bit shorter. Her breaths became shallower and more ragged and she started shaking as she responded to my touch. She'd come a long way in such a short time, but now it wasn't about me and she was the centre of attention she was still anxious.

To distract her from her nerves and move things along, I took hold her top and lifted it off, just pulling my lips away for long enough to do so. Now with more exposed flesh to play with, I moved around her neck and into her cleavage. I pressed her breasts together through her bra and sighed through my teeth. I could only dream of having a body like hers.

I don't know if she was getting impatient, just full of lust or trying to be helpful, but she removed her bra so I could have a full view of her magnificent peaks which I could now fully enjoy. I used my tongue and teasing teeth and her nipples hardened in my mouth. I flicked my tongue across them, moving from one to the other. As I suckled on them, I continued to nip them gently with my teeth—enough for her to feel, but not enough to hurt.

Soon she was moaning again, but certainly not complaining! Once more she was purring with the pleasure I was giving her.

She held my head close to her, cradling me gently as I went to work. It was one of those rare perfect moments that I sometimes write about when the whole universe collides into flawlessness. I felt protected, loved and safe with her arms around me and I don't know what she felt, but if it was only a little bit of what I was feeling then it must have been truly amazing for her too.

I was ready for more so I released her and slid down her body and as my face reached the level of her intimacy, I firmly pulled her jeans down and pushed them below her knees where they bunched and got caught up. She stepped out of them, or at least tried to, as they refused to budge over her ankles. For just a moment, as she fought the obstinate material, any thoughts of romance or lust were lost and forgotten in the clownish comedy that was playing out before me. As she wrestled with them, they turned inside out and she stomped her way out of them unceremoniously and then bent to take her socks off.

The slapstick moment was over and was nothing more than a fleeting moment, a momentary distraction to our desire. Now she was almost naked she was almost ready. She was wearing a sporty thong that rode high up her thighs from her magic triangle, almost like a swimsuit. I remained crouched in front of her and kissed her between the two little risen bumps of her outer labia and could smell her sex and feel her moisture. I don't know about her getting turned on, but my fire was burning again.

I couldn't be selfish. I had to lay my own greed aside, she'd pleasured me unconditionally and now it was her turn. I resisted the urge to reach underneath and feel my own sex. She might be *too vanilla* for this, for the time being anyway. I could coax her in baby steps and she had plenty of time to evolve.

And that was part of the adventure. We were still discovering each other. It was exciting, it was the explosive intensity of a sparked match, a burning passion, and each moment was just another small step into something bigger, more daring and more pleasurable.

I kissed her again between her legs through the material of her knickers and pushed my mouth against her intimacy as though it was her mouth. As I pressed and sucked on her I reached up to her hips and found the sides of her thong which I eased down. I pulled my face away to behold my favourite part of stripping off—the part that I like to call *the reveal*.

It's that moment when the part of the knickers that is the final defence of her inner bastion often kind of stays in place, even when the rest of her knickers are half way down her thighs. Then suddenly the material gives way and her flower is revealed in full bloom. This was no exception and it's always a surprise to me, like the sudden opening of a treasure trove or the unveiling of a perfect diamond.

I love it.

I eased her thong down to her ankles and she stepped out of it before I thrust my tongue once more into her channel. Her slime gave testimony to her arousal and I tasted her salt, as I lapped at her and pressed my tongue hard inside her. I used my hands to part her petals and slid my tongue up to her guarding hood. I flicked my tongue against it and she put her hands on my head and groaned. I let go, but only momentarily as I pushed a finger inside her. She was tight, but her wet made the invasion easy; all the time I kept my tongue on her open button, now a growing bump, as I tried to bring her flower into its fullest glory. She wasn't as wet as I get, but soon my chin was covered in her natural lube as she responded to my orchestrations.

Then I decided to try an experiment—I could always say '*oops!*'

With one hand already busy I reached around with my other and wiggled it between her ass cheeks until I found her little knot, which I touched just tentatively before I started stroking it. It's something I love; it tickles and is very sensual with just the hint of being on the threshold of being slightly naughty.

She flinched and I felt her body tighten as though surprised, but then she relaxed and let me carry on. I was already at her limits, so I resisted the temptation to push inside. I'd have loved to do that, l love it when my forbidden entrance is played with. But she's not me and caution won out because that might be too much for her.

I licked and lapped at her for some time until I finally stood up again and took hold of her elbows. I guided her as I walked her backwards until her knees hit the back of the bed and she collapsed gracefully with the help of my supporting arms. I helped ease her onto her back so I could get to her. I climbed between her legs and up her body as though I was going to fuck her like a missionary, but then I kissed her. She didn't complain about the taste of her sex, which was all over my tongue and mouth and now consequently hers too.

'I need to take this slowly. If it hurts tell me.'

I reached across the mattress and took the strap-on which was within easy reach. I didn't want to risk hurting her and decided to try it for size before fucking her with it. I pushed two fingers inside her to gather up as much of her wet as I could. Then I rubbed it all over the head of the phallus, before introducing it to her by just parting her lips and placing it maybe just a centimetre inside.

OMFG! It's like fucking a virgin.

I pushed it a bit further and paused while watching her face constantly for any signs of extreme discomfort or pain. Confident she was taking it, I fed her some more before giving her some time to adjust and repeating until it was about halfway in. Then I gently fucked her slowly with it a few times to make sure she could take it.

Satisfied she was ready, I moved on.

She looked a bit disappointed when I slid it completely out of her and took it into my mouth and sucked it like a cock. All the time I was tasting down her moisture, I was working her clit with my other thumb.

'Patience, Elwira,' I teased when I took it out of my mouth now soaked with a cocktail of my saliva and her arousal.

The truth is that I don't wear a strap-on very often, I am normally the one getting fucked, so I had to fiddle with the straps a bit to get it just right and I only hoped she didn't lose her fire or dry up while I was messing about with it. Once I had it on properly, I climbed once more between her legs and positioned it at her entrance. I pulled her hips closer and lifted her legs to rotate her tunnel and then as I had done a few minutes before I slid it centimetre by centimetre into her. She groaned in open mouthed pleasure as it went in and when I felt it was far enough in I began to rock up and down on her. By now I was balanced over her hips and pushing slightly downwards into her.

I pushed the back of her knees up to my shoulders so she was almost bent in half and pushed once more, going as deep as I could. She groaned as I impaled her, but I watched her face all the time, knowing I would have to stop if I went too deep. I guess for a man it is easier because he can feel it, but I was penetrating her with firm latex and couldn't feel a thing.

Suddenly, once I was most of the way in she pushed against my hips with the palms of her hands. I understood this to mean that I'd gone as deep as she could take. I used this as a measure to fuck her with. I started slowly and increased both my speed and stroke length by pulling further out of her and then pushing back in, but never more than she'd shown me. To begin with she kept her hands in a guarded position on my hips, but she moved them away as she became more comfortable and lost in pleasure. Her eyes flickered, half-closed, in an unsaid expression of her pleasure. Her mouth opened wider as she sucked in more air and her bodily movements attuned to my rhythm.

I'm quite fit, so for me to go at her like this was easy, although it was a bit frustrating not being able to feel anything. All I could do was focus on the expression on her face and listen to her grunt, every time I pushed into her to get some idea of how she was feeling, and at least I was serving—which is my natural role—and this more than made up for my denied pleasure. It was her turn anyway and I was determined to give it to her as good as I could. Taking on the masculine role was so unusual for me, but she deserved everything I could give her.

After all, she'd given so selflessly to me.

After a few minutes, I sat up and eased my thighs below her so my knees were either side of her ass. Then I pushed her legs down and allowed them to part either side of me. Her hips were now between my knelt thighs and my knees were pressing against her sides above her hips. I grabbed hold of her belly, one hand on each side near my knees, but just below her ribcage. This grip meant that I could fuck her harder and pull her against me in opposition to my plunging motion. I could also see the firm latex sliding in and out of her and her labia stretching as it did so. Her breasts rocked to my rhythm and her mouth opened as though trying to breathe in everything that was happening to her.

Then I took another risk.

I let go of her belly and took her right hand and placed it on her lower belly before stretching out one of her fingers and pushing it directly onto her treasure.

'It's not a spectator sport,' I joked, not jokingly. 'Join in!'

She seemed embarrassed, but then she seemed, almost as though she made a conscious decision to let go and embrace the moment. At first I kept my hand on hers to offer her encouragement but then I moved it back to her side and carried on fucking her as I had been doing. She didn't stop masturbating when I let go, and once more I got lost in her face and enjoyed the view as her ever-changing expressions were giving me a constant commentary on what it was doing for her.

And this is where my memory begins to fade because I remember fucking her long and hard and her masturbating as I did so. I remember changing positions a few times. I think first I rolled her on her side and fucked her while raking one of her hips backwards and forwards and then I fucked her like a dog from behind and finally I pushed her flat on the mattress and fucked her until she grasped the sheets and shuddered under me in the throes of her release. I think once I'd encouraged her to touch herself she didn't let go and held on for the rest of the ride.

Of course. my memory is a bit blurred here, but no one is perfect.

What I clearly remember though is what I did when we finished. I eased the dark wand out of her and undid the straps before taking the latex once more into my mouth. I sucked and licked it clean of her taste and her sex. Dirty and disgusting I know, but primal passion was taking over and it just added to my lust and desire. She just watched on, too exhausted to move or too shocked to comment.

I was fairly sure she'd never seen anything like this, but by my so-called standards I was still being extremely *vanilla*. I have very few limits when it comes to sex. I just couldn't stop myself, even though I was conscious that what I was doing could well have taken her beyond her limitations.

Sometimes I overthink things and maybe this was one of those occasions.

My libido was fired up again, but Elwira needed some time to recover from her exertions so we just cuddled up together and pulled the bedding over us. She laid into my arm with her head gently resting on my shoulder. An idle hand stroked my belly tenderly and it rose and fell as I breathed. Words were unnecessary and my fire ebbed in the glow of our intimacy.

Before we knew it we both fell asleep—entwined together as once again our two bodies became one.

I hadn't even noticed that I'd fallen asleep and only realised because I was awoken with a start as a hand slid between my legs. I jumped and was even more confused when I opened my eyes and realised that it wasn't Dominika. Luckily, my wits hadn't completely deserted me and I quickly remembered where I was. I was fortunate that my momentary shock didn't lead to me blurting Dominika's name out loud.

That could have been a disaster!

My instincts, so attuned to being submissive couldn't be hidden though and at Elwira's touch I automatically responded and before I even knew what was really happening, I opened my legs to let her in. My reaction was completely instinctive and thought never came into it. I live to be used sexually and with Elwira there was no reason why it should be any different. Serving means giving and that was exactly what I was doing.

No is a rare word in my vocabulary. Dominika and I have an alternative safe word for this.

Elwira wasn't even trying to arouse me, she was just trying to be intimate, but once we started we weren't going to stop. She lifted her head from my shoulder that had stiffened as we slept. My hand was numb and my arm was tingling because the blood had been cut off.

She kissed me again—I have never met anybody who likes kissing as much as she does.

My open legs were an invitation for her and once more she started fingering me. As she did so she rolled around and sat astride my face and lowered herself onto me and in a replay of what we'd done on Thursday and we tasted each other's sex at the same time. She was even saltier than she'd been earlier, but I can't speak for my own taste.

After a few minutes of this though, she suddenly stopped. 'My turn,' she declared with an almost childlike enthusiasm. I don't think she even realises how charming she is. She jumped off me and before I even had chance to answer she grabbed the strap-on and started to put it on. Her expression was one of bemusement as she was trying to figure out how all the straps the buckle worked. After watching her struggle for a few minutes, I helped her out a bit.

'What should I do?' she asked now it was finally in place. 'Should I lick you first or what?'

Poor innocent Elwira!

'Can you remember on Thursday I told you I find pain exciting?' I didn't wait for her to answer. 'So just put it straight in. If it hurts me it's ok and if it hurts me too much I'll tell you to stop.'

'But…'

'Just try and see. I promise I won't let you hurt me, not too much anyway. I'll press my hands on your hips if you go in too far—just like you did to me— if I have to.' I said it all sweetly knowing all the while that I more than didn't mind if she did hurt me. I live for pain and my soul feeds on my suffering.

I opened my legs for her and invited her in. She lay on top of me and I could feel the fake dong banging around me as she tried to push it in.

'You might need to actually *put* it inside me,' I suggested helpfully.

She smiled, slightly embarrassed, but reached down and put the head on my eager sex and pushed. I yielded with a gasp as she went further in than she probably expected and then she pushed again. I had relaxed while we were sleeping and was a little unstretched and tight. So it did sting a bit, as she entered. It was inadvertent on her part and more than a little bit uncomfortable, but for the first time, Elwira was combining pleasure and pain and giving it to me how I really like it. For me it was like fire to paper—instant combustion.

If taking on the masculine role was strange for me it had to be a completely new experience for her. It took her a few minutes to get her coordination just right but as she got into her rhythm, she lifted herself slightly off my belly and rested more on her arms. Now I could, I pushed my hand down to my divine pleasure button and began to roll my fingers around and on it as I had encouraged her to earlier.

I'd have been a hypocrite if I hadn't done so.

Between her sliding in and out of me and my own stimulation, it felt so good. From time to time I caught my fingertips on the latex as she pumped it into me, but nothing was going to knock us off our rhythm. I reached up with my other hand and grabbed at one of her breasts dangling fully in front of me. I lifted my head and licked and sucked on her other nipple as I tried to give her back at least some of what she was giving me.

We fucked like this for a while and then changed positions, she fucked me like the bitch I am from behind and then she lay on her back and I climbed on top of her and impaled myself on her. I was so tempted to push the phallus into my dark hole instead, but I wasn't opened—although my natural love lube is usually enough—and once more I chose the more conservative way because anything more might be too much for her.

One day… I thought to myself …and it can't come soon enough!

Elwira grabbed hold of my hips and held me tight as I bounced up and down on her and I was almost twerking on her artificial erection. I reached down and kneaded her chest. Her delicious flesh rolled in my hands and her buds, already hardened, pressed into my palms.

Each moment brought me nearer. My greed utterly consumed me, as I neared the end and while she continued to fuck me, I let go of her and leant back. I stabilised myself with my right hand behind me, on her knee, and once again I finger fucked my clit in tune with my bodily demands. I closed my eyes and Elwira's fucking became more sporadic and less rhythmic as she tried to coordinate her upward thrusts with my downward ones. This breakdown of our love dance meant was more bucking than fucking and I could hardly hold on. It's wasn't a smooth ride, but it was all the more intense for it.

Between her and my agitating fingers, I was never going to last long and blurred fingers took me over the edge into oblivion. As I cum, she continued to pump inside me and fill my lust as I squirmed on top of her. I gyrated my hips with little control or coordination and pressed down to take as much of the black cock as I could. All the time she didn't stop and my orgasm became painful—this wasn't just any mountaintop—I'd climbed Mount Everest. It was a perfect culmination of our sex as pain and pleasure rocked my body in almost unbearable harmony. My heart was bouncing out of my chest and I rode my odyssey to the end while she continued stabbing me from below. She only stopped when pleasure waned and I finally couldn't take any more, I collapsed forwards onto her body with my head buried on the pillow next to hers.

My heart reverberated audibly against her ribcage after the mountaintop had left me breathless and reduced me to a sticky, sweaty mass of used and utterly consumed flesh. She wrapped her arms around me lovingly and protectively and we rested with her still deep inside me and unlike a cock it was going nowhere.

After a few minutes, the coolness of the room began to caress and chill my clammy body. My insides began to tighten and the penetration became increasingly more uncomfortable and tender. Unlike a retreating cock, that gets spat out as it becomes flaccid and muscles contract, the strap-on wasn't moving—it was in too deep. The forceful fucking Elwira had given me had also heightened my senses which now meant it was becoming more acutely painful with every passing moment until it began to reach my limit of endurance. So, somewhat reluctantly, I was forced to climb off her. Once again I found myself cuddling up to her, intimate, close and without the necessity for words. She kissed me passionately and once more grabbed at my chest. She quickly found a nipple and moved down and nibbled on it again.

I was spent, but could understand why she was aroused and hungering again. This is the problem with using such a toy as a strap-on, one is pleasured and it leaves the other always wanting more.

Of course, a double-headed dildo is a solution, but I'd left that at home.

It'd happened to me earlier and now it was happening to Elwira. For the time being I was sated but she was hungry again. There was only one thing for it, and as a submissive it's my natural inclination to want to please others and serve their needs—even if I am tiring. My mind compelled me and drove me on. My inner sense of responsibility left me with no other choice but to attend to Elwira's obvious needs.

I wanted to be creative. She deserved that and if I took my time my own body would have time to recover and we could probably for the first time truly make love together while focusing on each other instead of taking it in turns as we had been doing so far.

I roused myself from the bed and went once more to the plastic bag and took out the second item I had brought with me. Now was the time for us play with it. While I was choosing what to bring I'd been so tempted to bring my big butt plug—but I was sure she would've panicked if she'd seen it—even if I only intended to have it for my own use. Rather, I'd opted for the somewhat more conservative blindfold. It'd give more than hint of naughtiness without being too much for Elwira.

I climbed on top of her belly, with my knees almost into her armpits, and blindfolded her. She had to lean forward for a moment, so I could get the elastic behind her head. When it was snuggly in place I tested to see if she really couldn't see by lifting my hand and bringing it down near her eyes as though I was going to slap her. She didn't even flinch so I was convinced by her blindness.

Of course, I would never have actually hit her.

Once more it led to me being in the more dominant position and, if truth be told, I'd rather it have been the other way round—with me blindfolded and subject to her every whim. I am no dominant so I didn't use this position as an opportunity for some kind of sexual power play.

I simply started massaging her.

Memories are vague, but I remember sliding down her body so I was sitting at her feet. I think I started on her legs and worked her calves and teased her thighs close enough to her hidden place to tantalise her, but not so close to directly stimulate her. Then as I once more moved up her body and sat on her legs I bypassed her intimacy and circled round her thighs and followed the contours of her hips up to her ribs and when I reached her shoulders I lifted myself up and rolled her onto her front. Then I lowered myself again on top of her with my treasure resting on her ass. I rubbed her shoulders and really worked my fingers into them and she groaned in pleasant pain—or so I would like to think. It is probably the first time in my life that I have ever inflicted possible discomfort on anyone and it was breaking down her tension so I don't think it really counts. She was shaking a bit again, but unlike Thursday's first-time nerves I was sure it was out of pleasure and nervous anticipation.

It was time to turn up the heat and take a risk. Slowly and naturally I moved my massaging hands down her back and stroked and rubbed her kidney area for a while before I slid my body down so I could sit on the back of her knees. Now I had a full view of her ass I began to play with her tight symmetrical globes. As I rolled them in my hands I pried them open and caught glimpses of her tight little knot and just below that the outer entrance to her promised land.

At some point I must have started tickling her because even though I couldn't hear her laughter I could feel her vibrating and shaking underneath me. I spanked her playfully and laughed too.

'If you don't stop moving my finger might slip by accident,' I joked, but I wasn't joking!

I ran my finger down her crease from the top of the valley to the unseen crevice below. I felt her wet and lingered on it for a moment before taking some of her damp to my fingertip and teasing her just inside before coming up the valley again between her two rolling hills. I paused at her unnatural opening, just to see how she would react.

There was nothing. She didn't tighten or squirm away in dreaded anticipation, so I pushed my finger inside, just a little bit. I felt her body protest and her ring resist, but she didn't say anything. Encouraged I pushed a bit further to my first bendy knuckle. I didn't want to hurt her so I wiggled my finger around a bit to stretch her muscle and she groaned—as if she liked it.

Maybe she is less vanilla than I thought!

I eased my finger very slowly to the mid-finger knuckle and she gasped in slight discomfort as her second ringed defence gave way. I could still feel her ass trying to reject me, but still she didn't say anything.

'Are you alright, Elwira?' I asked in a tentative voice, despite feeling emboldened by her silence.

'Yes,' she mumbled into the sheet. 'You just surprised me.'

Again I was presented with being in a peculiarly dominant position, but at the same time I felt like I was *educating* her into the things I like and what I'd like done to me. If I was educating her, I wasn't in the unnaturally unfamiliar position of dominating her.

I was feeling my heat again and could now take us both up a level. I had an idea where I wanted to go, but needed to get her there too.

From behind, with her on her belly it was really difficult to reach her on switch, but I was sure, that as I dipped into her natural hole with two fingers, I was inflaming her lust while the at the same time my already busy finger in her ass was holding her steady. I worked my fingers alternately like a pumping engine, but was careful not to move the one inside her ass too much. I am almost certain that before today she was untested there and I didn't want to ruin it with something impetuous that could hurt her.

She started wiggling again under my touch, but it wasn't in resistance. It may have been her first double penetration, but she was handling it well. After a few minutes, still restrained by me sitting on the back of her knees, she lifted herself to present more of herself. Only her ass was more or less on my chest now and I had no room for movement. So I had to slide back.

This actually worked in my favour. I carried on working her body with her ass almost in my face and then after a few more minutes I suddenly withdrew my hands and rolled her onto her side. I lifted one knee so she was almost forming a letter A and then I slid in so our labia exchanged the sweetest of kisses. I wasn't as hot or aroused as she was so, while leaning on my right side I used my stronger left hand to bring me up to speed.

Elwira is so sweet, open-minded and quick to learn. Like a mirror, she started to copy me and as we rubbed our intimacies together she too began to drive her motor with her fingers. It's harder than it looks, but I'm an old hand and she's a quick learner so very soon we fell into our own natural rhythm. The thing I remember most about those first moments in that position was we had to be careful not to catch each other's fingers. After a few painful scratches, especially on the bottom of each other's nails, we found our tune and then I abandoned my masturbation and just lent back on both arms and let my body do the work. Again Elwira did the same.

We bucked and we fucked and we rode each other, our swelling lips responding to the grinding of our hips. The only problem with our position was that we could only stimulate each other directly and it made all other play impossible, but it was enough!

It was good that I'd shown her to carry on beyond the orgasm because even a casual observer could see from her reactions that she'd reached hers before I reached mine. Her breathing became more ragged and her gyrations less rhythmic as she overheated and became a raging furnace. In an ideal world we'd have cum together, but this is the reality and as I keep repeating, Dominika demanded the truth and not some glamorised or shiny version of what happened.

Dominika—again! This is my full confession as you demanded.

As she shook and rode through her tempest, I too entered choppy waters and was soon swept up into a climaxing whirlpool. We rode the storm together with her being slightly ahead of me and returning to still waters before I did. I was very happy that she continued to grind on me until I joined her again in that peace that followed the torrent. Because neither she nor I were totally sure of where the other was we carried on until our hips ached and we couldn't go on any more and then we slowed our momentum together like the slow docking of a large ship.

It was fucking amazing.

Scissored together we both leant back and rested, which on such a small bed was difficult to say the least. My hips ached and our bodies were stuck together. Elwira's chest heaved before slowly coming to a rest as her excitement came down and her body recovered. It wasn't particularly comfortable and quite precarious. There was a good chance at least one of us would fall off the bed. In fact I am fairly sure that holding on to each other as we were was the only thing that was stopping this from happening.

I think we must have both been aware of this so we disengaged momentarily and I got off the bed. She shuffled across to make room for me and now it was more comfortable we cuddled up together. Our sweaty bodies felt hot and clammy as we held on to each other, but we didn't care. Closeness was more important than our stickiness. As we lay there we just switched off in our intimacy. I closed my eyes as the last of my sexual tension finally drained away.

After a few minutes, I was aware that Elwira's breathing become slower and more shallow and I realised she must have dropped off. Her arms were holding me protectively and I felt safe.

We only allowed ourselves to doze for a few minutes and when we stirred again we suddenly realised it was the middle of the afternoon.

Once more Elwira was a bundle of energy. 'You know, Ania as good as it is, we should do something more than make love. It's way too late for second breakfast. Shall we go and grab some food and browse in Uni Lubelski?'

I'm not sure how I felt about leaving our love pit, and not just because the shopping at Uni Lubelski isn't particularly good. Getting up meant the end of our pleasures, but Elwira was looking for more than sex and it was the least I could do for her.

She wants to spend time with me.

That's what really mattered.

Firstly, we had to wash the remains of our sex off and soon we were squeezed into her small shower. We washed each other down, it was intimate and close and sprinkled with kisses, but there was no more sex, as tempting as it might have been. I was careful not to wash my hair; Dominika would smell a different shampoo tonight when she came to bed—even if it was long after I'd fallen asleep.

Dominika!

My lust and physical workout had leeched the anger from my body and I had been feeling an inner satisfied glow that'd come about in the aftermath of our lovemaking. But with one thought the strange calm that had been about me and Elwira and our lovemaking was quickly supplanted by fear.

I'm not brave enough to confront Dominika, especially when I've done something so wrong,

As thoughts of her became stronger, fear became mixed with a pang of guilt that gripped my stomach. I had to do something to change my thinking. My remedy was right in front of me.

I distracted myself and the best way to do this was to admire once more Elwira's pure innocent naked form. Drinking her in with my eyes pacified my guilt as I remembered how unlike Dominika Elwira wanted me around. Thursday had been great and then today… it was only getting better and better. My lust for Elwira soon evaporated any thoughts I had for Dominika.

I am sure that anyone who is reading this completely hates me by now, yet you are still compelled to read to the end. I must say again, Dominika is completely innocent as is Elwira and all of the fault is mine and mine alone.

On the whole, I was able to ignore and compartmentalise my feelings towards Dominika, especially after so many months. But once in a while, throughout this time when I was lost, they came back to haunt me even in the midst of making love to Elwira.

After showering we were soon dressed and out of the door. We browsed in the shops for a while. It was lovely to walk arm in arm and just be happy in Elwira's company. It didn't take long to go around the shopping centre, there wasn't much to see so afterwards we genuinely did go to a coffee shop; well more an ice cream parlour—Grycan a great Polish café with perfect ice cream, sundaes and cakes. We chatted and laughed all the time; Elwira's not only great at being intimate but she really is such a lovely person to spend time with too.

And she chats more than enough for the two of us so that is more than fine by me.

I knew it was a kind of honeymoon period when everything was new and fresh, but at this moment she was just about as perfect as anybody can be.

The ugly idea of a relationship entered my head, not ugly because of her, but ugly because of the situation. I wanted both Dominika and Elwira, but my heart was still Dominika's. What could I do? It was a horrible position to be in and I was completely weak and gave in to my lust that had been both reignited and found a new focus.

Choosing is impossible for the greedy, not that choosing would ever come into it, because despite everything I knew Dominika would win.

I dismissed the idea that I could be in love with Elwira and decided I was *addicted* to her. My mind could handle that. It was better than considering that it could be the first flowering of love. It wasn't what I feel for Dominika nor was it the special closeness I have with Emilia. It was different. Yes it was vibrant and exciting, it made me high and I demanded more, but it doesn't even come close to what I have with Dominika.

Elwira will always be second, but when Dominika isn't even running Elwira is the clear winner.

After we had finished in Grycan, Elwira saw me to the tram and we went our separate ways after a polite Polish kiss and hug. It is better to be cautious on Polish streets and I am not commenting on if one of Dominika's friends saw us—

even though that was a possible risk. Many Polish people, especially older ones, are still not too open or tolerant to the idea of same-sex partnerships. This is thanks in no part to the attitude of our PiS-led government.

As we parted, we agreed to meet again tomorrow. I'd send her a text or something in the evening to organise it.

It took a little while to get home, although I didn't repeat the mistake I'd made in the morning and I came back by the longer but faster route that I should have used this morning.

When I arrived home, Dominika was still on her computer and immediately upon seeing me she put her work aside and came to me. She kissed me deep and hard and held me tight. Despite being sexually worn out I would've gladly torn my clothes off there and then to serve her, but she suggested going to the kitchen.

'I need a break and we haven't been spending too much time together lately. I'm tired of studying and being no fun.'

And so we went to the kitchen and drank tea and talked. I felt really awkward, but kept up the pretence of normality and hid my feelings from her. It was nice to actually talk and she was lovely, but I couldn't break her heart.

'So back to my books,' she said after a while and dutifully returned to her studies.

And that was it. She left me alone again.

Dominika why can't you see me?

I wasn't as angry as I'd been in the morning, more saddened and disappointed.

I immediately reached for my phone and messaged Elwira. I suggested meeting up with her again after breakfast and she replied immediately with the simple message 'Great,' followed by lots of hearts and kisses. I wrote back that I'd message her when I was on my way.

Dominika wasn't interested and like most addicts I was only thinking about my vice and I knew exactly where to get my next fix.

Sunday 5 May 2019

Dominika and I both slept in on Sunday morning.

She must have been so tired after working until well into the early hours. As is often the case nowadays, I wasn't even aware of her getting into bed next to me. I slept through and when I woke up and turned to face her I saw her still sound asleep through gritty light-stabbed eyes. It crossed my mind that it would have been easy to get up and sneak out, with her completely unaware, but I didn't want to run out on her until we'd at least spent some time together.

Distracted as she was, Dominika had tried really hard last night to at least spend some time with me. I'd more than noticed, and aside from my guilt, which her presence made worse, I had appreciated her time and effort. But then she'd gone back to her work and I'd ended up feeling disappointed. Unsurprisingly I found myself alone dwelling once more on Elwira—the corrupter of my already broken soul.

We'll breakfast together and then I'll go to her. Maybe today she'll be more in charge. I'd fucking love that. I'm addicted and I need my fix. I can't wait.

With lustful thoughts of Elwira and hot decadent temptation filling my mind, I got out of bed being careful not to disturb Dominika. I grabbed a shower, shaved the slight stubble that was appearing between my legs and cleansed myself thoroughly, including deeply in all of my intimate places as I always do when expecting sex. I knew it was unlikely to get any use, but I even cleansed my unnatural hole.

I'll spare you the details but better to be prepared for all eventualities.

My expectations raised a pang of guilt, but I determined that I had nothing to feel guilty about. There was love and acceptance on one side and rejection on the other. The choice was so simple that, in fact, it didn't even need thinking about. I put thoughts of Dominika out of my mind, but remained mindful of my intentions for the day.

Once I'd prepared myself for the day, I went to the kitchen and started making coffee. A few minutes later I heard Dominika moving about and soon she came and joined me. So I prepared a second cup and made some food and we had a relaxed breakfast together. We chatted, about nothing in particular and I maintained my poker face. I was so fake, but I was so fixated on getting my fix that I was a perfect actress. During the course of the conversation I reminded her that I was going out for a few hours again today so she could concentrate on her work.

Again I made my lust and sin sound like I was doing her a favour.

I didn't promise, but said that I'd try to be back before Emilia and Kasia got back from Sopot, which I expected to be sometime during the late afternoon.

With that said there wasn't much else to say so as she turned to her books I finished getting ready and was soon on my way.

The weather was similar to yesterday, overcast with the threat of rain and I wondered if the choice of a T-shirt, skirt and bare legs was wise. I was soon to learn that my decision turned out to be perfect and it had nothing to do with the weather.

But I must be careful not to get ahead of myself...

I'd learnt from yesterday morning's mistake and decided to use the much more indirect route that I'd used when coming home yesterday afternoon which although longer and a bit inconvenient was quicker overall. I had to get a tram just a few stops and then one bus for another couple of stops before finally taking another bus the rest of the way. The latter the same one I'd used on Thursday when I'd gone with Elwira to her flat for the first time.

Time flew and before I knew it I was on my way to Stary Mokotów and I was more than warm enough on the bus. Actually, with the windows closed and the air-conditioning off it got quite humid and sticky. I don't come this way too often and I was disappointed that the steam on the windows obscured my favourite view of Warsaw city centre as we were driving over the Siekierkowski Bridge.

I messaged Elwira while I was on my way so she knew roughly when to expect me. I reassured her that I was coming a much quicker way this time.

From the bridge, it took about another half an hour to get through to where we were meeting in Mokotów. As the bus continued I peered as best as I could through the windows to keep my bearings. Finally, as I was approaching the bus stop I got up and went to stand by the doors ready to get off. My heart jumped when the doors opened and I saw Elwira waiting there. I almost ran off the bus to get to her, such was my joy in seeing her. If it's even possible she looked even happier than yesterday.

It was such a relief to get off the bus. The humidity had become almost unbearably uncomfortable and my back in particular was getting damp and sticky. Stepping out into the chilled air made me feel cold, but it was so much better than the stuffiness inside.

We greeted each other in our typical way and, as with yesterday, our hug lingered just a few seconds longer than what is usual in Poland. She did however keep her hands in the publicly acceptable zone near my shoulders.

It's so sweet that she came to pick me up again. She was so attentive, at least as much as she could be in public, and she was… just… well… just lovely.

As we stepped back from each other I took her in again. Her blonde hair, pushed over her ears was cascading gently down her back and her red-lipped smile was wide and toothy. Her eyes glinted with the hope of pleasures promised but yet to be discovered and for just a moment they mesmerised me and held me. I broke first and with averted eyes I looked her up and down with the sure knowledge that she'd soon be mine again. She was wearing a white vest top and a light brown crocheted cardigan to cover her shoulders and ward off the chill. They combined to create a perfect picture frame around her ample cleavage. I lingered for maybe a few seconds longer than I should have before looking down and admiring her legs and thighs in her tight black jeans, and only wished I could get a glimpse of her luscious ass.

Soon Ania, soon!

'Shall we grab coffee and cake in Grycan?' she suggested brightly, to my disappointment.

'Ok,' I replied noncommittally.

It must have been really obvious what I was thinking about and she quickly tuned into my disappointment. 'Don't worry, Ania, we'll get to bed soon enough.' She then paused dramatically for effect, 'Besides, it's my turn to surprise you today.'

She flashed me such a cheeky playful grin that I wanted to have drunk my coffee already and be in her warm bed or at least have her *inside me.*

As we made our way to the coffee shop I thought absently about how I'd showered so thoroughly this morning. I was ready for everything and anything, even the implausible (I won't quite say impossible, although that might be wishful thinking).

I will spare the details, but we had a nice coffee and cake and laughed and joked constantly. I loved the way we were getting on and the spark between us hadn't dimmed, as we fell into easy conversation naturally and without effort, while at the same time accepting a need to be slightly reserved in public.

As good as it was, all I could think about was making love to her and self-restraint was hard work. As we chatted my eyes flitted around and not for the first time I admired her breasts and slender neck and dreamt of kissing them and when I looked at her face I longed to taste her lips, adorned with blood-red lipstick. It was easier now to imagine her naked as I knew exactly what she looked like. My lips and eyes had tasted every part of her body and busy fingers had explored her intimate depths and soon… and it couldn't come soon enough... pleasure would once again be realised. I'd like to think she was being consumed by the same lust and passion for me that I was feeling for her.

Burning as I was, my lust was slightly tempered by curiosity.

She was up to something and I had no idea what, but I daren't dream too much. I love surprises and it was obvious that it was going to be something deliciously naughty. I'd dropped enough hints that I wasn't vanilla and so far she'd proven to be open and adventurous. She hadn't even resisted my finger in her ass yesterday. So just maybe she could push my boundaries? Even so it seemed unlikely and I couldn't help but feel that I was probably setting myself up for a disappointment.

I just hoped I might be wrong and I found out how wrong I was sooner than I could have ever imagined.

Plates had been reduced to a few crumbs and mugs were empty. We were ready to leave and she suggested walking. The weather was still holding and it wasn't like we were in a rush (well maybe a bit!). We had all day to enjoy and feast on each other and I kept this in mind. A good wine is better savoured than rushed.

Maybe fifteen minutes later we were walking along Odynca Street and suddenly she hooked her arm inside mine and pulled me into the road. I was so surprised that I had no time to react and before I knew it we were going into a park that seemed to run the entire length of the opposite side of the street. Once inside she let go of my arm and kept walking, slightly ahead of me. I had no idea what she was up to, so I followed her slowly and looked around as I did so. I saw a small restaurant in a corner and a large open landscaped garden that was ringed by trees.

I knew that I was about to find out whatever it was that she was up to. Uncertainty and nervous expectation excited me in a way that evoked powerful memories of past adventures.

Elwira was different today. She seemed completely assured and for the first time, even if not overtly, she was in a more dominant position. The submissive in me was awakened and the perfect storm of excitement and nerves became a swirling maelstrom in my stomach. My heart was fluttering in anticipation and if my ribs had cracked open at that moment a thousand butterflies would have escaped. She was looking around until she found what she was looking for and then started moving more decisively and I naturally followed. She ducked into the shade of some trees and went behind a particularly impressive trunk where a second or two later I joined her.

Once hidden she put her hands on my hips and—after another quick look around—she pulled me close and kissed me. It was more than a kiss, it was a lusty, hungry invasion. Her tongue flew into my mouth and sought mine. I responded readily as my surprise was replaced by my need to have her. Our tongues danced together hidden in their secret cave as we exchanged the first of our bodily juices for the day.

While all the time kissing me, a hand moved to my front and pressed through my skirt onto my treasure. I was confused by her boldness, but loving every moment of it.

But she wasn't done.

With her lips sealed to mine, she quite deliberately pressed her body as close to mine as she could. Her breasts pushed against mine and she pushed her hand under the hem of my skirt between my thighs and slid her hand up until it reached the soft cotton of my knickers. She stroked my lips momentarily through the material before continuing her upward journey to the elastic and then she pushed her hand inside. Her hand was cold against my hot flesh and it tickled as her fingers reached my intimacy.

But she still wasn't done.

She wasn't satisfied with just touching me. She wiggled and stretched her fingers inside my knickers to make room to push them down slightly and I naturally opened my legs to let her in. Now she had enough room she thrust her hand deeper and a finger stood at the threshold of my inner space. It only stayed there momentarily though as she then began to rub up and down my moist slit.

I groaned into her mouth and still stunned I just stood there motionless and allowed her to do what she wanted to me. I wasn't even thinking. I just knew it felt good and I wanted more. It was so unexpected and thrilling and my heat was growing literally by the second. At that moment she could have done anything she wanted to me.

I can't put it any more directly. I fucking loved it.

Should I touch her too?

Her breasts were squashed against mine—so no room there. All I could do was with some difficulty was reach around her back and play with her ass. She'd become a revving lust machine going at full throttle. Her desire was infectious and I groped her with grasping fingers that only fuelled her up even more. Her face would have been inside mine if she could manage it and her manipulations only became firmer as she pressed my delicate flesh. My button hardened as she finger-fucked me in such a way that the heat of her friction stoked my inner inferno.

I threw my head back as my fire burned hotter and hotter and if I'd been able to speak I would have begged her for more. Her fingers were racing across my clit and almost along the full length of my slit. From time to time, her fingers caught in the material of my knickers and she had to stop and readjust before carrying on. Her face remained glued to mine as she worked my gap. I groaned my pleasure as a series of small squeals into her mouth. I was getting closer...

Then suddenly she stopped and pulled her hand away, guilt written all over her face.

She stepped back with tears in her eyes and said, 'I'm sorry. I just couldn't stop myself. When I saw you in a skirt this morning I wanted you and it was all I could think about while we were drinking coffee. I should've waited till we got back to mine. I shouldn't have done that. I'm really sorry.'

Shit! Elwira's feeling guilty.

I hadn't expected this and it'd come from nowhere. It has been a revelation to me that she'd been as least as consumed by lust as me as I was for her while we sat casually drinking coffee in Grycan. I wanted to grab her and pull her to me again so once more she could carry on and incinerate my yearning and cremate her guilt. She was close to freaking out so I did the only thing I could.

Thinking about it I shouldn't have been as surprised as I was. It seemed that Elwira was very open-minded, but again she had the habit of retreating when she reached the edge of her experience.

'Elwira, it's ok,' I reassured her, 'It's more than ok. I can't tell you how much I love you touching me like that. Was that my surprise?'

I flashed her a smile, but she wasn't at all convinced. Her neck flushed with hives as her self-consciousness took control. She had absolutely no reason to feel guilty. What she'd done was closer to what I am into than she could ever even begin to imagine.

Besides, I thought to myself, *if anybody should be feeling remorseful and ashamed it should be me, as an image of Dominika fluttered into my mind.*

'No I was going to do something else,' she almost whispered while looking at the ground. Her shame was such that couldn't hold eye contact with me.

I had to act and I had to act now.

I now stepped forward and kissed her and slowly, but surely, she responded. I then lifted my skirt and took her hand and very deliberately put it back inside my knickers and cupped her now cool fingers over my treasure and while, she didn't resist; she didn't go back to strumming my instrument again.

'There is nothing to worry about, Elwira,' I whispered. 'It was a nice surprise—even if it wasn't the one you have planned for me. I keep telling you that I love it when somebody else is in control, even if they hurt me.'

Fuck! Ania, you stupid bitch! Wrong words!

'Did I hurt you?' Her face was anguished, but her hand remained as though she feared losing me.

'No, that's not what I mean. Forget about pain, but I just loved how you took control and what you did to me. That's exactly how I like it. For me we can carry on if you want to, but I don't want to make you do something you don't want to. As for me, it was like one of the best presents ever and the best thing you've done to me so far.'

'Really?' She exclaimed in surprise.

I still wasn't convinced that she was convinced, so I headed off the conversation. She had touched me in such an incredible way and now the whole thing was in danger of becoming more than awkward.

'Let's go back to yours, and carry on. It's a bit cold today anyway.'

With that, I took her hand from my knickers and kissed her sodden fingers before leading her back into the open with her sticky hand still in mine. We left the park the way we'd entered and once we reached the street we reverted back to arm in arm and carried on in the direction of her flat. I might have mentioned that it's better not to draw too much attention on Polish streets. As we set off again, so to avoid that elephant in the room, I asked her about her plans for next week and after a few moments of awkward minimal answers she dropped her embarrassment and warmed more to the conversation. I naturally became quieter as her natural chattiness took over.

Normality had been restored, but really I was quite disappointed. What she'd done had been so exciting and I would've loved it if she'd carried on, but her self-consciousness had got in the way.

She's still learning and it was a big step for her to do something so bold, I chided myself in the recesses of my mind. *Give her time and space.*

Elwira's boldness had surprised me and I immediately understood that she was on the verge of a new threshold, a limit for her to pass. It was a boundary into greater deviancy that with a little encouragement she'd cross.

The more she embraces her kink, the better it'll be for both of us.

As exciting as things had been so far, and not just today, it boded well for the rest of the day and whatever every else might happen in the future. She may be inexperienced, which naturally was manifesting itself as insecurity, but she's no *vanilla* and may even be a dominant.

How good would that be!

The park wasn't that far from her flat so it only took a few more minutes to get there. It was familiar territory by now, so I had no problem with just walking in, taking my jacket off, slipping my shoes off and making myself at home. I did it even more casually than I'd done on Thursday and yesterday just to prove that I was still comfortable around her.

I naturally assumed that we were heading towards the kitchen, but before I had a chance to even take a single step she said, 'Come straight through to the bedroom, we have unfinished business.'

That was direct! Maybe she is bolder than I gave her credit for.

I cast my mind back to the park. It'd only been a few minutes ago, but now I was keen to know what was coming. She was only a few steps ahead of me but by the time I got in her room she'd already taken her top off and was unhooking her bra. I didn't need an invitation and I practically ripped my clothes off and soon we were naked and giggling under the bedding. All hints of self-consciousness that had inhibited her after the park had been extinguished and she was back.

In fact she was more than back and that suited me just fine.

She pulled me close and kissed me and again, her forceful tongue penetrated my soft and receptive mouth. She then grabbed my wrists and we rolled around and playfully wrestled until she was on top, the bedding became a dishevelled twist of soft cotton which entwined around us.

I'm not sure if she's physically stronger than me, but as she pinned my wrists and used her body weight to manipulate me onto my back it served only to excite me more as I truly submitted to her. Maybe what I'd told her after the park had hit home and she was ready to push more limits. I love being dominated and there was no way I'd ever do more than feign fighting back—it's just not in my nature.

Then when she'd got me exactly where she wanted me she slid her face up to my ear and whispered, 'you were very naughty yesterday—so now I need to punish you!'

A surge of electricity hit me. I was already turned on by her physically overpowering me and it had reignited the fire that'd cooled during the last part of our walk here. Even so, I couldn't believe what I was hearing.

Keep it real, Ania I reminded myself so I wouldn't get too carried away. Getting too worked up would only set me up for more disappointment and there's almost certainly a world of difference between what Dominika would call punishment and what Elwira was capable of. I wasn't sure what I'd done that'd been so naughty, but I had my suspicions, which were immediately confirmed.

'You pushed your finger in my bum.' (I remember she used the more polite Polish word *pupa* rather than *dupa*—ass.)

'You didn't complain,' I laughed.

'Actually no,' she said emphatically. 'It was a bit weird, but you're right, I didn't mind. It was exciting in the moment, but now I want to surprise you. You told me you like pain?'

Elwira! Where are you going with this?

The thought flashed through my mind, but question seemed rhetorical so I didn't answer.

She didn't say anything else, but she sat up and pulled me around until I was lying across her lap with my ass facing upwards. I couldn't see anything, but it wasn't a totally unexpected thing when she gave me a tentative spank.

She paused and there was silence.

'Was it too hard?' She asked gently. Once more she was unsure of herself, just as she had been every time she reached one of her boundaries.

I laughed. So she spanked me again a bit harder.

'Ow!'

But it wasn't me who squealed. It did sting a bit, but poor Elwira hurt her hand when she hit me.

'Curve your fingers before you spank me.' I suggested helpfully.

She then laughed as she started spanking me. Her slaps were fairly delicate and at most probably reddened my cheeks a bit. It was obvious for Elwira it was just a game, she was laughing and that made me laugh too. I squirmed, but not out of a need to escape or even in pain, but because it was so funny—it was almost like being tickled.

For me, it was a very light pain, but also highly unusual because I've been so rarely punished in this way. I had a flashback of Dominika who is highly unconventional even in BDSM terms. BDSM usually involves tying and a lot of spanking or flogging. Dominika never ties and very rarely spanks or flogs. It's just not her way of doing things.

Dominika—get out of my mind! If I think, I feel guilty because I know exactly what I am despite the way you abandoned me.

Elwira's final spank, harder than those which had preceded it, brought me back to the present and an urgent need, probably at least brought on in part by my laughter.

'Elwira, I'm sorry,' I said suddenly between gasped breaths, 'but I really need to pee.'

She laughed and tickled me under the ribs as I got up. That really wasn't helpful, but somehow I held my bladder. She might just have got a little upset if I'd peed on her or her bed. She let me go and I got off the bed and quickly did what I needed to do and washed my hands before getting back to her as quickly as possible.

As I joined her once again I saw that she was pretending to be asleep under the duvet. So I suddenly pulled the bedding up and saw her naked form on her side, but sprawled like a spider with her back towards me. She didn't move so I jumped in with her and went straight for her ass as the bedding settled on top of us. She turned to face me, still smiling and unbelievably happy and, no surprise here, she started kissing me again and her hand meandered down to my hungry treasure.

I wanted to surprise her now and I felt like taking a risk after her more dominant behaviour so far today.

'Hey Elwira, do you want to see a cool trick. Give me your hand.'

Reluctantly, as though putting her hand in a pit full of vipers, she gave me her wandering hand. Then on second thoughts, I realised it might not have been fear; she might simply have been begrudging about releasing her prize.

'Don't worry, I'll put it back in a minute,' I said with a smile as I turned and inspected her hand in my own. Her hand was slender, almost dainty which was good. There was no way I'd be able to do what I wanted without lube if her hand was much bigger or if it'd been a man instead of her.

It'll hurt but should be possible.

'You'll need to take your ring off.'

Totally trusting now, she obliged without doubt or question. I kicked the bedding aside so we'd have plenty of room and nothing would get in our way. I reclined in a slightly raised position propping myself up on her pillows and opened my legs with my knees up at a 10:10 clock position.

'Sit or lay comfortably so you can get inside me with your finger,' I instructed her carefully.

It'd have been so much easier to ask her if she watched porn, but I had no idea what her attitude to porn was and I didn't want to risk asking her. Even if she did, where I wanted to go might have been too much for her anyway. Small steps are always better than huge leaps when introducing somebody to something new.

Maybe that thinking is just the trainee teacher in me!

She put her face between my legs and after an initial delicate kiss and taste, I felt her warm tongue begin to lap at me. My flat button offered little initial resistance to her tongue, but as she pressed and teased it responded and hardened enough so that she could now flick at it by switching her stiffened tongue over it. When she felt I was ready she tested my gash with a finger. I was more than wet enough and her finger slid comfortably inside using my natural juices. All the time she continued to lick and enjoy my taste.

'Deeper and faster,' I demanded uncharacteristically.

She responded by doing so, although her licking slowed down and then only became intermittent. Her touch however was igniting me and I began to pant as she finger-fucked me. I closed my eyes as my mind drifted back to the park. Delicious thoughts, so hot and exciting, of being fingered by the tree drove me to greater arousal. My only regret then had been that she'd stopped just as things were heating up.

At least now we could more than make up for it.

Under her hands and mouth my pot started squelching at it filled with honey. It was exactly what I wanted and it'd only make what I wanted easier. I dropped my knees to open my legs further so I could take even more of her in. My body felt like it was being caressed by a million kisses, as it tingled in excitement at her touch. Both the raw pleasure of what was happening and the anticipation of what was to come were driving me crazy with greed.

I was still a bit nervous about whether she could do what I wanted.

As she moved in and out of me I felt myself getting looser and when I judged that I was more than ready so I encouraged her to go further, 'Keep going, Elwira, but add another finger. You won't hurt me, I promise.'

This wasn't a barrier for her; she'd already had two or even three fingers inside me this weekend so it was nothing new. She withdrew almost completely and then with a broader push re-entered me. I felt a bit of a stretch, but not too much, I was already prepared for more. My excessive wet must've been completely coating her fingers by now and soon she was sliding in and out as rapidly and deeply as she'd been with just one finger.

'Add another,' I suddenly demanded between heaving breaths that were the outward manifestation of my growing internal need.

She did so. She's so obedient, I thought ironically, and then another level of irony hit me when I realised in a way I was dominating her again. She was using me, but exactly according to my wishes. This is impossible I thought as I contemplated the paradox before me. I was only able to dismiss my unnatural state when I decided again that I wasn't dominating her rather, like I had on Thursday, I was *educating* her.

So far her limits hadn't really been tested and I was still well within mine. It was almost impossible that she'd ever exceed mine.

Now the first of three big tests—each getting harder—for both of us.

'Now add your little finger, pull it inside your other three fingers like a kind of arrowhead and push them in as far as you can. I promise if it hurts I will shout *stop*. If I say anything else, ignore me and keep going. Only stop if I specifically say stop. I really want this.'

I wasn't aware of it at the time, but I now realise that in this moment I introduced Elwira to the concept of the safe word, but it was more for her benefit than mine. I didn't really care about any pain and in fact craved it, but she was in unsure territory and was naturally slow and careful. I, on the other hand, had been penetrated, quite extremely many times in recent years and so it was nothing new for me. It wasn't easy what I wanted to show her—especially when only relying on my natural juices, but I've done much harder things and taken much more.

With such a broad assault, she wasn't so far inside now as she had been, but I could feel myself stretching more and more to accommodate her which meant she was pushing ever harder. As she persisted, my most intimate spot opened in tune with my heightened passion and she was once again getting deeper, even if it was with a bit of a sting. I was surprised that aside from this, there was no pain in the depths of my loins, which can happen. It felt like she was almost knuckle deep again.

'Now tuck your thumb inside and try to get inside me to your wrist.'

I was surprised Elwira didn't balk at this, but maybe I was teaching her well—after all I am studying to be a teacher—and I'd built her up to the fist in easy incremental steps. She was also giving me total trust.

I felt some stretching stinging pain as she pulled her thumb in and started rocking her hand into me. I tried my hardest to fuck back against her with my hips to make it easier. She had completely given up on licking me and was just concentrating on getting her hand inside.

Without warning, there was an excruciating sting that seemed to go beyond my insides and stretched across my stomach. I screwed my face up as I resisted the need to cry out. I knew what it was. Her knuckles were the widest and least flexible part of her hand, even if she was curling them slightly. Pressing bone against my soft flesh and resistant inner muscles was the meeting of two opposing forces that can only lead to intense agony. Being who I am, this extreme discomfort was not only something to endure but something that excited me and something I needed, if not physically at least psychologically. I would be lying if I said it was pleasurable, but my arousal and desire were at the fore and nothing else mattered.

Elwira looked at me all concerned, but I nodded repeatedly. *Carry on, please don't stop.*

Elwira didn't stop and she continued pushing me through the pain barrier. My body was screaming against this unnatural insertion and then without warning the sting eased off as I finally took her whole hand. Once she was wrist deep, my body relaxed slightly and tightened around her. She also felt my body give because once all the way in, she stopped.

'Do you like my little trick?' I asked her all innocently.

'I… I don't know what to say,' she half stuttered, amazed that her whole hand was inside me. She was just staring at what she'd done, disbelief etched on her face.

She just had to ask the obvious question when curiosity got the better of her, 'Doesn't it hurt?'

'Not now, maybe just a bit as I took your knuckles.' I demonstrated what I meant by showing her. Across my belly, so I wouldn't fall off my elbows I formed a fist with one hand and pinched in a vice-like grip across my knuckles with the other. It had the desired effect when she saw that they didn't flex too much.

I was tempted to explain how sometimes it can hurt deep inside, but this time remarkably it hadn't, I quickly decided that now wasn't the time for such a conversation. I knew that if I spoke too much about pain, it might put her off and at this moment she was as close to the edge as ever and I might still freak her out, besides I was ready for more.

'Now fuck me with it and lick my clit,' I demanded hungrily.

I guess it was hard for her to do anything else and so she began to move her arm back and forth while at the same time using her tongue on and around my hotspot. I was still a bit worried that I'd taken her too far, but so far so good. She didn't seem uncomfortable. At the very least she knew I'd been with at least one other girl and so I guess she was trusting in my experience.

The fisting hurt a bit. My natural oils are enough, but I totally understand how lube makes it much easier. Maybe I'd rushed her, but the combination of pain and orgasmic pleasure only heightened my senses and made it more intense. Unseen by her, I couldn't stop myself from cupping a breast in each hand to push myself on. I rolled them around and tweaked my nipples until they were completely erect and then I pinched them as hard as I could. They hurt, but not enough, I really wish I had some bulldog clips nearby—now they really hurt!

That would definitely be too much for Elwira!

Then I realised I was being selfish, but she was completely out of reach. A bit like with strap-on sex, we'd end up alternating again. It's always nicer to share, but what could I do? What she was doing to me was so intense, but my need had suddenly switched to wanting to satisfy her too.

I loved the way she was using me but I couldn't bear the thought of not giving her anything back. It just felt so wrong and there was only one way I could start reciprocating. It screamed against my nature, but I pulled her hair firmly, but not harshly, so she had to bring her head up to mine. As she struggled for balance, her hand had to come out of me. It was soaked with my inner juices and they felt hot and sticky when she rested her hand on my belly. A short sharp stab of pain tore across my body as her sudden withdrawal made my insides collapse back in on themselves.

She looked like she was going to say something, but I started kissing her. In our short affair I had learnt that she loved nothing more than kisses—and the more the better. It was also the best way to shut her up and avoid unnecessary conversation. I kissed her for a few minutes, with my tongue lashing against hers inside her mouth before sliding down the bed. When we got to the point when she was sitting on top of my face my tongue was perfectly positioned under her. I used my fingers to part her petals and began to tongue-fuck her, in and out and along her groove. I quickly found that if I lifted my head I could just about reach her little hood. She held on to the hair on top of my head and started fucking my face back.

Now I'm where I belong, and it feels so right.

She reached behind her and once more found my puffy gap that was still loose from the fisting. She began running her fingers up and down. Even with her thighs half blocking my ears I could hear the squelching as penetrating fingers once again met my wet. Although my fire had cooled slightly since the fisting, it'd not been sated nor dowsed and so it wasn't too long until my inner inferno once more began to rage.

I could see too that Elwira's fire was also burning bright and her skin began to feel clammy as her heat rose. Things were going so well that I was surprised when she suddenly climbed off me and pulled me more to the middle of the bed. She then climbed back on board, only this time facing away from me so she could bend over my body. Now we were both able to use our tongues to satisfy each other as once more we settled into a *sześćdziesiąt dziewięć* (69). She remained on top, of course. I'll spare you the details, this is supposed to be a confession after all, but through lapping tongues and manipulating fingers, we got each other off and this time almost at the same time.

After the tension of what had happened outside, the indulgent depravity of her fist and the delight of each other's tongues, I almost literally exploded as my body finally gave in to the ravishes of the morning. It seemed to me that Elwira's peak pretty much matched mine. Perfect orgasms are shared orgasms but, unlike in the movies, my experience has shown they are quite uncommon.

When we stopped, we rested as we were. Her head was turned to one side on my upper thigh and mine concealed between her legs. I closed my eyes in the afterglow and again as I did the other day I breathed in the smell of her sex and she probably did the same and inhaled my natural scent too.

It's strange but sometimes when underneath somebody I feel trapped and restricted. It resurfaces memories, dark memories that I hid from for far too long, but have learnt to confront as I have become more whole. I also accept that these shadows in my life are at least part of the reason that I am a submissive.

But with Elwira it was completely different, I felt contained and safe.

In that moment she reminded me of Emilia, but although she'd been quite bold today, Elwira lacked Emilia's decisive and wilful confidence. Emilia is both the most secure and sweetest person I know and while Elwira definitely matches her sweetness, that's as far as it goes. The park had shown me that Elwira is quick to retreat if she feels like things are going too far. There are lines that she seems unwilling to cross. She also lacks Emilia's sweet steel—that special strength that makes Emilia who she is. I'm not saying she isn't strong; it's just not the same as Emilia's unique quality.

If Emilia knew what I was up to now, I'd definitely know her steel.

We settled in the intimacy of the moment and probably both dozed off wrapped around each other. The next thing I knew for sure was being startled by a sudden SMS notification.

Isn't it strange when you hear a phone, you always check your own even when you know it isn't yours?

Elwira dragged herself off me and found her phone and fiddled with it for a minute before making a call. When she had finished she told me it was one of her flatmates, who would be back in Warsaw Central Station in about three hours. She then told me, that one of the others would be back in the evening and apparently the third wouldn't return until early tomorrow—cutting it a bit fine for classes in my honest opinion.

It meant that we only had four hours or so left together when allowing for the time it'd take for her flatmate to get home from the station. It marked the point when we'd have to go back to our ordinary lives. A pang of anxiety hit me and it was weird because although I was still with her I was missing her already.

'Hey,' Elwira announced, 'we should make the most of time we've got left. Doesn't mean you have to go when Marta gets back, but she perhaps shouldn't see us in bed together.'

I laughed and she climbed on top of me and kissed me again. I tell you I've never been kissed so much in my life! Not that I was complaining. As she kissed me, she once more reached between my legs which I duly opened to her advances and as she touched my threshold her kisses turned into small pecks that travelled down my chin and neck with an alluring insistence until they found a hard nipple, which she flicked her tongue over before taking it into her mouth. As she sucked and nibbled on my swollen cherry, urgent fingers pushed beyond my intimate gateway and found their way inside again. I instinctively opened my legs wider to ease her access. I was physically tired, but my submissive nature demanded that I had to give myself wholly to her and I was ready to go again.

And that's how we started to make love again. Much of it is a blur, but I do remember using the strap-on again (I hadn't taken anything back home last night, I'd figured that it was less of a risk to sneak them back home only once and I was fairly sure Dominika wouldn't even check whether they were missing). We alternated with her fucking me first and then I dragged my weary body behind her and fucked her from behind like a dog. I playfully tugged at her hair as I did so and from time to time, I reached under and groped at her breasts. At one point, she changed how she was leaning, so that her forehead was resting on her forearm. I couldn't see, but I guessed that she had reached underneath and was helping herself with the hand that she'd liberated. I had encouraged her the first time to masturbate during our lovemaking to make it as pleasurable as possible and I was pleased to see she was doing this now without me having to push her. I amused myself with the thought of how well I'd taught her. I rode her until my hips ached and she could take no more and in doing so I fucked her to the height of her crescendo.

Her arms stretched out and grasping hands clawed at the sheet as I pounded into her deep and hard and she muffled what I assumed were screams of pleasure and surrender by burying her head into her pillow until she was truly done. When she couldn't take any more I eased my momentum to a steady rocking before finally stopping. I rested on her sinuous back and our sweat mingled as she heaved up and down with every breath which slowly steadied as she recovered from our exertions.

As I rested I found myself in awe of Elwira. I just love the way she is. It perfectly explains my addiction to her. I'm not saying she is a sex addict or as perverse as me. Maybe it was inexperience, but she was very open and willing to try so many new things—at least for her. I enjoyed teaching her and her attitude, even if it meant me taking the lead more than I ever do and definitely more than I really wanted to.

And who knows maybe I should give her more credit. Is it possible I'd unleashed another deviant?

If I had any doubts about my eventual career choice they were now completely dispelled. I am convinced I can teach, just look at the last few days.

Although I am sure there are no classes available to learn how to teach the things I was showing Elwira.

We still weren't done though. We took some time, at first just enjoying the quiet in each other's arms and then quietly chatting as we relaxed. Somehow we'd changed position and we were lying on our sides. She was laying into my back and her fingers were nonchalantly stoking my outer lips in a pleasurable but non-arousing way. It was like a dream and I just let her do it and I genuinely thought our lust had cooled and we were just relaxing in our shared intimacy. After some time though I realised I was mistaken when her finger became a bit more insistent and found my clit. It soon hardened under her manipulation and I felt her finger begin to flick across it, first one way and then the other.

She wanted more…

I was getting horny again and an idea popped into my head. It was an idea that she'd be far too vanilla for—or would she? I reasoned that I should ask anyway because if a girl doesn't ask she doesn't always get. It was worth a risk…

'Hey Elwira,' I started. 'Do you want to try something really crazy?'

She carried on working her finger on me, but looked me straight in the eyes, keen as a lapdog to please. She could only smile and nod her head.

'It's something I find really exciting, but you might find it disgusting. You must tell me if you can't or won't do it though and it doesn't mean I expect the same from you. Do you agree?'

She nodded wordlessly and now I hesitated.

Am I pushing her too far?

'Do you remember when I pushed my finger into your bum?'

'Yes—it was *interesting*.'

Not the word I would have used, but it makes the point. I suddenly felt how Elwira must have been feeling when she started that conversation all that time ago about shaving down below. Pandora's Box was opened and I couldn't leave my thoughts unspoken. I just had to go for it. I took a breath.

'Well,' I paused for effect, 'I absolutely love having my bum played with and would love it if we could do something together.'

'I'm not sure what you mean,' she said quietly. My dramatic pause had had its desired effect. She stopped stroking me and stared at me. Her eyes betrayed anxiety, she was definitely getting uncomfortable.

'We'll use the toy, only you don't go through the front door.'

That was about as delicately as I could put it.

'But it's not for that, it's kind of disgusting.'

Her face was set and serious, but her objections were polite and measured. Nonetheless, I still thought I was losing her and my inner voice started cursing my boldness, but then she surprised me with a smile.

'If you like it we can try,' she smiled. My heart nearly missed a beat. 'I can do it to you, but I don't want it. Is that ok?'

I cradled her head in my hands and kissed her. 'Sweet, sweet Elwira of course it's ok. I never want you to do anything you aren't comfortable with.'

She smiled shyly, 'have you done it before?'

'Yes, but I want to try doing it a bit differently. Then, after we are done, I will give you a special treat.'

She smiled and nodded. I had no idea what I'd do as a treat for her. It was a spontaneous offer, a kind of reward. I didn't really care or dwell on it though since the conversation had taken a positive turn. My desire became compulsion, and it was only natural to offer her something back. But that's for later, for now, I needed her inside me again.

I'd been fucked in the ass before, but never how I wanted it to be right there and then. 'You'll need to wear the strap-on. So put it on again for me, I need to prepare myself.'

Elwira got off the bed and took the strap-on and began fiddling with the straps. Meanwhile, I reclined fully on the bed and started masturbating. I was still damp from Elwira's ministrations and anticipation of what was going to happen next probably added to my wetness. As I finger-fucked myself vigorously I dipped inside my honeypot to get my juices really going and then I lifted my knees to my chest so I could reach down and touch my knot. Using my wet hand I began to finger my ass and stretch it. The strap-on was obviously much bigger than my finger, but I needed to transfer my natural lube and begin to open myself up so I could take it in.

I was briefly reminded of when I'd masturbated on Friday morning and my dark daydream that had left me used by Elwira and murdered by Dominika. Shame and guilt for a moment threatened, but I determined they wouldn't break the surface. It wasn't quite the same feeling as Friday, but it was close enough. I cast thoughts of Dominika out of my head, and focussed only on Elwira. This brought me back to reality and her back to my consciousness. I looked at her and there she was standing with a big black cock ready and waiting for action. She was stroking it gently as she watched with a bemused look on her face. I was absolutely sure she'd never seen anything like what had been happening all weekend and now her limits were going to be smashed out into the cosmos.

'Come here a minute Elwira.'

Obediently she came to me and the phallus was now in my face. I took it in my mouth while still continuing to finger my ass. I sucked it and tasted the last residue of our most recent sex. I took it in deeper, knowing exactly what I wanted. Elwira pulled it out of my mouth.

'No Elwira we need to do this. We can stop if you want to,' I said not knowing if I could stop. 'Put your hand on the back of my head I need to take it as deep as I can. You'll see why in a bit.'

Poor girl must have been really freaking out, but she nodded and did as I asked with unspoken trust.

Once more I took it into my mouth and took it in until it was almost in my throat. I held steady for a moment to control my gag reflex and then rocked it in and out for a few minutes before withdrawing. As I did so a huge ribbon of my thick sticky phlegm came out with it. This was what I wanted. I quickly abandoned my ass and used both hands to wank my disgusting throaty goo into the cock before any of it was lost on the floor.

'Lie on your back,' I told her.

As always when showing her something new she was quietly obedient. It crossed my mind that I might be traumatising her, but I'd given her many chances to back out and now I only cared about my dirty desire.

Once on her back, I reached into her groin area and took the gooey phallus and held it upright before climbing astride her with my knees on the bed just either side of her ribs. I balanced myself with one hand on Elwira's chest between her breasts and lowered myself onto her while using my other hand to keep the black cock steady. Latex touched my knot and it immediately yielded the first few centimetres. I flashed Elwira a smile and when she smiled back I suddenly realised it was going better than I could have hoped. I rocked back and took a bit more and I felt my sphincters stretch as they surrendered. The stretch hurt a bit, but no more than I've experienced before. Now I was positioned and ready, I lowered myself in one slow but continuous motion so that I was impaled on almost the entire length. Taking it so deep gave me the characteristic and not unfamiliar dull ache across the stomach but that'd soon pass as we got fucking.

'We're still making love, so let's do it together,' I suggested.

I began to ride the length up and down and she too after a few seconds got into it and began to fuck me back. I took hold of her hands and put them on my hips and held them in place to help establish our rhythm. When I rose, she withdrew, almost to the extent of it leaving my ass and when I slid down she rotated her hips up creating the deepest possible penetration we could manage. Initially it was very uncomfortable, but after a few strokes the pain passed as it was supplanted by pleasure. I was literally fucking its whole length. It was disgusting, it was hot, and I was on fire.

After a few minutes like this, she began to tire and so as she steadied we got exactly to where compulsion and fantasy had driven me.

'Rest Elwira, and enjoy the view.'

With this, she stopped and it almost felt like she sank into the mattress. I leant forward and rested my right hand on a breast while my left found its way between my legs and my rocking honeypot. I found the spot I was looking for and I finger-fucked my way into delicious ecstasy while pounding my ass on the latex spear. My ass slapped against her upper thighs in an intensity that matched my greed until I reached upper orbit. As I cum, my heart nearly exploded out of my chest. I rode the shuddering pounding waves and gave myself completely to the moment and tossed my head back as I groaned my guttural release to the ceiling. Elwira still had hold of my hips, but I think she was holding on for the ride even more than I was.

Sadly it is impossible to remain in such a state. My flow ebbed and the last waves lapped my shoreline as pleasure finally departed my body. Now I had more self-control I bent forward and rested my head next to hers. My hot steaming breasts pressed against hers and my racing heartbeat rattled against her ribcage and reverberated back through mine. We rested like this while my ravaged body came back into equilibrium and when my pulse finally settled I climbed off her to the relief of my finally released ass. I wriggled my way into her armpit and she wrapped a protective arm around me.

As we lay there I was acutely aware that time was getting on and I'd promised Elwira a treat. I needed some quick inspiration, but my mind was failing me. In the end what I came up with wasn't particularly imaginative, but it was the first thing that popped into my head.

'Elwira, I promised you something. So here it is. I've always had a slave fantasy and from now until I leave I'm your slave to do with as you wish.'

Elwira let the idea sink in for a moment as though she was thinking.

'We should shower,' she suddenly suggested brightly. I roused myself and followed her into the bathroom.

'Take this off me and clean it,' she said imperiously.

'Yes Mistress.' I said automatically and then immediately regretted it.

Dominika is my mistress and nobody else can ever be! Dominika, get out of my mind!

I dutifully removed the strap-on and started cleaning it in the washbasin. I pride myself on my cleanliness and even though it'd been in my ass it wasn't as disgusting as some might imagine. It all comes down to good hygiene and deep cleansing. If I'd been at home, I'd have done it with my mouth first, but this was Elwira and not Dominika or even Kasia.

Elwira came up behind me and gave me a double spank on the ass, one to each cheek. It stung a bit, but she hadn't caught me by surprise because I'd seen her sneaking up on me in the mirror. So it probably wasn't the shock she'd hoped for.

'You've been a very naughty slave today and you should be punished.'

I almost spluttered as I fought down a laugh.

You have no idea what it means to punish me. You are so sweet in your naivety. If only you knew...

I was pleased that I managed to get a grip of myself. Otherwise she'd have thought I was mocking her and she wouldn't have seen the funny side of it.

She spanked me again, just once this time and I playfully squealed with laughter. She laughed too.

'And now my slave, my flatmates are coming back soon so you'll help me shower and for the last time today you'll serve me and if you are good I'll serve you too.'

She giggled lightly, and so did I. We both knew exactly what she meant.

And so the last time we truly made love, rather than what followed later, we were squeezed into her little shower with warm water cascading over us. I was supposed to serve her, at least at first, but that wasn't the way it worked out. I tried to go down on my knees to pleasure her with my mouth, but there wasn't really enough room, we could have opened the shower door, but then the water could have gone everywhere. Elwira had similar problems. I think it is because we are both quite tall and long legs just meant our asses mashed against the glass long before we could get low enough.

It didn't occur to me until later that we could've just turned the water off.

Consequently, it had to be fingers down below and hands and mouths on our faces, backs, necks and breasts. All this lovemaking became cloudy, but I do remember when she pushed me against the shower screen, my hot nipples pressed against the cool steamy glass. Surrendered and completely at her mercy she fucked me from behind with her fingers. It was the nearest she got to truly dominating me and although she didn't fist me again, I was sure she got three fingers inside. It was the most submissive she'd made me feel all weekend, and that added to my enjoyment and ecstasy. I groaned and squealed in pleasure while hoping that the cascading water would drown my sounds out and spare the neighbours.

I too gave back at least as good as I got—or so I hoped. After all I was playing the slave. For the last time we made our aching and worn bodies cum before soaping each other down and rinsing each other off. Exhausted and clean, we finally came to a rest in each other's arms as warm water rinsed the last of our stickiness away.

Done with the shower, the end of our day of lust was really romantic. She completely forgot that I was her slave, as we dried each other down with warm soft towels and then took time to dry and brush out each other's hair, which although hadn't been washed had got wet during our exertions. She did mine first and it was so nice to be pampered like this. It was still running with cool rivulets of water down my back when she started brushing and she pulled any knots out gently as she used her hairdryer. I then did the same to her before getting dressed and reapplying my makeup—which actually was just a bit of lip gloss and mascara—I'd deliberately kept it simple when I left home just in case I needed to fix it later.

At the same time, Elwira just pulled on a pair of leggings and comfortable T-shirt.

In an ironic echo of what I'd done in the morning with Dominika, I didn't want to just run out on Elwira. We made time for tea in the kitchen and she made some sandwiches. We chatted while we ate and I told her I wanted to take the blindfold and strap-on back home because it could be embarrassing if her flatmates found them. She readily agreed, although I knew full well that it wasn't out of consideration for her that I was taking them back. We smoothly moved on with our conversation and compared timetables to see when we could lunch together, but agreed we probably wouldn't be able to meet outside school until next weekend.

Finally, I decided I should leave before her flatmates got back because while Elwira isn't quite what could be described as clingy, she definitely loves kisses and affection.

I was proven right as it took me twenty minutes of non-stop holding and kissing to get out of the door. She explained that she wanted to come with me, but she had to stay in for when her flatmates get back, just in case they needed something. She was really sorry and it made it harder for her to let me go.

It'd been so nice to feel wanted, but I couldn't help but feel a bit paranoid that she was abandoning me by not coming with me to the bus stop. Maybe I'd pushed her too far today? She was so sweet though that I cast my fears aside while not completely dispelling them.

My biggest reassurance was that although we were probably both sexually exhausted, I may well have stayed longer if her flatmates hadn't been coming back. Who knows?

She wants me and it just pours out of every single pore of her existence.

By the time I got home, it was late afternoon and Emilia and Kasia were already back from Sopot. I'd originally hoped to be back before them, but when I'd indulged myself and persuaded Elwira to fuck me in the ass and then played slave it meant I ended up running much later than expected. It didn't matter though because there was no harm done (discounting what I'd already done to Dominika anyway). I quickly went to Dominika who was reading something on her computer. I kissed her, the taste of my gloss disguising my betrayal.

She actually turned away from her screen and looked at me fully and intently, in the way that only Dominika can.

Shit—she knows!

Fear almost made me pee myself there and then.

'I love you, darling,' I said in an attempt to reach her and expunge my guilt.

'I love you too, darling,' she said sweetly.

She hasn't noticed. Maybe I'm just being paranoid.

At long last, she isn't looking at her work and she's giving me some time. Everything that has happened this weekend doesn't really matter. Dominika... She hasn't seen my deception or smelt my guilt... I'm in the clear and we can...

Suddenly Emilia appeared at the door.

'I'm making some tea, does anybody want some?'

I love Emilia, but right at that moment I hated her.

'Yes please,' I said as I masked my irritation and Dominika nodded. Emilia smiled and turned and left.

'Go with her, darling, you haven't seen her and Kasia for a while and I'm sure you have lots of catching up to do. I just need to finish this. The end is in sight, but I just need a few more hours.'

I'll go fucking crazy if I hear *I just need to finish this again*. Unlike Elwira, Dominika was pushing me away again.

I joined Emilia and Kasia in the kitchen and after Emilia had made tea for everybody I took Dominika's to her, just hoping I could stay with her. I had a bit of trepidation, a fear of her smelling my sin, but the attention that she'd almost given me was all I could think about and my desire to be by her side overcame any nerves.

I passed her the tea, carefully rotating it so she could take the mug by the ear and she simply took it and turned her head back to the screen.

'Thank you sweetie.' She smiled warmly. 'Can you close the door on your way out please, darling?' She said as she shut me out again.

Tuesday 7 May 2019

I had betrayed Dominika and nothing could change or even mask over that fact. I'd spent Sunday evening with Emilia and Kasia and they'd filled me in on their trip to Sopot and everything was seemingly normal, but in my mind it was an echo of the old normality and a poor reflection of how things should've been. Inwardly the contrast between what should be and what actually was, constantly resonated sharply in my brain while we were talking about the banal normality of their trip.

It wasn't just Dominika that I'd betrayed, but it was our whole little family. Of course, Dominika first, but the thought of what I'd done to Emilia and Kasia made what I'd done to Dominika seemed even worse. In particular, Emilia's light shone brightly and only served to illuminate my darkness.

Later on Sunday night, when I climbed into bed alone, it all came together as my guilt finally overwhelmed my greed. I'd gone too far, way too far. My insides were slashed to pieces and my veneer of normality was struggling to hold in my inner self-loathing.

And now it was already Tuesday and it'd been two whole days since anything had happened between Elwira and me. True to her word it seemed like Dominika had almost finished her thesis. She was still focused on it but seemed to be spending more time reading and making small adjustments than doing any new research or work that required her undistracted concentration.

Coincidence of all bad coincidences, Dominika was suddenly giving me the attention I'd so sorely been missing. It was more than a little obvious that she spent a lot more time with me on Monday evening after classes. We even went to bed together at the same time for the first time in ages. Nothing happened, nor did we have any great or deep conversation, but at least she was cuddling up to me before she fell asleep.

It should've marked a new threshold, the rekindling of lost love and refreshing rain in the barren desert. Dominika was coming back to me and the end was in sight. I should've been happy.

But I wasn't.

It was too little too late and now she was there again it only made me feel worse.

One thing became very clear to be me though. There was no way I could ever go back to Elwira. It might sound harsh, but her idea of what it meant for me to be her slave was just too *vanilla* and while the sex was good ultimately she'd never be able to give me what I needed. I know for her it was just a game. My offer to be her slave for the rest of the afternoon had been spontaneous and an easy thing to offer as a treat, but she just couldn't be hard enough to be a true dominant and consequently there would never be any true submission on my part.

And if you really want to know me, look back at what I've just written, as I just have and see the fullness of my selfishness revealed.

Things were only made worse when I went to university on Monday and she was there, in the same class, as usual. I made excuses for not spending too much time with her, but it was impossible to avoid having lunch with her without making it an issue. Try as I might, I was trying to 'normalise' our relationship—whatever that means. I was non-committal to any suggestions she had and it has always been a natural thing for me to hide my lesbian leanings in public so at least that part wasn't particularly hard.

I was still attracted to her and she was such a temptation. Even though she could never ultimately give me what I needed, the sex had been good. I know how easy it would've been to tread the path once trodden and go back to her. But I was determined to go cold turkey with my addiction. I needed to, and in the long run it'd be better for Elwira too, but she wasn't making it easy. She is stunningly attractive and so open and nice and it didn't help when she kept sending me sweet, caring messages, which were only to be expected after everything that'd happened. She was still making me feel wanted and filling that gaping hole in my life.

To makes things look as normal as possible, I always replied and even sent her unprompted messages with kisses and hearts, so it didn't look like it was all one-way traffic from her to me.

I was being a coward and I wasn't prepared to face the consequences, even from her, and so I continued the lie.

On Monday night when we got into bed together, Dominika's returning love only served to pour even more condemnation on me. I lay awake for endless hours with Dominika cuddling into my back. I was fully aware of her closeness and her warm, gentle breath tickling the back of my neck was a gentle reminder of lost intimacy. I was cuddling the right girl, but all it did was remind me of how badly I'd treated her. My insides were bursting with grief and horror because of my sin, my crime and my shame. I was in a pit of my own making. It's exactly where I belonged and there was no way out.

Yes, I was feeling sorry for myself, but it went way beyond self-pity. I couldn't even look in a mirror without hating what I'd become.

Tuesday at university was a nightmare. I couldn't concentrate, but unlike Monday I was better able to keep my distance from Elwira, without looking like I was doing so deliberately. It didn't really matter though because her shadow was everywhere I went. No—let me rephrase that—her shadow had possessed my mind and I couldn't shake it. Yet still, I kept up the act, in front of Dominika too, both at home and when we were out and about going between university and home.

I needed to talk, but who could I talk to? I was too ashamed to tell Dominika the truth. Emilia and Kasia were just too close. Emilia had already told me what I should've done before I'd fallen and I hadn't heeded her advice and spoken to Dominika. So what wisdom was there left for her to offer? Kasia has no forgiveness and would undoubtedly want to crucify me, probably upside down to satisfy her satanic urges, if I told her what I'd done.

It'd be nothing less than I deserved.

So with nowhere else to turn, I visited my social media for the first time since I'd broken divine law and destroyed everything. I have two sets of social media, my regular or *vanilla* profile and my submissive one where I can explore and meet likeminded people and explore my interests. I was too ashamed to look for one of my *vanilla* friends to talk to. So I went online looking for a fellow deviant. Only online with such a person did I have a chance to be completely open.

I was looking for somebody in particular who is unlike most people who I have contact with on these sites. He isn't too bothered about turning the conversation to sex and fetishes or asking me for naked photos all the time—a persistent problem I have. Don't misunderstand, because we met through a specialised website he's just as comfortable to talk about all the kinky stuff—it's just not his driving force. He's on the outside, but close enough to have a real conversation with, without demanding a naked picture of me.

By the way I don't send naked pictures.

I messaged him and was then browsing other pages and filling up time when I suddenly noticed he'd messaged me back. It was a brief moment of happiness in the maelstrom that was engulfing me.

We 'chatted' probably only for about twenty minutes and he was so sweet and kind and very supportive. He wasn't judgmental and I tried to tell him how bad I am. It might have come across as attention-seeking and fishing for compliments, but I promise it was all heartfelt and genuine.

How could I think about myself in any other way after what I'd done?

He refused to accept that I was bad and told me it was temptation and that I'd made mistakes. That was all I'd done and that didn't make me a bad person. While telling me that it was entirely up to me what I do and that he'd be there for me no matter what, he strongly encouraged me to tell Dominika. His driving motivation was that he wholeheartedly believed that honesty was the best way forward. It might mean the end for Dominika and me, but whatever the consequences at least there'd be no more lies. He warned me that such a secret could become toxic in our relationship, but he also said if I could hide it from Dominika for the rest of our relationship—however long that might be—it was a possibility. He did keep coming back to the idea that I should confess and be straight up with Dominika.

He was very clear on this point, so Dominika, when you read this please see that he's a good guy and a far better friend than I deserve.

I was fearful of confessing. It isn't that I am afraid of Dominika. Even though we're living a BDSM lifestyle she is actually very gentle and isn't violent at all (and there is never any excuse for wanton violence). Yes, she inflicts pain on me, but it's never more than I yearn for as a submissive. Dominika is very principled and never gives in to anger or the urge to lash out. She is far more measured and self-controlled than that. My fear came from the knowledge that because of what I'd done I could lose everything. I could lose my home, my friendships with Emilia and Kasia and worst of all, my love and my life; my Dominika.

Another good person was now trapped in my web of lies and abomination.

I was getting more and more upset as the conversation went on because what he said made sense and it was the right thing to do. The problem with the truth is that it is often brutal and I am a coward. The truth just confirmed my shame and hastened my condemnation, and his kindness was undeserved even though that hadn't been his intention. I had to end the conversation because I could feel tears coming. I was in the same room as Dominika and my distress would surely stir her curiosity and concern. I wasn't ready to face her and I needed to get away from her before my face cracked.

So I went to have a shower.

I closed the bathroom door and stripped off before tying back my hair. Then I got into the shower and turned it on. Once I knew the running water would drown out any other noise I broke down and wept in shame and disgust and pure, unadulterated self-hatred.

I took the soap and lathered myself up and then rinsed off the bubbles that'd foamed all over my body as I cried. My skin was cleansed, but I knew my repulsive whore body and filth would never know purity again. I looked at myself, my tight skinny body that many people find so attractive, and felt disgusted almost beyond words. My beauty wasn't a blessing, it was a curse.

I am Babylon, a whore, destroyer of souls, bestowed with beauty, but twisted with my own desire and depravity. I am sin, I am lust, and destruction is my fate.

Mum's words came back to me again and again. 'Keep yourself clean, stay away from sin and keep your eyes on God.'

Her words echoed in my mind, heaping further condemnation on me.

It's too late for that, I am what I am.

I was trapped and saw no way out. With tear-filled eyes, I looked on the side of the bath and saw my razor.

My fate is sealed. I am lost. Maybe I should just end it now. Death is better than shame. How easy it will be to fill the bath and open my wrists and let my blood flow.

I began to shake as each passing moment made suicide more of a reality. Death or shame was in the balance. Shame always wants to hide in the silence so unsurprisingly death was calling louder. My last moments on earth would be my most honest—at least to myself. Finally, I understood and knew what I am and what I had to do.

I picked up the blade.

Adrenaline was tearing through my body and making me tremble violently. Eternity and damnation awaited me. I looked at the three sharp parallel edges knowing that they could be a quick instrument to end my mortal torment and cast me into the raging fires of hell where I belonged. Judgment awaited and I couldn't go on any more.

I sat down in the bath, and let the water from the showerhead run down my chest and belly. This was it. I looked at my right wrist still thinking clearly enough to wonder how to cut myself the best.

I'll fill the bath with water in a minute and soon spill my lifeblood. As I fade the water will turn crimson and my life will ebb away and with that, I'll know the end of mortal agony.

Eternity was calling enticingly, and beckoning me to join her…

Then from nowhere an image of mum and dad flooded my mind. I thought about them at my funeral mass, saying goodbye to their only daughter and ending their line. They'd be heartbroken. My death would destroy them and I would've done it to them. This'd be even worse than what I'd done to Dominika. Mum is strong and will eventually get through it, but dad dotes on me. I'm his little universe and he'll never ever understand or recover from this. Killing myself will kill him too.

Dad!

That one thought brought me back from the brink. With still shaking hands I looked at the blade.

I am ready to do this to myself, but I cannot do this to him.

I am lost to Dominika, Elwira, Emilia and Kasia, but not to mum and definitely not dad.

I'm selfish to even consider killing myself.

And with this thought I confirmed for sure exactly what I am; a self-seeking greedy little whore.

I am Babylon.

Despair still lingered, but now I knew I didn't have the strength or will to kill myself. With a new-found inner determination to live, even though it was ill-deserved, I consciously and quite deliberately put the razor aside and forced myself into the semblance of normality. I got up and towelled myself down before shaking my hair out and brushing it. The moment of madness was dissipating and with rationality returning, I sorted my face out and creamed my body and face before putting my dressing gown on. I paused long enough to let the puffiness in my eyes go down before giving myself one last look to make sure there was no visible evidence of my brokenness. I saw the dullness of my breaking heart in my eyes, but was sure no one else would. Satisfied that my mask was in place, I left the bathroom and went back to our room.

It was still quite early, but I told Dominika I was tired and going straight to bed. She kissed me firmly on the lips and wished me good night and in a mirror of what Elwira had done on Sunday she even playfully spanked my bottom as I turned away from her.

Memories resurfaced and made me feel even lower. More unseen tears formed in my eyes, I was fortunate—if I can use that word during this time—that my back was already turned and so I hid my disgrace and anguish from Dominika.

I can't show her any emotion because if I do the whole thing will come out.

It was what my friend had urged me to do, but I am weak and pathetic and like an eggshell, I was brittle and if I were to crack, everything would come out unstoppably.

I'm not even brave enough to kill myself, so how can I be expected to have the courage to tell the truth?

Obviously, I wasn't tired, or even if I was, my mind was so full of negativity there was no way I'd fall to sleep easily, but I got into bed anyway. I went through the motions of looking like I was falling asleep but I just lay motionless with my eyes closed. Just a few minutes later I heard Dominika leave the room and heard her pottering about in the bathroom. Soon she was back and I was surprised when she almost immediately turned the light off before the mattress squeaked and moved slightly as she climbed under the covers next to me. A protective arm came over my shoulder and gentle toothpaste scented breath wafted over me, but soon her breathing shallowed as she fell asleep. I'm sure the stress of all of her work had left her exhausted and now she was reaching out to me.

It's all very nice, but too little too late. I know my name. I am Babylon and I don't deserve her love.

Wednesday 8 May 2019

I must have fallen asleep eventually, but when the alarm went off, I was instantly awake. Sleep had been a refuge for a few short hours, but with the rush of daylight flooding in through the window, the darkness returned almost instantaneously. I looked over at Dominika and couldn't bear being near her so I got up.

I went to the bathroom and showered again and unavoidably, as water cascaded over me, my mind was drawn back to last night. Stormy clouds gathered threateningly only now I refused to allow them to consume me again. A plan was beginning to form in my mind and it was enough to keep the shadows at bay. I'd teetered over the edge of the abyss last night and the darkness still had a grip on my soul but with a newfound purpose for today, I was no longer suicidal.

I'm the most disgusting creature ever, and today I'll show just how true it is and how little I'm really worth.

I'd gone to shower mainly to avoid Dominika, but I was being totally unrealistic. I needed the routine to look as normal as possible so I dried myself off and threw on my bathrobe and went to the kitchen. Dominika was up and about too so while I made us coffee she made sandwiches for breakfast, I honestly can't remember anything about whether we saw Emilia and Kasia. I think they popped into the kitchen to get breakfast, but as you can imagine my mind was elsewhere.

After we'd breakfasted, I finished getting dressed and did my makeup and sorted out my hair. I quite deliberately picked out a white and grey pinstriped dress. The weather had been changeable all week, but I decided to take a chance on the basis that I'd only be outside for a few minutes at a time between buildings and on the buses. A dress would also serve what I had in mind far better than my usual jeans.

When Dominika wasn't looking, I quickly took a selfie and sent it to Elwira with a simple message:

'See you soon xxx.'

It was a deceit, and it was seductive and, worst of all, it was quite deliberate on my part.

We finished getting ready and soon we were on our way. Our journey to university has been complicated recently because the city is working on the tramline from the Windmill Roundabout (Rondo Wiatraczna) and the bus company are running a 'Z' bus (Zastępstwo—*replacement*) instead. However, to get to university it's actually easier to go just a few tram stops from home and then change to another regular service bus.

I wasn't very talkative and neither was Dominika. My reasons were fairly obvious, but I guess Dominika was thinking about her work again. Whatever her reasons it suited me fine. Talking to Dominika had become so hard, even if I'd got quite good at pretending.

While we were on our way I got a message back from in the form of a kiss and a ':D' smiley. When we arrived I saw that Elwira was waiting for me near the main entrance. She grinned enthusiastically when our eyes met, but I doubt if Dominika even noticed. I played it cool until Dominika went inside and then I turned my attention to Elwira, who was struggling to contain her excitement. A moment of self-loathing surfaced and a pang of guilt gripped my stomach as it lurched in disapproval of the course I'd planned for us today.

Unlike the weekend, I was going to quite deliberately and consciously use Elwira to demonstrate to both of us my sheer depravity. Depravity is a strong word, but not strong enough to convey my scheming. I knew exactly what I was doing.

I am Babylon, a whore and nothing more.

'Hey Elwira.' I smiled warmly, all sweetness and light while disguising the self-disgust I was feeling.

'Hey Ania,' she smiled back, all cool and casual too.

She was wearing a tight top that became an inverted triangle as it accentuated her breasts before tapering down to be tucked into her black jeans. She was an image of perfection and for just a moment I wavered. How easy it'd be just to carry on as though nothing had changed. My mind screamed that I shouldn't give in to weakness and let things carry on as though everything was fine. Nothing was fine nor would it ever be fine ever again.

I know my value. I just have to stick to my plan.

There was no conscience left to guide me. She was stronger than addiction, she was an irresistible compulsion. I didn't even care where we were. To embrace fully who I am there was no other choice.

Time to go to work, Ania.

'Did you like the picture I sent you?'

'Yes it was lovely,' she replied with a playful smile.

Elwira's arm twitched involuntarily as she resisted the urge to reach out and touch me. It'd have been the easiest thing in the world to grab her arm and pull her to me and kiss her—*but not here and not now*. But…

'Come with me,' I said insistently.

I then went along the corridor and she followed. I went into one of the female toilets with her following me like a shadow. As expected it was empty. Lessons were due to start at any moment, so most students were already sitting in their classrooms. I opened a cubicle and gestured for her to go in before following after her. There wasn't much room, but as soon as we were inside, I squirmed around and managed to close and bolt the door behind us.

The moment I turned to face her she was on me and her lips met mine. She drank me in as if she hadn't tasted water for a month and I responded by kissing her back even more passionately. Her hand went to my hips and she reached down to the hem of my dress. Her lips had to leave mine as she slid a hand down my front, and then she slid her hand back up my thighs and her cold hand pressed straight onto my unprotected little treasure.

'*Kurwa,*' ('*Fuck*') she said as she pulled her face away from mine. 'You really did it! I thought the picture was just to tease me.'

I knew I must have shocked her because I've never known her to swear—she's always so terribly polite. Surprised as she was, I noticed her hand hadn't moved and she was now gently cupping her fingers around me and her fingers felt like they were pulsing slightly as though wanting to penetrate and pleasure me there and then. One finger rested along my slit enveloped in the folds of my fleshy bumps just itching to be inside me. She was just waiting for a word from me and then she'd go even further.

'This feels so naughty!' She smiled, clearly getting quite a thrill out of it. So it seemed that *naughty* wasn't bothering her. I guess after what we'd done at the weekend, and especially on Sunday, I shouldn't have been surprised.

I must admit that I was turned on by the moment too, but this wasn't what I had in mind. This was just to get her going. My bigger plan remained at the front of my mind and I couldn't let temptation and a quick fumble derail it. So I reached down and took her by her wrist and she reluctantly let go of me. I lifted her hand to my face and quite deliberately sucked her fingers.

'Just a taste of what's to come,' I whispered mysteriously before kissing her briefly, 'and now, we should go to class.'

Her face flickered disappointment, but then she smiled, 'I guess so.'

What she didn't see though was my face as she turned her back on me to open the door. I wasn't happy, quite the opposite. I felt myself sneer at her and for a moment I thought I hated her, but just as soon as that thought entered my head, I realised it wasn't her that I was in such contempt of. She was a mirror and simply a reflection for my own feelings. I now understood what I am more than ever, and while I was embracing it, I hated myself all the more for it.

I am so sorry Elwira, but today you are going to treat me exactly as I deserve.

I followed her to class and went in. She took her usual seat near the front and I sat further back. After our brief encounter in the toilets it was hard to concentrate and now I'd given myself over to total debauchery, unrestrained depravity, I was getting more and more turned on. I kept thinking back to that moment when she had discovered I wasn't wearing any knickers and how she had reacted. I'd barely started what I had in mind for today.

It was frustrating that I couldn't touch myself there and then, but the idea more than crossed my mind.

The lesson seemed agonisingly long and when it was over I hung back to make sure most students had gone so I could leave with Elwira. We grabbed coffee in the little café area and took a seat in the corner.

Now comfortable, Elwira smiled cheekily and got straight to the point, 'I wish I'd known what you were up to before I left home. I could have done the same and then just imagine what kind of fun we could have had.' Her face went all coy, 'Only I'm not so sure I could be so brave.'

No Elwira, I'm just a nasty little whore.

'Yes, your jeans will be a bit of a problem, but we'll find a way.'

That was a statement of intent which gave her some insight into what I had in mind today. She knew I was looking for another shared adventure, but I'm sure that she had no idea that I needed to be treated badly. Regrettably, I was pretty sure that Elwira wasn't capable of such cruelty, so I decided on another approach. I smiled as seductively as possible and reached my hands across the table without quite making contact with her.

'Hey Elwira, you said earlier that what I did was naughty and you know not just from today how naughty I can be, so now it's your turn. Tell me how naughty you can be.'

She seemed surprised and hesitated, 'What do you mean?'

'I'm feeling really naughty today.' I decided that it made sense to stick with the same word she'd used originally as I explained, 'but like always, I don't want to make you uncomfortable. So I guess I am just trying to find out how far you are willing to go.'

Permission is, always has been and always will be important to me. Even now I wasn't ready to do anything without specific consent.

'Ok—I think I understand, but I have no idea. This is all new to me.'

I knew she wouldn't go full Dominika or Kasia on me and to expect so would be unrealistic, but I couldn't help but feel disappointed. She'd drawn a red line on Sunday and there was no reason to think that she wouldn't again. Elwira won't hurt me or humiliate me or treat me like the whore I am, but I thought she'd at least offer something. I'd managed to persuade her to fuck my ass although I was less than convinced that she was really into it. On her own, without my prompting, she'd also spanked me and fingered my bum, and that is without mentioning what she'd done to me in the park.

Memory of the park suggested a dominant trait, but it wasn't enough.

Dominika if you are still reading this, it's yet another reason why you are exactly right for me. Whatever potential she has is irrelevant because in you, dominance is fully realised and besides I don't belong to her.

'I have some ideas for later, but first of all for lunchtime. But like on Sunday I don't want to make you do something that you don't want to do. It's very naughty, but it's up to you.'

'So let's see. If I don't like it though we can stop?'

'Of course.'

'You are a very strange girl, Ania,' she smiled.

'I know.'

'You excite me, but are kind of scary at the same time.'

To me, it sounded like she was describing Kasia and I laughed inwardly to myself. It was humourless and ironic. It was a comment and total validation of the monster I had become.

No let me correct that. I hadn't become a monster—I am a monster.

'What are you doing after classes this afternoon?'

'Spending time with you,' was Elwira's immediate answer. She laughed at her own smart comment and I smiled back. My plan for the evening was better formed than for the rest of the day so I was already ahead of her because I'd told Dominika earlier on that I was meeting *friends* later. It was an excuse and a cover for me to stay out later into the evening.

'Good. So it's decided.'

My next two classes weren't shared with Elwira so we finished our coffees and then went our separate ways. The truth was that I didn't have a definite plan for lunch but was hoping she'd have her own ideas. I couldn't concentrate during lessons because I was too distracted by trying to think something up. It had to be something that tested her limits but at the same time not too much for her. I had a couple of ideas, but one of them was weather dependent. I looked at the sky, a tapestry of blue and grey and had my doubts.

I tried to catch Elwira in the corridors between classes, but we missed each other. By chance, I saw Dominika briefly and I quickly fixed my fake persona. We chatted as is our norm whenever we randomly come across each other like this. My timetable didn't mesh with hers so spending lunch together was never a possibility anyway. As always, at university, we were very *vanilla* and I reminded her that I was staying out later today. She simply smiled and said that she'd see me later. She was completely oblivious, without even the slightest inkling that something was wrong between us.

I'd accepted the consequences of my actions and had switched off emotionally. I was now just a sexual creature, the whore of Babylon and I needed to embrace it. Babylon's appetite must be satisfied before she is thrown into the lake of fire and cast into hell.

I just hoped Elwira would be up for it.

The next lesson dragged on, but it was the last one before lunch and as each minute passed my anticipation grew. I was unusually nervous but knew it was because I had set my course. Despite my tension, I couldn't wait for her to get her hands, and whatever else, on me. I was also trying to work out how I could get my hands on her. Elwira's jeans in particular were a bit of a barrier and might prove to be a bit of a challenge.

At last the lesson was over and I went to the main entrance area and waited. Although it was a bit chilly, especially on my bare legs, it wasn't unbearable. The sky was still a patchwork of grey and blue, but looked like any rain should hold for at least the next hour or so. So with this in mind, I decided that it'd be better and less risky to go outside rather than try anything inside the university building. She was only a couple of minutes behind me and as always she flashed me her smile the very second she saw me. I forced a plastic smile back.

'Let's go outside,' I said simply.

'I have a surprise for you, Ania, but will show you in a bit. Where are we going?'

'To be naughty,' I answered cryptically, knowing I hadn't answered her question.

There's a large carpark in front of the main building and across the road there's a kind of strip of trees, which is just a few metres wide. When I got there my first reaction was disappointment. There wasn't enough cover, as the trees were sparser than I'd hoped they'd be. Further back there was a metal fence, the kind that is often found surrounding building sites that might offer some cover, but not much. Loads of cars were parked along the pavement and if anybody came to their car there was a significant risk of discovery.

Added to that, it was the middle of the day.

Just when I was about to abandon my idea I saw a thicker tree that offered me some hope. Its trunk was just about wide enough and its branches were decorated with a fair amount of broad foliage. Elwira had no idea what I was up to until I pulled her into the trees.

'In here,' she exclaimed.

'Unless you don't want to?' I teased. I was confident that she couldn't refuse me. After all, she'd done the same to me in the park at the weekend.

'Come on then.'

We ducked behind the trees far enough to be concealed from the road.

'Here should do,' I said as I pulled her to me. 'If we hear anybody though we'll need to freeze and stop what we are doing.' I looked at her again, straight into her eyes as if to dare her.

'Are *you* naughty enough?' I asked.

In answer to my question she kissed me and reached around and eased her hands down my body until she reached the bare crease at the back of my knees. She then slid her hands back up under my dress and grabbed my naked ass firmly. I reached around and did the same to her through her jeans.

The way I'd imagined our encounter was that she was supposed to go straight under my dress and directly assault me both front and back in an inescapable pincer. It wasn't a bad start though. Then very quickly she let go of me and grabbed my left hand with her right and took a step back.

Disappointment is an understatement of how I felt.

Come on Elwira, I am a whore, treat me badly, like I deserve.

My frustration was short-lived. With her free hand she undid her belt and opened her jeans. I wasn't sure what she was doing at first but the sound of her zip sliding down seemed to confirm what I was thinking. She then pulled her top out of the way and thrust my hand down her belly and I felt naked flesh.

Her knickers had disappeared! Now I looked at her, surprised.

'Do you like it? Is it naughty enough for you?'

I couldn't believe my luck. I answered by rubbing my fingers up and down the top of her groove and looking down into her jeans where my busy fingers were obscuring a perfect view. She responded by pushing her jeans down just a few centimetres at the hips. This gave me just enough room to loosen her jeans from the inside. I now had room to get into the space between her jeans and crotch. She was already wet and I could even feel her moisture on the back of my fingers from the seam of her jeans. It seemed that anticipation had made her hot too. I slipped a finger inside and she groaned more in expected pleasure than anything else. I clamped my free hand over her mouth.

'Shsh—not too loud.'

I can't believe what she said next.

'What, Ania? Too naughty for *you*?'

Despite my dark mood, that had left me on the edge of the dark bottomless pit last night, I genuinely laughed. Nobody has ever suggested such a thing before. I am not boasting or being immodest when I say this, but I am probably the naughtiest person I know.

With that, she lifted my dress and I was suddenly exposed from the waist downwards. Then with one hand in front and one at the back she ran her hands down my body until they almost met in the middle. Now she was giving me what I'd fantasied about and what I'd really wanted from the very beginning. With two fingers she parted my labia and used the middle one to penetrate my sopping honeypot. I then felt another finger on my ass and playing with my forbidden button. She was making little swirls and I could feel my circular muscles slowly stretching as her dry fingers pulled and caught on my unprepared flesh. I hadn't expected Elwira to be this direct, but her growing boldness excited me even more because it was so both unexpected and high risk with us being outside.

As she toyed with my ass it crossed my mind that I'd done well in deciding as usual to deep cleanse before coming out today. It's a habit I got into a few years ago—it's always better to be prepared for anything and everything.

I am disgusting, but I am not unhygienic!

She had me in a vice and, for the first time today, she was using me as I deserved. Somehow we managed to make it work so that we could share our masturbation even though we were sideways on and couldn't look at each other. She was doing more to me than I was to her and for just a few minutes I was happy again, as I was living in the experience and embracing my destiny. For the briefest of moments I escaped into the present, but I knew it was only a short respite. Elwira was completely unaware of what was going on in my mind and for her, I'm sure we were just being a bit naughty.

It was probably the riskiest thing I'd ever done because there was a real danger of exposure. We were in quite an open public space in the middle of the day not far from our university building where there were hundreds if not thousands of students and that's not even mentioning the tutors or even Dominika. Discovery by a stranger would be bad enough, but being found by somebody who knows us would be worse and Dominika discovering us was the ultimate risk. I've exposed myself outdoors before in more secluded locations, but Dominika has always safeguarded me by acting as a lookout or at the very least asking Emilia or Kasia to keep an eye out.

Today it was just the two of us, with no lookouts and no precautions.

As I dwelt on the danger, I felt greater urgency that paradoxically was wrapped in excitement.

What if somebody sees us? We are fair game, well I am anyway. Do what you want with me and then throw me out with the trash. It's what I deserve.

Shit! It's my waking death fantasy!

I was horrified by how fear of discovery and death invaded my mind, but at the same time my fever grew. I gritted my teeth held the sounds of my rising passion down. I saw that Elwira too was fighting to keep her pleasure silent. I only wished I could have played with her breasts and tasted her nipples while we played.

We fingered each other into our personal oblivions and as orgasms rocked our bodies we quaked and fought to keep ourselves under control. I clenched my jaw firmly shut so not to let out even the slightest squeak and I saw Elwira wrestling with her need to cry out too. After a few minutes, we came down together with hands still holding protective vigil on each other's satisfied sweetnesses.

Words were unnecessary or simply hard to find. I wasn't sure which. The silence wasn't the golden afterglow of making love in private. It was more of a shock, after the intensity of what we'd just done.

Normally, I'd have loved it, but my driving motivation polluted any enjoyment. There is a world of difference between sexual release and true joy.

We couldn't stay like this forever, so we stepped back from each other, but before she had a chance to do anything else I took her wrists in both of my hands and sucked her fingers. I tasted my own sex and my ass before I let her go and then as seductively as I could I sucked her sex from my fingers.

'Well that was lunch, later we'll have supper,' I joked but with my intentions absolutely clear.

She laughed, the first sound she'd uttered since we'd finished.

I wouldn't have dared to say this a few days ago, but it seemed that as she grew in confidence Elwira was getting more and more adventurous. It looked like Sunday hadn't freaked her out as much I thought it might have.

Tonight after classes we'll meet again and I'll stretch her boundaries even further and fall deeper into my debauchery and just maybe too even push my own limits.

In another world she would've been a perfect addition to our little family.

I flattened down and straightened my dress and she pulled her jeans back up and with a clang of the buckle on her belt she once again was decent and ready to face the outside world. We left the narrow wooded space as though nothing had happened, but we both had a spring in our steps and certainly for me it was hard not to grab her by the hand. It was an instinct that naturally followed the intimacy we'd just shared, but I had to suppress it. Not only was it in public but it was a lie too.

Looking back now I realise we were really lucky not to have been discovered.

Once back inside the building we had just enough time to grab a quick sandwich before going back to lessons.

The rest of the afternoon was agony, as lust filled me to my bones. I couldn't wait to be in Elwira's hands again. She was sitting tantalisingly in front of me and I so wanted her there and then. I frequently found myself following the contours of her sinuous back and only wished I could see her luscious ass which was hidden behind other students and the back of her chair. Learning was impossible, but inevitably the day finally came to an end... and now I could really test how far she was willing to adventure into the darkness with me.

As I'd done at lunchtime, I hovered back after class and asked Elwira to wait there while I just popped to see my flatmate for a minute. I at least owed Dominika that, and to be honest she expected it because we always had a quick chat if one or the other of us wasn't going directly home.

As far as Elwira was concerned I just made it sound like it'd be easier to find her by doing it my way, but the truth was I didn't want Dominika to see me with her. Dominika didn't have even the slightest inkling of what I was up to, but it was better to avoid a situation than risk one.

It only took a couple of minutes to find Dominika, and when I saw her I reminded her that I'd be back quite late. I reminded her that I had my phone and she mouthed 'I love you' before we parted.

I love her too, but my destiny and my destruction are preordained.

Dominika left for home and I went back to find Elwira. She was waiting just outside the classroom when I found her.

'Let's get something to eat,' she suggested out of nowhere and to my complete surprise.

I was hoping we'd go somewhere hidden so she could tear my clothes off and break me with forceful fingers and a hot tongue.

'I love spending time with you, but it can't be just sex,' she explained. 'We'll make love later. Let's go to Francuska Street, there're a lot of restaurants there. Unless you've got other plans?'

I did actually. More direct plans.

Elwira clearly had some kind of a date night in mind. She was taking us to another level. It wasn't a place I could go, but what could I do? I was trapped by my own deceit. I could hardly say no. Almost as soon as I realised I'd ensnared myself I understood that I'd have to go through the motions, at least for now, to get what I really wanted out of tonight.

The end was all that mattered to me now and not the journey.

Stupid little bitch, I'll play the date thing for now, to get what I really want from you.

Once again I was filled with contempt for her and just as quickly recognised that I was projecting my own self-loathing on to her.

She is not the stupid little bitch—I am!

Francuska Street, in the district of Saska Kępa, one of the more fashionable parts of Warsaw, was only a short bus ride away. The late afternoon weather had turned surprisingly pleasant and because we hadn't made a reservation we didn't have an exact plan, but we had plenty of choice. We got off the bus near the National Stadium on the George Washington Roundabout and decided to walk. It gave us a chance to see what was available. With each step I was beginning to suspect that Elwira was caught up in the romance of walking together in such an attractive area even if we were limited to just linking arms.

In the end, after roaming up and down most of the street and looking at all the possibilities we went simple and chose an authentic-looking Italian place. It looked very classy and expensive but was intimate and cosy inside. It was more what she was looking for than me, but to achieve my endgame I had to keep her sweet and play along.

The prices were probably higher than we could really afford, but it's not something we do every day. Elwira took pizza and I took pasta which we both washed down with a nice cold beer. As we ate and talked I could see Elwira's eyes shining and she was almost staring constantly and blinking rarely. She leant attentively into our conversation and rested her chin casually on her hand as she listened intently in the few instances when I was speaking for more than a few seconds. She looked so adorable, but she wanted something I couldn't give her.

I'd already guessed, but as I looked at her now I was left with absolutely no doubt. She'd gone and fallen in love with me.

You fucking bitch, Ania! I hate you!

I had to drive my thoughts out and keep my feelings separated. It was hard enough anyway, and emotions only get in the way. If I simply owned up and did anything other than what I'd planned tonight it'd end very badly for Elwira.

Of course, I was just delaying the inevitable, but there and then I just couldn't bring myself to break her heart tonight. Her quiet charm almost melted me, but I knew that I had to break my addiction. I needed to concentrate on the moment and get through this evening. I had to what needed to be done, and that was all that mattered to me right there and then.

You fucking selfish depraved bitch, Ania. You deserve to rot in hell.

I was fully immersed in playing my role. As far as she was concerned, I behaved like it was a date too. I was attentive and interested but offered little of myself. Over the weekend everything had been quite chatty and easy-going, but she'd carried a lot of that. I've never been a great conversationalist and as usual she had plenty to say for both of us and so she probably hardly noticed anyway.

What I'm doing is sick and twisted, but I can't help myself. I have to do this. At least this way Elwira won't get hurt.

I even started to believe my own lies.

We'd finished eating and the beer was long gone and we weren't going to order anything else. It'd been a while since our table had been cleared and it got to the point when we needed to get going.

We paid the bill and while we were waiting for the change Elwira asked, 'Can we go back to yours?'

'My flatmates will be home,' I answered. That was probably the only honest thing I said all night.

'Same here,' she replied disappointedly.

Perfect! That suited me just fine.

I had no intention of being inside, whether at hers or mine. Time to put my plan into action. 'How did you like your lunch? Do you want to do something crazier?'

'Depends how crazy. But if it's like earlier then why not?' She flashed a cheeky playful smile. 'Only if I don't like it we won't do it?'

The question was implied and probably rhetorical, but needed an answer. 'No problem. I've always told you that.'

I will respect her sexual limits even if I no longer respect her.

'So let's go. We don't need to go too far.'

With that, we got up and left. I was ahead of her and as she followed she struggled to keep pace with me. We headed back in the direction of the stadium and then across the roundabout into the park. It was still quite light even though it was now nearly seven o'clock. There were still people walking around and enjoying the late spring evening and to the causal passer-by we wouldn't have stood out. We were just another two people anonymously doing the same as everyone else. We were chatting as we walked, but I was getting more frustrated with each passing moment.

'Too many people,' I finally said exasperated, 'and besides this place is so well-known that too many people know where the hiding places are. Let's go somewhere else.'

Babylon will get what she wants.

We came out of the park and got yet another bus that went roughly in the direction of my home near a large railway junction. It took a while and finally when we got off the bus, darkness was descending and the evening was beginning to really close in. Nearby, there are more woods and in fact, it wasn't my first time here. The woodland almost stretches to where I live and Dominika and I have done stuff in there before.

I have always been traumatised by forests and in recent years, Dominika has helped me come to terms with my fears. This place, more than any other, has become a sacred place for us. It was a place of personal liberation, and the thought of entering without Dominika's knowledge had never even crossed my mind before. Now here I was revisiting the place where Dominika had saved me from my phobias and helped me become more complete.

Going there without her, crossed every last line and completed my fall into complete depravity. I was disrespecting everyone and everything that ever mattered. It was almost as though I going into a church and spitting on the cross.

I am Babylon, I am a whore, I am Babylon and I must fall!

After what had happened earlier Elwira probably thought that she had some idea of what I had in mind. Despite this, she was still wide-eyed and surprised, but not resistant.

Over the last week or so I'd awakened the adventurous side of her personality and she was enjoying it. She was reassured that I wouldn't make her do anything that she didn't want to. My simple motto is that without consent there is abuse.

At first, we saw a couple of people walking their dogs, but soon we found ourselves alone. There's a concrete path going through the woods, especially near the railway, but soon it was possible to leave the path and descend further into the shadows that loomed with ghostly foreboding. In the past it would have terrified me, but compared to my inner darkness ghouls and spectres couldn't even come close. The undergrowth was a challenge, but we made it through and I didn't even scratch my legs. I envied Elwira's jeans though, which made it easier for her to walk through without a care.

'This'll do,' I suddenly announced and with that, I hooked my bag on a branch and unzipped my dress and lifted it over my shoulders. The cool air that I hadn't been paying any particular attention to suddenly pressed and caressed my skin. I realised I must have looked ridiculous standing there in just sneakers, socks and a bra so I quickly removed my bra too and even though I was obscured by shadow I exposed myself to her and the whole world.

'Ania! Are you crazy? What are you doing? Somebody might see you.'

She may have objected with her words, but it didn't stop her from putting her own bag down and grabbing me in a rough embrace. Even though I'd only been naked for a few seconds her body, now pressed to mine, felt really warm. Her tongue found its way inside my mouth and she didn't hold back in groping me. One hand was on my breasts and the other on my ass. It almost seemed like she didn't know what to do. She was grabbing my flesh so roughly and randomly as though she wanted to utterly consume all of me and not leave anything untouched. I reached behind her back as she likes and grabbed her ass fully with both hands and pulled her tighter to me.

Engulfed in passion, we stayed like this for a while with our mouths and tongues working overtime to the point where my jaw began to ache. She loves kisses, but eventually we pulled our lips apart and my hands moved to her front and tugged her T-shirt out before undoing the button and opening the zip of her jeans. My hand slipped inside and as expected she hadn't bothered putting her knickers back on. I touched her hot flesh briefly with my cold hand and she groaned in anticipation, but I wanted more. I took hold of her jeans by the waist and started tugging them down. When I got them to her knees, she grabbed them and for the first time resisted my passion.

'Stop, Ania please. No more.' She was almost pleading.

My strongest, and probably only, principle has always been *consent*. Even lost as I was, my absolute commitment to permission was unshakeable. In reality, it was probably all I had left.

My past has shown me the value of permission and I'd suffered the consequences when I was growing up before I moved to Warsaw. Dominika had only reinforced this throughout our relationship. Dominika has always insisted on explicit permission...

But in the forest with Elwira, while this one value endured, Dominika was far from my mind.

I let go of her jeans to send Elwira a clear signal. 'It's ok. Elwira as far as you are willing to go. That's what we agreed. Do you want me to stop?'

'No, I just can't get naked like you.'

Then to prove how 'brave' she was she reached under her T-shirt and removed her own bra. She wrestled the shoulder straps out of her sleeves and over her elbows before carefully pulling it out and hanging it up. Then she lifted her top to present me with a shadowy view of her beautiful breasts that I'd been denied all day.

What could I do but take them in my hands and nibble on her nipples and bring them to life? The cooling weather and my instant touch quickly roused them as they hardened in my mouth and palms. As I played with them it suddenly struck me that although Elwira had stopped me from taking her jeans down any further she hadn't hitched them back up. She'd drawn a line but hadn't retreated.

Somehow that made me feel a bit better. I'd pushed her to the edge, but when it came down to it I'd respected her boundaries as promised.

'Has anyone ever done this to you?' I asked rhetorically as I turned her around and slid my hands down her body and crouched down behind her. I parted her meaty globes and probed my tongue straight into her asshole and started licking. So long as consent remained I was no longer worried about her constraints.

I am a whore and this is our last time. I will take her as far as she will let me.

Lost in the moment I managed a cheery thought when she moaned in unexpected pleasure and pulled her own cheeks apart to help me get further inside her ass. Now my hands were free I reached further between her legs and found her little button already hardened and standing, her slit wet and ready for me.

'That feels so good, Ania,' she said in a drawn-out groan, as I continued to flick her button and tongue her ass.

As a reward, I slid two fingers inside her and began to fuck her with them while all the time keeping my tongue in her ass. As I worked her over, she started panting and shaking. She rolled her hips in tune with the beat I was setting. Her fire was rapidly kindling and her heat was rising. Despite her best efforts to stay silent the occasional sigh and squeal escaped as the magma rose inside her volcano.

I let go of her suddenly so I could move my hands to her hips and pull myself up. As I stood up, I ran my hands up her sides and under her T-shirt. I grabbed her breasts firmly, her nipples were firm, whether from the cold weather or her heat, I didn't know. They pressed into my palms as I squeezed and enjoyed them. I wasn't going to stay there and within seconds, while still standing behind her, my left hand had found its way between her legs again. I rubbed as though my life depended on it, and stoked her fire until she was white-hot with swift strokes over her clit and swollen labia while my other hand massaged her chest and teased a nipple. She threw her head back over my shoulder as pleasure became overwhelming and in doing so she exposed a bit of her neck. I nibbled and sucked on her neck with passion, but not enough to mark her.

Touching her neck electrified her and pushed her over the edge.

Still behind her, I pulled her tight to me and helped her ride through her extended orgasm as her body convulsed and she involuntarily gyrated against my furious fingers. Her ass pounded against my unused cunt (*for that is all I am*) as she spasmed in her pleasure dance. Her hands reached behind her and grabbed my naked hips and she steadied herself as uncontainable tremors overtook her. It was almost as though she released more than the immediate orgasm, but also the tension from earlier. Necessity had demanded restraint near the university, but now such constraints no longer held her back. Her hands felt clammy against my cool flesh and her nails sharp. She didn't really dig them in, but they caused just enough pain to excite me.

My turn, I thought impatiently.

Despite my keenness to fulfil my own desire, I rode with Elwira until she naturally came back down and as she did so I eased my rubbing until finally I was just holding her used intimacy protectively with curved fingers. As intensity waned she too eased her grip on my hips.

When she was settled I released her and she stepped forward a few steps before turning round to look at me. Even in the shadows, I saw the glint in her eyes as she lustfully admired my nakedness.

'Ania, you are so beautiful, and so … *so* naughty.'

She seemed to hesitate and I thought she was going to declare her love for me, which would have made things really awkward. Fear of expressed affection knotted my stomach, but then, to my relief, she simply stepped back into my face and kissed me. It was another one of those long lingering kisses that I'd become accustomed to over the last week or so.

Fuck—it's been almost a week since my Judas kiss.

She wasn't satisfied with just kissing me though. Her hands were warm on my firm breasts and my nipples were sensitive and erect in response to her attentions and the cool air. For a fleeting moment I wanted her to hurt me, but this passed when she moved from my mouth and first took one nipple and then the other into her warm mouth and sucked on them. As she finished with each one she playful teased them with a nip of her teeth.

My skin tingled as she then ran her lips down my body. She paused only briefly at my belly button and jabbed her tongue in it a few times before moving on. I grabbed the back of her head. I knew what was coming, and couldn't wait…

She continued to migrate south until she was facing my treasure. She put her hands between my knees and firmly and insistently splayed my legs. I moved to accommodate her and keep my balance as she dived in. Her hands found my outer lips and she parted me with impatient fingers. Her warm tongue soon found its way inside and began to work on my wet slit. She was working hard from her crouched position and clearly struggling. So within minutes she switched to licking on and around my button while finger-fucking me with a steady pumping hand using at least two fingers from below.

I fought to stay quiet as she worked me over.

She had no idea, but I was ready for pain now. So I let go of her head and moved my hands to my breasts. Unseen, as I often do, I played with them and pinched my nipples harshly. The cool air had made them quite sensitive and my self-inflicted torture made them hurt more than usual. The pain, as always, only added to my heat and the more intense the better it was.

Elwira was so focused that she was oblivious to what I was up to. The truth was that she was so lost in herself that she was hardly being gentle herself as her desire to ravish me took over. She was ramming her fingers in and out of me almost mechanically and her licking was more and more sporadic as she failed to coordinate both her fingers and mouth at the same time.

Like a smoking volcano, far from dormant, the explosion followed and she too rode me through it and didn't relent, even when it became uncomfortable to the point of agony. The contrasting feelings of torturous pleasure made me feel alive so I wasn't complaining—even if, as I often say, I was moaning. Silence was impossible, as a stream of thunderous pleasure overwhelmed my mind and body.

As I began to come down my brain was freed to think again and that's when the guilt hit me harder than a punch to the stomach. I had knowingly and deliberately used this sweet girl for my own ends. She'd made the mistake of falling for me and now the beast I am was revealed in its full decadence—at least to me anyway. Guilt was swiftly followed by another wave of self-loathing.

This is Babylon's reward.

I had to suppress how I was feeling though. Elwira was still there. Everything had to be normal as far as she was concerned. Keep smiling, and carry on…

You fucking using, nasty, evil bitch, Ania!

I'd known what I was doing all along, but I couldn't stop myself. The last vestiges of my conscience held some sympathy for Elwira, but no sorrow and no shame. It was Elwira, but it could have been anybody. I'd given myself over to my nature. A sudden realisation came over me, I was colder than Dominika and more evil than Kasia.

Fucking bitch is too kind. I am much, much worse than this. Smile, Ania. Fucking smile...

I forced myself to be light, despite the darkness that was consuming me and I allowed Elwira to hold me close and kiss me again and responded in kind to disguise my contemptable soul. Finally, we physically separated and I watched as she pulled her jeans up and I caught a last glimpse of her most precious part. She straightened her top, but didn't bother putting her bra back on. She simply, put it in her bag. We were finished for the night, and actually forever.

I slipped my bra back on before recovering my dress and putting it on. She helped me zip it up at the back and kissed the back of my neck as she did so.

Dressed and decent again, we left the woods. Elwira didn't really know where she was or how to get home so I explained to her that she needed to take two buses, but I'd go with her and wait until she was on the second bus. The first bus, the 135 service, starts near where we were so we went there and it was already waiting. So we got on and, because there was nobody but the driver, Elwira even held my hand. Such a small gesture.

Of course, I continued playing the role.

After a few minutes we set off. It was about 21.30 and at that time of night there is little traffic, so the journey to the Zamieniecka bus stop on the edge of Gocław only took about 10 minutes. Unfortunately, we'd just missed the 168 service which goes directly by her home and had to wait another fifteen minutes for the next one.

I couldn't abandon her, even though I knew I no longer cared for her. In fact, I was beginning to hate her—not her fault—but because she was a mirror that illuminated my dark soul and she unconsciously reflected everything that was bad about me. As before when I felt such negativity towards her I realised very quickly that it wasn't her that I hated, but myself as our relationship sharply contrasted the contradictions between us.

Relationship—that's a joke. I'd used her plain and simple. Even the sex over the weekend had served only to fill a void in my life. Everything we'd done had been all about me and me alone.

We chatted a bit while we waited, but talk was difficult after the adventures we'd shared and I wasn't being particularly communicative as I wrestled with my own feelings. She was making suggestions for lunchtimes and maybe the weekend and I just kept saying, 'We'll see,' or words to that effect.

It was with much relief that I greeted her bus as it came around the corner. It meant the end and I didn't have to talk to her anymore. I played the role and wore a mask of sadness to match how she was feeling. I could tell that she wanted to kiss me, but we were too much in the open and she had to settle for the Polish three cheek kiss. It was the last time she would ever touch me.

I watched the bus disappear into the distance and knew I should have gone home, but my guilt was engulfing me. Although I'd come to understand that mine is a life of loss and shame, it was still deeply disturbing and upsetting. Accepting the truth didn't make it any more palatable. Peace was forever lost and replaced with a heavy stone in my stomach. There was no way back.

No way back. The thought echoed round and round my brain and I realised that I wasn't ready to go home yet.

I crossed the road and went to the corresponding bus stop so I could return to where we'd just come from. This time I was very lucky, I even had to run a bit to catch the bus. Within ten minutes I was back on Szaserów Street just one bus stop before where I'd caught the first bus with Elwira maybe just a bit more than half an hour ago. All the time the stone was getting heavier and heavier. I checked another bus and found that had I'd just missed it so I walked. From here I could have been home in maybe 20 minutes, but like I said, I wasn't ready and I had something else in mind.

There's a forest, I think it is actually part of the same forest Elwira and I had just been in, very close to our home. It's the kind of place where nobody goes, secluded and isolated, but full of shadows and imagined horror. This was the exact place that Dominika had used to exorcise my demons and face my phobias. It was a special place and I believed that here, and only here, I would find my true self.

I looked around cautiously to make sure no one could see me. It was dark and quiet and nobody was around so I slipped into the shadows. I was immediately among the trees, but went deeper into the gloom mainly because it made the slight chance of anybody and especially the police or Straż Miejska finding me was even less likely. As I entered the stone in my gut was finally displaced with a stronger emotion. It started lower down in my bowels and I felt my ass clench involuntarily, but I kept going.

In the dark everything was monochrome and my footing was unsure. I stumbled further into the darkness and when I thought I'd gone far enough I stopped. I was next to a vast tree and once more I took my dress and bra off and allowed nature to see me just as I am, uncovered in the naked shame of Eve. I hung my bag and clothes in the waiting tree bough and just stood there. The cold air was closing in and danced in swirls on my skin serving only to cover me in goose pimples and exacerbate my anxiety.

What am I doing here?

Fear had taken over and I was confused. I'd come here with a plan, but fear had cast out all thought and I really couldn't remember why I'd entered this accursed yet sacred ground. There must have been a reason.

So rather than abandon what even I thought was beginning to look like a stupid idea I decided to go with it. I just followed my instincts and slipped a finger into my slit. Even I was surprised to discover how wet I was and once I touched myself I couldn't stop.

It's not the first time I have entered a forest on my own to masturbate. I remember doing it in England once when we were visiting for a summer, but unlike on that occasion, this time I had lost all reason and understanding of what I was doing there.

I want to be discovered and abused. Babylon must meet her end.

Fuck! Where did that thought come from?

Then the fog cleared. I knew from last night that I just couldn't kill myself, but at the same time I couldn't just turn off the self-destruction button either. It's not that easy. Fear had clouded my earlier thoughts, but unlike guilt, I knew how to overcome fear and now everything was clear again. I was still afraid, but there was a part of me that wanted to be found and brought to justice.

I didn't want a rescuer, a knight in shining armour. I wanted worse than my darkest fears could conjure up. I wanted a demon to possess me, use me and then discard me without even the slightest thought…

Was this my waking dream and prophecy? Is now the time?

Thoughts of destruction, in this the most fearful of places, only excited me more and I quickly brought myself off with rapid fingers that left me physically drained, but emotionally numb. I was frustrated and the physical release hadn't touched me how I'd wanted it to. I didn't understand why, but it'd done the opposite to what I'd hoped for. I was caged in self-inflicted oppression and had nobody else to blame.

Disappointed that I wouldn't be discovered nor reach some sexual mountaintop on my own my next thought was naturally to hurt myself. I fumbled around on the ground until my hand found a broken branch. I thought about whipping myself with it. It was thin and it'd tear my flesh painfully without really damaging me too much. I raised my hand to strike myself across the top of my thighs and then I stopped. If I mark myself unanswerable questions will follow.

How can I hurt myself, but not leave any marks?

Then I had an idea. I felt along the branch and found it had smaller twigs branching off it. I broke them off leaving sharp nubs in their place. I tested the rough bark stubs against my thumb and while there was a bit of give, it'd still scrape and scratch. I opened my legs and used one hand to separate my labia. With my other hand I put the branch in my love groove and made sure the sharpened stump was facing upwards so it would scratch my clit and protective hood.

Hopefully, it'll hurt my inner parts too.

I drew it slowly across myself and while it hurt, it didn't hurt me enough, so I did it again. It scratched slightly but it was impossible to get it on my clit how I wanted. So I tried a third time. I felt the rough bark bite into my skin and I gyrated against it and used it to masturbate, obviously not for pleasure, but to at least try to feel something. It was uncomfortable, but there was so little pain. Physical agony and brokenness were escaping me. The branch simply wasn't strong enough.

It had, however, caused enough pain for me to realise that it wasn't even touching my mind as I wanted. Nothing was working. I was looking for a physical torment that would break my body, without marks and appease my sin. Breaking my body was supposed to be a punishment that'd bring closure and set me free.

There was no release, no pain, no just punishment and no liberation. There was nothing.

I still felt the same, or if anything slightly ridiculous. Maybe a stronger branch would do? Only, I didn't feel like rummaging around all night looking for the right branch that might just hurt me enough.

I've run out of ideas.

I paused, naked and getting colder by the minute. I was exposed, and vulnerable, but my brain had deserted me. Nobody was going to find me and nothing else was going to happen.

Go home, Ania! That still rational part of my brain screamed at me.

Disappointed that I hadn't got what I wanted I retrieved my clothes and got dressed. It'd been so much better that time on my own in England. Tonight was so different, a pointless failure.

Why can't I find myself tonight?

That was the moment when I realised in my numbness that I was still breathing and conscious.

The dead can't feel and neither can I. I am dead inside.

I am an animated corpse, but not a brainless zombie. Cruel fate has left my awareness trapped inside my dead body to face the memories of everything I'd done. It is a horror movie and it's set on repeat.

Resigned to this new truth, I fixed my mind on getting home and quickly left the forest and crossed the road. It was less than a ten minute walk back to the flat and just before I went in I took a moment to compose myself. I set my all too familiar face and went inside. I said a quick hi to Emilia and Kasia, as though without a care in the world, before going to face Dominika in our room. She got up from the sofa and came to me before pecking me affectionately on the cheek and asking how my evening had been. I lied with a plastic face to reassure her that it'd been fun, but before giving her the chance to getting any deeper into it I told her that I was going to grab a quick shower.

But it hadn't been fun.

Unlike the pleasures of the weekend, my time with Elwira today had been devoid of anything other than selfish desire that had, as the day had gone on, left me increasingly more devastated inside. Yes, I'd cum, but an orgasm isn't everything. The day had left me unfulfilled and empty inside. Elwira had given herself to me and I was pretty sure that she had fallen in love with me. I'd taken her beauty and trust and twisted it to serve my own ends. Today had been very different to the tenderness of the weekend, even if at times we'd stretched the boundaries—particularly on Sunday.

I'd used her—it was as simple as that.

Today had been wanton lust shaped only by my perversion and depravity. I hadn't gone as far as forcing myself on her but taking a huge risk just outside the school and then taking her in the forest had been all about me. She had been right on her edge as demonstrated when she refused to take her top off or let me take her jeans down further than her knees. The only thing that I'd done that could even vaguely be described as moral was to stay within her boundaries. At least I'd respected her with that.

The truth was that she'd been a means to serve my loss and self-disgust and there was no disguising it.

With my last shred of decency, I resolved that I'd stay away from Elwira. She deserves so much better than me.

Worse still I'd cheated on Dominika who is my everything.

When she first met me she really had saved me from myself and now that I'd turned my back on her I was back to where I'd begun.

No that's not true.

Now my sick desire has led me to an even worse place. Dominika will never forgive me and everything is lost. Judgment has been made and now I am on death row.

I just wasn't brave enough to face the justice that awaited me.

I hate myself and everything I am.

A pretty face and a desirable body are temporary and this is all I have. Beauty can be a curse too. I'd realised that last night and today had just confirmed it.

As well as betraying Dominika and using Elwira I'd crossed the line with my closest friends. When it all comes out I will feel sweet Emilia's steel and know Kasia's hate.

I'd been ready to die for my sins, but at the last moment I'd cowered away from doing myself in. Now I was just left with a terrible sneering, cynical contempt of myself. I'd live on, a shallow and empty life. There would be no redemption, only destruction.

Even sexually I was just a shell, a physical husk awaiting deserved abuse, that'd leave me dissatisfied and hungry for the two things I needed the most.

Love and acceptance were now lost forever. My heart was still beating, but I was dead.

Part 2: Ania Is Lost
Saturday 11 May 2019

To celebrate completing her thesis, Dominika had organised a girls' night out and the four of us found a nice bar and drank and chatted the night away. On the surface, everything looked like it was back to normal. I played my part, smiled when I needed to, and kissed and cuddled seemingly without a care in the world, while at the same time I drank to numb my feelings.

Numbness is only a temporary cure. As blindness impacts vision, alcohol erases memories. In the moment it does however, make my life is easier, at least until I wake up the next day.

Before I met Dominika, I used to drink more than I do now. Dominika has slowly taught me how to feel and let go of the past. As I sat next to her seemingly in blissful normality, I continued to deceive her. I drank more than I had for a long time but did it steadily, so not to draw her attention. In the past, I'd mastered the art of hiding my drinking and so I returned to old habits.

It was all in vain though. The drink wasn't touching me and no matter much I tried to push my terrible secret deep inside, I still felt the weight of my betrayal. Teaching me how to *feel* was proving to be a two-edged sword.

Dominika was as sweet as she'd ever been and so attentive. She told me again and again that now her thesis was done things, would go back to normal. She admitted that she'd missed me and finishing her thesis had been long and arduous, but at least now it's done she needn't worry any longer. She almost sounded like she was feeling guilty and trying to make up for it. Discretely and whenever she could she was touching me under the table, a little pat on the knee or a little stroke here and there, and giving me everything I ever wanted and all I ever needed…

But it was too late. I was dead inside and I didn't know how much longer I could play the role. I hated myself and the last ten days had shown me to be a whore who was totally unworthy of her.

Her attention and love shamed me.

When we got home she was in the mood for something more and I only wished it was to punish me. It was the least I deserved, but when she suggested that we shower together, she clearly had something more romantic in mind.

We climbed into the shower together as we have done so many times before and dowsed each other down with warm water. When she first touched me I was so disgusted that I had to fight off the urge to flinch away from her. The feel of her hands on my body and her flesh in my hands should have reignited our passion, but touching her was killing me.

I'd be lying if I said that her touch and the closeness of her naked body weren't arousing me but there was no longer any passion because I was dead. The horror of what I'd done to her was in the forefront of my mind and I felt sick and yet my mask remained in place. It had to.

My dearest Dominika was gentle, attentive and just happy with the intimacy. As far as she was concerned it seemed that the closeness was all that mattered and while it was obvious she wanted more she wasn't pushing me. I was silently grateful because for now it was letting me off the hook.

How could I give myself to this divine creature after what I'd done?

I glanced from time to time at the razor on the side of the bath. It'd only been four days since it'd originally called me and as my thoughts drifted back there it called my name once again in a sibilant whisper. But I knew I was too weak and pathetic, I wasn't even brave enough to do myself in, If I was ever going to kill myself, it'd have been on Tuesday.

On Tuesday I'd saved the dead, my inner voice mocked bitterly.

We dried each other off and took it in turns brushing each other's hair out. My hair is longer than hers so it meant she was far more indulgent with me. What we were doing exactly mirrored what Elwira and I had done barely a week ago. I forced myself to suppress yet another damning memory, but nobody can ever imagine how that churned up and convulsed my insides.

This is my Dominika—so perfect. Her light shining over me just made my darkness darker.

As the last part of our nightly ritual, we brushed our teeth and I consciously and deliberately made sure I finished before her and went straight to bed. She hadn't made a move in the bathroom but once in bed it was likely to be another matter. I had to get ahead of her.

She soon joined me and snuggled up to my back and grabbed my ass. I muttered under my breath, but acid shot into my throat from my stomach and it took all the strength and will I could muster not to flinch away from her.

'Are you ok, darling?'

'Just sleepy—I think I probably drank too much,' I murmured in my best attempt to sound drowsy.

There was a seed of truth to what I said, but it was a delicate shell concealing a greater lie.

'Ok, darling, just sleep. We can have some fun tomorrow.'

She moved my hair aside and kissed the back of my neck and then rested her head on my pillow behind me. She stroked my hair gently for a few minutes before her arm slipped down onto my shoulder. Normally when she holds me like this I feel protected and safe, but tonight her love and affection left me feeling trapped. My mind was filled with bitter irony that only gnawed relentlessly at my guts.

I am a whore and have been a complete bitch to you—you will never forgive me for this. I hate myself and you are worth so much more than me. Almost anybody in the world can touch me and use me, but not you, my Dominika. You are better than this and I don't deserve you.

I closed my eyes and thought once more about Elwira; my sin and my downfall.

I'd been so confused and lost last time I was with her. The weekend had been all about passion and lust, but Wednesday had only been only about my depravity and I'd taken her down with me. I'm sure that as far as Elwira was concerned it looked like we'd crossed another threshold and reached another level in our budding relationship. Our longing had hit a new intensity and it must have seemed like I was giving myself to us.

But there was no us nor could there ever be.

She hadn't understood my motives and evil intentions. I'd used her. It was as simple as that and I had been wrestling with what I'd done to her ever since. There was no way around it. I'd become nothing, but a nasty self-serving bitch and since the forest, my shame and sin had been weighing more and more heavily on me. I was already condemned by what I'd done to Dominika, but I hadn't exactly respected Elwira either.

On Thursday and Friday, I'd kept Elwira at a distance without it looking deliberate. It was unavoidable at university and, even though my heart jumped every time I saw her, it hadn't been easy to resist her. Elwira was really sweet, with her little messages and her smile every time she saw me. I guess it was to be expected, after all, she'd fallen in love with me. I was fighting a massive inner battle, to run to her. The sex had been so good and the truth was that we simply got on really well and I have to admit the magic was still there. I was addicted and my body ached for us to make love again. She may have been inexperienced, but her enthusiasm and openness had more than made up for that.

But tempted as I was, Wednesday had marked a point of no return.

I knew this, but there was still no escape from her. It'd been ten days since we'd first had sex and I'd been fantasising about her on and off for a lot longer, ever since she'd asked me that rather strange question a couple of years ago. Even now, as I was trying to break away, her spectre continually haunted me and tore my soul apart as lustful images of her filled my mind accompanied with a sense of fear and dread and terrible doom.

She deserves somebody better than me and in this she had something in common with Dominika.

The only way I could win the battle with my addiction was to keep my overpowering feelings of revulsion at the front of my mind. A small rational part of my mind fought for clarity in the chaos. She was like vodka to an alcoholic, or heroin to a junkie. My habit was extremely toxic, dangerous and destructive, if not for Elwira, then certainly for me.

I am so selfish.

I'd done everything to get my fix, to get what I needed and to be treated as I deserved. Even when I had returned to the forest later, I hadn't cared if I'd lived or died. My only limit was my own cowardice.

Thoughts of the forest just reminded me once again of how cold and empty I'd become. What if somebody had found me? Maybe I'd be dead among the roots of the trees. It was everything that I deserved even if I was too afraid to carry out my own death sentence.

The only solace I had was that at least I now understood that I couldn't carry on with Elwira. I was afraid of hurting her and a big part of me didn't want to lose her, even though I knew I must. My heart, soul and mind still belonged to Dominika, but Elwira was my weakness. I had to be strong. She was still desperately keen to meet up and I'd even fended off her suggestion about meeting today by using Dominika's girls' night out to avoid her, but in doing so I'd heavily hinted that we'd meet up again soon. It was easier than facing the truth.

My deceit knew no bounds.

I longed for the day when once more Dominika would be mine and I would be hers. Going out last night should have marked the first day of a new chapter in our lives; a new beginning. Dominika was back and I loved her more than ever, but what I'd done was ripping me apart; my soul was a slick; dirty, slimy and utterly corrupted.

Stupid Ania. Dominika always warned me that pleasure has a price and that price has left me morally bankrupt, broken and cast adrift.

Finally, inexorably, sleep finally dragged me under and at least in that, I found some respite.

Sunday 12 May 2019

I was feeling bad, really bad.

The moment my eyes opened I was fully conscious and aware. The darkness attacked me immediately and relentlessly without mercy or respite. It gnawed at my guts and twisted my intestines into tight, painful knots far worse than any cramp I've ever known. It felt like a vast chasm had been torn open across my stomach and I felt like vomiting. I pulled me knees up in a futile attempt to alleviate the pain but I just knew that there was nothing physically wrong with me.

As bad as it was, my bodily torment was nothing compared to the turmoil that was crushing my mind like an unstoppable migraine. I had nowhere to turn and nobody to turn to, not even Emilia. There was no way I could own up to what I'd done. Shame and guilt had isolated me and I was trapped and alone in a cage of my own making.

I rolled over in bed to see Dominika still sleeping. Her face was perfect; her smooth pale features were gently masked by a wisp of vagrant hair. Looking at her didn't help. I turned away, tears in my eyes as the depth of what I'd done to her hit home yet again. Last night's personal psycho-analysis had somehow brought more clarity but had almost launched me over the edge again. I was bursting at the seams. I wanted to die. I needed to escape.

I'll go mad. I need to get out.

Quietly, so not to disturb Dominika, I got out of bed and took my clothes and crept to the bathroom. I quickly got dressed and fixed my hair. I daren't apply any makeup. I was barely holding back my emotions anyway and I didn't want to end up looking like a panda when my emotions finally gave way. Even being in the same place as Dominika rained condemnation down on me. Her purity and presence were more than I could handle and in my agony, I knew only one thing.

I need forgiveness, a salve to my soul.

Mum and dad have always told me that forgiveness was the root of hope and hope was the trust in the unseen made certain. I'd pretty much rejected the religion of my upbringing, without necessarily abandoning a belief in God, Christ and Mary. I'd wronged Dominika in the worst way possible and I desperately needed this unseen and elusive God of my parents.

So, being especially careful not to make a sound with the lock or my keys, I sneaked out unseen, and found myself on the way to church. Butterflies lurched in my stomach and damnation raked its claws into my lost soul as the darkness tried to claim me. It was nothing more than I deserved. The flames of hell were licking at my feet and my mind was caught in a maelstrom of death. Hissing demonic voices taunted me and harried and hustled me with constant reminders of what I'd lost and how I'd gone beyond even the forgiving hand of God to reach. It almost felt they were literally pulling and tugging on me, such was the heaviness in every step I took. All that remained was for me to give myself over to judgment and hell.

I am worthless, despicable and lost.

Despair, the opposite of hope, was crushing me.

There can be no forgiveness for what I'd done and yet something unknown and unfathomable compelled me to ignore these despicable angels of hell and seek God, his grace and ultimately his mercy.

Mary, I cried inwardly. *Show me the way.*

I arrived at the church in time for the Mass and went in and ritually washed my hands before entering the nave. Almost automatically I paused before genuflecting to the altar as mum had taught me. Outwardly respectable I was internally contemptible.

Even though it was an early Mass the church was already quite full. Soaring ceilings reached to heaven and offered God's protection to all within. It was a haven, but I felt so alone, ashamed, dirty, unredeemable and worst of all insignificant and irrelevant to the divine power radiating from the carvings and images. I hovered near the back. I daren't go any nearer. To approach the altar would have been to approach God's purity and shine an even brighter light on my filth.

God, are you there? I wondered.

My heart was pounding in my chest as the Mass began and the darkness that had left me teetering on the edge of the abyss finally overwhelmed me. God too was judging me and now I was in his house his glare fell fully on me. Eve couldn't hide in the garden and now neither could I. Condemnation, like a mighty weight. fell on me. I was more than a sinner, I was a total disgrace and utterly detestable, a cheat, liar and deceiver.

This is how mum and dad describe the Devil.

This sudden realisation was an epiphany.

Stunned by the sudden perception of my true nature, I lowered my face. I could no longer look at the altar or the crucified Christ in agony on the cross. I was the Devil and I'd put him there. I couldn't even recite the words of the liturgy, which had been drilled into my brain since childhood. Mum had often berated me when I got them wrong and wasn't paying attention.

If only she were here now, to guide me and support me, to hold me up.

She wasn't here, nor could she ever be. That'd mean her seeing the twisted and perverse creature I'd become. I was as far from being a child of Christ as anyone could imagine. I was the spawn of Satan.

It's often said that confession is good for the soul, but I'd fallen so far that salvation was impossible. How could I confess to a priest? My sins were of such a magnitude that nothing could absolve them. My damnation complete, no penance or amount of Hail Marys can rescue me. I was hell bound and there was nothing anybody, even Christ, could do about it.

God may have been there, but he wasn't helping. As each moment passed, I felt smaller and smaller, and more of a shade, as my humanity seemed to fade. I forced myself to lift my head and my eyes met with the downward gaze of the statue of Mary, but it wasn't her benevolence that I felt, rather it was disdain. I was the most disgusting creature in the world and now God, Jesus and Mary had seen everything and judged me for it.

I was humbled before God and my disgrace confirmed.

I couldn't stay, the horror of what I'd done washed over me again like a spiritual tsunami. There was no forgiveness in this place only a taste of my future; eternity, alone and destitute, without love without life, without hope.

I was lost. Forever.

The church is a place where a light is shone on humanity and the true nature of the soul is unveiled. For me, it wasn't a beacon of hope or a guiding light. It was a dungeon, a cage.

Even stronger than my desire to get away from Dominika earlier, I had to get out. I couldn't stand to be before God any longer. I turned and fled. My feet couldn't carry me fast enough. I didn't even turn and genuflect as I should have done. To have done so would've been to mock God in his own house even more than my presence already had done.

As I reached the door and slowed down I stepped out of the church into the brightness of the morning sun. But I only knew darkness.

I was in a daze and I reached the street with no idea of what to do or where to go. People and buildings were of no moment and I barely noticed anything as I drifted without purpose and without hope. I couldn't hold back anymore. I could feel the warmth of tears as they began to run down my cheeks. I rubbed them away, but more flowed. I did my best to stave them off because the last thing I needed was a well-meaning stranger reaching out to me.

I don't deserve anything from anybody and certainly not compassion or mercy.

Then before I knew it, I was entering Promenada, where the whole thing had started. As I passed through, my thoughts returned to that first coffee with Elwira

Why had I met her? Why had we gone to her flat? Why had I asked her that stupid question? Why had I kissed her? Why? Why? Why?

The truth was I'd met her and gone to her flat because I knew what I was looking for and I got exactly what I wanted.

You stupid little bitch, Ania!

Promenada also meant something else and as it dawned on me it punched me in the stomach. My chest tightened and for a moment I thought I might even faint.

Since leaving the church, I'd been drifting on autopilot, just walking, putting one foot in front of the other. Subconsciously, although I hadn't been paying particular attention, like a light coming on, I suddenly realised that I was heading home. As I comprehended this, I immediately understood that the road to forgiveness wasn't God, Jesus and Mary.

Dominika is my forgiveness.

I wasn't sure if it was a second moment of enlightenment or yet another curse. All I knew was that I had to confess all to her. Maybe God had directed my steps after all.

I don't know how I'll do it, but I'll confess everything to Dominika and then throw myself on her mercy. It's my only chance…

I'd sinned against her and only she had the power to forgive me.

God, I pleaded silently, *give me the strength and words.*

I don't know if he heard me or whether he even cared. Renewed determination didn't give me any hope. Quite the opposite, in fact Dominika's black and white outlook on life could mean that anything was possible. I could find myself both single and homeless before the end of the day. But even this would be a better fate than living with the eternal condemnation that was constantly crushing me from all sides.

Hope is lost and only darkness remains. Soon my life will be over.

I rehearsed many times, in those last twenty minutes or so as I neared home, what I'd say to her. I wrestled with words and created scenarios in my mind and tried to imagine her response. The only thing I knew was that I needed to tell her everything, maybe not every single sordid detail, but everything I could and be completely honest about anything she asked too. Questions might be a good thing, it'd mean she's still talking to me. A brief flame of hope flickered and died.

Questions might also be a way of uncovering the fullness of my depravity and sin.

I was minutes away and the knot in my stomach had formed into a hefty lump that was almost incapacitating me. Somehow I kept going and even though time lost all meaning, I soon turned into our street and was passing the houses before the big apartment block. Our flat was in the next building just behind it. Two more minutes and then I'd meet my destruction. Then before I knew it, I was entering the building and I was ascending the stairs like a convict climbing the scaffold to be hung.

It was unbearable. I paused, unable to go on. A hand was tightening around my throat and bile came up into my throat. I really thought this time that I'd vomit. My knees knocked and my body shuddered. I felt my bowels loosen as though they could betray me at any moment.

Then I recognised what had possessed me for what it was. Fear was now my centre. It'd driven out everything else that was smothering me. At least now I understood. I know how it paralyses and takes control and this is exactly what happened as it overwhelmed my self-pity and self-loathing.

When I first met Dominika fear ruled my life and she taught me how to take control of it.

On some instinctive level, I knew the symptoms and with this half the battle was already won. I took a moment to ease my breathing and bring myself back under control. Then as my throat was released, I clenched and relaxed my muscles a few times and focussed myself on mastering my oldest demon.

The greatest irony was that it was Dominika's strength that empowered me to push through my temporary paralysis.

Fear had gripped me and now I had a grip on my fear, but it wasn't a victory. All it did was prepare me to step into the abyss that now lay open in front of me.

Carefully I turned my key in the door, so not to disturb anyone just in case they were still asleep. However, when I went in, I saw that all three girls were up and chatting in the kitchen. Finished coffee cups and empty plates indicated they'd been up for a while.

As I entered, Dominika looked up and straight into my eyes. She immediately recognised my distress. Her face dropped and without hesitation, she crossed the space and came to me. She was there in a flash and pulled me close. Her cheek touched mine, and another tear escaped. I closed my eyes in a vain attempt to keep my tears contained.

'What is it, darling?' She whispered as her lips closed in on my ear,

'What's happened?'

This wasn't the scene or even a variation of what I had played out in my mind. Fear, which had been oddly comforting in its familiarity, was displaced and once more condemnation took over. Her closeness and attention, all I'd craved for the last few months, was finally here, undiluted and pure.

Too late to save me now.

'We need to talk,' I blurted in an attempted whisper, but my emotion betrayed me and it came out louder than intended.

I opened my watery eyes, and through the mist, they met the concerned eyes of Emilia. Her worry very quickly turned into an unspoken *finally*. She knew how difficult I was finding the growing distance between me and Dominika and she'd encouraged me to tell her.

She almost certainly thought that this is what I was going to do.

If only it were that simple. Her relief would soon be replaced with disgust when the truth came out. Soon even her hope will be corrupted.

'Come with me, darling,' Dominika whispered softly in a voice dripping with concern. She took me by the hand and started leading me to our room.

Just as we left, Dominika had enough presence of mind to ask, 'Could one of you girls fix us some more coffee.'

This is my Dominika. She's here.

This was all I'd ever wanted and all I'd ever needed, but it only served to heap more misery on me as my guilt increased a hundredfold.

The difficult had just become almost impossible.

We were back in our room and she closed the door behind us. Tears betrayed me again, but now it was just us, I no longer needed to hide them. Release came, and tears cascaded like a mighty waterfall. Somehow I stopped myself from wailing as a part of me remained conscious that Emilia and Kasia were elsewhere in the flat. I also recognised this was my last moment of intimacy with her and I longed for it to last for as long as possible.

This is the final calm before the storm. She's still blissfully unaware, but the dark clouds were already on the edge of my vision and soon they'll consume me.

I was foolish to believe and hope and I was even more foolish to believe in Dominika's forgiveness. The end was near…

And now this is the full confession that Dominika demanded that I write. It represents my best attempt at full disclosure. There was so much to tell and so much to confess. When she reads this, Dominika will be finding out things for the first time. I'm beyond trying to hide anything from her and it wasn't that I didn't want to tell her, but there was so much to say that it was impossible to mention every eventuality and certainly when limited only to my present recollections of what happened.

As you read on please remember this situation was entirely of my own making and both Dominika and Elwira were innocents, as were Emilia and Kasia as they too became caught up in the fallout that followed. Especially remember this when it comes to Kasia.

Judge me, but don't judge Dominika, Kasia or any of the others.

Dominika was all worry. She clasped both hands into mine and we sat on the sofa. I could feel her eyes on me, but shame meant that I couldn't bring myself to look at her. Her virtue bore into me more than the crucified Christ had in the church. Yet like Christ, her compassion remained…

But not for much longer.

'What is it, Ania? Tell me. What's happened?' she urged insistently.

I still couldn't look at her, but knew I had to get straight to the point. Dominika hates talking in circles. I took a breath, knowing what would follow, but fearing even worse if I dallied.

'I cheated on you last week with Elwira from my class,' I said quietly as I stared at the ground, still unable to look into her face.

One short sentence, but it encapsulated the whole truth. Dominika continued to hold on to me as though my words hadn't landed. A stunned delay followed by widened eyes.

'What?' She kept her voice calm and level, and not only because we weren't alone in the flat.

Such is Dominika's self-control.

I tried to tighten my grip on her hands with a desperate need to hold on to her, but I watched something die as the light in her eyes dulled and my betrayal hit home. She suddenly yanked herself away from me and got up and went to the door. My heart sank. I was sure this was the end. Judgment had been passed and Dominika had reacted in the only way she knows. Her polarised view of absolute right and wrong had thrust an unbridgeable chasm between us. This was it…

She's walking out on me.

However, judgment was deferred; for a little while anyway. She opened the door and, in a calmness contrary to reality, she called out to the kitchen. 'Hold the coffee girls; we won't be needing it.'

Then she closed the door and returned to me in silence. Her remaining in the room with me brought no relief. Rather it felt as though an executioner was approaching the condemned. The axe was sharp and the passing of my sentence was imminent.

I still couldn't look at her, but I was completely aware of her every movement. She's always had a powerful presence, especially for someone so diminutive, but now even more so. It was as though divinity had flooded the room. Her light was too powerful and I was fully dazzled by it. Soon her light will vanquish me. All that remained of me was pure darkness, evil, nasty slimy sin.

I'm fucked!

Foreboding punched me in the stomach and I consciously clenched my buttocks to overcome that feeling that my body was about to give way. I did it automatically, not sure what would follow from Dominika. The one thing I held on to was that despite our BDSM lifestyle, Dominika, by nature, isn't a violent or even aggressive person. Whatever was coming she wouldn't attack me. I found myself in that moment, the brief hiatus between my confession and what followed, wishing she'd lash out at me, but this is not Dominika.

She sat quietly next to me, and with one hand she lifted my chin. 'Look me in the eyes and tell me everything. Don't you dare take your fucking eyes off me.'

Her voice was calm and measured, again this says so much about her, and it only made it harder to carry on. Her eyes were mesmerising and I wanted to break her stare, but when she is like this her sheer will is irresistible. She is often unreadable when handling negative emotions as she internalises and holds back and now I was seeing it for myself.

I've only ever seen her lose control once and it came as a shock when it happened. She was truly terrifying and I didn't know what she was going to do. I was only a witness and that was bad enough. On that occasion she'd turned on her dad, who was drunk as usual, in defence of her mum and sister. Believe me, seeing it even once was once too often. It showed me that she will scream like a deranged banshee to protect others, but is deathly calm when it is all about her.

I'd have preferred the screaming.

'It was on Thursday during the long weekend I met up with Elwira.' The start of my explanation seemed so mundane, 'I'm sure you remember her—from my class—and we hung out in Promenada. Then we went to her flat for something to eat and we ended up having sex. You were so busy with your thesis and you told me to go out and have fun…'

'Are you fucking blaming me?' she said flatly. 'There is fun and then…'

'No Dominika, I'm not—'

'And now you are interrupting me? Has your respect for me gone so far that first you blame me and then, when you are clearly in the wrong, and there is no doubt about that, you have the nerve to interrupt me?'

Sometimes, she uses similar words in our BDSM play, but this was no game.

'You know it's an important year for me and I asked you just to be patient.' As usual, she retained her self-assured composure and her voice was still calm, almost as though explaining to a child. 'As of now I only have the bibliography left to complete and then revision for the final exams—but that won't take so much of my time.'

Dominika was so detached, but then she paused as the façade cracked just a little.

'You know what? Why the fuck am I even explaining myself to you? I didn't go and fuck somebody else. So what happened?'

Her language was stronger, but her voice remained steady.

'I was feeling lonely and when I got some attention I was stupid. I told Emilia how I was feeling and she kept telling me to talk to you.'

Her face set, harder than concrete. 'So she knows you cheated and that means Kasia knows too. Are you trying to humiliate me in front of our best friends? Fucking hell, Ania, who the fuck are you?'

She was cold, harsh and emotionless and worst of all she was right. I knew I'd hurt her badly and this was her way of coping, to be a cold edifice of stone unfeeling and hard. As soon as I saw her harden, the fate I'd feared went from being almost certain to absolutely inevitable. This was the moment when I knew that I'd lost her.

Again I wished she'd screamed at me anything would've been better than this steely detachment. All I could do was try to explain.

'No Emilia knew I was feeling lonely without you. You study all the time, come to bed late and never have any time for me anymore.'

'Are you blaming me again?' Dominika asked in a dangerously low tone.

'No Dominika. I'm just trying to explain.' Honestly, I was beginning to get really frustrated and angry with her too. It seemed that each moment when she could, she was turning the screw to make me feel worse. It was what I deserved, but it was getting in the way of my explanation.

'You know what, Dominika?' I said with surprising strength. 'Fuck it!'

My uncharacteristic defiance wasn't borne out of a desire to stand up for myself, rather it was an acknowledgement that there could be no worse consequence than that which was coming anyway. I was lost and so were we. So the least I could do was have my say.

'I am the one who cheated, I am the one who was wrong and I'm not blaming you at all. I'm just trying to explain and that means telling you how I was feeling so you might know why I did what I did. I was wrong, it was all me and nobody else. Or do you just want me to say I cheated—do what you want with me?'

She glared at me. 'You'd fucking love that, wouldn't you?' She said in her most cutting voice. 'But you make a fair point. I won't jump down your throat again while you are explaining.'

My Dominika, so reasonable, so in control.

I love you. I screamed silently with the entirety of my being. *I need you.*

'So,' I hesitated as I struggled for words, 'and I'm not blaming anybody but myself, but I was feeling lonely and somehow it happened with Elwira and me. I have to be honest—and maybe it is the worst thing—but I was looking for it and the moment we agreed to meet, I was kind of hoping something would happen. You remember our conversations about her a couple of years ago?'

Dominika wasn't interested in answering, so I carried on, at the risk of over-explaining. 'She was the one who told me about shaving down below and we agreed it was some attempt to show some interest in me and it turns out that we were right. So to get straight to the point we spent all afternoon in bed enjoying each other. I was her first girl and so had to kind of show her the way and I guess she must have liked it.'

If I'd done this with permission, Dominika would have smiled or even laughed, but she had no joy today. I'd started and I just knew I had to be completely honest with her and hold nothing back even though it's often said that there is such a thing as too much information.

'Then we met up again on Saturday and did it again and then again on Sunday. I even encouraged her to show some dominant behaviour to me and she spanked me a few times and we made some anal play. I even took a fist from her. She was shocked this was actually possible, but it is the truth. After Sunday I kind of tried to stay away from her, but we got together again on Wednesday and did a bit more too. It wasn't the same as it had been at the weekend…'

'So more than *once*?' Dominika drew out the last word into a serpent-like hiss to make her point.

'Yes. I cannot say how many times as you can imagine, but on three different days during the long weekend and then again on Wednesday. It was like a forbidden drug and I needed more. I got stupid and became addicted to her and kept going back for more. I knew I still loved you, but I couldn't stop myself. Like I said a minute ago, I tried not to be with her after Sunday, but I was so low on Tuesday night after what I'd done to you. I was weak and stupid and went back to her on Wednesday, but it was very different to how it'd been at the weekend. It was more risky and dangerous and I was totally selfish, even more than I'd already been. She doesn't know about you and thinks she and I are going somewhere as a couple. After Wednesday I knew I'd gone too far and I couldn't go back to her again. Since then I've kept my distance, but we've been messaging and chatting a bit between classes. She has been sending me love messages and I've been replying in a similar way, mainly to make everything seem fine. But it isn't. Everything's changed. She wanted to meet yesterday, but I told her I was going out with my flatmates. I tried to make everything look normal between us, but I felt so awful. I wasn't being fair and nothing was her fault, so I wanted to at least try to make up for it and treat her well.'

'And how about treating me well?'

'I got lost in my stupidity and desire, Dominika. I can only be honest.'

'Honest? Fuck you, Ania. It wasn't a stupid moment it was several times and you planned to fuck her, even on Thursday, which makes it even worse. A stupid moment of passion is one thing, but wilful cheating is something else. Both are wrong, but you've cheated on me in the worst possible way. I'm not even going to ask what you meant by *I went too far on Wednesday.* I am speechless. You disgust me you fucking slut.'

Her voice was still calm and again she was using the same language as we do when we play, only now she really meant it, and she was absolutely right.

'So why after a week are you telling me now?'

'Because I realised I was stupid. I knew I was in danger of losing you and I love you so much. I was already feeling bad, but last night reminded me of what we've got. The only thing I don't regret is that I didn't meet her yesterday. It'd have been so easy to go and meet her during the day and then come out with you all in the evening, but I didn't because you are my everything.'

I paused to see if my words were having any impact. Her face remained hard and cold.

She despises me and I'm totally lost.

'I can't live with the guilt or lie to you anymore. I'm so sorry. Please forgive me.' I begged her.

She was still a statue.

Knowing that there was very little that I could say, I pleaded in a last gasp chance to save us.

'I'll do anything you want. I need you, Dominika, you are my life and I'm nothing without you. I've probably lost you anyway, but the only chance I have for us is to tell you everything and hope you can forgive me. I'm so sorry, Dominika. I'll do absolutely anything to make us right again.'

'Take back your lying cheating ways? Too fucking late for that,' was her barbed response.

I didn't get chance to answer even though there was no answer to that.

'Right I've heard just about enough,' she said in unfeeling business-like manner. 'Just two more things.' She continued in an. 'You know I have always been accepting of your libido and you have open permission to go with Emilia if you want to so long as Kasia agrees. If you needed something and I was too busy, firstly why didn't you tell me and secondly if you can't control your sexual urges and you needed to be fucked so much why didn't you go to her? Doing something secretly like this has destroyed our trust.'

As she said trust it fell like a hammer. I tried to explain. 'I really couldn't, Dominika. Because of your work, we've grown so distant and I couldn't go to Emilia because I wouldn't be going to her for fun, but as a sign that something was wrong with us. Emilia's too close and I'd feel so guilty about involving her. It just wouldn't be fair on her.'

'So you decided to go with someone else; a stranger, a nobody to me? I'd have accepted Emilia and the whole point is that she is close. Ania, you have created this in your own mind and destroyed us.'

'You stopped even noticing me,' I finally retorted out of pure frustration.

I regretted it as soon as I opened my mouth and burst into tears. The last thing I wanted to do was seem to be turning the blame around. Yes, I'd cheated and gone behind her back, but it was down to her neglect and I hoped she'd see it without me blatantly pointing it out. I was prepared to take the whole blame, the last week of hiding such a dark secret and my trip to the church had stripped my soul bare and had brought me into the full magnitude what I'd done. My emotions were so churned up that I hardly knew what I was doing and I could tell that I had nothing left to lose. It was lost anyway.

She paused, as though considering what to say, as though swaying between two thoughts and then she made her mind up.

'We were always wondering what to do with Kasia's room. Well now we know. I can't leave you on the street, but I want you to move your stuff out. You'll do it now. I don't want to speak to you or even see you. I'm going to the kitchen and I'll tell the girls we are breaking up. I'll only be a few minutes and I want you gone before I come back.'

No emotion, absolute zero from Dominika.

Breaking up.

The two words I most dreaded. Has it really come to this? I'd broken us and only had myself to blame.

'But Dominika…'

'No buts, I've made my mind up. I want you gone before I get back.'

With that, she got up and walked out.

In stunned silence, I didn't know what to do.

Should I follow her?

I quickly realised this would be the worst of a whole lot of bad ideas I could come up with. It'd take our problems out into our communal space and unnecessarily involve Emilia and Kasia. This would cross even more lines than I already had—if that was possible. Besides, Dominika had already said that she was going to tell them anyway.

I grabbed my dressing gown and computer and some cosmetics and took them to Kasia's old room. I will *never* call it my room because I will never accept this. I dumped everything on the end of the bed and then too slumped onto the bed. I rested my head on the pillow and began to sob uncontrollably. I could feel myself shaking and the pain of separation actuality physically hurt, like some giant claw had ripped my stomach out, it was similar to how I'd felt when I woke up this morning, but far worse. I curled into a foetal position and clenched my aching stomach, but there was no relief and no comfort that could console me. The pain and the separation couldn't be eased by anything—only Dominika and I was as sure as she was that that wasn't going to happen.

I couldn't stop crying and the pillow was soon soaked. I can only imagine that my eyes were puffy and red like overripe tomatoes.

Suddenly the door opened and I lifted my eyes. My heart jumped.

Dominika! Hope!

'I told you to move out! That means everything. Believe me, it's better for you if you do it.'

Then she was gone again. Hope crushed. Despite my pain, I didn't want to make things even worse—and there was something very dangerous about her last comment that made *whatever is worse* a real likelihood.

I dragged myself off the bed and went back to our room. Dominika was already there, reclining on the bed with her laptop. She had her music on and was listening to it through earphones. She never even looked up. As I walked across the room, I glanced across in an attempt to make eye contact, but she was fixed on her screen and was clearly doing so deliberately. It was really obvious that she was looking, but not necessarily seeing anything. The worst thing was that I knew there was absolutely nothing I could do to reach her.

I opened my side of the wardrobe and pushed all of the hangers together before scooping my dresses, skirts, blouses and trousers out with both hands. I carried them back to Kasia's room and laid them out before going for a second load of my stuff. I noticed that Emilia and Kasia were nowhere to be seen. They too, had probably retreated to their room. The atmosphere in the flat was unbearable and it was entirely my fault.

It took several trips and Dominika absolutely refused to make eye contact with me or say anything. On my last trip, I cast one last lingering glance across to her in the desperate hope that I'd get something back, but there was nothing.

Once everything was in Kasia's room I had a quick thought and went back out and knocked on Emilia and Kasia's door. Emilia opened it and even she turned her back and went further back into their room when she saw it was me. At least she didn't slam the door in my face.

'Sorry to interrupt, and I know you probably hate me too.' I spoke haltingly, really unsure of what to expect from them. 'I've moved everything out of our room and I know Dominika is using some of my books for her thesis and she needs to finish her bibliography. Can I leave them in here so we can both get to them? Sorry to ask, but I've made things so bad the least I can do is try to make things a bit easier for her.'

'Like you fucking care!' Kasia snarled.

'Kasia! We need to keep out of it,' Emilia said flatly, before turning to me. 'Leave the books here on the floor.' Then she explained, defending Kasia, 'Ania, of course, we have our opinions, but it's none of our business, whatever we think.'

With that, Emilia also made her disapproval clear.

I went for the books and it took two short silent trips. On the second trip, as I was leaving, Emilia came to me and grabbed my hand. 'We'll look after Dominika.'

She then let go and turned her back on me. I clearly wasn't welcome and I didn't feel like talking anyway. I went back to Kasia's old room and as I closed the door another sob spluttered out. They all hate me, even Emilia, lovely sweet Emilia. Her comment that was so supportive of Dominika was also very clear in its unsaid message—they won't look after me.

I drew in a deep breath and got some kind of self-control.

I wanted to collapse once more onto the bed, but couldn't. It was covered in my stuff so I forced myself to put my things away. Forcing order might order my thoughts. Nice idea, but it didn't really work. All I could think was how I'd messed everything up.

Stupid, stupid Ania!

The bed was clear, but my mind wasn't. Once more, I crashed onto the mattress. I didn't want to nor could I actually do anything. I just stared vacantly at the ceiling. The flat seemed quiet. I don't know if it really was or if I'd simply fazed myself out of my surroundings. My mind was a void and so was the space that I was physically inhabiting.

Minutes and hours unknown passed my unblinking eyes. Eventually, after some indeterminable time, hunger invaded my stomach. Only I couldn't eat. I couldn't do anything. I didn't want to do anything. My life was lost and no longer worth living. I found myself staring into the same darkness as I had on Tuesday. Only this time I knew for sure that I wouldn't cross the line into eternal darkness. The abyss was no longer calling me and I knew to live would be the first part of my just punishment.

And this was how it was for the rest of the day. I just stared at the ceiling, a cold, broken stare that would've rivalled a corpse. I forced myself to go to the toilet when necessary and finally in the evening I went to the kitchen and picked at some food I found in the fridge. With my senses dulled, it was grey and tasteless, devoid of life and a perfect reflection of my loss. Nobody was about, although I could hear the murmurings of low voices coming from Emilia and Kasia's room. Dominika's door was shut and the light was off.

I'd broken her heart and I could imagine she was feeling just as bad as me, and probably even a lot worse. After all, she'd been betrayed and I was the betrayer. Dwelling on this brought a new eruption of emotion and tears ejected from my sore eyes. I wanted to go to her, throw myself on her mercy, beg her forgiveness and allow her to visit any punishment onto my body and mind.

Anything; any pain, any humiliation and any torture is better than this.

I didn't even feel like showering and doing my normal evening routine so after I'd picked at just enough food to take away my hunger, I went back to bed and just laid there, without even getting ready for bed. I just lolled on the bed, listless and lost and not too infrequently as emotion welled up again I broke down again and sobbed silently in shame and disgust. It crossed my mind that somebody might pop in and check on me, but nobody—not even Emilia—did.

Finally, sleep took me and at least with that some temporary escape from my agony.

Monday 13 May 2019

I kept waking up sporadically throughout the night.

Each time I turned over, I expected to see Dominika next to me… then in that literal blink of an eye when reality returned, my loneliness and guilt closed in on me and threatening to smother my very life. I cuddled my pillow and wept softly at my loss until once more after another indeterminate time, relief came again and sleep rescued me for another hour or so.

Daylight brought my world crashing down again, and this time there was no escape. I was lost in darkness and now I had to force myself to get up. I went to the window, opened the blinds and caught sight of the gloomy, overcast weather. Rippling puddles on the ground showed that it was going to be a bleak day. There was no reason to move so I just stood and stared out of the window.

What's the point? Without Dominika, there's nothing to live for.

More time passed, lost in my glazed eyes and my bladder was demanding release. When I couldn't hold it anymore, my need forced me out of the room into the hallway. All was quiet. I was alone. Normally on Mondays, Dominika and I go to university together, but she'd gone without me. I guess it was only to be expected. Emilia and Kasia had left too.

I tore at my jeans and got them down just in time before releasing my morning flow and giving myself a wipe. I stood up and dropped the toilet paper into the pan and flushed…

Momentum…

As I released the handle and closed the toilet lid I knew that now I'd started I just had to keep moving. Somehow I had to function and the best way to do that was to throw myself into my timetable. It didn't matter how I was feeling, I had to get to university.

But first I needed to get out of yesterday's clothes. I stripped off and quickly showered and dried myself off before wrapping my hair in a towel turban. Then as I took my makeup bag I caught sight of my face in the mirror. I welled up again, and as much as I tried I couldn't hold back another wave of pent up grief. Tears cascaded down my cheeks, but mixed with overwhelming loss there was utter contempt. I sneered at myself for what I'd done and the price I'd paid. I'd brought everything down on myself and that brutal fact was inescapable.

Emotion undulates, it comes and goes like the swirling wind, and so it was with my tears. In the calm that followed this particular gust, I fixed my makeup as usual and brushed out my hair to create an external veneer of normality that was in sharp contradiction to my inner turmoil.

Soon I was ready to face the day, but at the same time I felt weak, pathetic and listless.

I ran through the rain to get to my tram and then changed over to a bus. Although I made up some time I was still late and so I sneaked in and took a place at the back of the classroom. As I sat down, I scanned the room and immediately saw my sin and my downfall—Elwira. She was sitting at the front as usual.

I tried to focus but couldn't. My brain was buzzing; too much stuff going on in my head. I was already regretting coming, but at least in the presence of others I had to hold myself together and I'd have to face Elwira.

After the first class she came to me wearing a playful cheeky smile. My stomach clenched in fearful anticipation of what was coming. She too had done nothing wrong, it was all on me, and now it was time to own up and face my second execution.

'Shall we grab a coffee in the café, before our next class,' Elwira suggested enthusiastically. She was all sweetness and light as usual and it yanked on my inner longings.

I had a sudden flashback of that amazing week, first the weekend and then last Wednesday.

I was still deeply attracted to her, and both she and the sex had been amazing. It wouldn't have been difficult to persuade her to go with me into the trees again, and even if the rain might have put us off, I was sure we could have found some little nook to explore once more our shared desires. The toilet cubicle where I'd shown myself to her last week would've done, if nothing else.

This was never going to happen though. The truth was that I could never go back. Since owning up to Dominika, everything had changed. My conscience, which had deserted me, had returned.

Plain and simple, resisting this heavenly temptation was the right thing to do.

I knew that I could just pretend, but my mind flinched at such an appalling idea. Elwira would love me and care for me and give me her whole soul—of that I had no doubt. She'd never need to know about me and Dominika, but to go there would've just been so wrong. Everything Elwira and I had—*if I can use that word*—was built on deceit. Any thought of Elwira and me, was a house built on sand, regardless of Dominika. Technically, Dominika no longer had any hold on me, other than my emotions.

I was free and yet I found myself in chains.

'Ok,' I said simply.

I agreed readily, knowing that I had to kill desire and focus on my conscience. It was better to climb the scaffold and get the noose around my neck as soon as possible and get it all over and done with. I was dead anyway, so nothing really mattered any more.

I insisted on paying and she took a seat in a corner, which I was grateful for. At least we wouldn't create a scene in the middle of the coffee area. I ordered the coffees and as I was waiting, I saw Dominika in the corridor. She looked straight through me, but I'm sure she noticed Elwira sitting nearby.

I wanted to drop the coffees and run after her.

I realise now that this was a stark choice that had presented itself to me. I reasoned quickly that Dominika probably won't forgive me anyway, but if I made a scene here and now, things would only get even worse. Although my actions would suggest the contrary, in not running after her in that moment, I actually chose Dominika. Even so, my mind was in renewed turmoil, a vortex of negativity and self-loathing, but I had to force myself to do the right thing.

Elwira.

I took the coffees and went to join her.

As soon as I sat down she started with barely concealed lust in her eyes. 'Ania, I can't wait until I get you to myself again…'

She touched my hand tentatively, but aware we were in a public area she pulled back after a fleeting touch, before I even had chance to recoil.

'Shame about the rain, but maybe we can do something this weekend? Go shopping and then find somewhere quiet to be on our own?'

She smiled, a cheeky little grin that made it clear what she meant and for the briefest of moments, my body longed for her touch and my mind for her sweet love. It'd only been a day since the breakup, but she was offering me an immediate cure to my banishment.

No, I can't go back there…

But now she was into her rhythm. 'We could go back to Uni Lubelski Square, and then…'

'Elwira,' I cut her off. It was the only way I'd get a chance to speak. The more she went on, and the more she planned, the angrier she'd get. 'I need to tell you something.'

She stopped, confusion written all over her face.

'It was great last week,' I said before choosing my next phrase carefully, 'but I already have a girlfriend.'

That was it, blunt and to the point but with her mind racing away with fanciful ideas I had no other choice…

Did I?

Elwira's eyes widened, 'But…'

She was lost for words. There was an awkward silence which I needed to fill.

'You're so lovely and amazing and just wow, but it really is me. I'm not saying this just to be nice and make you feel better. It really is me. I'm a stupid bitch and you didn't do anything wrong. I promise you that. You're great and in another world who knows?'

I paused for a moment before getting the whole truth out. 'You know my flatmate, Dominika? We've been together since October 2015 and I cheated on her with you.'

'What?'

I could see tears in her eyes.

Now she hates me too and is right to do so.

'I… I can't…'

With that, she got up and started to walk off.

I got up and followed her. 'Elwira, please. Just let me explain and then go if you must.'

She kept walking, 'Just leave me alone.'

What could I do? She stabbed me in my already broken heart and I'm sure it ruptured. It certainly felt like it. I had to hold it together so I went back to the table and took my things and left two lonely untouched coffees on the table.

***

I was in danger of having a meltdown in the middle of the school corridor. I needed to be alone. I knew telling her was going to be bad, but this was even darker than my worst imagining. I thought she'd at least talk to me.

I went quickly to the toilets and locked myself inside a cubicle and just sat there shell-shocked. I had lost everything and my depravity had left me destitute. I stayed in there, unable to compose or console myself. From time to time, I heard the comings and goings of other students from within my confinement, but when it was quiet my demons drew me back to Tuesday evening and once more I truly wanted to die.

My world really has ended.

Broken, but at the same time knowing that I was incapable of doing myself in, I sat for endless uncountable minutes, or hours—*who could tell?*—in the cold imprisonment of the cubicle. I couldn't face classes or anybody. My solitude was agony, but the company of others would be worse. Like this morning in the bathroom, the gust of emotion intensified before it waned and in the quiet eye of the storm, I managed to find enough strength to leave the toilets.

The corridors were quiet, everyone was in class, but I was right on the edge. The only thing I knew was that I couldn't face anyone or anything else today.

I had to go home.

I really don't know how I got there. I guess I just put one foot in front of the other in a repetition of what I'd done yesterday when coming home from the church. I found my way onto the bus and then the tram and then once more I walked in a daze from the tram terminus for the last few minutes until I got home.

Coming home early meant that I arrived to an empty flat. The quiet only amplified the chaos in my brain. I needed comfort and reassurance and I wasn't really thinking when I went into our room and got undressed and climbed naked into our bed. I saw Dominika's dressing gown sprawled over her pillows so I grabbed it and pulled it close and pressed it to my chest. Its warmth and comfort somehow brought me into her presence. She was so close that I could smell her. It was if she was there and, just for a moment, when I closed my eyes the nightmare was over.

Who was I kidding? I was just being stupid again. Dominika couldn't have been clearer. She doesn't even hate me; that'd mean too much emotional investment. I don't even exist in her mind. She no longer sees me, only through me. Guilt unleashed itself on me again in its full irresistible power.

How could I have been so stupid? I need you to hurt me, like I deserve.

I closed my eyes and remembered the needles and clamps and other games we played. I pictured my naked submission and my complete trust in her. This was how it should be, perfect love, the matching of two perfect halves, Dominika and me were the very essence of this. We were one burning candle in two people—a twin flame!

But now I had extinguished our flame.

I was hoping visions of punishment would somehow appease my guilt, but it only served to do the opposite. At the centre of our BDSM life had always been trust—it had to be—but now that was gone and my memories only served as a painful reminder of what has been and what will never be again.

For just a moment, I thought about hurting myself to make the pain go away, but again I knew this would only make things worse. I don't know how, but somewhere inside that rational part of my brain that'd saved me on Tuesday and got me to university this morning was still working. I understood that, as I hadn't been able to find myself on Wednesday, today would be just the same.

No amount of pain will ever expunge my guilt.

Once more, I smelt Dominika's dressing gown, as I closed my eyes and tried to draw myself back into her presence. Tears started to flow again and pain washed out of me, but still my shame remained. I don't know how long I lay there, but as with last night, sleep finally gave me some respite from my inner agony.

I was awoken with a start when I heard the flat door open. Surprised, I just lay there as footsteps approached across the hallways and the door opened and Dominika walked in.

I don't know who was more shocked.

'What the fuck are you doing in here, and in *my bed?*'

The way she said *my bed* cut like a knife. I opened my mouth and nothing came out. *What could I say?*

Dominika recovered from her shock quicker than me and said coldly, 'Actually, you've done me a favour and saved me from having to find you later. I've got something more to say and something to give you.'

At least we are talking, I thought hopefully.

'I had a surprise today.' Her tone was matter of fact, but there was an edge to it. 'Your little friend came to find me and insisted on buying me coffee. She told me what you did to her this morning. Can you imagine what that was like?'

'I'm sorry…'

'Sorry isn't enough and besides I'm talking, you have no right to speak to me. Shut up. Let me finish and then you can go.'

That was brutal and it shook me to the core. Her words stirred me and I suddenly became acutely aware of where I was. I was still naked and vulnerable in our bed, and it should have bothered me, but it didn't because she hadn't even noticed.

'So it turns out that Elwira is actually quite nice. She was so embarrassed and nervous. Do you know how many times she said sorry to me? She told me that she had no idea about us and if you think I'm angry, it's nothing compared to how she feels. And I can hardly blame her. You gave her hope and made her the third person in our relationship. She's better than that, better than you and decent enough to come and see me.'

Dominika paused for a second to let her words sink in and to think through how to carry on.

'At first, I wanted to shut her down and walk away, but unlike you, she deserves my respect. She was so stressed that she was shaking like a leaf. But she was taking responsibility, a lesson you could learn and learn well. She really didn't do anything wrong and she's earned my respect today.'

She paused again but this time as though fighting for self-control.

'You lied to me and betrayed me and you did exactly the same to her. You really are an evil little bitch, breaking her heart like that.'

'I know,' I confessed. The truth is the truth and even more so when it is brutal and bare.

'You don't even realise what you have done?'

'I…'

'Why the fuck do you have to keep talking?' Dominika snapped. 'Just shut the fuck up. I'm telling you how it is. This is not a conversation,' then she threw another dagger at me. 'You lost that right when you cheated.'

She glared at me and took a breath, 'And do you know what, Ania? I do remember Elwira and if you remember a couple of years ago when we spoke about her I said that I'd let you play with her if she was up for it. Why did you have to hurt me?'

That was the first time Dominika admitted that I'd hurt her, even though it was patently obvious.

'I'll tell you something else too. I was trying to arrange for a special visitor to come and visit us last weekend, but originally he was working. Then Emilia and Kasia decided to go away, so we were trying to reorganise it just for you— probably in June. It was going to be a surprise. So you have fucked that up too.'

'Dominika…'

'How many times, Ania! Just shut the fuck up. I don't want to hear your voice. Now, I have something to give you, and Ania, if I ever come home again and find you in my room, I want you gone completely, even if that means on the street. This is my space; you have your own room.'

She paused again and then said, 'Now, where is it?'

Despite phrasing it as a question, Dominika knew exactly what she was looking for and went to her bedside cabinet and took something out and gave it to me. It was my submission ring, or safety ring, that I wear during sessions. As marriage represents total love, this ring symbolised our relationship and in many ways goes much deeper than even a wedding ring. It speaks not only of bonds of love and eternity but of absolute trust, safety and control and a perfect symbiosis. She pressed it into my hand and words were unnecessary. She was releasing me from her ownership. I no longer belonged to her.

'Now get out!'

I got up and gathered my clothes. Looking back it's strange that I'd lost all self-awareness and was totally unaware of my unimportant nakedness.

When I got out I closed the door and paused briefly, just long enough to hear Dominika take in a deep breath as she tried to stifle her own emotions. It was the first and only time I'd ever heard any emotional weakness from her.

I've done this to her, indomitable Dominika the unbreakable, is in reality, more fragile than I ever expected.

Once I was back in Kasia's old room, I broke down again and as a corpse, I just stared for endless hours at my ring clenched in my palm. It'd meant everything and if possible more than even that.

What it meant was lost and so was I.

Part 3: Ania Is Alone
Saturday 18 May 2019

Kasia's birthday was on the 15th May, just after Dominika and I'd broken up. Normally a time of delicious shared pleasures, this year had been markedly different. We'd gone out for Dominika's birthday in March and then Emilia's, just before the long weekend. With Kasia's birthday falling midweek, it wasn't very convenient, but I knew the original idea was to do something the following weekend.

Plans, of course, were changed because of me and what I'd done.

So on that Saturday evening, I found myself in Kasia's old room and doing my best to stay out of the way. This had become the norm in the week or so since we'd broken up because frankly, it was easier than facing judgment every time I had a chance encounter in the hallway, kitchen or bathroom.

Through the walls, I heard Emilia and Kasia talking and giggling as they got ready. I strained my ears to try to figure out exactly what they were saying. I really wanted to know if Dominika was going with them. I really couldn't tell and soon the sound of closing doors announced that they'd left and I had the impression that Dominika hadn't gone with them.

I had no idea whether this was by choice or not.

Maybe Emilia and Kasia just wanted the night to themselves. It was ok double dating, but going on a date night with a third person just doesn't work.

My actions have ostracised Dominika too.

It was bizarre, to say the least, that we were home alone and shut away in different rooms. I was in a prison of my own making and she too was imprisoned and facing the repercussions of my stupidity.

Five whole days had passed without her even looking at me. The flat was now unwelcoming and cold. It was fast becoming my habit to move around the flat while doing my best to keep out of the way and, fairly obviously, they were all doing the same back to me. I found myself getting up early and using the bathroom secretly and quickly so not to be seen. Kasia was still angrier than anyone can imagine, and as far as Dominika was concerned, I no longer existed. Emilia, who has always been a much gentler spirit, was just keeping out of the way.

So there I was, sitting on the bed and I couldn't stop thinking about Dominika sitting on her own. I wanted and needed her so much. I wished I could just go to our room and she would love me and throw me on the bed and forget everything that I'd done. We'd cuddle and make love and she'd hold me close and everything would be alright again.

I tried to distract myself by browsing on the internet for a while and did some writing.

Even before Dominika asked for my confession, I'd started writing down everything that had happened. I find my expression through writing and I hoped that through my words, I could understand where and how I'd gone so terribly wrong. Writing about Elwira and our adventures meant revisiting necessary feelings that just reminded me of how lonely I'd become.

Naturally, as I typed, I found my memories caused a paradox of arousal and self-loathing. Line by line, like an unearthly serpent of lust, my words appeared across the screen. I write how I write, and even though perhaps I shouldn't have indulged so much in describing the sex, it's just the way I am. My descriptions, lurid and honest, both excited and disgusted me as I remembered once more what a depraved sinful creature I am.

More importantly, my words helped me to order my thoughts, even if they brought greater levels of condemnation. They showed me where I'd gone so wrong. As I wrote, I remained centred on Dominika and I wept bitterly as my fingers stroked the keyboard, understanding more with each passing moment what I'd done and the dreadful consequences my actions had wrought on us.

I stopped typing.

I couldn't carry on. The memories stirring in my mind were just too painful. The words stared back at me. They were an unfeeling indictment, documentary evidence and proof that would secure certain conviction in a criminal court.

Dominika, I need you.

I don't know how long I sat just staring, but there was a moment when my mind crossed a line. It was sudden and demanded immediate action. I decided there and then that I'd get Dominika's attention, whatever the cost. I quickly devised a plan that was irresistible in my mind.

Dominika, you will notice me!

She had to either take pity on me or grab hold of me and punish me. I'd make it so that she'd have no other choice, but to respond—ignoring me wouldn't be an option. Both had a certain appeal and especially the idea of suffering punishment at her hands, after everything I'd done to her. The thought of pain obviously held a greater attraction for me. It was nothing less than I deserved.

Convinced it'd work I put my plan into action.

I had a shower and washed my hair and did my makeup to make myself as perfect as possible. I used my favourite perfume that Dominika had bought as a gift and when I was satisfied that I was ready, I took my pillow and a blanket and put them on the floor outside our room. I then lay down and waited for Dominika to come out and find me. I didn't cover myself up and only used the blanket because it was cleaner and softer than the floor. The floor was hard and uncomfortable, but if I got what I wanted it'd be a price worth paying.

I was naked and exposed and ready for her to take and use as she desired. I was hers unconditionally and without limit. I'd considered putting my submission ring on, but one of the things the ring represents is limitations and safety and it somehow seemed inappropriate. I wanted to present myself as God had made me with no expectations of mercy from Dominika.

Please take me and do as you will. Do what want with me, Dominika.

I strained my ears to listen for the slightest sound or some indication of movement. Her light was on, so I guessed she was probably reading or on her computer or revising for her exams.

My stomach was churning in anticipation of discovery. It was the familiar combination of fear and dread, but as always and somewhat perversely the nervous anticipation excited me too. I felt my body reacting in the hope of renewed desire and could almost feel Dominika's touch. I refused to touch myself, despite the overwhelming temptation to do so, as I repeated played out in my mind how I imagined my plan unfolding.

At some point she'll open the door and see me pathetically lying on the floor. She'll only need to look at me for the briefest of moments before offering me her hand. I'll lift my hand and she'll take it into her own and pull me up in a simple gesture that more than represented my redemption. I'll rise lovingly in response to her grace and she'll lead me to our bed and take me home. Once more I'll be safe and secure, loved and protected by the only one who has ever really mattered.

As I got more excited, the urge to play with myself got stronger and stronger, but I pushed such thoughts out of my mind. I wanted and needed to present myself just as nature intended me to be. Once more I'd be untouched and pure, ready to submit to her will. I wanted to be innocent again.

I am yours, Dominika. I am ready.

Time passed and still there was nothing. All I wanted was for her to come to the door. I just knew that if she saw me, anything, and everything, was possible.

Please, Dominika, find me and take me back to our bed. Why won't you come out?

Please, Dominika, I need you. Show me something... anything...

Minutes passed in an endless blur and hope began to fade. Even though I wasn't that comfortable, and the floor was hard through the thin blanket, tiredness was inexorably winning the battle for my consciousness and I was slipping further into the painless oblivion of sleep. With an unnoticed indifference my mind was overpowered and my eyes collapsed into darkness as my mind drifted into night.

I was brought back to reality with the ringing of the intercom and less than a minute later a key was rattling in the door. I was disorientated for a moment, confused about where I was. Then I remembered. Now finally, Dominika might come out and it couldn't have been at a worse possible moment.

The door to the flat opened and it was followed by the sound of footsteps entering. No light came on, but through gritty eyes, I saw the shadowy forms of Emilia and Kasia close the door behind them. Even in the darkness, I saw Kasia open her mouth, but she wasn't as fast as Emilia, who deftly cut Kasia's words off with a quick finger.

'Go to our room,' Emilia whispered tersely with her finger still on Kasia's lips. 'I'll be with you in a few minutes.'

Kasia looked like she was about to object, but Emilia gently pushed her on her upper arm. I know I repeat myself, but Emilia's gentle steel constantly astounds me as does Kasia's willing submission to Emilia's will. Kasia may appear to be the dominant one in their relationship, but this would be a fundamental misunderstanding of them both.

Emilia came straight to me and put a gentle hand on my shoulder. I was surprised that it was warm to the touch even though she'd only just come in from outside.

'Come with me quickly, before we disturb Dominika,' she whispered in a low even tone.

She offered me her hands and pulled me gently to my feet, almost in a parody of how I'd envisaged Dominika reaching out to me. Even with her help, I stood up slowly on aching legs, stiffened by the hard floor. I immediately started to follow her, but she stopped me with a hand on my chest just below my neck.

'No Ania, bring your blanket and pillow. You're not going back there.'

I had no will to object and the window for capturing Dominika's attention had well and truly shut anyway. She led me to Kasia's old room and closed the door behind me before flicking the light switch on. The sudden light stabbed my eyes and I blinked as my nakedness was brought into the light. I had no shame left and didn't even think about covering myself up. Emilia, beautiful Emilia, had other ideas and was already reaching for my dressing gown that was strewn across the bed. She wrapped it around me and in that simple gesture of covering my disgrace gave me some of my dignity back. I automatically eased my arms into the sleeves and as she pulled it around my stomach, I tied the cloth belt to keep it in place.

She put firm hands on my shoulders. 'Ania, I know you are hurting and you know what you did was wrong. I am not judging you or anything…'—she paused briefly—'Oops! I guess I just did!'

There was no answer to that.

She threw me a reassuring smile to make it clear that she hadn't meant to pass judgment or say anything bad. It really is impossible to be angry with Emilia, and even if she had judged me—so what! At least she was talking to me and telling me something I already knew.

'The thing is, Ania, behaving like this won't work and you'll only feel even worse than you already do. Whatever you thought you were doing, Dominika would've just ignored you, believe me. And at the bottom of your heart you know this too.'

She let go of my shoulders and cupped my cheeks in her hands, forcing me to stare into her soft eyes.

'I can't begin to imagine how bad you feel, I know you still love her and regret what you did, but by lowering yourself you will only humiliate yourself to no end. It won't be the same as the sexual humiliation you crave and enjoy, it'll destroy you and I can't let you do that.'

She tightened her grip on my face and pulled it closer to her. She was so serious; probably the most serious I've ever seen her.

'Promise me you won't do this again.'

I tried to look away. Her love and compassion, yet again, were exposing my wretchedness. She'd covered my nakedness and shame with my dressing gown, but nothing could take away my guilt.

'Promise me.' She wasn't letting go of my face.

'I promise,' my eyes were darting everywhere, anywhere but the purity of her eyes.

'Again. Look at me.'

'I promise.' I finally conceded and looked her in the eyes, even though the condemnation I felt made me want to tear myself away from her.

'Good, so that's the end of it.'

Emilia then let go of my face and caught me completely by surprise. She pulled me close to her in the tightest hug she has ever given me. She held me wordlessly and suddenly I felt safe and loved. Her warmth was security and her sympathy broke my heart again.

Then as quickly as she had embraced me she let me go. 'I should go. Get some sleep.'

She then left and carefully closed the door behind her. I'd barely been able to contain myself when she held me, but once the door clicked behind her I let go and burst into tears. I was confused, the slightest bit of love and I'd melted. Her love had both condemned and redeemed me. It made no sense, but it'd touched my inner soul, that flickered with the first sign of life since I'd betrayed Dominika with that Judas kiss.

Where there is love, condemnation soon follows. Once more my sin and depravity crashed down on me. A well of emotion erupted from deep within and I threw myself on the bed and buried my head into a pillow and sobbed my heart out.

What have I done?

It wasn't the first, nor would it be the last time that I asked myself that same question. I'd caused the catastrophe and there was little sign of anything ever changing. Only Emilia, sweet Emilia, had reached me in the only way she knew how to.

I shuddered at the thought of what Kasia might have done if Emilia hadn't insisted on dealing with me. Kasia's only restraint would have been not to upset Emilia, but she was still so angry that she may not have even considered Emilia's feelings. That in turn might have had implications for them too—and it would all of been my fault.

Emilia I love you and despite my betrayal maybe you still love me too?

There was small comfort in that, but it only made me feel even more isolated from Dominika.

***

The next morning nothing had really changed, and as far as I know, Dominika never found out about what I'd done last night. It may just be that her reading this confession may be the first she hears about it and how Emilia stepped in and stopped me. I realised almost straight away that Emilia was right. She'd saved me from a condemnation worse than death.

Whatever happens, I will always remember and be grateful to Emilia for what she did.

Living in the flat was so difficult and the hardest part was that as far as Dominika was concerned, I no longer existed. To be irrelevant was the worst feeling possible, a tiny little atom meant more to her than I did. I wasn't even worthy of her hate and anger. This meant in her world that I was even worse than her dad. Even he, quite rightly, deserved her anger.

Kasia continued to blank me and, when we did meet in the hallway, she glared at me with her dead vampire eyes.

Emilia was quite different, and since she'd found me naked at Dominika's door she'd thawed rapidly. That in itself, might be a bit unfair. It's not in her nature to stay angry with anybody, even for a few days. Life's simply too short. She was open but minimal, especially in front of Kasia, but what had changed, since she'd found me, was that she was a bit more chatty, especially when no one else was around. When she could she flashed me reassuring smiles, unseen by the other girls. I totally understood her. She couldn't break solidarity with Dominika and Kasia, but at the same time she recognised it wasn't her fight or her problem.

She was in a difficult position and I totally got how she handled it, although I didn't always show her as much respect as she deserved. From time to time, as days and then weeks passed, when we found moments to talk I'd inevitably try to turn the subject to Dominika, but Emilia wasn't interested in getting involved. She always found a way to steer me away and although she was talking to me, I felt that she was still more for Dominika and I couldn't really blame her.

By pushing her, I was disrespecting her and I should've been grateful that at least she was talking to me.

About a week after Dominika broke up with me I reconnected with my social media and started chatting with my online friends. Over the last few years, I've joined several specialised dating websites and made contact with a lot of likeminded people. There were two main reasons for this, the first was to share my experiences within a community of shared interest and secondly to meet people for possible hook-ups—with Dominika's full approval of course. This was to help me further explore and understand my sexual boundaries and desires.

When I reengaged with my social media, I quickly discovered there were three types of people on there. The majority just carried on and contact was just the same as it had always been, although they generally accepted that I wasn't really into it anymore because I was mourning the loss of my relationship. It took me a while to recognise that my loss was indeed a form of grief.

The second group, a tiny minority, are quite predatory and the kind of people everybody should be wary of. They wanted details of what I'd done and they didn't really care about me. A couple of them even asked for pictures (obviously no pictures exist of Elwira and me).They just wanted to use me to further their wank fantasies.

Brutal as that sounds maybe this is all I am and all I am worthy of—to be a *wank fantasy* for lonely men.

There is thankfully a third group and they were (and are) real friends who really took care of me and supported me. They didn't judge, but they never condoned what I did either. They were real and they were there and they saved me from complete isolation. If you are reading this you know who you are and I can never thank you enough, you probably literally saved my life.

It was one of these very supportive friends who encouraged me to write a letter in order to win Dominika back and I started thinking about how to do this. It needed to be perfect, to show how I feel, but without any emotional manipulation, intentional or unintentional. She'd see straight through anything like that anyway. She's too smart to fall for any stupidity or even inadvertent emotional blackmail and it'd inevitably backfire terribly with unfathomed repercussions.

In the meantime, I somehow got my routine back in order. I had to.

My exams are important. There is never a good time to experience a breakup, but this had happened at probably the worst possible time, during an end of year exam session. I studied as well as I could, but everything was empty and meaningless without Dominika. The only thing I can say is that at least my exam preparation gave my life some purpose and a direction.

At university, I attended lessons and focused on my revision, but Elwira could only stare at me with pure hate. I tried a couple of times to talk to her, but she just walked away, or when I cornered her in the corridor, she told me to leave her alone. I backed off each time because I genuinely believed she'd start screaming at me and create a scene. I soon realised any efforts to reach Elwira would be futile so I gave up and let her be.

I still have no idea how she felt about this.

I went through the motions of conversations with friends, the truth is I don't have that many friends, but I guess it's the best way to describe those who I share classes with. Normality was an act, and I was grateful that at least Elwira hadn't gossiped about me and made things even worse.

On reflection, this last sentence just shows how selfish I am. I've just read this again, a few months after originally writing it. Elwira was probably heartbroken too and couldn't share her pain for embarrassment or fear of rejection. Ironically, the nearest she'd probably had to a real conversation was with Dominika of all people on the day after we'd broken up. Of course, I didn't recognise this at the time and could only see things through my eyes and from the limitations of my own self-pity.

I'm sure she was hurting and she had nobody. At least I had my online friends.

All of my conversations were echoes, meaningless and hollow. I smiled and played the role, but was always looking over my shoulder to see if Elwira was lurking somewhere in the shadows.

Living in the flat continued to be difficult. I got into the routine of setting my alarm earlier and taking my breakfast to Kasia's old room before anyone else got up. The other girls must have been aware of what I was doing as I could always hear their doors, subdued footsteps and whispered conversations once I returned to the room.

I did my own shopping and even started labelling my own food—we'd never done that. We were a family and it was something we'd never needed to do, even when we'd been relative strangers at the very beginning. When it came to paying my part of the rent and the bills I simply gave the money to Emilia who then gave it to Dominika who's always been in charge of that kind of stuff. With Dominika already living in the flat when we moved in, it had always been this way and there had never been any reason to do it any differently.

Using the bathroom to do anything was always awkward, because of the risk of bumping into Dominika or Kasia. Bumping into Emilia wasn't so bad, but because she was caught in the middle she too tried to keep out of my way when the others were about. I resorted to doing my hair and makeup in Kasia's old room so I was only in the bathroom when I really had to be.

Every night, I'd sit in Kasia's old room while the other girls chatted and went about their own lives. I was no longer welcome at the kitchen table or to join in with anything they were doing. They probably wanted me out, but I had nowhere to go.

One of the things that I found the hardest was that I was now excluded from seemingly normal activities that I'd always been a part of in the past. Even simple things like sitting and drinking tea together or just gathering in one room to watch something on TV. I felt this most acutely on the night of the Champions League final. Emilia is a huge football fan and important matches have become major social occasions in our diary. It is nice to spend time with Emilia supporting something she likes because she gives the rest of us so much.

As usual, the girls gathered, but I wasn't invited and I found it unbearable to be excluded. I could hear them laughing and cheering and enjoying themselves. I wanted to shut everything out and pretend they weren't even there so I had an early shower and went to bed.

On reflection, that one evening was a microcosm of the anguish and emptiness I was feeling. I was sharing the flat with three beautiful girls, but had no one.

I was so lonely.

***

By now, it was early June and things couldn't get any worse at home. At least I'd got through my exams and passed everything that I'd already received my results for. As you can imagine they weren't great, but at least they were passes. I was still however, awaiting results from my written exams that'd be the difference between passing and failing the year. We were all in a similar position and for Dominika, being in her final year it was even more important.

Even though the academic year was as good as finished, we all remained in Warsaw waiting around for nothing. We all could have easily gone back to our parents and checked our end of year results online, but for a variety of reasons we ended up staying.

Normally we have a summer plan, but I'd messed everything up. For me, I just couldn't bear going home. Mum especially would see that all wasn't right and would fuss around me and drive me mad. She and dad had kind of accepted my relationship with Dominika, and it wouldn't take a genius to see that we were no longer together. No mask could hide the truth and it was a truth I wasn't ready to face. Mum, in particular, is very religious and conservative and I wasn't sure she wouldn't use my unhappiness as a divine knife, to try to turn me away from what she believed to be sin and back to her God.

Honestly, I don't think she would, but I can't say for sure. And that's why I didn't go home.

I was desperate to stay close to Dominika too, even though that light had completely gone out.

Knowing Kasia, she really didn't want to go home either, for which she has her own reasons, so Emilia chose to stay with her. Dominika probably was staying because now she'd done studying she had to start looking for a job and June is the best time for giving CVs to prospective schools. I was sure she was lonely and longing especially to meet up with her sister, but now she had other priorities.

With the turning of the new month, the weather had turned unbearably hot, most days were around the 30C mark and it was hard to believe that in the last few days of May the authorities had been worried about the Vistula flooding. The river had been so high that the beach near the National Stadium had completely disappeared and on the other bank water was lapping on the top step of the restraining concrete. In four years of living in Warsaw, I'd never seen the river so high before.

With the heatwave, the flat became an even more hostile place to stay and I found my days filled with going outside. It didn't matter where I went, and it wasn't just to get out of the way of the girls, but it was to avoid being baked alive. With the flat having windows on both the east and west there was no respite from the evening sun in Kasia's west-facing old room. The only place I actively chose not to go even near was Promenada. It aroused far too many memories of Elwira and everything that happened afterwards. I'm guessing that the girls had similar ideas because I didn't see or hear them too often either. Only in the late evenings, was I sure that everyone was at home.

I was still pining for Dominika and wanted nothing or nobody else.

Without university to distract me, she was all I could think about. As I walked the lonely streets of Warsaw or lay sweating in bed at night, she was the centre of my thoughts. Then one evening the suggestion about writing a letter came back to me and I decided it was worth a go.

Just maybe it'll save us. Things can't get any worse—can they?

I knew it'd mean more if I wrote it by hand. A pen-written letter would show more effort and commitment, which in itself would make a point and stand for something. I had nothing to lose.

I don't know how many times I wrote and rewrote the letter. I definitely wasn't being very environmentally friendly as the pile of screwed up paper that was surrounding me testified to. Sometimes, I got no further than *Dear Dominika...* or *My Sweetest Dominika...* Even starting the letter was impossible, because I was determined to put absolutely no expectation on her. I'd wronged her, it wasn't her who had wronged me and I needed to take full responsibility for that without the slightest hint of pressuring her.

Finally, I resorted to at least saving the planet and ordering my thoughts in a Word document. I reasoned that doing it this way meant I'd be able to make as many changes as I wanted and then finally write it out by hand with some last adjustments if necessary.

Anguished tears poured out with every word as I tried to take full responsibility. Unlike here, I skimmed over much of what had happened between Elwira and me as it seemed unnecessary. I wrote about how things had started and when we met without going into every sordid detail. What made writing it so hard was that I didn't really want to say that it all happened because I was feeling ignored and abandoned, that'd somehow flip the blame onto Dominika and I already knew from our breakup conversation how she felt when this was even hinted at. This was something I wanted to avoid at all costs.

I already knew that I'd tell her everything if she asked, but the letter wasn't the place for this.

I explained how I felt and how I feel and how I need her to be my centre. I didn't go fully into the depths of my despair or how close I had come to ending it all because I didn't want anything to come across as emotional blackmail. Even then, I understood that I couldn't try to win her over on the basis that I might kill myself if she didn't take me back. I just wanted her to see the truth as it was and my remorse as well the all-consuming loss that was now engulfing me in a living hell. My message in many words was simple.

Dominika I am sorrier than words can ever express and I will love you forever.

It took me about a week to reach the point when I decided it was as good as I could make it. I transferred it to paper in my best handwriting and put it in a pink envelope that I'd bought especially. I wrote her name on the front and decorated it with some pretty hearts. It was as perfect as I could make it.

I then waited for the right moment and I didn't have to wait long.

It was a Saturday evening, a couple of days after I'd finished writing. Once more, I'd been out again to escape the furnace that our flat had become. I was caught slightly by surprise when I passed Emilia and Kasia who were on their way out as I was on my way back in. Emilia smiled at me discretely but never said a word and Kasia, as usual, was the ice queen who sent another shiver down my spine despite the weather.

Her hate knows no bounds, if only Dominika could hate me it'd be something.

As I went through the hallway a quick glance into our room confirmed that Dominika was home. She'd left the door open probably to try at least to get a breeze blowing through the flat and reduce the oppressive heat. She was sitting on the sofa lost in her laptop and lost in her own little world. I went to Kasia's old room and changed from my dress into a vest and shorts, which were cooler and far more comfortable. There was no point in showering before changing because the air was so charged and sticky that as soon as I stepped out of the shower the humidity would have saturated me again anyway.

My nerves were only adding to my stickiness, as the anticipation and fear of facing Dominika made my heart pound and my body shake. I focussed on my fear and bringing it under control as Dominika had taught me and I made the purely mental decision that I just had to go for it. I'm not sure how much bravery came into it. I just had to force myself to give her the letter and with it my last hope of saving us.

I found the discipline to wait a few minutes more, just to be absolutely sure that Emilia and Kasia wouldn't come back and disturb us. I clock watched for a long agonising ten minutes before deciding they weren't coming back in a hurry. This was it. It was now or never. I went into the hallway and saw that Dominika's door was still open.

Lost in whatever she was doing, I took in once more her natural beauty framed by her gentle blonde hair and was hit once more with a contradiction of longing and loss. *Time to get on with it, Ania*, I urged myself silently. I respectfully knocked on the door gently because I didn't want to enter uninvited.

It is probably the most courageous thing I have ever done…

She lifted her head and saw me. Her face revealed nothing. There wasn't even the hint of a smile or anger. She set her laptop aside and got up and came to the door. I feared the worst. Dominika not inviting me in had to be a bad sign.

I held the envelope in front of me. I moderated my voice and made sure that I didn't whine, as she abhors brattish behaviour.

'Please Dominika, I have something for you. Please read it. I beg you. It's all I ask.'

Wordlessly, Dominika took the envelope off me and turned it over in her hands, inspecting it carefully, before looking at me. It took all my willpower not to avert my eyes as my sin and shame flashed once more before my eyes. The tension between the thought of being either totally crushed or elated tore at me as uncertainty and insecurity ripped through my mind.

'Come with me,' she said flatly, revealing nothing in her tone. They were the first words she'd said to me since we'd broken up completely. As clear as day I remember the day when she'd disowned me by giving me the ring back.

With that, she passed me and I followed her into the kitchen.

'I have a lesson for you. You see this? All nice and pink with its cute little hearts? Well, watch and learn. This is exactly what you did to my heart.'

She then lit the gas hob and quite deliberately set fire to a corner of the envelope and as the flames took hold she moved it over the sink. Ashes began to cascade like grey snow as it was consumed.

I couldn't hold back, tears ejected from my eyes and my lip quivered as I fought for self-control. Finally, she was striking back and it couldn't have been more brutal. The pain and anguish I'd poured into that letter was literally going up in smoke and beating me would have been kinder. She'd never do this. What she was doing was far worse and it hurt like hell, far more than any physical pain could ever. I had to escape. I started to turn away…

'Don't you fucking dare. Watch and learn.'

I am *compelled* to obey Dominika and she made me watch as my last hope died in those hot flickering orange tendrils. The little piece of my soul that Emilia had resurrected with her tenderness died too as the letter burned. As the fire got nearer her fingers, Dominika twisted what was left of my efforts to utterly incinerate it until she could no longer hold it. She then dropped it into the sink and waited a few seconds before turning the cold water on. She rinsed everything down the plughole and then opened the window to ventilate the smoke out.

'Done,' was her final comment and I didn't know if she was talking about us or the destruction of the letter. It didn't matter though because the end result was the same. With that she returned to our—no now it was *her*—room.

I tried to follow. I was just a pace behind her, but she closed the door on my face and I heard a heavy intake of breath from inside and I knew she was fighting down her own emotions. I wanted to reach out to her, but knew I couldn't.

The closed door and end of hope condemned me even more than everything that had led up to this moment and before I knew it my own self-loathing once again consumed me as the flames had the letter just a few minutes earlier. I went to my room and threw myself on the bed.

Hate, pure self-hate, filled my mind. Why should Dominika give me another chance? I've done this to myself and only have myself to blame. What a stupid little whore I am! Dirty little fucking bitch, worth less than nothing!

It truly was the end.

The isolation I felt was similar to how I'd felt the first night after I'd confessed, only worse. Pain ripped my stomach and my heart pounded in the devastating realisation of total loss. She'd not only left me but had crushed the last vestige of hope that remained. Burning the letter up so coldly, without feeling, perfectly represented my place in her life. I was paralysed and I just stayed there lost and alone. I fazed out of reality and time became an eternity of nothingness. I didn't move for the rest of the evening other than when I needed to drag myself to the toilet and even when I did that my body felt heavy and lifeless. I stared at the ceiling with empty unseeing eyes and nothing would distract me. I'm sure the girls came home at some point, but I was totally oblivious.

Everybody was dead and so was I.

The next day was the same. I didn't change or shower and I barely ate. Life was meaningless. My soul was gone and only emptiness remained. This stupid little bitch was without purpose or hope. My beating heart and brain was just a machine, and not even a shadow of vibrancy and vigour remained.

Occasional thoughts of ending it all resurfaced, but I knew I was too weak and I couldn't do that to mum and dad—better for them to have a zombie than a funeral I reasoned. At least I could save them if not myself. There was nothing left from Dominika and my passing would mean nothing to her—she'd made that abundantly clear. Kasia would probably go to my grave, just so she could piss on it. Just maybe Emilia would have some compassion for my departure from this cruel empty world.

Second after second, followed by minute after minute, and then hour after hour dragged as time seemed to stop. The agony from the rip in my stomach didn't let up nor the overpowering grief that tore at my body and burned deep into every recess of my mind.

Time had lost meaning and had become a blur of the barest of existences. So I think, and I am far from sure, that it was probably late on the day after the letter had been burnt when Emilia politely knocked on my door and walked in without invitation. I guess I should have expected her. It was just a case of *when* rather than *if*. Emilia has always been the most sensitive and aware of us all. Her soft face was all concern as she walked across the room and parted the curtains and opened a window. The sudden bright light from the evening sun stabbed my eyes and as I blinked she came and sat next to me.

'Why are you still in bed?'

I ignored her and looked away. Part of me wanted to break down and cry on her shoulder and reveal all, but she'd then get sucked into my maelstrom of death and self-loathing. I had hardened myself to my fate and part of that meant letting no one in—not even Emilia.

'You should get up. You'll feel better.'

Nothing.

'Come on, Ania, let me in. You know I still love you, despite all the shit you caused.'

This is so Emilia, I think it's called brutal honesty. She wasn't sugar-coating anything, but still reaching out to me. I almost softened and as I nearly relented I remembered that I deserved absolutely nothing from anybody and certainly not compassion. So quite deliberately and consciously I shut her out again. My mind was constantly reminding me in a silent scream that I don't deserve any kindness.

'Please Ania talk to me,' she touched my hand with hers.

I pulled back as though stung by a wasp. Shocked, her face flickered for a moment before it reset. She grabbed my hand forcibly and looked straight into my eyes.

'Look Ania, it's really simple. I'm here for you and you are far from alright. Let me in.'

I tried to look away from her, but she tightened her grip on my hand until I once again caught her gaze.

'You *will* talk to me before I leave here, and that's final. Give me all the silent treatment you like. I'll just wait you out. You know me well enough by now, don't waste your time and test me.'

She'd made her point, so she let go.

Emilia's sweet steel was bared, sharper than a dragon's teeth and I knew it. Irresistible, compassionate and caring, Emilia was also indomitable and indefatigable. It may not be obvious to outsiders, especially those who only know us through our social media, but out of all of us Emilia has the strongest will and even Dominika won't contend with her. Emilia is probably the most secure person I know. By default, this means Kasia is a pussycat in her hands. Emilia very rarely shows her steel, and, in fact, only does so when she really needs to.

Steel unleashed, I knew she wouldn't leave before I talked to her.

I surrendered possibly even sooner than she expected, but there was no point in holding out. I had no pride left and the sooner I gave in the sooner she'd leave me in my sorrow.

'Ok, I'm struggling,' I acknowledged in a whisper.

'I know it's hard, but what's changed?'

'I just need a few days,' I lied. 'I now understand that me and Dominika are over. I just need to work it out and let go. Then I can move on.'

Emilia cast me a sideways glance, she wasn't buying. Her glare demanded more.

'Em please, I really don't want to go into it. All I'll say is that Dominika and I kind of talked last night while you were out with Kasia. When we were done, I understood that it was the end. I always hoped she'd change her mind, but now I know.'

At least this wasn't a lie. Emilia's eyes melted and she reached out her hand to mine again only this time I accepted it.

'I know it's over, and I just need to get used to it,' I repeated sadly, but with my mask still firmly in place.

Emilia wasn't letting go, 'What do you need? How can I help?'

I don't want kindness and compassion but I knew I needed to give her something more than silence back.

'Nothing; I just need to get a grip of my feelings and figure out what I am going to do. It's enough to know that at least you still care.'

We sat like that for a few minutes longer and she held my hand in silence and I wasn't sure if she was lost for words or waiting for me to say something more.

'Thank you,' I said eventually.

She squeezed my hand once more and got up. It was obvious to her that I'd said as much as I was going to.

'You know where I am if you need me. I won't push, but come to me any time. Don't worry about Kasia.' With those parting words she let me be and left.

Despite what I'd said it wasn't thinking space that I needed—it was my destruction.

Emilia had been so lovely, but it was sympathy that I was totally unworthy of and I just couldn't accept it.

I'm sorry Emilia, but I'm too far gone for even you to save.

Once she was gone I slipped back into my melancholia and remained there until finally exhaustion overwhelmed me and sleep provided some relief.

On Monday the weather changed. It was cooler and gloomier with heavy rain showers. It seemed like God was setting the weather to match my feelings. The new day didn't bring any new hope and I remained hidden in my room. I stayed in bed and again I only forced myself to get up when I had to. I barely ate and only left my room when absolutely necessary.

Tuesday and Wednesday blurred into a void, the light filtered through the shaded windows and the temperature rose once again, only now unlike last week the humidity had risen even higher and it made the room feel so much worse. Once more my room turned into an oven, a foretaste of hell which was beckoning me.

I suddenly realised that I'd stopped thinking in terms of Kasia's old room and now only *my* room. The change was significant and represented my fall into complete darkness. I then, just as quickly, remembered I'd been thinking of it as my room from the moment Dominika had closed her door after burning the letter and with it any last hope for us.

I couldn't see any point of carrying on so I just let myself rot in the heat of my sweat. The decay of my sin now finally had a complete hold on me.

The only slight relief to my suffering was a nightly cool shower, which was a pleasure that I no longer deserved.

Hate, nothing but self-hate, was all that remained.

I was existing; but no longer living.

Part 4: Ania Is Impetuous
Friday 21 June 2019

It was another long weekend, almost six endless weeks since Dominika and I had broken up and just about a week since she'd burnt my letter and with it my last hope for us.

Devastation reigned and I was an empty shell, a husk of my previous existence. I was isolated and alone and even though Emilia had tried to reach out, I'd even completely withdrawn from her. My inner voice, which had so often conflicted with my outer expression, now spoke in unity with my whole being.

I am nothing and my life is worthless.

Thursday was *Corpus Christi*—or in Polish *Boże Ciało* (literally Christ's Body)—which always falls on a Thursday. In my current state it meant nothing to me and even now it only stands out because it was on this day, imprisoned in the oven-like cell that my room had become, that my mood found new expression.

One band more than any other band reaches into my inner being and connects with my deepest sorrow. One song in particular has always stood out as an anthem and it's a song of disappointment and an inability to feel. Words used to describe people as nothing more than unfeeling machines resonate to my very bones and especially with the overlay of disappointment in that as human beings we should always have been more.

Life should simply have been different.

So in my solitude it was my music that I turned to. I locked myself into my earphones grabbed my phone and went to the playlist I was looking for. Only today I scanned through my anthem and settled on another song by the same band. Maybe it was my particular mood, but the words of this grabbed hold of my head like never before.

Nothing is forever, the vocalist explained in terrible angst, and things change so quickly. One moment everything is fine and then it all slips away like sand running through your fingers, and the more you try to hold on the more you lose.

This is me and this is my loss.

Every time the song came to an end I played it again. I've always been a bit obsessive with music and it's not unusual for me to do this. The difference was that normally the constant repetition diminishes the power of the music and lyrics, but today they reaffirmed my feelings even more powerfully. Each line passed through me like a jolt of electricity and only served to remind me of my loneliness and despair.

My existence had become unbearable and the only certainty I had, was that I knew my self-imposed exile was fully deserved because of my crimes. I'd done it to myself. I'd given in to temptation and now I was paying the price. It'd left me heartbroken and even though I knew it was the end, I was still in love with Dominika, probably even more so than ever. The finality of her burning the letter, which I'd so carefully written, had been the cremation of our relationship.

How could I have been so stupid?

The old saying really is true, you don't know what you've got until it's gone. And now it was well and truly gone. After six weeks and especially the last few days, I'd reached my breaking point and needed to get out. My guilt wasn't dissipating and there was no release. I knew probably only Emilia really cared and I was so loathsome that I couldn't accept even her love. I didn't deserve anything, but disgrace because I was so contemptible. I'd spent too long cooped up in what I'd finally accepted was my new room, with each lonely moment being a terrible reminder of my sins. My chains were heavier than Jacob Marley's, but no Dickensian ghost could save me from my past, present or future.

Guilt demands punishment.

Where the hell did that thought come from? It hit me like a hammer, a brutal blunt force trauma and suddenly I understood.

In a second my mind was made up. I knew what I had to do. It was time to embrace my judgment. I wasn't brave enough to do myself in, but maybe someone else can!

What a fucked up thought! I'll hand myself over—even to death.

With that stupid rash thought my mission for the night was determined. I'll go out and find my own obliteration. I was no longer committed to anyone or anything and could do what I wanted. I was free and yet the very things that made me free locked me in dark shackles which clanged as an indelible reminder of how far I had fallen.

I didn't even need to tell anyone what I was going to do. A plan began to form in my mind. There was nothing and nobody to restrain me.

Dark thoughts gave me focus and a reason. With greater resolve than I'd had for ages my plan steadily evolved as I was getting ready. I had a cool bath and, as I'd done so often in the past, I deep cleansed and prepared myself for the onslaught that I was looking for. I brushed my hair out properly and made myself up all nicely before choosing a nice summer dress and clutch handbag with just enough room for my phone, keys and some money.

It was quite easy to achieve the look I wanted. It was simple and elegant at the same time. It also meant minimal accessorising. It was a bit *girl-next-door*, but as I stood back from the mirror, I immediately saw that my unadorned modesty would achieve exactly what I wanted. Dressing as a slut, even if in many ways it'd have been appropriate, would be too obvious. Besides, just putting it out there would deprive me of the hunt beforehand.

Guys like the hunt too and find an easy hunt unattractive.

The girls must have noticed me getting ready. It was the longest I'd spent in the bathroom for weeks. It was almost totally predictable that, out of the three of them, it was Emilia who came to find out what was going on.

When she asked what I was up to I lied and told her that I was meeting friends and getting on with my life. I reminded her that I'd finally accepted Dominika and I were over and I needed to start going out again and rebuilding my life. I'm not sure she believed me, but she had no other choice other than to accept what I said at face value.

As usual, during the summer months, the flat had been uncomfortably hot, but when I stepped outside it was immediately obvious the weather was quite strange. I wondered whether I'd made the right choice of what to wear. It was quite sultry with the ominous threat of a storm. Angry dark clouds had gathered, darkening the sky and oppressing the air which was almost thick enough to be suffocating. It crossed my mind briefly that it might be a bad omen for the night, but I quickly dismissed it as superstitious sentiment from my childhood.

I walked, the ten minutes or so to the tram terminal and by the time I got there I was clammy and my dress was sticking to my back. I felt strangely detached from my surroundings and was lost in my own thoughts as I played out in my mind how I thought the evening might go. It was like I'd entered some kind of a trance. It was almost as if my consciousness was separating itself from what I'd decided was my destiny. Physical torment and brokenness might appease my guilt, but even in my darkest imaginings, it wouldn't go far enough. Nobody could do to me what I deserved, however extreme.

My body needs breaking and so does my mind. Only then will I know release, even to the point of death.

The possibility that I might not survive the night was a twisted, paradoxical comfort. My earthly sin will finally be paid for and I will know peace one way or the other. Accepting my fate didn't lessen the potent fear of imminent catastrophe. My old friend fear had me in his grasp. I recognised him immediately as that familiar feeling that had dominated my life. The big difference now being that, unlike when I was a child, fear now gave me a modicum of control. As much as fear knew me, I knew him too and I was able to rationalise and use it to help me focus.

A quick flashback to when I owned up to Dominika reminded me that it was she who'd given me the strength to overcome fear. Bizarre as it sounds, it was Dominika's strength that gave me the power to do what I had to do tonight.

I had to cast Dominika out of my mind. If I die judgment before God will be hastened, and an eternity of fire awaited me. It was a bitter, but just, pill to swallow.

It's my true reward for the sum of my life on the great scales of justice,

The tram took about twenty minutes to get to the city centre and I went directly to a hotel bar. It was the same place where I'd picked somebody up just a few months ago to fulfil a personal fantasy. Dominika had allowed this, as a special present to celebrate our third *first date* anniversary. As I stepped inside the atrium my minded flooded with bittersweet memories. Things had been so different in back in October.

Stupid reminiscing will only get in the way.

I had to put any pleasant thoughts out of my head and think about the here and now. My course was set and my path was laid out before me. All I needed to do was reach out and take hold of it.

Now the moment had come, I must admit that I was terrified. I took a sharp intake of breath and set my mind. I quickly ordered a neat vodka and sat on a stool at the bar. Destruction is the key to my freedom so *best just get on with it*, I thought to myself pragmatically. I downed it very quickly and ordered a second that soon followed to give me the courage for what I needed to do.

Emboldened, more by the mental effect of drinking the vodka than by any direct effect of the alcohol, I casually looked around and scanned the bar to seek out any potential quarry. I laughed inwardly at the bitter irony of what was happening. As when I'd directed Elwira's steps, it was a strangely assertive position to be in, but the contradictions ran far deeper than that. I was the hunter, the predator on the lookout, but ultimately I would be the prey; the victim, the carrion for the vultures to pick over.

There were a bunch of Germans, maybe five or six, sitting around a table and they looked like a likely target. I try to avoid contact with Polish people when hooking up because it's always in my mind that it could cause later complications. I was looking to be used and abused. I didn't want a relationship or a stalker. I wasn't sure whether I'd live to see tomorrow, I no longer cared for my fate, but just in case I survived, I kept my normal protections in place.

I stood up and casually drifted over to them and sat on an uninvited lap. I had no idea whether he was handsome or fit or anything because I wasn't even paying too much attention. I was looking for brutality in the shape of a big hard cock or more if I could find them and that was all I cared about. I'd fucked and played with ugly guys before and experience had shown me that they are much easier to manipulate than younger fitter guys—simply because they can't believe their luck.

'So who's going to buy me a drink,' I murmured in English.

'Go home little girl,' my unwitting new friend answered patronisingly in broken English as he stood up suddenly to shake me off.

Dislodged and off-balance I wobbled on my heels and nearly fell. I was lucky that I didn't twist my ankles.

My reaction was immediate.

'Fuck you!' I growled like a spurned alley cat as I caught myself and stood up pushing my face right into his. My frustration and anger of the last few months finally found a voice, only this time it wasn't looking inwards. Generally, I'm not that belligerent, but I've always known the potential was there as an unseen undercurrent. Having said that, I was surprised when it came out so aggressively, but now I'd shown this face I couldn't back down. I still had a little pride left.

He must have felt threatened and looking back now I'm not surprised. He pushed me firmly on my shoulders and I had to take a step back so not to fall over. As I recovered my balance he put his hands up in a pacifying gesture, 'I don't want any trouble. Just go and leave us alone,' he protested with indignation echoing in his deep voice.

'You're no fun—boring, boring, boring!'

'Hey! What is this?' he protested irately. 'You are bothering us. Just go home.'

I retorted, 'Don't care for a bunch of fucking losers who don't know how to have a good time.'

One of his friends had seen enough and got up and came across to me. He put a hand on my shoulder and started to turn me around as if to direct me away.

Bad move.

'Don't fucking touch me,' I screamed, drawing the attention of everyone else in the bar.

The hotel staff too had now seen that I was causing a scene. I didn't care, I was beyond embarrassment. I was actually so pissed off that for the moment anger had displaced my pride, fear and inner self-loathing. A barman came over to us and tried to find out what was going on. Now all the Germans were talking at once, wagging their fingers at me and flashing angry glances in my direction. My German is non-existent, but it was fairly obvious they were blaming me.

Stupid cunts don't know when a girl is offering them a good time.

Can't remember exactly what followed, but I think I was just telling them to shut up, and I didn't care particularly about watching my language. I now had the sole attention of the barman, who addressed me with customary Polish politeness.

'Please young lady, I think you should leave. Perhaps you would like me to call you a taxi?'

'Fuck off! I don't need a taxi and I don't need your help. Besides your bar is shit and nobody's any fun. I'm leaving.'

And with that, I shrugged my shoulders, turned my back and with a nonchalant flick of my head I walked out. I should have been embarrassed but I was so angry and frustrated that I didn't care. If they didn't want a good time I wasn't going to waste time on them.

As soon as I stepped outside the vodka truly hit me and I went a bit woozy. I took a moment to allow the dizziness to pass and steadied myself before once more setting my course for another hotel bar. I remembered the Mercure is just around the corner. It's nearby and it'll be another convenient hunting ground.

It only took a few minutes to get there, but as soon as I walked in it felt all wrong. The atrium just didn't feel right, there was no bar and maybe at the far end there was something, but it looked more like a dining area and not the kind of place where guys hang out drinking. I knew I wouldn't find what I was looking for so I promptly left to find another bar.

It was proving to be more difficult than I expected, but I was resolute. It'd just take a bit more effort. There are plenty of guys out there and it was just a matter of time until I found somebody to fuck me into oblivion. Of this, I had absolutely no doubt.

It's good that there are so many bars situated together in the city centre and at least that meant I wouldn't have to wander around all night. It was only a matter of time and at least that made it easier.

The truth is that men with hard cocks can't resist girls like me.

So with renewed determination I started drifting towards the railway station and the Marriott, expecting it to be the first of several more hotels until I finally got what I wanted. The Marriott had been the first place I'd tried back in October. On that occasion, I'd used the overly obvious *girl alone at the bar* ploy and while it hadn't worked I'd still got some interest. It just hadn't worked out in the end. Regardless of this, I had reason to believe that I might find what I was looking for in there.

As it turned out, I never even got as far as the station. As I walked along I was mentally listing all of the hotels I could go to and was so focussed on my mission that I was caught by surprise when a disembodied voice called out from somewhere off to one side.

'Hey pretty girl, all alone? Want to join us for a drink?'

I glanced over to where the voice had come from, and despite the muggy weather, I saw four guys enjoying a drink on the pavement bar in front of the Hard Rock Café and they were English.

I fucking love the English and they've never let me down. I thought for a moment about Phil and Stuart and the other English guys I'd played with in the past. It was one of those moments in life when suddenly, without warning, exactly what I was looking for had appeared right in front of my face.

Disappointment dissipated and now I had a chance. I just needed to bait and snare them and then they'd be mine. Baiting would mean playing it cool and not offering them too much too soon.

'Why not,' I simply said.

He looked surprised and his friends laughed. They couldn't believe their luck. It'd been a playful fun comment and they'd probably expected, at best, some banter, and suddenly I was joining them. Now things were beginning to happen…

The bar must have been really humid inside because there were a few other clusters of people sitting outside and I remember there weren't enough chairs for all five of us. One of the guys had to beg one from another table.

As soon as I sat down, I realised I needed to be a bit more sensible with my drinking. I know I'd only had two vodkas, but I couldn't allow myself to get wasted. It wasn't out of any sense of self-preservation, quite the contrary. It was much simpler than that. Vomiting will get in the way of my destruction and the more I drunk the more it'd act as an anaesthetic and dull the very thing I was looking for. They got me a Coca-Cola although they tried to persuade me to take something stronger. Their inducements soon turned into a big joke for them and they started playfully joking along the lines of what's a party girl doing not drinking alcohol?

And that became my name to them. I was simply Party Girl.

I soon found out what they were doing in Warsaw as we chatted easily; that is they chatted and I listened. Despite what I was looking for my natural introversion can't just be turned off like a light switch.

They were on a lads' weekend and staying in the nearby City Centre Novotel. As soon as they said that I knew there was hope. Groups of English weekenders have a bad reputation in Poland, especially guys coming for stag weekends. Their disrespectful behaviour has made them notorious, especially in Kraków, but they are watched with wary eyes here in Warsaw too. Most come looking for sex and cheap beer and right before them I was there, ready, and more than willing.

They were all in their 20s or maybe early 30s and were much better behaved than the stereotype, maybe because they were a little older and more mature. I read between the lines, as they bantered with each other, that they were probably work colleagues and, as far as I could tell, they were all single because they didn't mention any relationships.

But then it wasn't the moment to be talking about such things.

They were definitely into me and I caught them eyeing me up all time. A quick glance at my bare legs or at my chest, as well as the occasional sideways lustful *up and down* was a dead giveaway. While we talked, I was attentive enough to show interest, but not too much, because I remained focussed only on getting what I needed.

My focus and mission hadn't changed.

Poor guys had no idea what their playful invitation had got them into. They all seemed fit, but their bodies didn't seem to be over-sculptured, like a lot of the macho monsters that go to the gym far too often.

After some time I tired of their light-hearted chit-chat. I didn't want entertaining, I wanted to be fucked beyond destruction. Their admiration of me was becoming so obvious that I decided that now was the time to really turn it on, so I started flirting outrageously. It didn't mean that I suddenly become a chatterbox. I couldn't even if I wanted to. It's just not me. Besides, it'd have been weird or even intimidating if I suddenly underwent personality change.

They were baited and now I just needed to lure them into my snare. So, I drip-fed them with overly obvious compliments while not paying any specific attention to any one of them. They didn't care and one thing that I know about guys is that they don't take hints. Any subtlety would've been lost on them.

Not that I was in any mood to be subtle. There is a certain charm to being direct.

Now I almost had them, I unleashed my full arsenal on them and there was no way they could resist my firepower and it was almost a matter of routine to wrap them around my little finger. I flashed my eyes at them as I diminished myself fully, knowing full well how they'd respond. In part, my self-depreciation was genuine because of how I was feeling about myself, but I also knew that it was the best way to fish for compliments and get them to pay even more attention to me. It also cut straight to the point, because now, by putting myself in their faces, they had no choice but to be drawn to my sex rather than stare from a distance.

They were probably a bit taken aback by my directness, but soon got into the spirit of it. Blatant attention-seeking, more than invited them to glare openly at my body. The looks they were giving me were no longer sideways, but were straight on and fuelled by lust and desire.

'My tits are too small,' I understated vapidly. I'm not really airheaded, but it has a direct charm to it.

'No, they're perfect, firm and so round. Besides in England, we say more than a handful is a waste!'

I'd heard this comment before and despite my mood, I almost laughed with them.

'My ass is bony.'

'Oh no, Party Girl, you have the tightest arse I've ever seen.'

Not sure how they could say this, I was sitting down, but such positive attention made a nice change and it was a bit of a turn on too. My spell had been cast and they were enthralled. I was sure that they were at the very least imagining me naked or probably they'd already crossed the line and were mentally fucking me already. I had them trapped and possibilities were beginning to turn into reality.

I had them exactly where I wanted, so now I was ready to, ironic as it sounds, move in for the kill. We continued to play flirtation tennis for a while longer just until I gauged when the moment was perfect. Suddenly mid-sentence I leant forward and casually touched one of them on the leg, quite high up his thigh, near the pronounced bulge in his jeans, where he was already hard in anticipation. It was a clear sign of his interest and what I was after—or so they thought.

The other three immediately leant back in their chairs with disappointment written all over their faces. So I reached forward and touched two of the others on their knees while looking at the third. 'Don't be disappointed, boys. After all, I am *the* Party Girl,' I winked.

We don't have *a*, *an* or *the* in the Polish language so it's hard to learn especially at the beginning, but I knew exactly what I was saying with my emphasis on *the*. Strictly speaking, my grammar was wrong, but the point I was making and my clear suggestion wasn't. I was *the one and only* and they wouldn't find anybody else as hot or available as me. I was putting myself on a plate as a feast and they only needed to partake.

'You're drunk,' the first guy said.

'No I am not.' Like a moment ago I deliberately didn't use a contraction to emphasise my point and stuck my chin out.

The vodkas I'd drunk earlier were rapidly wearing off. They'd served their purpose in giving me the courage to get me going, but funnily enough they'd failed me when I'd met the Germans. I'd been too brash and now with these guys, I hadn't needed any Dutch-courage to get me going. Perverse as it sounds, everything had evolved very naturally.

I was now so lost in what I was doing that there was no way I could back out, not that I wanted to. They were melting before me as my overpowering sexuality turned them into putty in my hands.

They were mine!

I let the moment pass and the conversation returned to easy topics. As available as I was, I couldn't let them know that, not yet. It might put them off the game. I suddenly realised that I didn't even know their names—and honestly, I never asked. They may have told me, but it was lost in the blur of everything that followed.

So now I will call them Adam, Barry, Carl and David. It's as simple as ABCD!

I gave them a masterclass in deliberate and conscious manipulation as I pulled and pushed them with overt flirtation and then retreating slightly so not to appear too easy. I drove them mad with lust and if they could have got away with it they'd have probably got their cocks out there and then and given them the attention they were screaming for. Finally, in one of those innocuous moments when they were using words to say nothing, I decided that I'd tormented them enough.

'So boys, you up for some real fun?' I suddenly asked, cutting across the banal and pointless conversation. I was more than ready and I knew they were too,

'You know a good club?' one of them asked.

In the end, despite everything that had let up to this moment, they were such innocents! Maybe they were just being polite or just couldn't believe their luck.

'No. I was thinking of taking this party back to one of your hotel rooms. What do you think?' I paused dramatically, suddenly all serious. 'I only have one condition. Condoms. You want me?'

I couldn't have said it more directly or made my intentions more obvious.

'Are you fucking with us, or a prostitute or something?' Carl asked sceptically.

'If you mean, will you have to pay me? No!' I paused again to let it sink in before quipping, 'But I'm not buying the condoms!'

They laughed, but Carl persisted, 'So who's going to get lucky?'

'You boys are so sweet.' I hit them with another vapid irresistible stare, 'It's an open invitation for all of you. So are you up for it?'

'Fucking hell girl! You're serious,' David exclaimed as his eyes flashed at the unexpected realisation of what I was offering.

'Yes I am.'

'Wait a minute. Let me get this straight. You mean all of us?'

'Yes, but I need to tell you some rules.'

'But why are you doing this?' Adam asked, almost as though he hadn't heard my last comment.

'That doesn't matter; but if you boys can have some fun why can't a girl too?'

Talk is getting tiresome. It's time to ramp it up a notch.

'You guys probably wanted to pick up some girls anyway so I've just made your life easier.' Again I paused before unleashing my most lethal weapon, 'Unless you don't want to fuck me of course?'

I knew my loaded question put them exactly where I wanted them. It was a stark choice and they were never going to say no. Even so, I still shot them a look that I know is devastating and tantalisingly seductive. After all, a girl has to use what she's got.

And with this one look I closed the deal.

'So are you going to let me down? Am I going home alone or are we going back to your hotel room together?'

Even though I suggested I might go home alone there was never any chance of that. The battle had been won long ago, probably even just a few minutes after I'd met them.

Armed with this certainty, I knew I could push them to the brink and still get away with it. They were all mine and there was no way they were going to resist my charms. Their agitating cocks had long hardened and their brains had disengaged.

Men are so fucking easy.

They chatted among themselves for a moment and it'd be tedious to repeat their exchange, but it all centred around one thought and one thought alone.

Why not?

Adam finally spoke directly to me again, 'You know what, if you're offering we're taking. And we can walk away tomorrow? No strings?'

'Agreed, even tonight after we're finished. That's one of the things I wanted to tell you anyway. No strings,'

'You won't cry rape?'

'How can I when I asked you? I'll even make a voice recording on your phone if you want and say I wanted it. Will you say I overpowered and raped all four of you?'

They laughed and it seemed that I covered Adam's concerns.

'I love fucking and I'm just up for some fun.' I repeated just to ram the point home.

It was a lie, I wasn't seeking pleasure, only destruction, but they didn't need to know that. Besides they might enjoy me anyway!

'Guys do it all the time, so why shouldn't I? Just coz I'm a girl—so what! It doesn't make any difference nowadays. You probably came to Warsaw to hook up anyway so I've just made it easier for you. So are we going? I'm getting bored.'

They quickly got the attention of one of the waitresses and paid the bill. Once done we set off together in the direction of the Novotel, but before we got too far, I asked about condoms because I knew there was a convenience store on the way. They reassured me that they'd already got some *just in case*.

See how right I am? Boys with their obsession with satisfying their lower brain!

They'd come for a fun weekend and were fully armed and ready. Thinking of our conversation I laughed and said mockingly them, 'I told you so'.

It's an old chauvinistic belief, handed down over centuries—or even millennia—that men like this are *studs* and girls like me are *sluts*, but the truth is that anybody and everybody who is quick to jump into casual intimacy (not to be mistaken by early intimacy with a longer-term partner) is a slut regardless of gender. The four guys and I were clearly on the same wavelength—sluts all round—and so, between us, we'd all found our natural level.

It wasn't that far and we got to the hotel and quickly found our way into one of their rooms. A key card unlocked the room and the guys, invited me to go in first. The irony of such a strangely courteous gesture wasn't lost on me. I am no lady and the fact they'd all readily agreed to fuck me proved they weren't gentlemen either.

As I crossed the threshold of the doorway into the unilluminated darkness my brain changed gear. The fun-loving slut I'd presented myself to be was gone. I'd done what was necessary to get me here and the dark room was light compared to the depths of my depravity.

Now, I am the whore of Babylon, dark and lost. I am in Gethsemane, Judgment awaits me...

Part 5: Ania Is Broken

The room was suddenly awash with brightness. One of the guys must have put the key card in its slot as he entered. Almost as soon as the lights came on the door closed behind me, and as it clicked, it resounded in my mind with the echo of a prison door.

This was it, the moment had arrived. Judgment was imminent, but they didn't need to know that. Somehow I had to bury my feelings and just play the part of the slut they thought I was. If they knew the inner turmoil that drove me they might just stop.

It was one of those moments when I had to put the mask firmly in place, grit my teeth and just get on with it. If I weakened, justice would be denied. Mask in place, I was ready. Almost too casually, I went and sat on the bed, seemingly without a care or a second thought as though what was about to happen was the most normal thing in the world. They just stood there and stared at me. Nobody seemed sure what to do.

There was a pause, but just when it was in danger of becoming uncomfortable, Adam asked, 'So you mentioned some other rules, as well as condoms?'

So it turned out that he had been listening to me after all.

Meeting and chatting with the guys had had an unforeseen consequence. I realised that I actually quite liked them. It wasn't that I fancied them, but they seemed quite decent—more in line with my previous encounters with the English than the stereotypical English stag party tourist we get around here. They'd been polite and respectful and in their own way quite charming, even though all four of them had jumped at the chance to *sharefuck* me. The problem was that while I still needed them to destroy me, I didn't want them to face serious consequences or even a murder charge later. I hadn't cared whether I lived or died, but now I was with them things had changed.

Concerning myself, I felt no different, but I couldn't take them down with me.

I had to survive the night, whatever they did to me and for their protection, not mine, I had to set some rules.

'Yes, just a couple more.' I was deliberately matter of fact and almost casual, as though I was creating in their minds the impression that I was in control, but in reality, I wanted to completely relinquish any sense of self and be given over to their collective lust and fantasies. 'You can do what you want to me, but no kissing, punching or kicking me. Don't pee on me either.'

I'd said the last one for dramatic effect and they all pulled disgusted faces, so I was safe on that one.

'I'll suck you off without condoms, but if you want to fuck my ass or cunt, you must wear one.'

My choice of vulgar language was totally intentional. I often use eloquent language to describe sex, but here and now there was more brutal honesty in my choice of coarse language. I knew for them my choice of words would be more disarming, and besides my so-called rules were just an extension of what I'd already told them. Despite this and my need for them to utterly humiliate me, in the midst of reckless abandon, somehow a sense of responsibility still pervaded. To put it simply, now I knew that I'd live to see tomorrow, I couldn't allow myself to get pregnant or get an infection.

In setting very open rules and by banning some other stuff I'd framed what I wanted, and even expected, by not forbidding it specifically. It was my way of making it clear that everything else was possible. They were almost certainly more conservative than me—*not difficult to imagine, especially with the mood I was in*—so it'd encourage them to be brave and perverse and to see how far they dare go. There was just one more thing I had to make absolutely clear to them.

'And one more thing, so long as you stick to the rules, don't worry about treating me badly and hurting me.'

Another awkward silence filled the room. I didn't know if it was shock or disgust. There was a hiatus; uncertainty and indecision that lingered tangibly in the air until Adam voiced what the others were almost certainly thinking.

'Are you fucked up?'

'Probably,' was my simple answer. At least that was honest.

Adam was a genuinely nice guy and I found his attitude both annoying and comforting. I didn't want or deserve compassion or decency. 'But that's not your problem and none of your business. Just enjoy me. Do what you want with me and take advantage of what I'm offering.'

Why are you talking so much? Shut the fuck up and just fucking take my word for it and get to work on breaking me.

With my mind made up, and a determination to move things on, I did the only thing I could. They weren't going to move first so I'd have to. I stood up and unceremoniously unzipped my dress and eased it off my shoulders before allowing it to drop to my ankles. I quickly stepped out of it and slipped my heels off before removing my knickers and bra with a *let's get on with it* attitude. Now naked, I couldn't have made my intentions any clearer, but they were stunned into paralysis.

Fucking hell boys, I'm sacrificing myself to you. What are you waiting for? Come and take me.

After another moment of hesitancy, Carl was first to move. He came to me and grabbed my treasure and roughly rubbed it. I opened my legs to make room for him and he pushed a finger inside, probably much more easily than he expected.

'She's right you know. Dirty little bitch is wet already.'

Finally! Somebody understands.

You can call me much more and treat me even worse. Can't you see that I'm begging you for this? I can take anything and everything you have for me and more.

It seemed to be the signal the others had been waiting for and suddenly they were all there. Hands were everywhere. My legs were dragged further apart and arms pushed behind my back. A hand went around my throat and others grabbed my breasts and ass roughly and somebody yanked my hair from behind.

I started shaking. I wasn't sure if it was fear or excitement—it was probably both. This was a first for me. I'd been in the hands of the girls before, but never so many men. Even when I'd pleasured the two guys with my mouth a few years ago, Dominika had been in complete control.

I was flesh, meat in their hands and they were butchers ready to go to work.

'You alright?' Adam asked. He was persistent and consistent and definitely worried about what was happening. As nice as he was, his kindness was getting in the way.

I was getting tired of explaining my wishes and needs, so better to show what I needed. Actions speak much louder than words. I didn't reply, I just dropped before them and as they let go of me I fell to my knees. Once on the floor, I started pulling on Adam's jeans. I unbuckled his belt and undid his button and zip before reaching in and taking out his meat. It was already swollen, so his apprehension can't have been bothering him too much.

I took him into my mouth while pulling the skin back to reveal his sensitive head. I flicked my tongue over his purple arousal and he juddered in initial pleasure as I tasted a hint of pee, but I wanted more. He didn't resist and now he was focussed on his own needs I'd effectively muted him, aside from some small sighs of pleasure.

With unseeing hands I reached up and found the swelling between two more of the guys' legs. Clanging metal filled my ears with the opening of belts and the distinctive sound of zips opening and suddenly I had a face full of cocks.

Good, I could see three, and one was in my mouth, they'd all joined in. Now I had to try to share myself. I'm no expert, especially when it comes to men, but I had to do my best. My experience was somewhat limited and I remembered again the two guys from a few years ago. On that occasion, they'd queued and waited patiently as I'd sucked one off and then the other. These guys were English too, but they weren't queuing and I was keen to please as they thrust themselves at me and gave me the badly needed attention I was craving.

I pushed Adam away. 'I'm more than a mouth.'

I then took another anonymous cock in my mouth and awkward hands reached down and groped my breasts and squeezed my little buds. One hand was over-enthusiastic and pinched a nipple harshly.

For the first time tonight, one of them was reaching me.

I spat the cock out. 'Yes, hurt me,' I groaned in encouragement. Then I took yet another cock into my mouth.

As exciting as it was I needed more. Even though pleasure wasn't my aim, I opened my legs and reached down to my honeypot and ran my hand over it. My fingers glided easily with the wet of my arousal and as I caught glimpses of the four of them they were smiling unabashedly at the display of my blooming little flower.

And in that moment everything else became irrelevant.

Guys are funny creatures because as far as they are concerned, a woman is all tits and ass until they see her inner sanctum and then suddenly her flower is all that exists to the exclusion of everything else.

Without warning, I abruptly stood up and climbed on to the bed. It worked out well that it was a double bed with plenty of room for all of us. A quick thought flashed through my head as I remembered Elwira's narrow bed and how it'd been a tight squeeze even for us.

With thoughts of Elwira invading my mind, guilt soared once more and I knew what I was doing was right. My resolve hadn't slackened and nor would it. Her momentary intrusion made sure of that. I reclined on the bed expansively with my delicate petals fully displayed between my spread legs.

'Right boys, will you stop fucking about and start fucking me.'

I've never seen people take their clothes off so quickly and before I knew it, Adam was lapping between my legs, David had stuck his cock into my face and I took it into my mouth while the other two went for my breasts again. I sucked enthusiastically using a hand to pump as I went. David's member was firm but slightly spongey as I worked my mouth around it. At the same time, warm tongues and groping hands covered my body with sensation.

They were warming up and slowly getting more into it, but they still weren't being brutal enough. I didn't want tender sex. Tenderness is compassion and compassion is a kind of love.

Love is incomprehensible and lost on me.

I wanted it rough and as hard as possible. How can I encourage them to hurt me without freaking them out? Poor regular *vanilla* guys had no idea what they'd got themselves into when agreeing to fuck me. Nobody had touched me since Elwira and masturbation just isn't the same. I had to show more initiative and get them going somehow. They were into it, but still playing quite safe.

It's really unnatural for me to take control, but as I'd learnt with Elwira I will if necessary.

The last thing I wanted was for them to politely take it in turns, doing me like a missionary, and saying their prayers afterwards and if I wasn't careful this was exactly what they'd end up doing. After all, as I previously mentioned, the English are the best queuers in the world and they'd even queue up for me, as though getting on and off a bus.

Even though I'd led Elwira when necessary I didn't really want to have to do the same here and now. With Elwira it had been her inexperience, but with these guys I got the sense that it was about them not being sure how far they could go with me. I needed them to be in control and for that, they needed to understand that my limits were far beyond theirs. I could only show them and then finally they might start giving me what I really needed.

Then I had an idea which would blow them out of the water while fulfilling a long-held personal fantasy too. I wriggled free of their attentions and to their credit, they let go and didn't try hold on to me. It was bizarre that they seemed to have more respect for my limits than I had for myself, but as contradictory as it sounds I found their restraint frustratingly restrictive.

'Adam, lay on your back. The rest of you just give me a minute, but get your condoms out. Give me one.'

I squatted next to Adam. Remaining stable on the springy mattress was quite difficult, but somehow I found my balance. I took hold of his cock and now pulled his tight skin up and down. While giving him a hand job, I dipped the fingers from my free hand into my honey pot.

Out of the four of them, Adam was the most hesitant and even a bit reluctant. I knew that he too wanted to fuck me, but he was just a bit too concerned about my welfare. Pushing him to his limits while giving the others some idea of what I can take, might just provoke them, in turn, to push harder and take me ever further.

Disarming Adam's inhibitions and allaying his concerns was a battle I just had to win.

From the constant dipping and rubbing, my fingers were now lubed up with my viscous slime. I reached further under myself while continuing to yank on Adam's staff I started toying with my little asshole. I touched it tentatively for a couple of seconds before penetrating it with one slopping ready finger, which slid in so easily that I immediately pulled it back out and did it again only this time I added a second finger. This was much tighter and while it had offered little initial resistance to one finger, two was almost too much. My inner circle constricted and tried to eject me. Ignoring the urging of my body I pushed deeper and forced my ass to stretch and give way. It wasn't that what I was doing was particularly painful; it was just that my ass was unyielding.

I must admit that from my squatting position, to focus on both fingering myself and stroking Adam up and down took a lot of concentration. It was a variation of patting your head and rubbing your belly at the same time. However, I've always been a good student of deviancy and this was a new lesson for me to learn.

I glanced around from time to time, and saw the other boys were standing proud and watching. Even though they couldn't see clearly what I was doing they must have had a fair idea and were, if possible, even further captivated by me. It seemed that they were almost too embarrassed to wank, but as their sprigs sprang and bounced none of them could resist the occasional stroke.

When I was ready, I rolled the condom onto Adam's cock. It was hot, swollen and agitated and its head was a purple balloon almost ready to burst—but not too soon I hoped. I held his member vertically while I stepped astride him and I then eased myself onto him while giving him a view of my tight cheeks and sinuous back. I only paused when his cock pressed against my lubed up asshole. Now I was precisely positioned and ready, I held his cock firmly like a pillar and lowered myself onto him. His cock bent slightly under my weight before my ass surrendered a bit at a time and I took it really slowly until I was almost sitting on him with his member most of the way inside me. I wasn't fully stretched and it became more painful the deeper he went.

I'd opened my sphincters myself, but my fingers aren't that fat or long!

A dull pain across the front of my belly didn't deter me and I comforted myself with the knowledge that the pain was all a part of the punishment I was so deserving of. I won't deny that it was terrible, more than uncomfortable, but to reach me it was totally necessary. His cock felt tight in my constricted ass so I started bouncing and almost screamed as I forced myself open in the most carnal of ways. I was determined to take it all and for it to hurt. When it came down to it, this was exactly why I was here.

Finally, punishment… it's started…

Thinking back, I'm surprised I didn't break his cock. After piercing myself with his bayonet for a few minutes my ass gave up the fight, and I found that I was more able to slide up and down his entire length. Muscles had yielded and as my body adjusted, the pain subsided. Now I was a bit more comfortable with the unnatural penetration, I stopped and leant back. I rested my hands on Adam's shoulders and kept myself impaled deep on his shaft. I opened my legs and gave the others a sight of Adam inside me and my greedy love hole. It was alone and unattended, but ready and eager to please.

'So who's coming *in* to play?'

No surprise when Carl was there. He seemed to be the alpha in the group and so it only naturally followed that he'd lead. He rolled a condom on and knelt in front of me and pushed his way inside and for the first time ever, I had a real cock in both my ass and love channel. It was really uncomfortable and more than a bit painful, but I bucked and fucked like I loved it. I groaned in what to them sounded like pleasure, but was really the natural soundtrack to the pummelling they were giving me.

The tension of the two cocks stretched and distorted me as they pumped with no coordination or rhythm and I forced a smile and uttered encouragement as though I was loving every second of it. This was especially hard when they both penetrated me deeply at the same time and the double stab threatened to break me. I even lifted my legs and clenched them around Carl's waist the best I could to maintain the fiction of my nymphomaniac greed.

Even though they were more into it now, I still sensed that they needed an unquestionably clear signal to show them that I was really into what they were doing to me and enjoying every moment of it, even if the truth was that I was taking a well-deserved punishment. I smiled and encouraged them and begged for more. The more they gave, the more I played the role of the fun-loving slut. Their banging against my loins was becoming increasingly painful and my insides started to really feel the abuse they were taking.

The paradox was that I needed the pain, but I couldn't show them that I was suffering. I feared that if they caught even a hint of my discomfort that they'd stop. There was no way I could allow that to happen.

It was hard, but I needed to keep going. I closed my eyes and just focussed on the moment and every time they raised their energy levels so did I. Whatever they did I mirrored it right back at them. My body was already suffering, but my mind was still strong and nowhere near the brokenness that I was so desperate to find. I had no idea how to break my mind and I began to doubt whether four guys was enough. All I could do was keep going and get the others more involved. Just maybe then it'd take me to the mental edge I needed and maybe even push me over it.

A broken mind will give me the oblivion I am seeking.

'Come here, Barry.' I pointed at my mouth and he quickly obliged and soon I was rocking against two hard cocks with another one in my mouth. Dave watched on in disbelief as my ass slapped against Adam's lower belly and Carl drove relentlessly into me from the front.

A girl has only got three holes so what could I do? I could alternate sucking, but another idea started to form in my mind. If they weren't aware of how dirty I was by now, they'd soon know.

My mind, drifting into fantasy, was abruptly brought back to reality when soon—too soon—Carl was done. With rasping breaths, quivering legs and a claw-like grip on my hips, he pulled me closer and shot his load into his condom that was burrowed deep inside the stem of my flower. He took a few minutes to expel the last of the shudders from his body, as pleasure waned and when he was done he climbed off me, with the same sentiment as one has when getting off a bus. I immediately closed my legs in a silent signal that shut everybody else out so I could concentrate on Adam and Barry.

Below me, Adam was getting more and more excited. His hardness felt huge inside me and as he neared his end, his grip on my hips tightened. His rough fingers dug into my delicate soft flesh in a mirrored repetition of what Carl had done just a few moments ago.

In the meantime, Barry too was getting close and it was a pleasant shock when he finally grabbed my head and started pumping it backwards and forwards. At last, they were beginning to understand what I wanted and the more abusive and the rougher the better. I quickly got control of my gag reflex, as his fleshy sword glanced off the back of my tongue deep in the recesses of my mouth. I sealed my lips against his sliding skin and his breathing became increasingly more erratic. He soon arrived and he announced it with trembling legs and knocking knees as he sprayed his hot seed into my mouth.

I could actually feel the fat vein in his cock pulse in my mouth and against my lips as he emptied his load into me. He tried to pull away, but I'd got him this far and I wasn't going to waste his cream. I followed him with my face and somehow, without losing my balance, I reached a hand behind him and pulled his ass in. There was no way I was strong enough to hold him there, but now he understood what I wanted he allowed me to suck him dry and only when he began to melt in my mouth, did I think about letting him go. Even so, I only released him after I'd swallowed every last drop, He still twitched from time to time as I ran my tongue along the underside of his rim to get the last of any stubborn residue that remained on his pathetic flaccid flesh.

Thinking like that reminded me for just a second of the contempt Dominika has for what she calls man meat. It stands all proud and then vomits before it withers and dies.

There wasn't any time for my mind to wander, because as I was finishing with Barry, Adam shook below me and let out a long groan as he too filled his greasy balloon that was firmly inside implanted inside my dark hole. As he came, his throbbing cock tightened inside me in its final throes of pleasure and my inevitable constriction started to strangle him, even before he lost the last of his potency. His momentum, so virile to begin with, soon wavered and finally faltered. His strength faded quickly and my well-trained ass quickly ejected him, spent and useless.

Carl was easing his condom off and seemed ready to dispose of it. Despite the distractions, I'd been watching and waiting for this moment.

And now they will see the depths of my depravity and understand they can push me even harder.

'Wait Carl,' I said and held out a hand. He came to me and I took the condom from him and sucked the sperm out of it and then I turned once more to Adam's shrivelled worm and took his condom too. His sperm followed Carl's that in turn had followed Barry's.

Three loads of sperm and salt was all I could taste, creamy dirty salt, a just dessert for the disgusting whore I am.

Actually, no, it wasn't dessert; we'd just only begun and if I had my way I'd take a lot more sperm before the night was over. It might have been breakfast and nothing more. Some calories to get me started if you like.

Then I was alone on the bed with only David's angry cock unserved. I could already see he was bigger than the others and even though I was already quite sore from the double ramming I'd just taken, I knew what I had to do. I propped myself up and looked at him between my beckoning knees with my flower opened and ready to be exploited again. He was already frustrated through the lack of involvement. I wondered how far I could push him.

I can always try.

'Come on then. What are you waiting for? Can't you get it up?' I teased.

It was like a red rag to a bull. He jumped on top of me almost faster than I was ready and grabbed me by the throat and thrust his throbbing monster inside me as far as it could go. Although my hole had just been used and was quite ready, such was his size that it stung as he rammed home, true and deep. There were no tentative or gentle strokes. He was a rampant animal, focussed only on serving his aching cock. His hand tightened around my throat and just for a moment I got scared, but then he relaxed his grip a little, so that I could at least breathe.

'Dare to mock me, bitch!'

He wasn't gentle. He withdrew almost completely and then stabbed home again as deep as he could. I flinched in pain—pain that I hated and desired at the same time. Now he'd started he kept assaulting me with long painful jabs and hurting me until my soft flesh yielded and taking his whole length became bearable. This is exactly the right way to describe what he was doing because it still felt like his mighty trunk could break me in half.

Finally, this is justice, this is my punishment...

I set my face and endured and our bodies merged as he found his rhythm. I felt strangely emotionless as he used me. I was a fuck machine and this was nothing more than physics, just friction in motion. There was nothing gentle about David, but his brutal beastliness reached me in ways that the others weren't even beginning to understand. As he continued his fuck stampede, my insides splayed and succumbed to his pounding might. My flesh was tenderised and my insides finally stopped stinging and yet this wasn't an end to my pain as his workout continued to inflict more suffering on me. Only now it wasn't my insides that protested. His rhythmic banging felt like the persistent hammering of a sensitive bruise each time his legs slapped against my lean, tight thighs. His stamina wasn't weakening and he was ramming like a bull. A sudden fear gripped me.

'Show me your cock in its glory,' I suddenly demanded imperiously.

It wasn't that I wanted him to stop, despite the pain. I thought his efforts might have ruptured the condom, but when he pulled it out, I could see that it had stood up to the rigours of his impaling. I must admit though he was huge, even bigger than before he'd penetrated me. He was definitely, as I'd originally thought, much larger than the other three. Armed and ready and with it standing proud in front of me, I'd finally found a weapon that really could destroy me. It was a sledgehammer and I needed to push him into using it with greater brutality.

I need to make him angrier.

'Now fuck me properly and hurt me if you dare. Show me what kind of a man you are,' I said before noisily clearing my throat and spitting in his face. A large glob flew out of my mouth and caught him squarely on his cheek. For the briefest of seconds, his face registered shock before a new rage started burning in his eyes.

He deserves this for treating me bad, and I deserve worse for betraying Dominika and destroying what we had. Seems like fair karma to me.

Dominika...

An image of her filled my mind. Her innocence and the pain I'd caused her reaffirmed once more that what I was doing was absolutely the right thing to do.

My pain was incomparable to the torment in my mind because of what I'd done to her and with that, I compelled myself to carry on.

He may have the weapon to break me but even he is failing to reach my mind.

Spitting and outright defiance is very unlike me. I certainly would never even dream of behaving like this with Dominika. David isn't her though and I didn't know him nor care for his feelings or pride.

I won't be swayed from my mission and the more I provoke the four of them, the harder they'll be and the more they'll hurt me and that's all that matters.

I'll make them so fucking angry that they might just dislodge my guilt and absolve my sins. David is already on the right path, I just need to get the others on board.

If David was driven before, now he was possessed. Lust and anger consumed him and he was turning it all back on me. With one hand he wiped the spit off his face, while reaching out, and grabbing my throat with the other. His grip was tight, but I could still breathe and he was using it more to balance over me. He smeared my spit into my face and now with his weight fully pressing against me, his dull blade seemed even more powerful. He carried on ramming home as deep and hard as he could without consideration or feeling. I looked at him and he was like a demon, full of spite and hate.

I groaned under the weight of his almost Neanderthal masculinity and the perverse pleasure he was giving me. I hadn't been looking for it, but I was so excited that I could have gone off like a bomb. As my arousal grew, I started to move my hips in the opposite direction to him.

Despite the pain, I was determined to fuck him back just as hard as he was fucking me. Each time our hips came together he went deeper and soon he couldn't match my lustful dance and pure energy. It forced him to change to rapid, shallower strokes that were almost beyond everything I had to give.

But my will was still stronger.

'Are you fucking me or am I fucking you, you fucking cunt?' I mocked in a deliberate ploy to goad him even more.

I cleared my throat of saliva again and ejected it all over his face. I really wanted to push him as far as he could go and over the edge if possible.

'Fuck me, you useless cunt,' I screamed in defiance.

My repeated use of the C-word was deliberate and it wasn't because I lacked imagination. As far as I know, it's the worst word in the English language and almost guaranteed a reaction.

Again he wiped it off and growled at me, 'You dirty little fucking bitch.'

He pulled his cock out of me and rolled me over before pulling my hips up. Then he was behind me. A quick finger found its way into my ass and he pushed it in without mercy or consideration. I already knew what was coming so it was no surprise when he quickly followed his finger with something much, much fatter.

Even though my sphincters had been open to Adam just a few minutes ago, they were reluctant to give way again, especially to such a brutal assault. The sting almost transcended endurance as he pushed inside with a single thrust. Instinctively, my body betrayed my wishes and tried to recoil from him, but he'd clamped down on my hips with his hands and pulled my hips against him. I was going nowhere. He went deep and I had to bite down on my bottom lip to suppress a barely containable scream as I took his entire length.

God never designed my dark space to be used as a fuck hole and even though, for a few years now, I'd given it over to be used in such a way, it'd never been assailed as brutally as this. I felt an intense pain deep inside my belly as he skewered me and I dreaded to think what he was doing to my insides. It was so much harder than when I'd impaled myself on Adam. The difference then was that I'd been in control. Never in my life had I experienced such penetrative pain.

Finally, we've arrived…

The thought hit me with a strange, cold, mental detachment that was contrary to the tears that began to well in my eyes.

'Stop, David! You're hurting her.'

Adam!

My face must have betrayed me. I couldn't disguise the torment from David's physical onslaught. My body was breaking, but my mind remained strong. I just needed them to push through and then finally my mind too will be released from the chains of guilt and condemnation that continued to fill my mind despite the obvious distractions. My purpose was still the same. Nothing had changed.

Shut the fuck up, Adam. This is my punishment.

David wavered for a second, torn between his lust and his friend's warning. I was in danger of losing him. I had to get him back.

'Fuck me, you cunt, ignore him; he doesn't know what I want.' I couldn't see him, so I added for good measure, 'Unless you can't stand up to it.'

With that, David renewed his efforts, but had little left to give and within a minute the inevitable tremor and tightening of weakening legs indicated he was reaching his zenith and seconds later he exploded inside my ass. As he did so, he pulled back on my hips to push his release even deeper inside. His spasming legs no longer supported him and I took his full weight on my hips. He then collapsed and I too gave way leaving me trapped underneath him and there we rested with me almost entombed in his body that covered my back and was pressing me into the mattress.

We couldn't stay like that though. After a minute or two I felt my ass begin to tighten as his spent member lost its power. It was another kind of pain as it tried to reclaim space that didn't exist and I started squeezing him out.

'Feed me,' I almost begged when my ass finally rejected his shrinking appendage. He pulled away from me and now free from his imprisoning body I rolled over and sat up and took his condom off him and tipped its contents into my mouth. It was disgusting but necessary and something I'd decided to do from the outset.

I'd eaten from the other three—so why should he be any different?

I tasted his cream, contaminated with the rubbery flavour of the condom and swallowed it down. When he thought the last drop has trickled out, he started to move away, but I took his hands in mine and pushed a finger into the teat to turn it inside out and then I sucked on it to get every last one of his swimmers.

To do anything less would be a waste.

What was happening was only fuel to my fire. I was still coherent and my mind was sharp. As sore as I was deep inside, with ass burning hot from the pounding it had received, I needed more. I ached all over, my muscles weren't used to being so abused—and certainly not recently—but the guys still hadn't hurt me enough. They were getting closer to giving me what I wanted, but still falling short. My mind screamed to be pushed over the edge and while it still demanded more it meant it still remained untouched and so my body just had to endure. I'd only just got started and destruction was still far off.

You've all cum once. How much more have you got left? You're not that old. Surely there's more?

'Is that all you've got,' I mocked with a sneer. 'You should be able to keep going all night.'

'Fucking hell, girl! Give us a moment,' David protested.

This was when a switch in my mind flipped and I realised that my appetite was beginning to freak them out. Adam especially was right on the edge. Whatever they felt, I couldn't help but notice that other than David, who was spent for now, their cocks were reinvigorated.

How can I train these sweet boys to give me what I need?

I only did what came instinctively. I rolled once more onto my back and began to finger myself. I wasn't particularly stimulating myself. I was doing it more for their benefit than mine. As I rubbed and teased, I parted my labia with nimble fingers to expose my inner depths, a place I just knew they all wanted to be.

My solo show will drive them mad with desire for me again and once more I will be ravaged by their hardened cocks.

I entertained them for a few minutes and witnessed a resurrection of Carl's dead bone, which I naturally went for when I got off the bed and went and stood next to him. I still assumed that Carl or David were the alphas in the group and so, especially now he'd hardened again, Carl was my natural target.

'What are you going to do with that, just stand there and point it at me? A gun is only useful if fired.'

I grabbed him and started wanking him off furiously and Barry came closer so I grabbed him too. Barry's swollen but less than firm cock stood up all proud literally as soon as I touched it. Two hard cocks meant that they were both ready to go again.

They groped me with clumsy hands, grabbing at my breasts and ass and now they were in range, I had a chance to educate them. I took hold of Barry's hand and positioned it over one of my breasts and took his finger and thumb and placed them over my nipple and squeezed them tightly together forcing him to pinch hard.

I groaned in approval, as I pressed even harder and told him he could do it as hard as he liked. Then I turned my attention to Carl, who by now had reached down and was stroking my used love hole.

'Not like that, like this,' I told him as I gripped his fingers together to form a blunt triangle in an echo of something Elwira had done to me. 'Now try to get them inside me. And give me your other hand.'

He quietly obliged. My normal need for submissiveness had given way to the need for these innocent naïve boys to hurt me, and they weren't even close to where I needed to be yet.

'Push against my ass, put a finger inside, if you want. You'll get a better grip as you force yourself inside me. I'll say absolutely clearly *no more* if it gets too much. Ignore anything else I say and carry on.'

Strangely, at that moment of all moments, I suddenly understood something new. It wasn't my usual safe word, but actually, I was offering a layer of protection and what's more, it wasn't for me, but it was for them. I'd never really thought of a safe word in such a way. I'd always considered it to be more of a restraint for Dominika and especially Kasia than a limit for me.

Dominika...

My emotions crashed back down on me. I'm sure she'd be disgusted, but she no longer had any claim on me. Once more a brief image of her burning the letter came to mind. The finality of that very act had closed every door and every chance for a future that we ever had. That more than anything had forced me into the situation that I now found myself in.

I'm not blaming you, Dominika, I'd set everything in motion, but that was the moment when all hope was lost.

Carl was pressing his fingers into me forcibly. One finger was inside my ass holding me steady while he force-fucked me with his other hand. It hurt, but now I was thinking about my lost love the physical pain was strangely numbed.

I felt like my mind and body were separated. It was almost as if it was happening to somebody else and I was just looking on. It then struck me that out of body experiences are normally associated with near-death experiences.

Is my mental detachment trying to tell me something?

I dismissed such thoughts. My mind was disconnecting, but it was going to take me a bit longer to understand why. I am what I am and I needed to fully embrace it, whatever the consequences. I was so in the moment that I wasn't even thinking of the guys any more. It was time to push them again.

'David, come and grab my throat again, like you did a few minutes ago.'

After the way I'd spat all over him, he was more than willing. Hands were all over me again, manipulating and hurting me. I was trying to stand still, but as Carl pushed and prodded at my delicate spaces, I found myself being pulled about in all directions. David's tight grip on my throat was the only thing that was keeping me upright as the three of them visited more abuse on my body. For his part, Adam was just watching in gaped disbelief.

Then David spat in my face—*and I can't say that really blame him.*

I looked at him and growled in defiance, 'That all you got, you fucking shit?'

He squeezed my neck harder and drove me backwards. Barry and Carl were forced to let go and he threw me on the bed. Then he was on me. He grabbed me by an ankle and forced me to roll onto my front and then as he changed his hold on me, he went straight between my legs grabbed my shaved pubis and pulled me up like a bitch on heat.

I heard Adam take a deep intake of breath as though he was going to intervene again, but I cut him off.

'Just remember the condom,' I almost screamed. It was as much to tell Adam to back off as it was a reminder for David.

David was so enraged that he was likely to forget, but then Adam was there.

'Use this one, mate.'

There was a brief pause. Then rough hands grabbed my ass cheeks and parted them. A hard finger found my little sore knot and was soon pushing its way in. My ass had already yielded twice, but it'd tightened once more and my ring protested even more than it had earlier. I guess it must have been bruised by now. Nonetheless, it was under attack again. It stretched unwillingly and once more my ass was violated—even if it was only by a finger.

'Yes,' I cried.

'Fucking bitch loves it.'

Then David lined his hips up behind mine and pushed all the way inside. As before, he pushed with a single brutal stroke. My muscles yielded and I stung as he distorted me with his crude implement. My stomach cramped, worse than cramped, as he went deep. He had been the last one I'd drained of his seed, but the first to enter me again. Angry sex is often the most passionate and I'm sure that I'd pissed him off the most. Only he'd suffered my imitation of a spitting cobra.

'Fuck me harder,' I begged as pain in the form of deep spasms that were racking my body tried to warn me against taking any more abuse. However close to the end of endurance my body was my accursed mind was still strong and unwavering. Until it broke, I'd keep going for at least as long as they could. My body was screaming *no more*, but my mind still needed to push through. Thoughts of protecting them were now lost in my quest for destruction.

Maybe I'll pass out and they'll continue using me. I don't care. Use me and throw me out with the rubbish. It's what Dominika would want.

Then Carl was there and he brought my consciousness back to the moment. He grabbed my head near my ears, pulled me towards his flaming standard.

David temporarily lost momentum but soon got it back. I opened my mouth and took Carl inside. He kept hold of my head and began to fuck my tonsils. For a moment I almost gagged as he banged the back of my throat clumsily, but well trained as I am, I too was quickly into my stride.

I was paralysed. I couldn't move. I was impaled in two directions as I was being spit-roasted and there were still two cocks out there to please. I rocked back and forth with absolutely no control.

Then it happened.

Like the slow measured approach of an army marching to the pounding rhythm of war drums it came upon me. The beat was relentless and to begin with the words were incoherent as they seized my mind. All I knew was sensation, no more significant than the pumping of pistons in a cylinder or the meshing of cogs. My body now disconnected completely from my mind and yet paradoxically I felt greater connection than ever before as the muffled chaos in my mind formed real words that began to reverberate inside my head.

My words, my song, my anthem!

Finally, I was nothing more than a fleshy mechanism, a device and nothing more. It was a mystery how I could be so detached from my mind and yet at the same time so finally attuned to what I'd become.

Then my body, mind and anthem merged…

Snippets of the song played round and round in my head, but always came back to the chorus that drove home exactly what I was and where I belonged. Now, at last, I was where I wanted to be and the tears began to flow. Everything the last two months had done to me finally began to find a release. Carl hesitated and pulled his cock out of my mouth. It wasn't just Adam who I was taking to the edge.

He really was concerned. 'Are you alright? Do you want us to stop?'

David couldn't see my face and just carried on regardless.

I felt a flicker of annoyance with Carl for distracting me, but I had to give him something so I smiled weakly at him for a second. 'No, carry on. Please. Hurt me. I need this.'

He was less than convinced.

'Please,' I repeated as I pleaded for him to carry on.

I needed to get back to what I had a moment ago. I didn't want a conversation I wanted oblivion, so I then reached up and cupped his balls in my hand and pulled him back into my mouth. Thanks to him, my anthem was lost and I desperately wanted it back, but in the meantime, all I could do was carry on.

His face was weirdly resigned, almost like he didn't want to carry on, but somehow deep inside he started to recognise that it was all about me and what I wanted and not his needs.

He'd lost some of his potency. He was noticeably less enthusiastic for a few minutes until he was once more convinced that I really was into the abuse I was taking. Of course, it might just have been that as his arousal returned his brain stopped working. The blood that was engorging his cock had to come from somewhere!

I went back to rolling my tongue around his enflamed head in my mouth. I jabbed the tip of my tongue into his small crease each time he pulled back and laid my tongue out like a blanket every time he pushed himself back in. Behind me I could feel David's rhythm become sporadic and once more as he passed the point of no return he lost control and dumped his load inside me as my ass massaged his meat into surrendering its seed.

As soon as he withdrew, another cock was there and pushing inside my ass.

'You really do like this, don't you?'

It was Adam, which was a surprise.

He wasn't as driven as David had been, but still, his swelling filled my black hole. He was smaller than David, but my ass closed in and was soon holding him snuggly and not too uncomfortably. Adam wasn't inflicting any new pain or harm even if his working me over was pressing against already damaged flesh. I was fully stretched and as he glided in and out of me, the pain in my stomach eased off. At the same time, his slow gentle strokes almost caressed my insides.

My attention was soon drawn back to Carl, who grabbed my head with renewed vigour. He sped up and then suddenly his legs tightened and he pulled me onto him and a spurt hit the back of my throat, quickly followed by another. I was expecting it, but I still almost choked as his seed clagged my throat. I had to push him back a bit so I could swallow, even then it didn't clear, but it was enough to be able to breathe again. Adam must have seen I was struggling and he slowed down.

I was fairly sure that I'd taken most of Carl's seed so I spat him out. 'Don't stop. Keep going, Adam.'

I looked at Barry with more greed.

'So what are you going to do?'

Then he did the perfect thing, but it was completely unexpected. He came and stood in front of me, where Carl had been just seconds earlier and he reached under me and grabbed my dangling nipples and squeezed them really hard.

'You like pain, slut?'

'Yes, give me more please,' I whined, gratefully.

Then he let go of one of my nipples and slapped me across the face. My head went with his hand.

'Barry!'

It was Adam again.

Stop protecting me please—it's not what I want. I want to be abused.

Normally, I'd be thankful for such protection—it's a role that Emilia usually plays, as a kind of guard, an additional layer for my safety—but it was the last thing I wanted here and now.

'Adam, let him be,' I breathed in a low tone.

I think Barry must have crossed his own limits after slapping me so he went once more for both nipples, but this time he started twisting like he was tuning an old radio set. New pain began to course through my body and it invigorated me. I only wished for some needles or clamps; that'd have taken my torment to another level.

Too much for them, I'm sure!

Then he grabbed me by the throat and rolled me onto one side. Adam popped out of my ass and the sudden internal contraction that followed caused a painful cramp.

'Let's swap, Adam. Don't take the condom off. Let her chew on the taste of her own arse. She'll probably love it anyway.'

I was getting confused. At first, I thought Carl was the alpha; then I thought it was David, but maybe it was Barry after all? Or maybe I just bring the worst out of people?

Although Carl had softened for a moment, only Adam seemed genuinely concerned for my welfare—not something I needed or wanted. I know I repeat myself, but destruction was my goal.

I think also, Dominika, that I need to remind you that they never went beyond any limits that I'd set. They were in control, but as contradictory as it sounds it was only to the extent of the control that I'd relinquished to them—and by that I mean all of them.

I was still on my side and Barry made a point of putting a condom on in front of my face—I think mainly to reassure me and then he squatted behind my ass. He lifted my upper cheek and pushed his fingers unthinkingly into my almost forgotten and neglected treasure like some kind of pathfinder. I was a piece of meat and he was a butcher. Then he pushed his fat English sausage inside my pink love tunnel and shuffled closer as it went in. Then with two hands, he grabbed my upturned hip and started racking my hip harshly back and forth as he slid his inflamed passion in and out of me.

Meanwhile, Adam had grabbed my head and turned it so he could position his cock. It was still a bit too high so he squatted down and eased it, still in its protective jacket, into my eager mouth. I know how I taste and it is always a matter of pride that I am clean but it was still a relief when all I could taste was ass and latex.

I pursed my lips around him to keep his helmet inside my mouth. Barry's workout was making it hard to concentrate as he pulled me about like a dog with a piece of old rag. It felt good though as he used my pink hole in a natural but somewhat mechanical way…

My mind suddenly filled with the relentless sound of my anthem and the words possessed me again…

I'm back where I need to be…

Suddenly, Barry was ready. He withdrew from me and pushed Adam aside and pulled his condom off, he almost grabbed it wrongly and caught himself just before it sprang back to cripple him. He got it off at the second attempt and he pushed himself deep into my throat. I coughed slightly fighting for control as he vigorously stroked himself a few times on the way in. The taste of latex was quickly replaced by the salt of his cum as he exploded. He too pulled me deep and pinched my nose as his lust rolled down my throat. I couldn't breathe…

…and all the time my anthem reminded me that everything that was happening was just and right…

He soon let go and I took his juice down so I could take an undeserved life-preserving breath of air. As his cum went down it clung to the sides of my throat and another cough helped it on its way. Then he pulled away and Adam was there, now without a condom and I took his load too.

I was losing count.

Have I taken eight loads now?

I was aching and felt so heavy, but my mind still hadn't crossed over. Now their passion faded my song too ebbed away. I wondered if any of them had anything left because, although I was tiring and hurting like one massive bruise, I still wasn't completely broken. My mind still screamed at me and my mission for personal annihilation was still incomplete. I needed more…

All four of them needed some recovery time—or were they fully drained? What could I do to keep things going?

'Come on boys!' I pleaded lustfully ignoring the pain. 'I want you to fuck me again.'

'What kind of monster are you? We're knackered, give us some time,' Carl complained.

Then Barry was on me again. He grabbed my hair and pulled me off the bed and onto the ground and rolled me onto my front and spanked my ass.

'You really are a bad girl.'

'Yes,' I said meekly. If I'd learnt anything recently, it was that honesty has to be the way forward. My lies and deceit had cost me everything.

He spanked me again. Dominika never spanks and even when Elwira had, it'd been nothing but a big game for her. Barry's spanks were harder than Elwira's but the sting didn't really do anything for me. At best it did make me feel like an object in their hands. I was nothing more than a toy for their use. Then they were all there and rolling me around as they groped me roughly and covered my body in slaps that stung and reddened my pale flesh.

I guess I should have expected it, but it wasn't long until fingers found their way inside me again. My ass and treasure were both invaded with no intention of giving me any pleasure. It was nothing more than a brutal invasion. This has always been the historic fate of the Polish—a two-pronged attack with no chance of survival. Like the Germans and Russians had decimated us during the war I too would now suffer the same fate for being Polish.

The guys were testing and probing just to see how far they could go, and as I lay there allowing them to do exactly what they wanted to me finally, they too now understood that I was nothing more than a machine, a device given over to serve their pleasure.

When I could, I tried to peek between their legs and I could see different levels of arousal. Adam was spent, and his cock drooped pathetically between his legs and had shrivelled almost completely into his jungle of untrimmed hair. He had cum last so it was probably to be expected. Carl seemed spent too. His cock was still fat but had no power left. It remained pointing at the ground and a miracle on the magnitude of divine resurrection would be needed to get any more out of it. Initially, I'd thought he was the alpha, but as the evening had worn on it seemed less and less so. David was hard again, his monster was aroused and ready to fight again and Barry was swelling and also showing signs of new life.

David was clearly in the swing of things now and his dominating personality had found its expression in my submissive defiance. I was a challenge to his man meat, his masculinity and his sense of self. I'd treated him the worst and he'd (literally) risen to my baiting. He pulled me up to my feet and spanked my ass hard.

'Barry, get on the bed on your back. We've still got some condoms left. Party girl, wake him up and put his coat on while I put mine on.'

I'd never it put that way before but it was obvious what David meant. I went to Barry and thrust my head between his legs and took him into my mouth. As I bent over David was once more presented with a rear view of my most tender parts and once more he was on my asshole with insistent fingers. I felt as my dark hole was violated with rough callused tips as two fingers entered and tried to pull me apart. My muscles tried to contract, to resist, but David's drive wouldn't allow them and intense pain ripped through my ass as his power overcame my feeble resistance. It made it hard for me to concentrate on Barry's cock, but somehow whatever I was doing with my mouth was working and his arousal was growing.

I knew what was coming and even though I too was almost on the verge of exhaustion and bodily collapse I had to somehow find the strength. I knew my ass couldn't take much more. Barry was filling my mouth and a condom was placed in my hand. I pulled my mouth away from Barry's cock while at the same time tearing the condom out of its foil, before rolling it onto his now rapidly hardening shaft. As soon as I'd done so, David pushed me forward so I was astride Barry. I then dropped myself on him and once more my treasure was filled. As he went in, it wasn't really too painful; rather, it was uncomfortable. I was most probably bruised from one of the earlier poundings, but at that moment I couldn't think who'd done it or when it'd happened.

As anticipated, David was immediately behind me and pushed himself once more deeply into my ass without hesitation. As he'd done twice already he did it with a single stabbing stroke, but at least this time he'd spent a few minutes opening me up with his fingers, not that he'd been particularly gentle in doing so.

'Yes,' I wailed in agony.

The pain was unbearable. He wasn't kind; he had no consideration for me at all. I was there to be used and used I would be. Don't misunderstand I'm not complaining. I was getting exactly what I'd been demanding from them all night and everything that was happening was down to me and me alone.

David was deeply embedded and I was shackled by the two fleshy restraints that now had me trapped, one was diagonally stretching my honeypot and the other more horizontal, pinned me helplessly. Grasping, pinching fingers dug into my hips and once more they rocked themselves in and out of my broken body. From underneath Barry's strokes were short and rapid, but David once again was determined to crucify me with his hammer. I felt every moment as long strong strokes, sped up the abject destruction of my ass and suddenly when it couldn't take any more I felt my delicate inner flesh tear and with it, I understood that I'd given almost everything that I could. My body was finally giving out on me. I just had to endure their final exertions. To deny them their cum, would be really unfair and their frustration would be their lasting memory of the evening.

The guys were oblivious anyway. They kept pumping me with their hard rods and even though I was through I was still determined and proud enough not to show any weakness and surrender to these men, who were finally overwhelming me. If I showed them my true state, they'd stop and both they and I would be denied.

I am nothing more than a machine, I reminded myself. I dug deep into my final reserves of power because I'd only be able to keep going if my will prevailed over my trashed body. It was now a case of whose stamina would last longer. I was in agony and every little movement only made it worse. David was wielding his hammer as he'd done all night with long, plunging, deep thrusts. In doing so, he was probably both making it as pleasurable as possible for himself and making my suffering as bad as it could be. The skin around my damaged delicate parts burnt constantly as they pumped in and out of me. Friction inside my ass had made it hot and more painful than can be imagined and it felt like a raging fire was burning. My hips ached and my inner thighs tightened with the worst ever muscle cramps as the constant bruising momentum pushed me headlong into final oblivion.

As each double stroke lashed me with ever more pain I scrunched up my eyes and endured. My treasure was spoilt and my ass destroyed, but finally, I was getting what I needed. *I can take it,* I thought, as I experienced pain like never before. Still my mind wasn't yet broken, even if my body was. I was close, I wanted to cry, but I *will* not show weakness.

I am a machine…

David especially had zero consideration, he was focussed only on his pleasure and had no thought for my comfort and pleasure, not that I wanted any. This may sound difficult to believe, but David more than the others was giving me exactly what I'd been looking for all night. I hated him for what he was doing to me, but secretly I loved him too, because only he was truly reaching me.

Thank you, David!

Then Carl was there again. He was in front of me, but had no strength left. He was still swollen slightly, but drooping like an old tap. His manly pride remained hooded in its little fleshy sheath, but he wasn't interested in fucking me again, he had other intentions. While one hand, vice-like, gripped my throat tightly the other squeezed my nose. I held my breath for as long as I could, but he wasn't letting go. Eventually, I had to open my mouth to take a breath and this was what he'd been waiting for.

A gooey splodge of phlegm landed on my tongue.

'Eat it up, you stupid bitch.'

I did as I was told, but he still didn't let go.

I think Carl too now, and especially with what had happened earlier, finally understood that this was my desire and my wish. As disgusting at it was, I felt that he somehow did this for my benefit.

Thank you Carl.

Still this wasn't the end of my endurance or suffering. David had other ideas.

'Barry, stick your cock in her arse too. She thinks she's a porn star so let's treat her like one.'

I didn't think it was possible, but while remaining inside me, David lifted me by my hips and Barry popped out. I felt him fumbling below and then he too was pressing on my ass. David rocked my hips violently and almost slipped out before I felt a stretch like never before. I yelped as suddenly I was double penetrated by real cocks in my ass for the first time. David still had hold of me and he pushed as deep as possible and I could tell Barry wasn't as deep, but was still rocking back and forth.

'Yes,' I screamed through gritted teeth and even though I thought it impossible, my agony reached new depths. My scream expressed my pain, but I still had enough wits about me to send a clear signal to Adam. I had to stop him from getting involved again.

Carl was still holding me by my throat with one hand but his other hand had moved to my breasts and he was twisting and squeezing one of my little buds as much as hard as he could. He really had come to understand me, probably more than any of the others. In some ways, it was a shame that I only paid scant attention to him because nothing could distract me from the double thrusting I was taking in my unnatural hole.

Being double-stabbed was a version of death by a thousand cuts. I didn't think it could be any worse than it'd been a few minutes ago, but how wrong I was. My flesh burned and I ached like I can't describe. I just had to hold on until they finished, as they shattered what remained of me with relentless double hammer blows.

This was it. I was getting the destruction I'd been craving. I hurt so much and still felt that I hadn't paid enough for my sins, but there was nothing left. *Please cum soon* I was begging silently as I fought back tears of genuine agony, and with this I realised that I was finally broken. I literally couldn't take any more and needed them to finish as soon as possible, to bring everything to an end.

Maybe God is still in heaven, because David, the most vigorous of the four, released his final load into my ass almost as soon as I reached this point. He pushed down hard on me and as he shook the final vestiges of his libido into me, I thought I was going to break in half.

As David withered, he withdrew and moved away to give Barry more space. In turn, Barry was able to get even deeper inside me and carry on. Agony had reached such a level that David's withdrawal had made absolutely no difference. One cock was hurting as much as two had. Within seconds he too fired the last of his seed into my darkness. As he did so, he reached up pushed Carl's hand aside, and grabbed my breasts and pinched them brutally from underneath. I was already in so much pain that the additional torture got lost in a cacophony of agony and brokenness.

As soon as his seed had been released and his spasms passed, he shrivelled and retreated, and for the last time I expelled an invader from my body. He got up slowly and left me alone on the bed.

Used and abused and then abandoned, my ass collapsed painfully in on itself.

I was fully aware of the four of them standing and watching me so I rolled away from them and in doing so I shielded my face and feelings. All they could see was my back and ass. In those first moments I forced myself not to hold my aching stomach and rested my cheek on my hands, almost like when I fall asleep and let my mind drift.

I was on the bed alone, a pile of disgusting fleshy sweaty corruption; destroyed, but finally at least partially punished for my wrongs. I wept silently as I contemplated the fullness of my depravity and sin.

I couldn't see or hear them, but was somehow remained conscious of their presence. They were probably too exhausted and stunned by what'd happened to do anything else.

They'd given me everything and it'd only just been enough.

I couldn't hold myself in that position any longer. I pulled myself into a foetal position to try to feel some physical relief. My stomach hurt deep inside and my ass was a festering sore, a constant scream of silent protest. I could only dread what the slightest touch would feel like. My used natural hole was in constant dull pain, and my legs ached like I'd run a marathon. My entire being felt lifeless and heavy.

This was the brokenness I'd craved and desired, but missing Dominika only compounded my loneliness.

Then a gentle hand touched my shoulder. 'Are you alright?'

Adam again.

I discretely wiped my eyes and slowly sat up, facing them. I was in so much pain, and it was on so many different levels. It was like every nerve in my body had been set on fire. I couldn't move any faster. *I am a machine.* I must force myself to do what I must and there was still one more humiliation to endure.

I held my hand out, 'Condoms please.'

They all looked at each other, surprised as if to say, *Really—after all that?*

Both Barry and David's cocks had gone completely flaccid, but they hadn't removed their balloons that now drooped with the weight of my feed filling the little teats. Both condoms were blooded in an icky brown slime. They'd made me bleed, but probably hadn't even noticed. I had to move quickly. It was best if they didn't see. It'd only worry them.

First I eased the condom off Barry's cock and swallowed down the last of his lust tinged with the metallic taste of iron while concealing the condom in my palm. I even turned it inside out and sucked it to make sure I got everything—mine and his—before giving him it back. Turning it inside out also hid the evidence of my inner wounding. He was about to step back but I reached up and grabbed his balls.

'One more thing,' I barely whispered.

I took his spent power once more into my mouth and cleaned the last of the slime from his withered cock, a taste of salt and rubber. He enjoyed it, but had nothing left, he didn't even twitch. Then I did the same for David, firstly I cleaned his condom out while hiding it in a semi-closed fist and then I took him into my mouth. He swelled slightly and jumped a couple of times in my mouth, but he too had nothing left and honestly, I too was finished.

I was done and needed to go.

'I need to use your toilet,' I announced when I'd finished feeding.

I stood up slowly and, although I shouldn't have been surprised, I was shocked to realise it wasn't so easy. I really was broken, even more than I thought possible, and my whole body protested in silent defiance. I forced myself to walk correctly, but with each step my stomach and lower parts shrieked in escalating pain and cramp as they objected to the suffering that'd been inflicted on them.

I was determined not to waver or weaken or give the guys any reason for concern. I didn't need or want compassion. It'd steal away the whole point of the night.

I made it to the bathroom and almost collapsed onto the toilet after I'd closed the door and was out of their sight. I rested for a couple of minutes and took another moment to pee before forcing myself to go to the basin. I leant on it heavily and knocked my knees together to better support my weight. It was agonising, but I had to leave and at least appear decent and together when doing so.

I checked my face. My makeup was a mess of spit and ruined mascara which I washed off, the mascara took a bit more effort, but soon I was as clean as I could be. I didn't have any makeup with me, so I just left my face natural, just the way God had made me…

God… hmmm… I no longer had a soul and so there was nothing left but emptiness.

I was ready to go. Anyone would think I'd have been embarrassed to leave the bathroom, but I felt nothing, only broken, physical soreness, that was a mixture of muscular aches and internal stinging. I took a deep breath and forced myself to walk, as normally as possible through the agony, to the door. I paused, hardened my face and took a deep breath before grabbing the handle.

I was determined not to show any weakness. My humiliation and degradation were complete and it couldn't get any worse.

I stepped out and I wasn't even ashamed of my nakedness and vulnerability. I cast my eyes around the room and saw that they were all in various states of getting dressed. They too had realised the party was over.

This was a small mercy; I literally couldn't have taken any more.

I put my bra on and slipped back into my dress. I somehow managed to fit my knickers into my clutch. I feared falling if I tried to put them on and I was so chaffed between my legs that the rubbing from the thin material would have been unbearable, like a razor blade being constantly drawn across an open sore. The constant rubbing, in my mind's eye, would have quickly become excruciating. And that's without even mentioning my ass, which was burning hotter than the sun.

Next my shoes.

That was a real effort. I had to sit on the bed to put them on, and as I sat down, my body felt like collapsing through the pain. As I leant forward I felt myself retch and for a second I thought I might vomit. Somehow I got a grip of myself, but sitting on the most painful part of my body only brought more agony. It was a necessary endurance, but I got there in the end as I slipped into my heels.

All done, my next challenge was to stand up again. I'm a quick learner and had already done this twice. So I knew what to do. I got up slowly, almost too consciously, to show absolute self-control and not attract any concern or worry from the guys and especially Adam. I don't know how I did it, but I didn't even wobble. Once upright, I forced myself to walk as naturally as possible to the door while ignoring the pain.

I felt their eyes on me. In the stunned silence, they had nothing left to say.

'No strings,' I said as I closed the door and walked out of their lives forever.

Part 6: Ania Is Rescued

As soon as I closed the door, I gasped in agony and bent over slightly in a vain attempt to find relief. I gripped my stomach with one hand and used the other to steady myself against the corridor wall. It didn't help. I needed a moment to get myself together.

I can't stay here. I might be seen, or even worse, the guys might come out looking for me.

I had no other choice, so with a reserve of strength that I thought had long been exhausted, I forced myself upright and, as my insides tightened and protested silently in agony, I staggered to the lift. Every step was an effort and even more so because I was determined to make my gait look as normal as possible.

I barely made it.

I pressed the button for the ground floor. My stomach was in knots, but I refused to hold it again. I needed to look as natural and normal as possible. I had to lean against the wall while I waited. I might be mistaken as being a bit drunk if discovered and I could wave anybody off with such a feasible excuse.

The lift finally came, and even though waiting had felt like an eternity, in reality it probably hadn't taken that long. The doors parted and I was grateful to see that it was empty inside, so I entered slowly. I immediately made my way to the back wall and leant heavily against it. I ached all over and I can't even begin to describe the pain that was racking the inside my body. It was sharp and unrelenting and spasmodically it intensified almost beyond all endurance. It was like nothing I'd ever experienced or wish to experience again.

I had no idea how I would make it home, even getting out of the hotel seemed to be a challenge too far.

On its way down, the lift stopped occasionally and a few people got in. No longer alone, I stood up straight but still relied on a supporting hand to look as casual and natural as possible and maintain the deceit that all was fine. I forced a poker face each time one of those higher waves struck with the only sign of my inner agony being my whitened knuckles as I grasped the metal bar tighter as I rode it out. When the lift reached the ground floor, I waited for everyone else to get out before stepping out last.

I needed to sit down again. I couldn't allow myself to collapse in public and risk discovery. A doctor would assume I'd been raped and I had to protect the guys. They hadn't done anything wrong and I knew that whatever had happened back in the hotel room, it certainly wasn't rape.

The hotel toilets off the atrium were my safest and nearest option. I didn't need to go, but as another wave of pain hit me and the weakness that followed threatened to take my consciousness, I knew that I needed to move fast and at the same time make sure I didn't collapse into a heap. I was surprised that the pain was only getting worse. I'd foolishly expected that when I left the room, I'd only get stronger with each passing moment.

Thinking like this brought me back to what I'd done. Judging by how I was now feeling, I assumed that I must have initially been so shell-shocked and numb that I couldn't feel anything. This, in turn, had given me just enough strength to get out of the room. But now just a few minutes later, I was confronted by the terrible reality of the consequences of my actions. And now I was worried that I might really have hurt myself.

It might have been better If I'd died.

But that wasn't the reality that I had to deal with in the here and now. I somehow kept myself together long enough to reach the toilet and lock myself in a cubicle. The lid was already up so I turned around and put my hands on the back of the seat. As I tried to lower myself gently, my legs gave way and I fell onto the toilet with a slight bang that slapped the back of my legs as I landed heavily on the seat.

On impact, a shot of pain ran through my body and I became acutely aware that I it wasn't only the internal pain that was a problem. My muscles were also aching like I'd run a marathon. They were so solid that even sitting gave me no relief. I've never known a toilet seat to be so hard. At least sitting down relaxed my inner parts a bit and there was some respite in that. I hitched my dress up to my hips and checked myself below, starting with my fuck hole.

This is all I am a fleshy fuck hole; used and abused. Actually no… my inner voice disagreed with itself… *All I am is nothing but a lost little collection of fuck holes.*

My flower was damaged and tender to touch, there was absolutely no doubt it was bruised and as I moved, I gently pressed a finger between my labia but didn't penetrate myself. It too was tender to the touch so I moved on quickly rather than risk exacerbating the discomfort. I didn't even dare to consider exploring my insides. They'd had enough attention. My inner thighs were almost as sensitive and hard as my muscles. The pounding I'd taken had left everything stretched and taut with overuse.

Then, because I knew I couldn't put it off any longer, I reached a bit further and dipped my fingers into my well-used unnatural hole. As expected, the constant resounding sting that had been my constant companion, even before the guys had finished using me, accelerated a hundredfold at the merest touch. It was like I touched myself with a burning ember. I could hardly keep my fingers in contact without wanting to scream and cry, but I had to. It was necessary to see what damage I'd done to myself. The skin felt flaky, which I kind of expected. I remembered with a shudder the moment when their exertions had shredded the delicate skin inside my dark hole.

I had literally felt my ass give way.

Too painful to touch for more than a second or two, I moved my hand away and saw my fingers were flecked with blood. It wasn't the dark red that had coated their condoms, rather it was an almost unnatural fluorescing red. At this unusual sight, a knot of fear tightened my stomach as I convinced myself that I'd really hurt myself.

My fear was strangely comforting because I understand it and demanded an immediate response.

I needed to confirm my worst fears so I took some toilet paper and touched it to my ass. It stung again like a thousand bees, and then I had a look. My ass was bleeding, but I was relieved to see that it wasn't excessive. There were spots, but no continuous flow. It seemed to be from the broken skin rather than anything more serious—but it still hurt like hell.

The relief was only momentary though as the fullness of what I'd done and who I'd become hit home in a torrid flurry of emotion. Over the last six weeks, and even as the guys had finished me off tonight, I'd experienced flashes of conscience and disgust, but nothing like now.

I was worse than filthy, I was less than a whore and I was more degenerate than the devil himself. I was lower than all existence and worthy of nothing. Shit was of greater value.

I wanted to hurt myself more, but had no strength or will to do so.

Dominika, why did I destroy everything?

I sobbed to myself. Waves of guilt-ridden pain washed over me with increasing power and attacked and tore at my stomach. I clutched myself and bent forward to find solace, but it offered no relief.

I hid my face in my hands, my pure disgusting shame open before God to judge. *I am nothing* I thought, *not even a machine.*

I wanted to hurt myself more, but had no strength or will to do so.

I hadn't been strong. I hadn't thought about my actions or the consequences. I hadn't had enough discipline. I hadn't treated Dominika as she deserved. I hadn't...

I wanted to hurt myself more, but had no strength or will to do so.

I had betrayed her. I had left her no choice. She had been right to burn my letter and I had brought my loneliness and judgment down on myself. I had deserved the destruction I had endured. I had deserved the pain I was in. I had deserved even more. I had...

A sudden shooting pain inside my ass lifted me from my depressing spiral. It was like a massive cramp as my insides rebelled against the repeated impalement they'd suffered. Another surge ripped through me and I almost yelled. I clenched my buttocks together for fear of my insides literally falling out and pressed my hands against the sides of the cubicle as I braced myself for another wave.

It helped.

I rode the pulsating pain out as its sharpness slowly dissipated in serious of receding ripples until, once more, my body settled into the constant agony that had become my new reality. I'm not sure if my changed posture really made any difference, maybe the physical bracing had just helped me to mentally prepare for each crashing wave.

The fresh waves of pain, as much as they'd startled me had achieved something in that they brought me back from the brink. They'd snapped me out of my abject desolation and saved me from straying too close to the abyss that I'd stared down just a few long weeks ago. Once more I was thinking clearly, probably for the first time since before I'd met the Germans in the first hotel bar.

I needed to get out of here and I needed help.

I need you, Dominika.

I reached for my phone and went for her number on autopilot as I'd done so many times before and then I stopped. In Dominika's world, I don't even exist anymore. She'd ignore a call, 20 calls, 50 calls. She'd ignore me forever. Yet I needed her.

Then I realised that only one person would answer my call. It was getting late, but I was surprised to see that it wasn't as late as I'd thought it'd be. I checked my phone—23.15. I placed the call.

'Hi Ania.'

'Hey Emilia,' I almost cried in relief. 'I need your help. Please come to me. Come in a taxi. I'll pay. Please Em, come quickly.'

'What happened?'

'Just come to Novotel Centrum.'

'Ania, you're scaring me. What is it?'

'I'm hurt. I need to come home.'

'How? What happened?'

'I hate myself. I want to die,' and I meant it even if I was too frightened to open my own door to the eternal darkness.

'Ania, of course I'll come, but tell me what happened?'

'I hate myself,' I repeated. 'I picked up four guys and let them use me. It's what I deserve after Dominika. I ruined everything. I wanted them to destroy me.'

There was a slight pause as Emilia absorbed the impact of what I told her.

'Did they rape you?' Emilia's voice had changed as her concern for me increased a hundredfold or even a thousandfold.

'No, I asked them to do what they did.'

'Why?'

'Not now, Emilia,' I said flatly, maybe even a bit harshly. 'Please just come. You're the only one who still cares—at least a little bit.'

'Don't hang up, Ania. Give me 20 seconds.'

There was a brief pause, the sound of a door opening, then talking in faded voices.

'It's Ania. Dominika, she really needs you. Call a taxi.'

'Tell her to call Elwira.'

That stung—even more than my ass. I nearly hung up, but then Emilia spoke again. 'It's you she needs. She was stupid with Elwira, but it's you she loves. Go to her.'

This is Emilia. Once she makes her mind up, there is no discussion.

'Ania, are you still there?'

'Yes,' I barely whispered.

'We're coming to get you.'

She didn't specify who *we* were, but I'd heard the conversation. It was Dominika who I wanted, but at the same time I was scared to face her and for her to see me in this state. Since she'd burnt the letter, I couldn't even stand the thought of being in the same flat with her despite my heart's constant yearning for her. I knew I was nothing and I didn't deserve anything from her.

'Ania, I am going to hang up now, but I'll call you when we get there. Novotel Centrum?'

'Yes. Please come quickly. I'm hurting really bad.'

Click—silence and I was alone again.

I stayed in the toilet and closed my eyes. I wanted the last two months to disappear. I wanted to wake up next to Dominika and for her to stroke my hair and tell me that everything was alright.

Dominika—shit—she's on her way! How can I face her?

Panic entered me and I started shaking. It was more overwhelming than the physical pain that continued to consume me.

Dominika and me; purity and abomination, sanctity and deviance. What will I say? What will she say?

The minutes ticked by slowly, From time to time I heard other women pop in and out to do what they needed to before leaving again. I stared at my phone just longing for it to ring. It was probably only 20 minutes, but it was an eternity. My phone finally rang—it was Emilia. I answered.

'Ania, where are you?'

'In the toilets.'

'Come out into the atrium. See you soon.'

Click—the call ended.

Emilia was here, but I couldn't hear Dominika. I didn't know whether to be saddened or relieved. As I pulled myself up, my whole body protested and I felt ten times heavier than ever. My leg muscles strained as they took my weight and the pain deep in my ass and lower bowels seized hold of me again. My ass tightened, as I straightened myself up slowly, my abused ring stung in an ever-increasing surge as a reminder of my debauchery and sin.

One foot in front of the other, I said silently to myself as I forced myself out of the protective cubicle that'd been a sanctuary, at least for a short time. Every step hurt. My ass chaffed as I walked and my lower stomach felt like it had been punched, and lower down near my intimate inverted triangle it felt even worse and I can't even describe how the inside of my ass screamed in objection to the slightest movement. I opened the door and stepped into the atrium and looked around.

It took me a moment and then…

Shit!

I saw Dominika—and she was on her own!

She saw me almost as soon as I saw her. She rushed over and took me by both hands and eased me into a nearby seat and perched on the edge next to me. I grimaced as I sat, but she didn't let go. She was oblivious to her surroundings or simply didn't care what others saw. Her eyes were on me.

'What have you done, you stupid girl?'

Her tone was harsh, but her eyes were soft.

'Can we just go home?' I cried pitifully.

'Do you need a doctor or to go to the hospital?'

'I just want to go home. I'm sorry, Dominika, so sorry. I need you. I'm sorry.' I was on the verge of completely breaking down.

'Enough of that,' she said sharply. 'Let's get a taxi.'

Her actions and words were a contradiction and I was confused. She did put a comforting arm around me and I wrapped an arm around her waist. She didn't resist my touch, but then she almost force-marched me out of the hotel. It was hard keeping pace with her, and every step hurt like hell, but her physical closeness was a reassuring support. I remember thinking how cool the air felt outside as we left. The mugginess of the early evening had somehow evaporated while I'd been in the hotel.

There's a small taxi rank in front of the hotel, so we didn't have to wait around. We approached the first one and she opened one of the back doors and helped me in before putting my seatbelt on. Once secured, she went and got in from the other side and put her arm back around my shoulder. I rested my head into her neck. Normally we are so discrete in public, but she only had thoughts for me and no consideration for the rest of the world.

'Is she drunk?' The taxi driver asked.

'No, she's upset. She's just had a bit of a shock,' Dominika answered plainly. 'She just needs to get home. She won't be sick if that's what you are worried about.'

In my state, I couldn't tell if he bought what Dominika told him or not, but it's a dangerous thing for any guy to disagree with her and all he could do was nod in mute agreement and take the fare.

Dominika told him our address and then we were on our way. We rode in silence, but she never let go of me. I know it takes about ten to fifteen minutes, depending on traffic lights, but time had become irrelevant. All I knew was Dominika was there and that was all that mattered.

I was grateful that the short journey was relatively smooth and didn't make me feel any worse. When we got home she paid for the taxi—after easily overcoming my attempted insistence to pay. Despite my ordeal I was fully alert and aware of what was going on around me. I'd only drunk two vodkas earlier and their effect had long worn off anyway.

How can I expect anything from Dominika?

Once she paid, she got out of the taxi and came around to my side and opened the door. She had to help me climb out of the taxi and back to my feet, but she never left my side and remained in constant physical contact with me. The steps in the stairwell were a challenge, but Dominika helped me all the way. When we got to the door she leant me carefully against the wall for a few seconds so she could free her hands. She unlocked the door and as soon as we entered both Emilia and Kasia rushed out of their room to see what was happening. Emilia fussed around me and Kasia kept a cool, detached distance while Dominika knelt in front of me and eased my heels off before removing her own shoes.

'Thanks girls,' Dominika said, as she stood up, to call an end to the fretting. 'I'll call you if I need anything. Ania, come with me.'

We went to our room and she gently led me to the sofa and beckoned me to sit down. As soon as I realised what she wanted, I stiffened and refused to go any further despite her urgings.

'I'm bleeding, Dominika,' I explained in a low tone.

'Let me have a look.'

I have absolutely no resistance to Dominika and so I passively allowed her to lift my dress.

'No knickers?'

I mutely nodded, not sure what to say.

For a moment she looked like she was going to say something more, but then decided against it and began her inspection. She started with my bruised treasure, it stung as soon as she touched it and I flinched slightly, so she moved quickly on. She took hold of my hips and turned me around and inspecting me from behind. She bent me over slightly with a light push in the small of my back and ran a finger between my cheeks. I yelped as she touched my broken, raw skin. I'm guessing that my reaction gave me away.

'It's not bleeding now, but probably best to be careful. Come with me.'

She led me to the bathroom and unzipped my dress before lifting it gently over my head. She then undid my bra and removed it, while at the same time being careful not to pull me about. Again, I was in her hands where I belonged, and for me, Dominika can do everything she wants to me. Now before her, I was reduced to exactly what I am; shamed, naked, exposed and vulnerable, but in the hands of my own deity. I suddenly understood how Eve must have felt in the Garden of Eden.

'Get in,' she said simply.

She offered me a supporting hand and I climbed into the bath while she remained standing. Every muscle protested and even the slightest movement only intensified my inner pain. I spread my legs slightly to widen my base of support and just hoped it'd be enough to hold me up. She took the showerhead and turned the water on. She tested the temperature briefly on her hand before splashing it on my arm.

'Too hot?'

'No, Dominika,' I answered meekly, but completely confused. Her words continued to be very matter of fact and cold, but her actions spoke much louder. It wasn't too dissimilar to how she behaves during a BDSM session when harsh words and treatments are a mask for her gentleness and compassion. I found this strangely reassuring.

'Good.'

She then began to gently hose me down and took the bar of soap. Once I was completely wet, she passed me the showerhead and lathered me up by rubbing the bar over my body and thoroughly cleansing me. The hard soap immediately went to work on my overused muscles and I felt a bizarre paradox of deep pain and relief as my tightness began to break down. She was very thorough, even to the point of running the soap down to my calves while pressing hard all the time.

She washed my treasure and pulled my labia about as she inspected me, as though handling a piece of meat.

I endured the renewed pain in silence. It was only fair; after all I'd brought everything down on myself. Despite my best efforts, I couldn't stop myself from wincing as my tender folds screamed for mercy. I suddenly felt her eyes on my face and she stopped for a few seconds before carrying on, but much more gently. Then to finish off, she took the shower again and rinsed my puffy bruised outer curtains clean.

'Turn around and go down on your knees if you can.'

I wasn't sure what she wanted, but I wanted to please her.

Obedience is my natural state when it comes to Dominika.

I laughed bitterly in my mind at the sad irony of that thought after all that had happened.

She showed me with firm hands what she wanted and gingerly I lowered myself down into the bath. It pulled on my upper legs but it didn't make the pain any worse. Once I was where she wanted me, she dowsed my hair and I realised why she'd wanted me to go lower. I'm much taller than her and with me being in the bath and her next to it, our height difference was exaggerated. Once my hair was soaked and water was running down my back, she passed me the showerhead to hold. She then took some shampoo into her hand and massaged it into my scalp and worked it into my hair that was cascading down my back. I closed my eyes and enjoyed her attention, it was the simplest of things, but it felt so good even though I knew I was completely unworthy. Then she again took the shower back to rinse the lather out and even used her other hand to mask my eyes to keep the shampoo from running into my eyes.

My beautiful tender Dominika.

I wanted to cry, but had nothing left to give.

Once more she passed me the shower. I faced it to my belly and the warm water splashed and ran down the front of my legs. She cradled my elbows in her hands and lifted me back to a standing position. Content with how she'd placed me she took hold of the top of my hips and gently, but firmly, rotated me around. I turned in small steps and she didn't rush me. When my back was to her, she pushed me in the small of the back again, just as she'd done when we first got home. I knew what she wanted and I bent over slightly in silent compliance. At the same time, I pressed my free hand against the damp tiles on the back wall to steady myself.

Dominika's hands were on my cheeks and she gently pried them apart and paused. I felt my abused knot distend slightly as she stretched me out and unsurprisingly, my agony sharpened as she did so. Then she rubbed a hand between my small hills and once more my ass was penetrated as she slowly eased a soapy finger inside me.

She barely got it inside me when it became too much. The intensity that came about from her slightest touch as she probed made me almost jump out of my skin and collapse as I came down. It was impossible to remain silent and I squealed in pain, in a vibrant echo of what I'd endured earlier.

She promptly removed her finger.

She rubbed more soap into a foam before washing my ass and the area around it. It was obvious that she was doing her best to be as gentle as possible but this was the epicentre of my agony so even the slight touch stung like hell. She went as fast as she dared until she was satisfied I was clean. Then she took the shower from me again and rinsed me thoroughly, but not before making the water slightly cooler when she rinsed my ass.

'Almost done.'

I was still facing away from her and couldn't see what she was doing, but I heard her open a cabinet and move about a bit and then I felt a gentle warm cotton pad kiss my ass. It was abruptly followed by a sharp sting and I realised she was applying antiseptic. It's always been a necessary element after blood play in our BDSM games, but today it hurt even more.

Maybe it was simply because the flesh was more sensitive and the damage far more severe than from anything I'd ever done before?

I bit my lower lip and closed my eyes as I poured all I had left into suppressing my scream and controlling my agony.

'All done,' she suddenly declared. I'm sure my sigh of relief was audible.

Dominika then took a towel and gently dried me off while being very careful where I was most tender and not drying the inner groove of my ass at all. She then offered me her hand and I stepped out of the bath. The first step over was hard, but she was there to prevent me from falling.

She is there to prevent me from falling.

That thought rattled around my brain with repeated ironic sadness.

Her eyes penetrated my inner being and drew me in. My soul flickered and life returned as my heart fluttered like caged butterflies. I stepped forward to kiss her, but she deftly ducked away and placed her hands on my shoulders and moved me in front of the washbasin and washed my face, taking away any last vestiges of my makeup. She then applied toothpaste to my brush and gave it to me before filling the small cup with water. Although I'd somehow managed in the bath standing again was a continual agony, so like I had in the hotel I supported myself by knocking my knees together.

The difference between now and then though, was that the pain was worth it because I would endure everything, just to be with her. She was so attentive and focused and for the first time in so long, I was truly her centre again—exactly where I needed to be. As I brushed, I kept catching her face in the steamy mirror and saw nothing, but love and concern.

What have I done to you? I thought not for the first time.

As soon as I spat the toothpaste out, she passed me the small cup of water. I took a gulp into my mouth and swirled it around and rinsed before ejecting the water into the sink. Even in doing this simple thing, she made things much easier for me in that I didn't need to bend down to the tap as I usually do. I dread to think how I'd have managed without her. I'm not sure, but I think she even ran water from the tap round the sink after I was done.

To complete the cleansing ritual, she brushed my hair out, and she was even careful not to entangle my brush or pull excessively on any knots that were forming. While working out my tangles she held my hair with her other hand so to avoid any pulling or yanking on my scalp. All done, she put my brush down and crouched down before me and parted my cheeks gently with soft fingers and checked my ass once more.

'Good you are all dry, we don't want it to get any worse because I left it wet when I put you to bed.'

I really didn't expect her to lead me back to our room, but nothing she'd done tonight could have been anticipated. So it really was a complete surprise when I entered her sanctuary. Other than just before we went to the bathroom maybe half an hour earlier, this was the first time I'd been in there for weeks. Even when I'd presented her with the letter she'd come to me and blocked my way in.

She pulled back the quilt and helped me to sit down. Then she lifted me from behind my knees and in one smooth rotating step, she eased me into bed before covering me up. As she tucked me in, it was like the best hug I've ever had in my life.

No, that doesn't even come close to describing it—it was even better than that. It was like being wrapped in an intense warmth and love that defied all description.

'I'll be ten minutes, but don't stay awake if you can't.'

'But Dominika, I need to…'

'No talking. Rest.'

'But…'

'Shut the fuck up and rest,' she said in that neutral flat tone of hers that allowed for no disagreement.

And that was the end of the conversation. I can't even begin to explain how confused I was. Dominika was perplexing me. My body was broken and my mind twisted. She was being so unemotional and detached, even cold, but her actions were shouting much louder and they were showing me nothing but unadulterated and pure love.

Dominika turned the light off and left the room. There was the brief murmuring of exchanged words from outside, but true to her word, she was back a short time later and climbed into bed next to me. I smelt toothpaste as her breath caressed the back of my shoulders. I was on one side facing away from her, and within seconds I felt her nakedness press against mine and an arm came over my shoulder—a protective, possessive arm.

I wanted to turn around and talk to her and explain, but as soon as I made the slightest move she tightened her grip on my shoulder.

'Don't move,' she whispered sharply. 'Sleep.'

She wasn't moving, and neither was I. I felt so heavy that I wasn't even sure I could. Silent tears ran down my face and I don't know how long I was lying there before sleep finally took me. All I knew was that she fell asleep before me. I know her well enough to recognise when her breathing patterns change.

At some point during the night I woke up. I didn't want to disturb her, but I turned my head and saw her. She'd changed position slightly but she was still there facing me with a sprawled arm reaching out to me. I woke up several more times and she was still there. My emotions were all over the place. I was so confused by her behaviour and it only served to make me even more ashamed of how much of a slut I'd been—and I don't just mean with the guys tonight.

But I was home.

Part 7: Ania Is Restored
Saturday 22 June 2019

I woke up before Dominika and as I tried to move, my whole body protested. Physically, I was a lifeless wreck, totally devoid of energy, but I was buzzing as thoughts flitted quickly from one to another. My broken body was testimony enough to what'd happened last night, but my mind was processing it as a series of detailed flashbacks. Memory after memory bombarded me and I somehow wished that the vodka had wiped out the whole evening, but everything was as clear as if it'd been filmed and I was watching it back in full HD.

I slowly and cautiously rolled over to face Dominika. It'd been hard enough to move when I was waking up during the night, but now it was even worse. Every slight movement raised a protest from my tattered body and my hip joints screamed even louder. At some point later in the night she must have finally turned away from me and left her back half covered. And now, I just lay there in the silence admiring her naked shoulders. I wanted to reach out and touch her, but the vast chasm, those unforgivable sins, was still there and I'd relinquished any right to love her. Guilt, that fucking stone, lodged in my gut, was back. Sleep had brought relief, but it'd only been fleeting.

Daylight and wakefulness brought renewed darkness into my wounded soul that had flickered with the slightest hint of resurrection when Dominika had taken care of me. The whole of last night had been so overwhelming and she'd crowned it with completely unexpected and undeserved tenderness.

I was so confused. I had no idea what today would bring, but she'd invited me back into her—*was I being too hopeful in thinking our*—bed?

Sharing the same bed, however temporarily, meant that she'd have to talk to me at least once. Such was my state, that I had absolutely no feelings, neither fear nor hope, about the thought of actually having a conversation.

I needed to pee, but didn't even dare to get out of bed. Honestly, I wasn't even sure I could.

I had no perception of the passing of time, but it must have been getting on because I could hear Emilia and Kasia moving around between the kitchen, bathroom and their room. None of us had anything specific to do and with it being a long weekend, Kasia had one of those rare weekends off. *Or was she finished?* I really can't keep up with her timetable. Thinking of Kasia, I'd still have to face her and for the first time, I began to think she might be even less forgiving than Dominika.

With everything she'd done for me last night, Dominika had at least acknowledged my existence, but nothing had quelled Kasia's anger.

The realisation that at least I still existed, somewhere in Dominika's consciousness invigorated me. The tiniest hint of forgiving grace began to creep into me and with this a sudden hope. My emotions began to well up again. I closed my eyes, to shut everything out and wept in the silent bitterness of my sin.

It must have been the steady shaking of my shoulders as I sobbed, that woke Dominika because I was suddenly aware of her moving next to me. I was surprised when I opened my eyes to see that she was laying on her side, her soft eyes staring at me and their purity penetrated my reviving soul. I wanted to reach out to her, but she reached out first.

She cupped her hand and slipped it between my face and the pillow and carefully cradled my cheek. It was too much and the last semblance of self-control gave way and I lost it and broke down completely.

I blubbered and wailed and between tears, I repeated endlessly, 'I'm sorry.'

I'm sure I was hardly coherent. As my emotions exploded, my nose ran and I snivelled. I must have been so snotty and ugly and still nothing from her. She still seemed unmoved by my outburst and her expression remained a constant unmoving stare. Just looking at her brought another wave of sorrow and more of the grief that I'd been holding on to over the last few months was released. Sorrow and grief weren't alone and I couldn't handle their third companion. As I looked at her, and she held me in her steady gaze, it was like darkness looking at the purest of light and with that wave after wave of condemnation washed over me again and again.

Elwira, my guilt, my shame, my sin, my frustration, my anger, my neglect, my pain, my despair, my sorrow, my loss; all washed out of me a tsunami of tears and agony, worse than anything I'd experienced last night. I was physically broken last night, but I'd been wrong about my mind. I thought the ordeal with the guys had completely broken me but now my mind finally capitulated before the grace and power of Dominika's presence.

I absolutely sobbed my heart out and soaked her hand and the pillow with my constant flow of tears and there we stayed until, after endless minutes, my storm finally passed and the tears ebbed. I felt strangely empty and now there was nothing, but a shell remaining. I'd lost all dignity, and couldn't be any more devastated both mentally and bodily.

'I'm still here,' Dominika finally whispered.

What does she mean? What should I do?

It was so unexpected and confusing that I responded in the only way that I knew how to. I shuffled forward to kiss her, but as I neared her, she restrained me with a firm hand on my chest just below my throat.

'No!'

That shot me down. I withdrew again, rejected and unwanted. Hope crushed. That all too familiar feeling of abandonment that'd been my constant companion for the last few weeks, returned. She then raised her hand slightly and tightened it around my throat. Her touch and assertiveness excited me, and sick as I am my physical longing for her and inner fire started to burn, even though there was no way my body couldn't take any more, even from her. She closed her hand tighter around my throat, but not enough to stop me breathing. My heart was beating faster as I responded naturally to her touch. As she pressed my neck, it felt tender and sore, another consequence of last night. A little bit of discomfort was worth it though.

'I could snuff you out easier than a candle if I wanted to Ania, especially after what you've done. But I won't, and do you know why?'

My eyes were fixed on hers and I've never seen her so serious before. I mouthed *why*.

'Because, you stupid girl, I never stopped loving you.'

Her tone was flat and even, but the impact of her words was anything but. My whole being lurched inside and her words resonated in my brain. They set off another flood and all the time she kept her hand on my throat, to remind me of her power and grace.

Was it really as simple as this? Has she forgiven me? Have the last two months just been erased like they'd never happened?

Then a darker thought entered my head, was she tormenting me, fucking with my mind and breaking me even more than I already was?

I'd seen what she'd done with my letter.

No—Dominika doesn't play this kind of game. She may tease and torment, but never about serious things. She's a lot more straightforward than this. Remembering the letter, it'd been the thing that had finally left me completely destitute, but she hadn't been playing stupid games then and she wasn't playing stupid games now.

The letter burning was probably just as symbolic for her as it had been for me.

But this wasn't like the letter. Her love was strong, unending and consistent and this sudden epiphany broke me once again, and as a volcano releases multiple flows of lava, I ejected more pain and guilt through my tears. Then another revelation struck me as I realised my soul was being renewed in pain and anguish. I was undergoing the labour pains of my rebirth.

It was a miracle. My dead soul truly was experiencing a resurrection.

She watched and waited until she judged that enough time had passed for the truth to sink in. Maybe she saw the dawning of understanding suddenly illuminate my face and only after that she released me. I knew all along that she'd only grabbed my throat to make a point and I was never in any real danger of violence.

'Let me have a look at you,' her tone was still flat, but everything about her was telling me something quite different.

She moved quickly and pulled the quilt back. The air felt cool, but I didn't care. She sat up next to me, her naked form a sight of pure beauty that I hadn't seen for so long. I had little chance to admire her though because she rolled me onto my back. I grimaced as I moved and obediently complied with her wishes. The slightest movement was a challenge. My legs ached and I was stiff all over. She must have seen me struggling but carried on regardless. She carefully, but firmly put her hands on my nearest leg, one above and one below my knee and she pulled my legs apart. I felt so heavy that I'm not sure I'd have been able to do it so easily on my own.

Now I was exactly how she wanted me she leant over and with a thumb and finger and gently parted my outer lips. I tensed up in anticipation of pain and her touch was a bit sore, but not too bad, certainly nowhere near as bad as I'd expected it to be. They'd recovered surprisingly well from last night's trauma, or so I thought until she gave them a firm tug, first one and then the other and I squealed quietly.

That hurt!

She then pressed my clit through its hood, I would have loved to say it excited me, but I was in no state, so I just passively lay there.

I know it sounds bizarre, but the power play when she had grabbed my throat had been more arousing than her direct touch. My mind was hers, but it might take a bit longer for my body to realise that I was undergoing a resurrection.

My little button hadn't really suffered, and it was totally unresponsive to pain or arousal. Her inspection wasn't over though. She put a finger on my abused slit and pushed a finger straight in, no lube and no stimulation and it bit sharply as broken flesh gave way to her force. Again I balled my face up in pain, but this time I managed not to utter a sound. It was then that I realised most of the damage was internal and outwardly everything was fine.

Content with what she'd discovered, she withdrew her finger and moved on to pressing my inner thighs in parallel with both hands. That hurt, more than I'd expected and I flinched under her palms. As I instinctively jerked away even more pain ran through my bruised flesh and overtight muscles.

'Must have been quite a workout,' she commented without emotion.

There was no response to that, but she'd already moved on. She ran her fingers in delicate circles over my hips. 'Bruised here too. Looks like finger marks to me.'

I remembered how my hips had been forcibly grabbed all night as they ravished me and filled me with their lust. 'Yes Dominika. They held on to me when they were fucking me.'

'I see,' was all she said. I'm sure that what had happened was so obvious to her that no further explanation was unnecessary.

She then moved up my body and checked my breasts. I was so happy she didn't press on my belly. At least she was now talking to me, and I didn't want to lose this precious moment simply because I needed to pee. My breasts hadn't suffered too much, having only been groped and pinched, so she quickly moved up to my neck.

'You've got a couple of finger marks coming up on your throat that weren't there last night. Did they throttle you?'

I couldn't remember telling her that it was more than one guy. Maybe I'd told Emilia on the phone and she had told Dominika. In the fugue surrounding my phone call to Emilia, I was less than sure what I had and hadn't told her, but it seemed to make sense. Later I remembered that indeed I had told Emilia that it'd been four guys.

'Yes.'

'Did you want this?'

'I wanted as much abuse as they could give me.'

'Even at a risk to your life?'

'Honestly, Dominika. At first, yes. I didn't care whether I lived or died, but they were decent guys and I didn't want them to have consequences later.'

'Decent guys?' She snarled irritably. She's never had much patience for men and now this. 'Can't you get it into your head, look at the state they left you in? In that first moment when I saw you, I thought I'd need to take you to the hospital. What would you have done if nobody had come to pick you up last night?'

'I don't know.'

'I don't know? What kind of fucking answer is that?' Fire that filled me with dread flashed in her eyes. 'This is just so like you, not thinking of the consequences of what you do. When have I ever left you in such a state after one of our sessions?'

I needed to cut her off. She was wrong on this—*sorry, Dominika, but it's the truth*.

They hadn't gone beyond the boundaries I'd set and yes inside our BDSM sessions she can be harsh, even cruel, but she never abandons me or leaves me so physically incapacitated.

I suddenly realised I was thinking in the present tense and I began to feel more than hope.

'I know, Dominika, but don't blame them.' My loyalty to them was real and it was part of our no-strings agreement. I had to explain,

'They stayed inside the limits I set. One of them was even kind to me all night and another stopped at one point when he thought it was going too far. I told him to carry on. No, that's not true. I insisted that he carry on. I'll admit there was a moment when I got scared, but then the guy who scared me changed his grip on my neck—so I guess that's how I got these marks.'

Seemingly satisfied with my answer she simply said, 'You may need to cover that with foundation when you go out. I don't want anyone to think that I did it to you. There don't seem to be any love bites or tooth marks though.'

'No, Dominika, I didn't allow any kissing.'

'Why no kissing?'

'Kissing involves emotion.'

And what about when you were kissing Elwira?'

If this is the way it needs to be, then so be it. I will never lie to Dominika again.

'It was emotion. I made an emotional connection with her. I was addicted. I really liked her, but knew I was still yours.'

'Go on.'

'I can't explain, Dominika. I can only be honest. Like I tried to explain before, I was feeling all alone and she was there when I was vulnerable. I'm not blaming you, but I was looking for something to happen and it only took a moment of desire to make it so. I kissed her and that led to everything else. I really am sorry, Dominika.'

Tears started to flow again.

'I really am, Dominika,' I repeated.

Dominika, as usual, had herself under complete control and no emotion was leaking from her. She cut me off and steered the conversation back away from Elwira, 'Now back to last night, what other limits did you set?'

'No kissing,' I repeated. 'I told them that they had to use a condom, if they wanted my ass or *cipku* (pussy sounds so much more delicate in Polish so I use it here as I did in the actual conversation) and no beating or peeing on me. I kind of gave them a safe word that we didn't use.'

'Anything else?'

'Not that I remember now, but I promise I will tell you if I do remember something. I will never lie or cheat again.'

It was important for me to get that last bit in.

'Right. Now roll over for me.'

Slowly, so not to hurt myself, as much as it was possible, I did as I was told and she helped me with delicately firm hands. The press on my belly became even more uncomfortable, but I could hold my bladder just a little longer. This conversation was far too valuable to lose for the sake of something as insignificant as my need to pee.

I felt Dominika on my ass as she gave my cheeks a quick squeeze. My muscles here too were tight and I clamped my teeth tightly together to hide the pain. Dominika was already done though and moving on. She then separated my little globes and ran a finger along my knot. It wasn't as painful as last night, but still stung and I instinctively clenched my cheeks and shut her out.

She pulled my cheeks open again, and like last night it caused my knot to dilate a little with a sting, but she didn't touch it again.

'And what happened in here?'

It was fucked several times.' I said frankly. 'I honestly don't remember how many times, but one guy was really brutal and pushed straight inside me with his whole length and only used long strokes. He was really hard and quite big and he really hurt me, a lot more than the others did. Then later he and one of the other guys both entered me at the same time.'

'Both in your ass?'

'Yes.'

'And it really hurt?'

'Like nothing I've ever known before. I was already hurt after the brutal guy and he wasn't the first one to fuck my ass.'

The truth is brutal, but I needed to tell her exactly how it was.

'And what about your safe word?'

'I didn't use it.'

'Why not?'

'Because I was getting what I deserved after the way I'd treated you. I'm so sorry.' More tears. 'It was my punishment and still less than I should've got. I deserved far worse.'

She turned me over again so she could look in the face.

'But they really hurt you.' For the first time her tone matched her soft and gentle face. It was the way I always remembered her.

'I know, but it still wasn't enough. I needed more pain. The more they abused me the more I felt the need for more. My mind was screaming for worse than hell and their punishment was hardly touching me.'

'So why did you stop and call Emilia?'

'My body was broken and it couldn't take anymore. They too were done. I think I took ten lots of cum and they were completely drained. Guys can't go forever.'

Dominika's eyes widened in surprise before she laughed mockingly, 'Yes, man meat is fucking useless. Stands there all proud, then vomits and deflates into a pathetic little worm.'

I already know Dominika's long-held opinions on men so she didn't need to remind me. A sudden memory of last night resurfaced. It was worth a risk.

'I spat on the brutal one a couple of times and called him a useless cunt and asked him if he was fucking me or I was fucking him. Actually, I think it was one of the reasons he was so brutal. I doubted his manhood.'

She almost cracked a genuine smile. She always appreciated anything that belittled any man. Quickly she masked her expression and her hard unfeeling face was back.

'And what happened?'

'I'm really sorry, Dominika, I promise I'll answer every question, but I really need to pee. Can I go? Please. I am sorry.'

It might seem strange I was asking permission, but the question was polite and purely rhetorical and more about appearances. I didn't want to look like I was escaping and risk losing the conversation. I'd held on as long as I could, but now I was in real danger of making a puddle in the bed.

I rotated myself to get out of bed and dropped my feet to the floor before standing. My legs strained and resisted. It was almost like the unnatural use of my body had made it to go on strike against even its natural functions. By willpower alone I forced myself upright—I had no other choice.

Then Dominika was there. Like she'd done in the hotel last night, she wrapped a reassuring arm around me and took me to the bathroom like I was a hospital patient.

We were both naked, but it didn't matter even when we saw Emilia and Kasia in the kitchen. It's not an unusual thing for them to see us naked, even if it's been a while, not counting when I'd been naked before Dominika's door. It looked like Emilia was going to say something, but Dominika put up a halting hand and Emilia let it go.

Dominika stayed with me while I peed and wiped myself and with her supporting me I washed my hands. Again like last night I knocked my knees together because in doing so it was much easier to stand. We then headed back into the hallway.

As we passed the kitchen, Dominika asked, 'could one of you girls make us some coffee?'

Unlike the last time she said this, I was sure we'd get these coffees.

We then went back to the room and Dominika helped me back into bed and climbed in beside me before pulling the bedding back over us. Snug and warm I was safe and next to all that mattered.

Dominika.

For a few minutes we rested in the perfect silence. Then there was a tap on the door and I was surprised to see both Emilia and Kasia enter with two steaming mugs of coffee. I'd kind of expected Emilia, but Kasia was a surprise. I am sure it was at least in part out of curiosity.

'Thanks girls,' Dominika said brusquely, but not quite rudely, and the girls got the hint and quickly and quietly left.

'Now we carry on and you will listen to me.'

She changed position so she could look me straight in the eye. 'I don't trust you anymore, Ania.'

It was a hammer blow, but she was far from finished. I fought back tears as her words seared into me.

'I'm no good at this emotional shit, so this is how it is. You betrayed me. I have pretty much let you fuck who you want when you want and supported your deviancy. Ok I know I was doing that almost as much for the kick I was getting out of it. It turns me on to have as much control over your desires as you do.'

This was a rare insight into Dominika's own deviancy.

'When you came to me and told me, despite my anger, I couldn't see you on the streets. At least you'd owned up freely before you were caught—that's the only redeeming thing about your behaviour and the only reason I let you stay here.'

Dominika paused before starting one of her psychoanalyses.

'I'm worried about what you did last night, but accept that it was something self-destructive that you felt that you needed to do. I don't like it, but I get it. I know you better than you know yourself and I've seen similar spirals before, just not as bad as this one. Last night you weren't tied to me so I can't or won't call it cheating.'

'But Dominika…'

'I told you I am fucking talking, that means *you* are listening.'

I fell silent and she carried on.

'But Elwira is a different matter. You went to her repeatedly and deceived her too. I'm livid, angrier than you have ever known. My dad's a cunt, but I've known that for a long time, but you… you were supposed to be different.'

My tears started again and she touched my cheek.

'You hurt me and worse than that you disappointed me, Ania, and just maybe you did feel a bit neglected. Deal with it, you're not ten. Grow up. You knew I was stressed about my exams and thesis and you fucking around was the last thing I needed. I asked you to be patient because I couldn't give you what you needed.'

Again I wanted to say sorry, but sat up and reached for my coffee instead, after passing Dominika hers first. Other than briefly glancing at the mugs, I kept my eyes on her at all times. I reasoned that if I was busy drinking it'd stop me interrupting. I just hoped that it didn't appear callous or light, like I wasn't giving her my whole attention. The distraction also served as an external focus to keep my own emotional state in check. I took a sip and so did Dominika.

'So this is how it is going to be. You'll move back in here with me and as far as I am concerned we are back together.'

More tears, but this time of joy. I must have flashed her my perfect Colgate smile.

'But,' she continued, 'things are going to change. You're mine and mine alone. Look at another girl—or anybody for that matter—and you are gone faster than you can imagine. As far as I'm concerned, you can die on the streets if you go there again. Another thing, you can keep your social media and special friends, but you're no longer for sharing and you should make this known. Don't give anybody any expectation of a hook up. For now, this is permanent and I almost certainly won't change my mind on this in the foreseeable future. I'll work out something with Kasia and Emilia, it's not fair to deny them, but you no longer have the right to go to Emilia—you never used that right anyway. We'll have to figure something out for Phil, because he's been nothing but good to us and especially to you.'

I nodded mutely.

Anything to have you back, darling.

'There is no point in dwelling on the past. What has happened has happened, it'll just be tedious and a waste of time. I do want from you though a full confession and you'll write it down, every detail you can remember, even this conversation and you'll give it to me. Later we may send it to Phil so he can understand why things have changed. It might just give you some insight into yourself too.'

'I've already started writing…' I started to explain.

'Ania! You must learn to listen. Who's talking?'

The question was clearly not for answering and I fell mute again.

'I repeat, I love you, but I don't trust you—that'll take time to rebuild—if it can ever be. Don't be surprised if I act more possessively, you have only got yourself to blame. I'll try my best not to be, but I think it is inevitable. In time as my trust grows, I hope it'll ease off and we can go back to normal, but only time will tell.'

I thought she was done, so I opened my mouth to speak again.

'Wait, I haven't finished. You won't keep apologising and going on about it because that insults me and shows disrespect to what I've just said about dwelling on the past. It also means you haven't accepted my forgiveness. I do believe you are sorry, last night proved it, so you don't need to keep repeating yourself. I absolutely forbid you from doing anything to hurt yourself. If you need to talk, but can't reach out to me, you can freely speak with Emilia or Kasia—I know that probably means Emilia.'

'Talking of the girls, I'll have a word, but don't expect any grace from Kasia. Your behaviour upset the balance of our little family and you know how sensitive she is about family. She might be less forgiving than I am. I'll work on her and I am sure Emilia will too.'

'Finally, for now, the BDSM part of our relationship is over. I'm still too angry with you and I've always promised never to discipline you when angry. My anger will only get in the way and might lead to excess. You can use that as an idea of where our trust is if and when we ever go back to it. I am tempted to hand you over to Kasia for a while, but you've already punished yourself enough and that'll be too much. You know she won't be able to control herself.'

The thought of Kasia unrestrained and unleashed filled me with horror and then relief when I realised it wasn't going to happen. She's the one who is sadistic enough to truly frighten me. She won't cross Dominika and even more so she won't cross Emilia, but unrestrained she doesn't recognise limits.

'Where's the ring I gave back to you?'

'In Kasia's old room next to the lamp near the bed.'

It was the first time I'd reverted back to calling it Kasia's old room in the week or so since Dominika had burnt my letter. It felt very liberating, like I'd been released from a prison cell.

'I'll take it back for now and on the day I give you it back, if it ever comes it'll mark a new chapter for us. Is everything clear?'

'Yes Dominika, thank you.'

It was just a few words, and they didn't seem to be enough even though I genuinely meant what I said. It wasn't just empty words, even though it was pretty much all I could say.

'So this is my olive branch and the only one I'm offering. It's up to you and it's the only chance you'll get. Break my heart again and you are gone.'

Typical Dominika, she'd broken it down into a black and white understanding of what had happened and what it meant, for her, and for me and more importantly for our relationship.

I love her so much, what more could I do, but accept it.

'I love you, Dominika and I promise myself to you forever,' I pledged earnestly. 'Thank you.'

I couldn't say any more, I was forbidden from saying sorry even though my resurrected soul screamed at me to apologise again. There wasn't enough time in my life to say sorry for how I felt about what I'd done, even if I lived to be 100. I just had to accept it.

'Now rest,' and with that, she kissed me tenderly, the first kiss of a new dawn.

***

For the rest of the day, she kept me closeted away and refused to let me leave the bed. The only exception was when I needed to go to the toilet, and whenever I did so she was always there to support me. I was terribly stiff and sore. I might've been able to make it on my own, but to have her next to me again was all that mattered and it was all the better for her help.

She kept Emilia and Kasia away from me too for that entire first day, even though they must have been burning with curiosity, and in Emilia's case, concern.

I'm sorry to bring up such a thought (one that total honesty demands), but I was so grateful that I hadn't needed to go to the toilet that day to use my ass. When I did eventually go on the third day I was well enough for it to cause no major problems. It stung and there were some spots of blood, probably because as I passed my soil, it rubbed and tugged against the healing wounds. The most hopeful thing was that it made me bleed far less than when the guys had finished with me.

I was slowly being restored—physically at least.

Dominika brought food to me and pampered me and in the evening she climbed in the shower with me and cleansed me. She checked me over and while she almost scanned over the bruises on my hips and gave my treasure scant attention she focused on ground zero, my damaged ass. Pleased that it was getting better, she didn't apply any more antiseptic. Once I was clean and my inspection was completed, she helped me climb out of the bath and gently towelled me dry and when I wanted to do the same to her. She wouldn't let me.

'You're the one who's recovering—not me.'

'I know, Dominika, but I feel so useless.'

'That's just the way it is. Now shut up and let me dry your back.'

With that, she turned my back to her and dried me off. When I was dry she helped me into my dressing gown and we cleaned our teeth before going back to our room, where she sat me down in front of the desk and brushed my hair out. Our makeup mirror, a small round one, had been left there, and through it I caught the reflection of her face. She was so cute, so focussed and I felt so wanted.

I actually smiled and I saw something I thought I'd never see again as she grinned back at me.

'Oh while I remember, open the drawer to your right.'

I did as I was told, and in the front was the ring that meant so much.

'So I've taken it back and I'll decide if and when you'll ever get it back. Until then it stays there.'

Her harsh matter-of-factness brought back the cold reality of the state of our relationship, but I guess I should be grateful. At least she'd taken me back. I can't expect things to go back to normal just like that. While her comment took the edge off my joy I was happy, happier than I'd been in a very long while.

She returned to brushing my hair as though what she'd said was of no significance and when she'd finished she helped me into bed and as my aching body fell into the confines of our soft mattress she climbed in next to me and pulled the duvet over us. I was facing away from her and she cuddled into my back and held me tight until I fell into a truly restful sleep.

Sunday 23 June 2019

I woke up naturally and realised I was alone. Panic hit me and for a few minutes I thought Dominika had deserted me, but then she appeared with breakfast on a tray. She helped me to sit up and we breakfasted together in a silent bliss that needed no words.

Later she let me get up and spend some time moving around the flat, but not for too long. As is often the case after a strenuous workout, I ached more today than I had done yesterday. I've never understood why muscular pain is always worse on the second day.

Although I spent some time in the kitchen and between the bedroom and bathroom, Dominika was still shielding me from everyone. She banned me from going online and even kept me away from Emilia and Kasia and encouraged me to sleep and rest.

This changed for a short time in the afternoon when she loosened her protective grip on me.

I was in our bed, it was still the most comfortable place for me, when I received my first visitor and it wasn't who I expected.

Dominika had left the room and there was a knock on the door and Kasia entered, uninvited. She came and sat on the bed by me and didn't stay for long. She had only sat on the bed so she could see me at eye level and her message couldn't have been clearer.

'Ania, we'll be ok for Dominika's sake, but cross her again and we're done,' and that was it.

Kasia was blunt and to the point and it hurt, but I couldn't blame her. There was little forgiveness in her words, but I knew it was a big step for her even to have gone this far and I was grateful that. She'd at least given me this. I knew Emilia would soften her in time because Emilia is both gentle and irresistible while at the same time being as hard as steel.

Almost as soon as Kasia left, Emilia came in and my conversation with her, while making a very similar point, went quite differently. She was warm and gracious and constantly touching my arm. She urged me to communicate next time and not keep it inside. She promised that she'd be there for me, but warned me that if I ever cheated on Dominika again she'd have to choose sides and I'd lose.

That's the steel I keep telling you about!

On this, she was in total agreement with Kasia and completely with Dominika. She did reassure me though, that while Kasia was trying to be *all Dominika* in her matter of fact attitude, she'd actually softened quite considerably after seeing the state I'd been in when I got home on Friday night.

This was the most comforting thing I heard after knowing Dominika had accepted me back.

'But remember you have just one more chance,' she reminded me just as I began to understand that they'd all let me back into our little family. 'And that's from all three of us.'

Emilia's steel is not to be taken lightly.

On a lighter note though, I asked her about her own deceit.

'So what happened to you at Novotel?'

'What do you mean?'

'You said you were coming, and then only Dominika turned up.'

She laughed, 'Well somebody had to do something. You were slowly destroying yourself—even if I didn't know exactly what you were up to on Friday night—that much was clear. You'd exiled yourself and were in limbo. I thought, after what you'd told me on Monday, that you really were trying to move on with your life. I was somewhat surprised that you'd moved so far in so few days and I didn't really believe you could let Dominika go just like that. And as for Dominika, she was lost without you. You may have an unconventional relationship, but you are *her anchor* and never forget it. I've never seen her so devastated. I've always known that she still loves you and I had to do something to push you both together. Friday was my chance. It was her you needed—*not me*.'

Emilia is so wise. Never ever underestimate her. Kasia's lucky to have her and we are also blessed to have her in our little family.

Once the difficult conversations were done, Dominika re-imposed my quarantine, and I didn't see Emilia or Kasia again for the rest of the day.

I snuggled down into bed as the second day aches were really debilitating and the tightness of my muscles were making it hard to sit comfortably anywhere else. The sofa was a possibility, but I decided on principle not to go there. It'd been my bed when I first lived in the flat, before Dominika and I had got together, and it'd only have reminded me of our separation.

Besides what is wrong with a luxurious bed that smelt of Dominika?

In the early evening, Dominika was really sweet and moved all of my stuff back into our room, I offered to help, even if I wasn't really able to, but she insisted on doing it herself. She kept me fed and brought me endless teas and coffees. She understands more than most, probably because of the now dormant BDSM element of our relationship that I needed looking after and she's really good at it—something I've always known. As more of my stuff was brought back to our room a growing reflection of normality began to return. The day had started as a mirage, but took greater form as the hours passed and the room was restored to how it had been previously.

As with last night, in the evening she eased me out of bed and took me to the bathroom. Only this time she'd already run a bath for me. She helped me to climb in and gently soaped me down and rinsed my body. Being submerged in the warm water brought some relief to my broken body.

But my broken body no longer bothered me because my soul had been restored,

Epilogue

To begin with, I wasn't sure if it'd be better for me to write this epilogue or for Dominika to do it. To me it's important, because I need to explain how I'm feeling after everything that happened.

Dominika has been amazing and she also felt that it was best if I use my own words, rather than have her speak for me. She did want to have her say on everything that had happened so we had to decide who'd go first.

In the end, we decided to do it this way round and it's probably only fitting that Dominika has the last word.

So why, after explaining what happened, do I need another chapter?

Simply I felt that I needed to make two things abundantly clear, if it's not already obvious. I'm going to try to do this without repeating anything that Dominika has written.

Before that though, I have to own up to what I did. Whatever the reasons, justified or not, I cheated on Dominika and in doing so I set in motion a sequence of events that almost destroyed me. The whole point of my confession is to take full responsibility.

Now I have done that I can move on…

The first thing is that I have physically healed from the punishment that I took and for now, there doesn't seem to be any long-term effects. I'm still in a kind of a shock and I think it's fair to say that everything and especially the night in the hotel left me traumatised. When I cheated on Dominika with Elwira all kinds of stuff came bubbling to the surface. It exposed not only the immediate problems that I was facing at the time but also much deeper underlying issues from my childhood. The demons from my past, that I thought had long been banished, had returned to taunt and drive me along the path I took and especially the dark road of self-destruction that I walked alone after Dominika let me go.

What has become obvious to me since then is that as my body has healed my mind too must go through a similar healing process. Bruises fade quickly, but psychological scarring often remains. Unseen, it festers quietly in the hidden recesses of the mind only waiting to emerge once again in the face a crisis.

The second thing is that I must repeat for the umpteenth time what I have been saying all along. It may seem repetitive and even boring as I keep reiterating what I am about to say, but I need to hammer the point home again so that it is clear beyond the shadow of a doubt.

The guilt is mine and mine alone and even when I went with those guys it was I who pushed the boundaries and it was me who was unhappy when they weren't abusive enough.

As Dominika will explain in more detail, that evening almost certainly crossed the line into abuse, but it was self-abuse, a kind of *self-harming by proxy*, and actually, all the way through the guys were ready to pull back from the extremes that I drove them to. Adam in particular, was quite protective and uncomfortable with a lot of what I wanted and it was I who overruled his cautionary urgings. To me it seems clear that he could even have restrained David, only I didn't want him to.

Did you see how they pretty much all responded to him?

It wasn't what I was looking for though and I deliberately provoked and pushed David into brutality and if anything, in the moment, I wanted them all to treat me as he was doing and probably even worse.

I was in such a state, that as far as I was concerned, they could have done anything they wanted and I only insisted on limits to save them from possible criminal charges, which I wouldn't have initiated anyway.

My point is this, and by constantly repeating myself, I can't emphasise this enough, this was *self-harming by proxy*. The guys were nothing more than innocent pawns caught up in my depravity and need to be punished for what I'd done to Dominika.

Yes, it was abusive and yes it was harsh, but I could have stopped them at any time, but I didn't want to.

I needed to make these things absolutely clear but will stop there so Dominika can have the final say.

Ania, September 2019

Afterword – Dominika

My writing style is nothing like Ania's. I am just simply not so flowery or descriptive as she is. If something needs saying, I just say it as it is and make no apologies for doing so. This approach means that I tend to write more formally, so some of this may not flow as well as her writing.

So now that has been made clear, and it is out of the way I shall begin.

So this is Ania's confession, the very thing I demanded as part of our reconciliation and in writing it not only has she gained a greater understanding of her behaviour and the calamitous consequences it brought down on her, but I have also been able to see more fully what was going on in her mind during those two dark months when she was effectively lost.

As a result, I too, have gained a greater understanding of both her and the wider circumstances.

Consuming her letter by fire, now I know the full story, has created mixed feelings for me. In hindsight, I probably ought not to have done that but, as things worked their way through, it probably worked out for the best. The confession that she has given me is far deeper and more heartfelt than anything she could have ever achieved in a simple letter even if her intentions had been the same.

It is also obvious, that as usual, Ania is very detail focused and some of her account was probably almost over-described. For her, erotica is what she knows and therefore it naturally follows that it is what she writes. I think that for her, going into every single element of what happened was ultimately therapeutic. It enabled her to confront what she had done, take responsibility and deal with it head on.

What was of greater interest to me, rather than her lurid descriptions of what happened, was her emotional journey which forms a subtext that runs throughout. In describing her angst on the day we broke up, the events of the Tuesday night before, and her response to my letter burning, the raw pain she felt clawed its way deep inside me.

More positively, it is impossible for me to ignore how she saw everything from the moment I picked her up at the hotel.

One thing that has become very clear to me since reading this, is that our problems started sometime between late January and early February. It is no coincidence that all went awry when I was distracted by my thesis. I invested all of my energies into getting it right; it was the culmination of five years of study and needed as much attention as possible. I must admit to being a perfectionist and it took me away from her. I was well aware that I was spending much less time with Ania than usual and that was why I asked her repeatedly to be patient.

Understanding why she felt abandoned is not a justification for what she did and she still needs to take responsibility for her own actions. She is not a child. What has become clear to me now, again with the benefit of hindsight is that, while I agonised over every word and phrase I wrote, it left me largely unaware of Ania's inner agony that was growing day by day. She summed it up perfectly when she wrote *that [she] longed for [my] touch, but [I] wished only not to disturb [her] sleep. Tired in the mornings, conversation was minimal and desire was unfulfilled.*

Some may think I need to take responsibility too, but I am straightforward and simply expected her to accept it. Maybe our main mistake was that we started taking each other for granted. We both assumed that we both needed space, me for my work and with her, because of my late nights, I assumed she must be tired and needed to sleep. She should have understood my need to study, but knowing her, I should have understood her needs too.

I was genuinely shocked at how much she has tortured herself since and even while she was cheating. Then, subsequently, she sought punishment in the only way she understands. I had no idea she contemplated suicide in her lowest moments or even when she could not bring herself to cut her wrists she no longer cared whether she lived or died. Somehow, and to her credit, she found the mental strength to keep going. It just showed me once again what I already know; she is damaged, but also remarkably resilient.

She endured so much unnecessarily and I definitely disapprove of the punishment she took from those men. Even so, knowing Ania, I understand why she did it. The only thing I can say about these men is that I recognise that they never went further than Ania herself wanted. While it was abusive, by my understanding of the word, they behaved within the limits she set. It really strikes me that Adam was more concerned for her welfare than even she was for herself.

On that first day when I accepted her back, she was quick to defend them, and although I found it hard to understand her reasoning at the time, I can now see why she did so.

Fundamentally, when it comes to the bottom line they did not do anything wrong, even if their actions were morally questionable. However, if we follow that train of thought Ania's actions also come under the same scrutiny, and she was far from an innocent.

Ania set the agenda all night. She went out with a singularity of purpose and a laser beam focus on her own self-destruction. She provoked whenever she could, to get stronger and more aggressive reactions from the guys when they were failing to satisfy her need. Spitting at a guy and verbally abusing him in such a situation was escalating things to a whole new level, but it is clear she knew exactly what she was doing.

It is almost a strange irony that she was most out of control with the Germans that she met in the hotel bar before going on to the Hard Rock Café.

Make no mistake, Ania was in complete control in that hotel room. She and I have often debated what can be called *the submissive paradox*.

I will never encourage her to do anything like that nor will I ever put her in a situation of such personal endangerment. When I met her in the hotel on that June night she was right on the verge of needing to go to hospital. Not only that but I was even more worried about her mental state and to be honest, I still am.

For now I must, with the support of others, nurture her back to health. Her physical wounds may have healed, but her mind needs more time to mend, I will pick up on this again a bit later.

All I could do that evening was give her the love that I had been withholding. The truth is that I never stopped loving her, even if I could no longer trust her. It took me until the following day to acknowledge fully to her (and probably to myself) that my feelings remained, although it seems that Emilia was never in any doubt.

Looking back, it was a perfect case of actions speaking louder than words as I brought her home and cared for her immediate needs. I am not a person of many words, but I seemed to know just what to say and nursing her over those first few days afterwards brought her back and it meant I could once more find my joy in her.

She often says I am her centre, but the truth is *she* is my centre. Things needed to change though.

I kept her in virtual solitude for the first few days and would not even let her near her computer. This may have seemed overly controlling and restrictive, but at that point, I was worried that interaction with others would do more harm than good. I relented briefly on the second day so Emilia and Kasia could spend some time with her and then over the next few days I stepped back more and more so once more in our home we could start becoming the family that we had been; restored and whole.

It was an easy thing for Emilia, but I have to give a lot of respect to Kasia for how she dealt with it—but more about them later.

For now, we are not going back to our BDSM life. I am still a Domme and nothing has fundamentally changed about either of us. She is still a submissive by nature and while I am not a sadist, my need for order makes me naturally dominant. While some may judge us, (and remember at all times we are both *consenting adults*) our lifestyle has shown me again and again that she truly is tough and can withstand almost any physical pain. Our lifestyle suits us and that is really all that matters. For me, it just happens to fit with my neat little picture of the world, but for Ania, it runs far deeper.

Due to her upbringing she has always carried a huge burden of guilt and felt the necessity to be punished for it; particularly because of the impact religion has had on her worldview and specifically, when it comes to the strong association she has between sex and sin. In her mind they mean the same thing and, consequently, it creates an everlasting circle of sexual deviancy going hand in hand with the need to be punished. Consequently guilt drives her need for greater punishment with each passing cycle or to put it another way the more she enjoys the sex the greater her inner need to be punished to restore her equilibrium.

To put it simply, the whole cycle drives her to greater extremes.

Primarily as her girlfriend, but also as her Domme, I am able to moderate these extremes. For those who understand our dynamic it really is not mindless cruelty that many perceive it to be. My need for control matches her need to submit and so in our relationship it really is her for her own good. It enables her to embrace her inclinations while at the same time I am able to protect her.

This tandem relationship between sex and punishment is so delicately balanced that, as events showed, if there is no punishment forthcoming she will go out and find it in some other way. That was the real reason she went back to the forest on her own on that Wednesday night after her last time with Elwira.

I immediately understood the whole point of the forest even if it escaped her.

If you really want to understand Ania, go back to the morning when she confessed and focus not on our conversation and break up, but on the whole morning beforehand and in particular how she approached the church and how it made her feel.

As we heal and grow back together, we may return to a D/s relationship, but not for the foreseeable future. The wounds from what happened are still too fresh and scars have yet to form. In time my anger will let go, but these scars may disfigure our future. It is my hope that we can put this chapter behind us so that we can build something new and stronger. In the meantime, I absolutely refuse to treat her as a submissive. It is just not possible to turn off what happened and if I discipline her in anger, it crosses the line into abuse. This line is vital for the domme who must always demonstrate complete self-control.

It is an often unseen factor, but in true BDSM, as contradictory as it might seem to sound, the dominant is under a greater pressure to show restraint than the submissive and this is why it can actually be quite liberating for the submissive.

The truth is that I have to bring any element of personal frustration with her under control to avoid the risk of an abusive situation developing. I have chosen with Ania, this life and it demands the highest levels of self-control and more from me than her. It must be remembered that violence is not only limited to being physical.

She needs to understand and accept this too.

She needs to find her value in herself and her own worthiness and not in what others, including me, imprint on her. As I have already mentioned, her mental state is still a worry to me and I have to know she is healing and it may well turn out that she will need professional help at some point. I really don't know, but for the time being, I will love her and protect her and do whatever I must to bring her back to full health.

Her quest for destruction—while I repeat I do not agree with what she did—does prove one thing beyond a shadow of a doubt. She is completely remorseful and, if she could take back everything that happened she would. Her confession communicated this far clearer than any, even well-written, letter ever would have done.

I am also absolutely convinced that she will never stray again.

For her mental health, it is important that while she is remorseful, it cannot remain as deep-seated guilt. I know she still feels guilty and the truth is that she is guilty.

However, we have moved on beyond that.

I made it clear to her very quickly, that we reached the point when her apologies were no longer needed, wanted or appreciated. This was for her sake. I had to draw a line in the sand. What happened in the past needs to stay there. Yes, I am still angry, and yes, forgiveness will take time, but if she lives only to apologise to me, she will continue to feel devalued and inadequate.

These are the same feelings that drove her to such extremes in the first place.

Love is our foundation and, until she cheated, trust was our rock, a place I really want to get back to. Whether we make it or break it, we will have to see, but we will not be broken by her cheating again. I am confident of this.

So now that is clear I want to give some consideration to Elwira.

I have a lot of sympathy for Elwira, who Ania completely deceived. The poor girl really did believe they were starting something. She was excited and really thought that in Ania she had met somebody special and that they were going somewhere as a couple.

I think it is important that I go even further in defending Elwira. Some might ask why she jumped into bed so quickly with Ania. It accelerated extremely quickly from hanging out for coffee to them having sex. Ania's motives and drive are clear, she was looking for it. Elwira's motives less so—*why did Elwira agree so quickly?*

The answer, as I see it, is really quite simple. Elwira had been holding a secret desire for Ania for at least two years and then suddenly Ania was there and offering herself to her. Ania kissed Elwira first and it was Ania who moved things in a sexual direction very quickly. Elwira only responded. She may have been confused, but her senses were overwhelmed with something she had fantasied about for so long.

When looked at in that light, it would have taken a heart of stone to resist Ania's advances.

Would you have been able to resist if you were Elwira?

I think very simply, Ania used Elwira for sex and attention and Elwira believed that sex would lead to something more. Although I thought this was the case when Elwira spoke to me, it was later absolutely confirmed by Ania both in word and writing.

One more thing I realised, but only later, was that Ania was right on Elwira's limits when she freely confessed that something had changed on the Wednesday. Unlike the weekend, Ania had deliberately used Elwira near the university and later in the forest to reaffirm how she was feeling about herself and so it touched on being abusive—or so I thought.

Then I remembered what Ania had written about what had happened in the park when Elwira dragged Ania into the trees when they were on the way to Elwira's flat. Ania was probably unaware that she unwittingly did the same back to Elwira as Elwira had done to her, even if Ania's motives had been less than pure. In both the park and outside the university, the risk of discovery had been high. Possibly the only difference was that Ania went with what Elwira was doing, but when it was the other way round Elwira stopped Ania when she reached her limits. If Ania had persisted at that point, then it would have crossed the line into abuse.

From what Elwira told me and Ania's confession, it is totally reasonable to see how Elwira got the idea that it was the first blossoming of a relationship. Elwira is lovely and if by any chance she ever reads this and realises it is about her I want her to know that I totally respect her. She was incredibly brave to risk coming straight to me as soon as she had the chance to, after Ania had confessed to her too. It speaks so much about her decency and integrity. I was angry, but recognised immediately that it would have been wrong to direct my rage against her.

In another world, Elwira and I could have been good friends and she could even have joined our little family so long as she is open to how we live. I can only hope she finds the happiness she deserves. Ania hurt her too and looking back I still feel like taking care of her, but that is just the way I am. I will explain in further detail in a bit, but I already look after the other three girls, namely Ania, Emilia and Kasia so another one wouldn't be any great strain.

Talking of the other girls; I want to briefly mention both Emilia and Kasia.

You will have seen Ania constantly describe Emilia as *sweet steel*, an apt description. Emilia has a well-developed moral core and unbelievable mental toughness and resolve. Some readers may think she was being fake or shallow in offering a secret hand of friendship to Ania during the worst of times when she was completely isolated. This is an unfair judgment. To some extent, Emilia was caught between her own conscience and Kasia's needs and what she did was all she could in the circumstances.

Emilia is just not the kind of person who can stay angry with somebody and she soon let go while maintaining that what Ania had done was wrong. There were hints of her kindness even on that first day when we broke up. I was previously unaware, until I had read this, that she had told Ania that they would look after me.

Why did she tell Ania this?

She could have just directed her energies and compassion to me. She didn't need to say anything to Ania and therefore she said it only to reassure Ania that I would be taken care of. She did this because she cares. While still being against what Ania had done, even in that moment, she didn't completely abandon her.

I had no idea that Ania had been naked on the floor waiting at my door on the weekend after Kasia's birthday and again it was Emilia who stepped in. I'm not sure how I would have reacted to Ania if I had discovered her, but based on what I did to her letter later we can assume the worst.

Emilia only stepped in when she could have a positive effect on the situation and ultimately after Ania had finally pushed her self-destruct button in the hotel it was Emilia who she turned to and again it was Emilia who pushed us back together. It should always be remembered that it was because of Emilia's attitude throughout that Ania had at least one of us that she could reach out to when she really needed to.

It was tragic that Ania refused Emilia's hand when it was offered after I burnt her letter. It would have saved her so much pain. Having said that, it was Ania's complete brokenness after going to the hotel that brought her back (and you could argue that it brought me back too). I will never wish that kind of suffering on her again, but I am grateful for it because of what it led to.

If Emilia had not done what she had done throughout, who would Ania have called from the hotel? Ania's own assessment was right. There was no way I would have answered and neither would Kasia.

That person always was and always will be Emilia, the sweetest steel you can ever meet. Ania has always called Emilia her best friend. I am not offended by this, quite the contrary. I have always known this and now have even greater reason to appreciate her. Emilia simply is great.

Now moving on beyond Emilia…

As you read, it might have surprised you that Kasia seemed even angrier than me towards Ania. It would be easy to label her as harsh, evil or even a bitch. Those of you who do so fundamentally misunderstand us, and her in particular.

I deal with things in my way and other people in different ways. As Ania wrote, I am not so good at this *emotional shit* (her words I believe—even though she was quoting me) and for me to cut her off was the best way of coping.

Kasia is more of a *wear your emotions on your sleeve* type of a person. She will never pretend or be a hypocrite, she will say it as it is and if you have a problem, it is your problem as far as she is concerned.

I know she has written some negative stuff about Ania on social media, but I also know that she wrote that she doesn't care if Ania sees it or not. Her harshness was not stabbing Ania in the back—it may have been stabbing her in the front, but Kasia is the way she is and it is as simple as that. There is a greater honesty in being like this than in how many others are.

I think Kasia will be fine with me writing this, without details, but her family background is tragic and when she came to live with us at the start of her studies she had everything she wanted, but nothing she needed. We collectively filled that gap and became her family. Emilia especially is an incredible light to Kasia's darkness.

When Ania's actions tore us apart, it was like a child watching her parents separate or even divorce. Even if Ania isn't a surrogate parent to Kasia (that would be bizarre Ania is a couple of months younger than Kasia) I am a bit of a mother to all of them. Kasia's anger is totally understandable. When a solid foundation, established from the very beginning, was suddenly destroyed through the actions of just one person how else could she have reacted? Ania had created this, no other and there was little wonder she was the sole focus of Kasia's fury.

Kasia actually showed great restraint by keeping out of the way, although I think that was probably more due to Emilia's influence than anything else. Whatever was going on in her mind the truth is that Kasia began to soften as soon as she saw how broken Ania was when I brought her home from the hotel.

When discussing Elwira above, I said I already look after three girls and now you have some idea how. I am a little older than they are and was already living in the flat when they moved in. I had been flat sharing, but the girls I originally shared with finished their studies and moved on. I had to move out, or with the help of my landlord, find more people to share with. Ultimately I had to live with the new people so the landlord allowed me a great deal of freedom to choose. This is how we all first met in summer 2015.

I was once described as a mother hen and I think this is about right. I can't help, but look after and protect all three of them. Ania has taken responsibility for her actions and both Emilia and Kasia behaved perfectly as they are entitled to in the given situation. It is also probably why a part of me wants to reach out to Elwira, despite everything that happened.

Anybody who thinks otherwise will find themselves at odds with me!

Life is a learning curve and the hardest lessons are those learnt through challenging times. This has proven to be no exception. Although I have already more than touched on it, I am not going to explain our BDSM relationship here, it will take far too long and it is far more complex and deeper than most vanilla relationships. I will however provide some insight starting with the fact that within BDSM the bonds are stronger and more intimate and this comes from a clear differentiation of roles.

As I have already said, and especially if you are not familiar with BDSM do not judge us, both Ania and I are consenting adults who have agreed on everything that we do and actually my withdrawal from the BDSM element of our relationship more than demonstrates my respect for Ania. She frequently writes it is not abuse, if it is consensual (and this means giving consent with full awareness of its implications), but I add too and reinforce the point that I made above, it is also abuse if I dominate her out of anger.

Another reason why I have withdrawn the BDSM element from our relationship is that Ania needs to learn self-control and self-discipline and this means at times self-denial. She indulged herself with Elwira and paid the price. On the other hand, I do not see what she did with the guys as self-indulgence. If you read carefully, she had no intention of getting any pleasure out of that evening and I recall her in her description she said very clearly that she never orgasmed at all. At most I think she might have described herself as aroused at one point.

The strongest sentiment that comes across is that of painful endurance, alongside a determination to push beyond that into the greatest intensity she could get from them. She defined this state as oblivion. She allowed herself to be punished and abused by them because she firmly believed that she deserved everything she got and more. Punishment and self-destruction were her reasons for going out that night.

Thirdly and finally I had no other choice, but to not continue (for now at least) in our BDSM roles. She is so damaged and close to the edge that she needs loving more than anything she might think she wants. For now, she needs to see the amazing person she is and for her confidence and esteem to be built. I love her so much and this has to start with me, especially at this time when she is fundamentally incapable of grasping how wonderful she truly is. I need to help her to find herself so that she can know true restoration and be stronger and a better person for it.

Additionally, in not offering her the BDSM element of our relationship, she will learn to be less selfish. It can never be all about her and her esteem needs to teach her that she doesn't always need to be the centre of attention. This hiatus will also give me time to deal with my own emotions. I have invited her back because I love her and she loves me, but forgiveness will take time and I will never forget.

As a teacher, I am always looking for an opportunity to teach and guide others and this is the main reason that I made the decision, with Ania's complete agreement, that she should publish this. Ania is a pure submissive and her behaviour perfectly demonstrates this. Within the BDSM lifestyle, in an act of trust, I became her owner and she passed all responsibility for her life to me. This is a responsibility to lead and guide and protect her, but also a responsibility to discipline her both for her sexual pleasure and on other occasions when necessary. For her, even the harshest of punishments means security, a sense of belonging and bizarrely protection. It does not mean she is not free to make any decisions nor that she does not have a voice, but it does create an amazing symbiotic relationship that offers so much more than a more conventional relationship.

Her 'sin' was a result of the loosening of her BDSM chains. I was distracted by my thesis and she had nobody taking responsibility for her actions because she had previously handed that over to me. Unrestrained and frustrated she looked elsewhere for what she needed and found it in Elwira. But then, when she realised what she had done she found herself unable to live with the sudden weight of responsibility and her world crashed around her. She suffered the consequences of the released submissive in that it made her feel even more isolated and even needier.

After recognising what she had done she set about a course of self-destruction that culminated in that night when she sacrificed herself to those English guys and everything that followed.

And that is exactly what she did. She sacrificed herself because on an altar of their pleasure that evening she reached an even lower point than she had when she had contemplated suicide. She even twisted her inability to commit suicide as a weakness. The loss of all hope for our relationship pushed her over that edge and she didn't care whether she lived or died and no punishment would have been enough for her. In fact, she saw her death as a shortcut to hell which still wouldn't have been enough for her. She wore out four guys (yes—if you read carefully she did make them cum collectively ten times and she further humiliated herself by drinking their semen) and her body was broken, but her mind still screamed that it still was not punishment enough for what she had done with Elwira.

The unfamiliar might call what we have in our relationship as controlling; I would however use the word *restraint*. The truth is that while the submissive is restrain*ed* it is actually the Domme, in this case me, who has to show greater restrain*t*. As I have tried to explain, I have to be disciplined and hold back or guide or provide limits for Ania to grow and feel safe in. In the context of our relationship, at the risk of repeating myself, it was when she no longer felt that I was taking responsibility for her that she betrayed me, as she is incapable of taking such responsibility for herself.

This is probably coming out all wrong, but I will try to explain. Ania's personality type is needy and this is one of the many complex reasons why our relationship works on a D/s level. Just see what she says about how she has overcome childhood trauma, beaten fear and grown in confidence.

This has all come from what, to many, may seem to be a contradiction. It is however a paradox, we have a non-abusive BDSM relationship and I would like to think it comes across in her writing how I do nothing but care for and love her. Even when I read back what she writes I am surprised by how she interprets love. She understood everything from the moment I picked her up at the Novotel as love, even if my words confused her. She came to the simple conclusion that love is less about words and more about what a person does.

So what I did from the moment I met her in the hotel communicated far better than any words could have ever done. It is also clear in her understanding that I never stopped loving her.

If I could impart one final lesson, and allow me this indulgence, when love is real, allow a little more grace and a little more forgiveness and hold on. It is the most precious gift anyone can ever have.

This is also a lesson to myself.

I hope that one day, we will return to what we were or be even stronger for this dark chapter in our lives.

Dominika, September 2019